Praise for *The Greek Persuasion*

"Robeson makes her protagonist's existential fretfulness about her future, and her feelings of uncertainty as she pursues a perfect romantic match, highly relatable   narrative will   nate with readers who are confronti   ."

s Reviews

"Kimberly K. Robeson's in.   ries combines modernity and myth in a tale that centers on multiple points of view without losing direction and is done with such ease. She embeds human life in time and space, while at the same time exploring ethnic, sexual, generational, and temporal fluidity. . . . One is awed by an ending that balances closure and pathos, becoming and élan."

—James Bland, PhD, recipient of an Academy
of American Poets Prize

"A personal and raw novel, full of honesty, about one person's journey to find her place as a woman in a modern society—because labels shouldn't matter. . . . What a joy to read."

—Amy Morse, former VP of Marketing, McGraw-Hill

"This narrative discusses age-old questions in a contemporary context. . . . Like every mind that actively seeks fulfillment as 'entelechy,' Aristotle's term for fulfilled potential, Thair must come to terms with her past—her Greek roots—and her future. . . . Robeson writes a novel that is both brave and sensual, and I look forward to reading her next book!"

r of Hawk, L.A.
e Moment More

The
Greek
Persuasion

The Greek Persuasion

A NOVEL

KIMBERLY K. ROBESON

SHE WRITES PRESS

Published 2019
Printed in the United States of America
ISBN: 978-1-63152-565-0
ISBN: 978-1-63152-566-7
Library of Congress Control Number: 2018958867

For information, address:
She Writes Press
1569 Solano Ave #546
Berkeley, CA 94707

She Writes Press is a division of SparkPoint Studio, LLC.

For Yiayia and Mama

and for my Love

Prologue

"Mama, tell me the story again. Please, Mama."

"Okay . . . " she says while taking my hand in hers, rubbing my palm lightly with her fingertips, hoping to lull me to sleep. "So, once upon a time, in Ancient Greece, at the top of Mount Olympus, all the gods would meet. Zeus would sit on his throne, with Hera beside him, and make decisions about the Greek people."

"Mama, was Yiayia alive during that time?"

"No, sweetie, that was a very long time ago, even before your grandmother was born."

"Mama, tell me again about Zeus and the ball people."

"Well, people back then were round, kind of like big soccer balls. They had four arms, four legs, and one head with two faces. Each face had two eyes, a nose and mouth."

"They couldn't see each other, right, Mama?"

"No, but one always knew that the other was close. One was stuck right behind the other. They shared one mind, one heart, and were eternally joined."

"And, Mama, they would roll around the earth, right?"

"Yes, Thair. They would roll around the earth, moving quickly, powerfully, as they used their arms and legs to travel at great speeds.

They were strong. And they were happy, really happy, because their other half was always right there, connected to them."

As she speaks, Mama notices that I am no longer smiling.

"What's wrong, *agape mou*?" she says as she takes a strand of my dark hair and moves it off my cheek.

"I guess . . . well . . . I was just thinking that it would be nice if people were still like that."

"Really? You don't think it would be uncomfortable to roll around instead of having two separate legs and two separate arms?"

"I was just thinking, if your other half was always stuck to you, then Daddy wouldn't be at work so much."

My mother lowers her eyes and in a quiet voice continues: "So do you want to hear the rest of the story or shall we save it for tomorrow?"

"Okay, Mama, we can save it. I already know that mean Zeus will take out his magic sword and slice all the ball people in half."

"Thair, the way you say that makes it seem like such a sad story."

"It is a sad story! I wish people had their best friends stuck to them from the beginning, and you didn't have to look for them."

Mama pats me on the head, "You know, sweetheart, you're right. Zeus was a mean fellow. It would be easier if we didn't have to look for our other half, and we were born with that special person stuck to us right away. But let's remember the great part of the story: that our other half does exist and one day, baby, when you grow up and are a young lady, you will meet a nice boy that will make you so happy, and all your worries will be over."

Part I

Change

1

Encinitas, California
May, 1999

James and I are both lying on the couch, our heads at opposite sides on the arm rests, legs and feet intertwined. He is studying a book of Henry Fuseli's paintings, and I am growing frustrated with Jane even though I have read and taught this novel more than ten times. After a few minutes, I can feel James's eyes bore into my book. I lower Miss Eyre and hesitantly smile: "What's up?"

"Are you familiar with the Scylla and Charybdis myth?"

"Yeah, they're the female monsters who drowned and devoured sailors—but Odysseus got away," I reply.

"Yes, exactly. Look at this painting," he says while passing me an art book.

It's an ominous painting. I can see James is waiting for me to react, so I proceed, "Odysseus's stance is powerful, the monsters look devil-like. The rough waters feel like turmoil, the colors like hell at night. But . . . to be honest, it's just too dark for my taste."

James stares at me through his dark-rimmed glasses. His intense features, velvet-black hair and aqua eyes, had initially attracted me, but now his eyes, almost translucent, seem too distant. James is a few inches taller than me, standing 5'10", but we both look longer with short torsos and giraffe legs. We share similar features: light eyes, sharp jaws, petite noses, wide smiles—except for our skin; his is so white, and mine, honey tan, with a glow year-round. So similar, yet so different.

He's still staring at me while I hold the heavy book, and not knowing what else he wants me to say, I set it down on the carpet since his arms are crossed.

James speaks slowly. "There's an expression 'between Scylla and Charybdis' meaning 'between a rock and a hard place.' Have you heard of it?"

"Interesting. No, I haven't." I try to remain calm, but the tumultuous scene in the painting is slowly rising up off the page and working its way into our living room.

"I want to ask you something."

"Okay."

"Do you ever feel like we are stuck?"

"What do you mean *stuck*?" I ask.

"Thair, apart from books and art, what do we really have in common?"

I'm unsettled. I sit up straighter, "James, don't they say opposites attract?"

"Come on, Thair, you love to walk, talk, hike, bike, go out for a cocktail, a sumptuous dinner—"

"And you like dark spaces, to come out at night, and restaurants are considered a waste of money," I continue, finishing his sentence. What I don't say out loud is *and when you have a showing, you hide in our extra bedroom, your pseudo-studio; you're absorbed, distant, unreachable. Nothing except your paintings matter.*

"I feel our life together is stagnant," he says while looking down at the swirling waters around Odysseus.

"James, neither of us wants children. We both agree that we don't need marriage to feel committed, so I'm confused. Where's this coming from?"

"Are you . . . are you in love with me?"

I kick his foot with mine. "Of course, I love you."

"That's not what I am asking. Are you *in love* with me?"

My body quivers. Trying to sound optimistic, I continue: "James, after almost five years, who is really *in love*? We love each other very much."

When we met at the gallery for his debut showing, more than six years before, his passion for his work captured one part of me, and I was smitten. James's gentle soul, kind arms, and smart words forced me to silence my inquietude, to continue to try to be open, but I knew my heart and mind didn't agree.

"Thair," he repeated, "Do you see me as your other half? The one who was created just for you?"

James doesn't believe in fairy tales; since our conversations are usually objective and analytical, rarely emotional—unless we are discussing his artwork—I'm taken aback, uprooted, even a bit angry.

"Thair, please . . . are you in love with me?" he repeats weakly.

I finally answer, "First, Aristophanes got it wrong in Plato's *Symposium*. There is no such thing as 'the other half.' I should have never told you about my mom's bedtime story. Obviously, this myth has persuaded you, too. This idea of being 'in' this thing that neither you nor I can define is stupid. We are happy. I love you. You love me. At least I think you do. Finish. End of story."

As I speak the words, inside I'm thinking, *I'm a part-time professor, living a part-time life. I don't want to marry James, and I don't want babies. My life is a merry-go-round. Every day looks like the other. I am pretending. Pretending to be happy. Just like most people I know. Core happiness is an illusion.* I want to scream: *Fucking deal with it, James!*

He looks straight into me, a rueful expression on his face. His eyes drop, and a barely audible whisper escapes his lips, "I think . . . it's time . . . for me to move out."

I don't fight. I don't beg. I simply accept. But beyond my control, tears explode from my eyes, stream down my face, and I cry for five hours. Our feet are still interlaced. We never get up off the couch. He just closes his eyes and listens to me whimper. Words are inadequate. Finally, at midnight, I get up, dazed and disoriented. I have to give a final exam the following morning at 8:00 a.m. and can barely open my puffy eyes. I shower and come back; he hasn't moved.

"When do you want to leave?" It's my place after all, only one name on the deed. "You know you can stay as long as you like."

"Yes, I know, and thank you," he replies solemnly.

Five weeks later, five suitcases and a pile of paintings sit by the door. I look at them and feel vacant.

2

Island of Kythnos, Greece
Late May, 2000

I get up from the table, pour myself a glass of water, and look out the window. I can't shake James from my mind. As I relive the day we separated, I can hear James's voice, see his tired eyes. My mind still misses him, the intellectual conversations, hours of talking about art and literature, but my heart always knew something was missing. Aristotle once said the mind and heart are one. I do not feel that way—mine never agree. I know logically, viscerally, I *should have been* satisfied, but my heart demands more. I couldn't tell James I was in love with him because I wasn't. He was my best friend, my companion; his good looks should have made me want to tear his clothes off, but sex was prosaic.

This past year, instead of feeling grateful for what I do have—health, home, a job—I've felt lost. I remember a Greek friend telling me when I was younger: "You Americans all say you are lost! Go look in a mirror. There you are!" I laugh remembering this while looking at the calm blue water below, but I also know the emptiness inside is real.

When I told my mother I had decided to spend my entire summer on Kythnos, the island of my grandmother, she was concerned. *Thair, women don't travel alone for such an extended amount of time. It's just not normal.*

5

I had listened quietly, not wanting to argue with her because, ironically, this trip was the sanest option at a time when my life felt like it was unraveling. Ever since my grandmother died, ten years before, I had dreamed of returning to the island of my childhood, and since there was no one to hold me back, I knew it was time.

I rented a traditional white-washed house, a pretty little place perched high on a cliff; not too big, two bedrooms, one bathroom with a stand-up shower, and a breakfast nook with a stunning view of a cove below. The owner cleaned up the place for me, cleared away the cobwebs that grow over the nine months when these houses go to sleep.

Leaning against the sink, sipping my water, peering around the kitchen at the turquoise paintings, the blue cups and white plates, I am reminded of Yiayia's home, yet this enchanted place is so much cleaner, better-kept. Every detail chosen by the owner captures the Greek isle's magic and makes me even more nostalgic.

From fifteen years old until twenty-one, there was no place I would have rather spent my summers than on the island of Kythnos with my grandmother. And, now, after ten long years, I have finally made it back—a single, thirty-one-year-old woman with no children. I wonder what Yiayia would say if she could see me today? I've been thinking a lot about my yiayia, about our summers together, about my mother, divorced now for more than a decade, about her decisions, her choices. She had escaped *from* Greece, yet this country had been my escape during my youth. Once more, just as I had felt during my teenage years, I hoped clarity would come if I returned to Greece. So, the last day of final exams, I graded my students' essays, submitted all the necessary paperwork, bought myself a brand new laptop, and had a drink with Rick and Frank to toast my birthday and show off my new cutting-edge purchase.

Rick's words ring in my ears: "I hope you're not taking that thing," he had said while playing with my computer, "just to have it sit on a table."

No, Rick, I plan on writing. Really. I remember sitting with the lovebirds that night in a dive bar in Hillcrest and Frank telling his partner to "give Thair a break. It's been a tough year. Not everyone is as lucky as we are."

"It wasn't luck, Frank. You and I were actively going out and looking," Rick had responded. Then Rick had told me: "You need to go out, darling. You need to meet people," and then he enthusiastically added, "I'm so glad you're finally doing *something*, going to Greece for the summer!"

Rick and Frank make a striking pair and are the most loving couple I have ever met. No two people love and respect each other more; they are my role models for a perfect union, and not just because they are in love and have been faithful to each other for more than nine years, but when they are together, there's this wonderful harmony present. They clearly complete each other. They want to get married, but our country, sadly, is not there yet. When I see them, there is no doubt in my mind that they were together before Zeus had his way with them. They were the lucky ones, the ones who found their other half.

"So, Thair, will you write a novel or stories, a memoir? What's your plan? I want you to write a big, fat, juicy bestseller. With lots of sex!" Rick had said. I chuckled and told him *I just want to write something.*

So, I have decided that for three months of pure isolation on the sleepy island of Kythnos, I will write stories, stories about my grandmother's life, about my mother's, and about my own. I'm hoping that writing about the past will help me make sense of my future, and maybe retracing my roots will help me find that thing I am searching for.

3

As I sit here in this blue and white kitchen, images of my youth are overpowering. Yiayia in her regular spot, I'm across from her, asking her question after question. During those long summers, as a young girl obsessed with falling (and staying) in love, I repeatedly asked my yiayia about my grandfather and if she loved him. She just laughed: "*Ti nomizis?*" What did I think? I had no idea. It didn't seem like it. She never talked about him, never seemed to be sad that he was dead. My theory was she did not love him. If Yiayia didn't love Papou (the handsome man from a bedside picture), and my mother had admitted to me, just years earlier, that she had never fully loved my father, did I ever have a chance of loving a man? That is, loving a man *completely*? Mind, body, *and* heart.

———

Even though I woke heavy, somber thoughts plundering my mind, it's another beautiful day. The morning sun penetrates the shutters and beats down on my body. I stretch my arms out and take a deep breath as the salty air tickles my nose; sliding my legs off the side of the bed, waking slowly, I saunter into the kitchen. I get the Loumides and a coffee cup from the cupboard and fill the briki with water. Struggling to light the stove with the flint, I finally get it lit and place the single-serving pot on the fire and watch the water boil.

I picture my plump, pint-sized grandmother sitting at the table, mechanically cleaning green beans. Whenever she saw me making my morning coffee, Yiayia always grumbled. She complained about her tired hands and sore feet, complained that she did all the work around the house, but when I asked her what she wanted me to do, Yiayia's response was always the same: "Nothing." She loved to whine. She whined all the time, but I knew that her routine complaining was just so that I would never forget to appreciate her. Yiayia complained incessantly that her daughter had forsaken her motherland for the land of air-conditioning, but at least, she would say, "You I have," and when I would turn around, I always saw her naughty smirk. "Tell Yiayia," she would say, "Where you go last night?"

All alone in my rented kitchen, I remember how our morning visits were the times when I felt closest to her. On the straw-thatched chair, I sat, telling her all my stories, how every night of the week, I found my friends on the main street in town where people—young and old—gathered. I told her how I had spent the evenings talking to boys and dancing. She would sit, cut, nod, and I would continue.

I told her who was dating, who was kissing, who was disappearing during the night, and Yiayia pretended she didn't want to hear anymore, "No more, Thair!" But every morning while she prepared the day's lunch, she always asked me about my night out. I was only a teenager, but life was so different in Greece, so much freer than the US with its many laws and regulations.

Our morning ritual consisted of me drinking Greek coffee and telling her all the local gossip. "I met a nice boy, Yiayia, at Aleko's bar."

"Who is his papou? What name he has?" She always asked me whose grandson he was; as if a last name would explain the boy's complete family genealogy—it almost did, on this island of only 1,500 residents.

"He's not local, Yiayia." Her eyes always flickered when I said I spent the night flirting with a foreigner, a *xeno*.

"He a German? Italian? A South African?" she asked, then added: "A good British boy?"

"He's Italian."

Her face turned downwards, "Why not English? You never like English?"

"Yiayia, I think I really like this one. His name is Sandro." She got up and walked out of the kitchen, onto the balcony, with her bowl of beans. The conversation was over.

So many memories, so long ago, and yet her raspy voice still penetrates the air.

As I take my coffee outside onto the balcony, I picture Sandro, my final summer love. His family had rented a villa on the island for a few months. Sandro was tall with dark eyes and olive skin. Very, very handsome, but sex was beige ceilings—me lying there, staring up, waiting for him to finish. He was memorable with his gallant manner and sexy accent, but it was simply young love.

When I would tell Yiayia my stories, she never asked if I cared for these boys. I think they were just characters to her, but one day plans about my life with Sandro spilled from my young mouth, and, for the first time, her body twitched and her face contorted in a way I had never seen before. I had kept talking, explaining how Sandro said that he wanted to marry me; that I was a mature woman, he a man who knew what he wanted. But what did we know? I was only twenty-one and he, just a twenty-four-year-old boy. Sandro wanted me to come back after I graduated from college, live with my yiayia for a while; he would open a café on the island, I could teach English, and we could be together forever. Finally, I could not ignore the look in her eyes. It's still with me today, peering deep into mine, so deep, I felt her dive and drown in them, then resurface as she said slowly: "Thair, you no marry. You no love this Sandro. And you so young. You not know what love is."

As I sit here now, I feel as frustrated as I did back then.

I had pleaded with her, "What is *agape* then, Yiayia? Tell me!" If my grandmother, Aphrodite, named after the goddess of love, didn't have the answers, then who did? "*What* is love, Yiayia?" I begged her to tell me about my grandfather. Was the love she shared with Papou *real* love? Instead she took my hand, leading me to the bedroom. She opened a drawer, handed me a small velvet box, and gave me a simple gold band that was inscribed with a man's name. *Henry Archibald Hadley*. And then she began—finally—to tell me her story.

4

Aphrodite's Story

Alexandria, Egypt
May, 1942

Aphrodite, or Dita as she was called, looked her parents directly in their eyes and with a vehement "*Oxi!*" said, no! She would not marry the young Greek fisherman. She was seventeen, having the time of her life, and would not spoil it with marriage. Dita said this as she slammed the door of the thin, two-floor building that was her home. She walked a few blocks, her body still shaking, knowing the wrath of her own voice would be paralleled by her mother's once she returned home. Unlike most seventeen-year-old girls, she was not afraid of her father. She worried about her mother, the towering woman whom she adored, but also feared.

Walking down the dusty street, she made her way to the military base. It wasn't Saturday, but she would see if they had any work for her. She loved her weekend volunteer work. The Allies had several bases in Egypt and since she couldn't enlist (what she would have preferred doing) she would wear her old overalls, a tight red blouse, a pretty checkered scarf, and every Saturday show up to change the oil of the Jeeps at the base. It was a novelty for the young men to see this buxom Greek broad offer her "services." The first day she showed up, Dita said she was handy with a wrench, could do almost anything on a car, could also change electrical outlets, knew how to build a wall—and how to tear it down. Dita's mom had a less than subtle way of introducing her daughter to activities that were anything but feminine. "Show her how to be useful!" she would bellow to her meek husband, who dragged himself off the couch, to show Dita the difference between a starter and a generator. And Dita loved learning those things. She loved pretty dresses but loved getting dirty more.

When Dita went to the base for the first time, the officer directed her towards the Red Crescent office. She responded that she couldn't stand the sight of blood, but give her an oil pan: she would show them what she could do. So that's how she came to be the local oil-changer. She loved sliding under a Jeep, feeling the oil drip on her face, the grease under her fingernails. Of course, she also loved the attention. Men would come to see the young girl in overalls who was working under their vehicles, and without trying too hard, she got dates; lots of dates with Americans, with Australians, with South Africans. And with a unique, young gent from England. In fact, she had become the most popular girl on the base. Her knowledge of cultures grew quickly as did her appetite. But she wanted more—more of what, she wasn't exactly sure, but she definitely wanted more. So when her parents told her she was betrothed to the Greek, she just would not accept it.

That afternoon when Dita went home, she found her mother, a large woman whose size equaled her patience, sitting at the kitchen table reading the newspaper. She said nothing to Dita, put down the paper, walked upstairs, and shut the door. Dita could feel her heart beat faster; she knew that her mother would end up getting her way, but Dita decided that afternoon she would not think about her upcoming doom. She was supposed

to meet the Greek any day now. They wanted her to marry someone she had never even met! Instead of worrying about a possible betrothal, Dita opened her armoire and selected a yellow
dress with small daisies on it. It looked a bit too summery and
light, but she wore it anyway and put on bright red lipstick that
didn't really go with the dress but went with the times. Then she
quietly went downstairs and sat in the living room. If her mother
came down, Dita would say she was going out with a group of
friends, but her mother never descended when the doorbell rang.
As she sat there staring at the floor, a long "Diiiiing" and a short,
but loud "DONG" echoed through the house. Dita opened the
door quickly, and in front of her stood a gallant Englishman by
the name of Henry. Henry Archibald Hadley. Despite his lean
contexture, squirrel-looking face, and intensely small hands, he
was dashing. Though awkward at times, he was certainly perfect—and a real gentleman.

Smiling with his exaggerated front teeth, he asked Dita if
she felt like going to the theatre or to the ice cream parlor. She
didn't feel like talking. *Gone with the Wind* was playing again,
having finally made it to Egypt years after being released, and
even though Dita had already seen it twice with other dates, she
chose the theatre. She loved Scarlett, hated Rhett. When Rhett
had the gall to ask Scarlett if she ever thought "of marrying just
for fun," Dita squirmed in her seat. Dita wished she had the
courage to tell her mother what Scarlett had replied: "Marriage,
fun? Fun *for men* you mean." Marriage. It was too much to think
about, so, like Scarlett, she decided she would not think about
it—at least not on that day.

The sun burned the afternoon sky as she escaped into the
dark theatre with Henry. His arm immediately wrapped around
the seat behind her, making her feel secure; then lifting it slowly,
he laid his arm on her shoulder. His hand hung like a dead fish,

his fingers dangling dangerously close to her perked-up breasts. She lost track of the movie and enjoyed the warmth of his embrace. After a few minutes, he moved his arm, put his hand timidly on her leg while the heat of his sweaty palm radiated up her thigh, settling between her legs to a spot that was getting hotter and wetter by the moment. Then she heard Rhett's voice: "With enough courage, you can do without a reputation." Dita leaned over and peered into the Englishman's eyes, without any hesitation, kissed him long and hard. They necked through the whole movie, tongues in a wrestling match, his gentle hands, cautiously, sliding up and down her legs—but never too far up. Dita could feel him trembling; she was pushing him to his limit, so before the final scene, he asked her: "Shall we leave and go for a drive?" Dita nodded, yes, that would be a good idea.

They walked, with urgency yet respect, arm-in-arm out of the theatre and to his Jeep. Once they got in, the necking started all over. She kissed him hard. He responded. He was pushing against her. She could feel him getting bigger. She pushed back. His arms unwrapped. Time slowed down while Henry delicately began unbuttoning the bodice of her dress, looking, so genuinely into Dita's eyes, begging for permission, and she could feel her insides throbbing. It felt so good and so right, so why was she suddenly pushing him away? Why were girls told over and over that these feelings were wrong? That only bad girls did these things? Bad girls, dirty girls; girls who men would not marry? It was only a few weeks before when she was doing these *things* with the South African. The only difference was that Dirk hadn't taken so kindly in the same situation, and when Dita told Dirk to stop, he grew angry and took her home. But Henry was different. He was wholesome. He was English. Suddenly he pulled back and said: "I'm sorry. I'm so sorry, my dear Dita. I don't know what got into me. I want you to know that you are very special. And when this war is over, I plan on marrying you." Her smile faded as she heard those dreadful words that she had been trying to escape all day. From feelings of guilt, she was instantly irritated. She coyly kissed him again and asked him to drive her home. Despite being a bit annoyed, she knew Henry was genuine, but it didn't matter and she didn't care; it was getting late, and there would be no time to change if she didn't bid adieu to Henry immediately.

Just as she was walking in the front door, with one last tender kiss on Henry's lips, she could hear the back doorbell ringing. Some houses in Alexandria had two entrances: guests entered from the front, hired help from the back. The back entrance came complete with a porch, door, doorbell, and number, so most foreigners confused the front for the back and the back for the front. For Dita it was perfect. Good-bye to English suitor at the front door, hello Dirk at the back. She had barely shut the door on hapless Henry when the second bell rang again, and again, sounding more anxious with every ring. Dita worried her parents would come downstairs, and her father almost did, until she heard her mother say to him, "It's probably a late delivery. Stay here. Dita can get it." Did her mother really expect a delivery at this time of the night, or was she in essence delivering Dita? Either way, she didn't have time to contemplate it further. It was Saturday night. There were social clubs, free food, and lots of young, strong Allies. She was having the time of her life.

Dita knew she didn't have time to change after all, but before going to the other door, she glanced over at the mirror, wiping her mouth where another man's kisses had been, and quickly reapplied her lipstick. She opened the back door as Dirk grabbed her and began to kiss her voraciously. He immediately slid his hand between her legs and under her dress—rude, savage—but she loved it.

"Stop . . ." she whispered, "We must go. My parents will come down." She knew she was in for a wild night because Dirk would not like being shut out three times. He was her bold South African "boyfriend," tall, rugged with Popeye arms. He had been away for a few weeks, but now he was back. He stared at her and smacked her bottom as they moved away from the house. Dita laughed. Dirk jumped on his motorcycle, patted the seat behind him, and Dita smiled as she spread her legs and got on, lacing her arms tightly around his waist, laying her head on his back. This was freedom. This was happiness. Dirk reached back and ran his calloused hand alongside her leg as far up as it would go in that position.

"Are you ready, Doll?"

"Yes!" And inside she heard herself say: *yes, yes, yes!* She would be courageous, and she would not allow others to dictate her reputation. She had decided. It was her body, her choice— one of the few choices she had left.

Tonight would be the night.

5

Early June, 2000

While making my breakfast, I put on a Parios CD in an ancient boom box that is on the kitchen counter. It skips a few times and then, as a familiar song begins, I see myself, nineteen years old, tan, svelte, dancing in front of my yiayia. My knees bend to a *hasapiko* dance, and she tells me that I look funny, that I am bastardizing the dance by "Americanizing" it with the slight shake of my booty. Then I dance *tsifteteli* for her; my arms are like snakes in the air, my hips move like a belly dancer's, and she pretends to look away, "You look like *poutana!*" She tells me the neighbors might see you and know that Dita's grand-daughter from the US is indeed a "whore." I know she doesn't mean it, using the word *poutana* playfully, but—one thing is true—appear-ances always matter here.

I get winded dancing a short *sirtaki*. Anthony Quinn has entered my body; I am Zorba—free, powerful, with an insatiable zest for life. Then, finally, I dance the *zeibekiko*. The man's dance. A strange look crosses Yiayia's face, one that I will never forget, reminding me of the faces of women I have seen in pictures who were marching for wom-en's suffrage: looks of defiance, strength, determination. She is still in this kitchen with me, her commanding expression so vivid. The words out of her mouth say: "Thair, stop! That dance *only* for a man!" But her eyes betray her real feelings, so I continue. I'm circling wildly with my arms outstretched; with each tapping of my hand to the ground, her strange look turns to one of inward pride at my stubbornness. Still pretending to be upset, as she stifles her smile, she exclaims: "You no listen to Yiayia, huh? You do what you want!" I jump to my feet as the song ends and run to her, planting a big kiss on the top of her head as she pushes me away and wipes her forehead.

But Yiayia is not sitting on the chair. Instead I am twirling around in an empty kitchen and I am alone. Just an orange cat lies on the cool tile floor, watching me as if I have gone insane.

Even though it's been years since Yiayia died, it feels like yesterday. She never made it to my college graduation. Days before the ceremony, she called to say that she was so proud of me and "Yiayia sew a dress to wear." She said it was green oyster silk, material that she had saved from after the war. "Yiayia save it for something special. Good I wear it for your diploma, not for wedding."

She hated to fly, but for me, she said in her husky voice: "I come to the land of big cars and air-conditioning." A few days before she was supposed to travel, a neighbor found her dead. Probably her heart, probably too much excitement, no one really knew, no one was there, all alone, on a cold kitchen floor with a piece of stale bread lying beside her, the stench of feta cheese and Kalamata olives on the table. Yiayia was strong, vibrant, only sixty-six years old. Her heart expired and mine broke.

"Can you meet me in Athens?" Lena asked through a buzzing phone line.

"Of course, I'll look for a ticket right away," I heard my mother say to her older sister. She looked over at me and her hands shook a bit, but she was calm, in control, and after the short conversation, she sat down quietly in the living room and held her head in her hands. But she never cried. I cried enough for the two of us. I had so many plans: I was going to return to Greece with Yiayia, live with her on the island, get a job teaching English.

The next day my mother flew to Athens, took the ferry to Kythnos, and buried her mother, missing my graduation, too. The only person there for the ceremony was Gordon Wright—the man I saw a few times a year, the man who would show up, take me out to lunch, buy me something expensive, then disappear again. As we sat in The Acropolis Garden, ate souvlakia and toasted my milestone with a bottle of Retsina, I tried to be cordial to my father.

"Honey, do you like it?"

"Yeah, thanks," I said while looking down at the diamond tennis bracelet that was indeed pretty but did nothing to raise my spirits.

Then there was the typical silence. "So what's next for you?"

"I don't know, Dad. I really don't want to talk about it."

He was trying, but I didn't care. I was in a fog. I just wished I could have gone with my mother to see my dear yiayia one more time. Instead, I was in a tacky Greek restaurant with pictures of Santorini plastered on every wall as if that were the only island in Greece. And the food wasn't even good; the wine was worse.

After two miserable hours of small talk, he dropped me off. I opened the door to my mother's home, the one I had shared with her for the last twenty-two years of my life, and plopped down on my awful pink comforter that had covered my bed since I was twelve.

When Mama returned from Greece, she brought me even more bad news.

"Thair, I need to talk to you about something," she said matter-of-factly.

"Okay . . . "

"I know how much you love going to Greece . . . loved spending summers with your yiayia, but—and I hope you can understand—I had to sell your yiayia's cottage."

Sell Yiayia's cottage? My body started shaking. Sand, blue water, sitting, laughing with Yiayia, *our* little cottage, *my* sanctuary! I barely heard my mother as she continued.

" . . . and I can't afford to have a house half way across the world. It's old. And it was falling apart."

I was livid, screaming at her in a way I never had before: "We could have figured something out! You did *not* have to sell Yiayia's house!"

My mother's eyes welled as she whispered, "I'm sorry. I had to."

For years, I would not forgive her, but she was right. How could I have afforded to keep up a property on an isolated Greek island? But God knows how I loved that house. The white-washed walls. The red tile roof. The blue door. The balcony with our thatched chairs. The little garden that gave us figs, grapes, plums, crunchy cucumber, gorgeous green peppers. And deep-red, delicious tomatoes.

———

I grab *Vanity Fair* from my suitcase, a tomato from a basket, and go out to my small, private balcony. Sitting on a plastic chair, I stretch my legs out in front of me and eat the sweet tomato, just like someone would eat an apple. After just a few minutes, my fruit is finished, my fingers are sticky, but I'm too lazy to get up, so I hang my hand loosely beside me. I watch the beads of sweat form between my breasts; little diamonds nestled in my cleavage. Perspiration drips down the front of my stomach. My thighs are stuck to the chair, moisture pooling between the plastic and my legs. And yet. I don't wish for air-conditioning. The stifling heat, the suffocating humidity, they allow me to *breathe* because I am back, after so many years, to the place that makes me feel alive, really alive.

6

Aphrodite's Story

Alexandria, Egypt
May, 1942

This was the day the Greek fisherman would be coming over. Instead of being tired from the night before, Dita woke up early, feeling anxious, nervous; completely uneasy. She tried smiling at her reflection, but her eyes welled up with tears because it had not been what she had expected. On the beach, sand between her toes, sand everywhere, it was painful, then uncomfortable, and fast. Too fast. She held it for years in her secret pocket, and in a matter of seconds, it was gone.

He sounded like a beast, but he wasn't rough. Dirk held her in his arms after and told Dita he would be back, but she didn't believe him, and it didn't matter. What mattered now was that she was *spoiled*, and though she mostly felt disgraced and dirty, more than ever before, another emotion sat with her that morning, pressed on her chest, one she had never experienced before: opening her mouth and letting it out, a deep sob with no tears, and suddenly, she was relieved. But that moment was fleeting. She was a mere woman with no hopes for a future, so her relief, her disdain for marriage, quickly turned into fear. The Greek fisherman would not want her now.

When the doorbell finally rang at noon, she ran downstairs and hid behind the large jacquard couch like a schoolgirl. Her father walked over to the door and opened it; the two Greeks exchanged a polite handshake and some other niceties, then walked in and sat at the far end of the room at the small dining room table. Two men ready to do business.

Dita could hear the man talking politely, his words polished, his mannerisms refined. He didn't sound like a fisherman. She knew he was from an affluent family from the island of Kythnos, but he was a villager nonetheless. His were not educated people, but they had stretches of land all around the island, some for their fig trees, some for the wheat that they harvested every July, other pieces of land for their herds of goats that produced the legendary cheese and milk of Kythnos. If Dita married this man, she would surely be a busy wife.

Dita's father asked Stavros about his family, how they were managing. The Greek's responses were slow and calm, his speech not typical, a soft, yet masculine voice (much like her father's). It was a voice that said: "I can take care of you. Protect you."

For almost an hour, they talked about the land. About fish. About cheese. About the war. Stavros said that he wanted to finish his studies in Athens that were interrupted when the war broke out, and one day he planned on being an engineer. Dita wanted to peer over the couch so badly but knew how ridiculous she would look (the day before a woman, today acting like a child), so she sat quietly on the floor, knees under her chin, sweat dripping between her thighs and in the crooks of her elbows while her dear father sold her life to this man whom they knew only by name, who was really just a stranger. Stavros would get a wife who would make babies, work the wheat fields, tend the goats alongside his family, and in return, Dita's parents would get consolation that she would marry and be protected for the rest of her life. The man accepted Dita without ever having met her; her photo and heritage sufficed. Stavros said he did want to meet Aphrodite eventually, but there was no rush. He would inform his family of the upcoming nuptials, so his mother could plan the wedding, and then he would call on Dita while on his next visit to port. The men shook hands once more, sealed the deal, and as he got up and began walking to the door, Dita raised herself just enough to see the manly shoulders of the person she would soon have to marry.

After he left, her father walked over, sat down, and leaned over the couch and looked into Dita's face: "What do you think? *Agape mou*, can I persuade you into believing that he is a good man?"

She wanted to start screaming, saying that her life was hers and she would not marry this man! She wanted to tell him her dirty secret and that his plan to marry her off was foiled, but her father's soft eyes silenced her. How foolish she must have been to think that she could create another destiny for herself. Her life had never been her own. So, instead, Dita succumbed: "Do you think he knew I was here, too? He probably thinks I am a fool." Eyes cast downward, she surprisingly cared what the fisherman thought of her. She didn't want to care, but she did.

Her father reached over, took her hand, pulled her up off the ground, onto the couch, and with open arms squeezed her. "No, I don't think he knew you were there, and if he did, he would not think you a fool. You will never be a fool to anyone, Dita." His icy blue eyes, so warm, held her gaze as he put his arms around her again. Then his face and tone changed, "Dita, I know you have been going to the Ally Social Clubs, but now that you are an engaged woman, you need to bid farewell to all your . . . friends."

Dita's eyes pooled with tears. "But, Babba, I just got a real job. I won't go there to change oil anymore or to meet friends. I was offered a position, a real position to work on an assembly line. I want to take this job!" Her voice dropped, her shoulders sagged, "Please . . . at least until I get . . . married."

"Dita, you need to talk to your mother about this. Stavros said that he will write to his parents and you can get married and go to Kythnos within the year. He said there is safe passage for those who want to return to Greece."

"Within the year! No, Babba, please! I don't want to leave you and Mama. Please don't do this to me." Her voice cracked.

Dita's father looked immediately frail. He loved his daughter and it broke his heart to imagine her so far away, but his work was here in Egypt, here at the Alexandria port. He loved Greece, a true patriot, but time and circumstance had led him to this country where work was plentiful and pay secure.

His voice was once again gentle, "Dita, didn't you like him? He looked like a decent young man. He's only four years older than you and so well spoken."

"Like him? I don't know him! Shall I tell you who I like? I like an Englishman named Henry! And I like a South African man named Dirk! And I like the way these men hold me! Kiss me! I like the way—"

Her father should have gotten angry at her outburst, but instead he stopped her from speaking with a finger gently placed on her lips. He did not want her to say something she would later regret. What he did not know was that she had already done something, not something that she necessarily regretted, but something she hoped the Greek would never find out about.

"Dita, please. Stavros is a good man. You will come to love him. I am sure of that. And when the war is over, and when your mother and I have enough money saved, we will move to Kythnos, and then we will all be together. By then, imagine, you will have several children, and I will be a papou." A large smile beamed off his face, "And we will be a big and glorious family. Won't that be good?"

Dita did not answer, instead she sobbed and sobbed, sweat mixed with tears. She held onto her father tightly, loving and hating him intensely at that moment.

Her staunch mother stood at the top of the staircase and just listened. As the words poured out of her husband's mouth, Dita's large-framed mother quivered slightly. The heat was suffocating, yet she looked chilled as if her big bones ached. She looked down once more without being seen, then disappeared into her bedroom. She had had no choice either.

7

It's already 10:00 p.m., but I'm not tired; in fact, I'm more alert than ever. I stand up, stretch my legs, get a large glass of water and return to my nook, my pseudo office, my space in the kitchen that has turned into my writing room.

Aphrodite's Story

Island of Kythnos, Greece
April, 1943

The Italians and Germans occupied several of the neighboring islands, but Kythnos had remained relatively immune with villagers milling around, daily duties taking precedence over anxiety. Dita always listened for news about the war, but the plethora of physical chores left her physically exhausted and mentally drained.

Her days began at dawn. Dita's first duty was to prepare her husband's breakfast: coffee boiled in a briki, bread, cheese, olives, and three types of jam set on the table. Stavros sat and ate and spoke very little. Their cold stone house was large in comparison to other properties on the island; she had indeed married well. Not white-washed, not picturesque, not quaint nor delicate, her new home had seven rooms and sprawling spaces, yet Dita felt isolated—ironically so, because her mother- and father-in-law lived in the same house. Family members lived in houses surrounding hers, each house but a stone's throw away. Her husband was also an only child so there were no brothers- or sisters-in-law, but the Mylopoulos clan was endless: cousins, old aunts and uncles, ancient people in black. Everyone in the village seemed related one way or the other, and like most new brides on the island, everyone expected so much from these young, strong women. Dita needed to invite family members for homemade sweets; that is, after she had tended the chickens, the goats; after she had washed the clothes, the linens; after she had made cheese, bread, and cooked for her husband, his parents, the auntie that was too old, the cousin who was recently widowed. And when all the work was done, and the guests had left, her mother-in-law expected her to hand-embroider intricate lace tablecloths.

Dita was too weary to cry at night, but when she accidentally poked her finger with the horrid thick needle, silent tears often mixed with the blood. She shared none of this with Stavros, who was a kind husband, because he, too, worked hard and was gone almost all day, fishing or tending to his family's land. He would rarely relax in the corner café with other men drinking Ouzo, discussing the war and other matters of less importance. In fact, he saved all his extra energy to read the pile of books by his bed by the light of a candle and, unlike the other villagers, he saved his conversation for his intelligent wife.

Shortly after Dita and he had met, Stavros decided he liked her. Truly liked her. Yes, she would make a good wife, but he also—quite surprisingly—enjoyed her company. The few dates that they had in Alexandria had surpassed his expectations because she was not only a fashionable, handsome girl, but she was also witty and confident, and he found her amusing. Dita would tell him stories about changing oil on Jeeps and about her short time on the assembly line; her knowledge of the war was extraordinary, especially for a woman, and once in a while, when he least expected it, she would shock him with a dirty joke. He was a serious young man, but Dita could make him laugh. And she found him charming in the way that she felt protected when she was around him, similar to the way she had felt about Henry.

Sometimes she thought about Henry, how life would have been in England, but he was too late because when the letter and the box arrived, she was already on her way back to Greece. She was taken aback when her mother gave her the package years later, but her mother had always surprised her. Sometimes she even thought about Dirk. But from him, she never heard a word—not after *that* night.

On the island, Dita would usually retire as soon as the sun went down, escaping into her bedroom to avoid her pesky mother-in-law, who was always touching her stomach, telling her: "It is time." Eidothea would wink at Dita, opening her mouth sideways, two gold incisors protruding from a mouth that only housed six teeth. Dita did not appreciate this swarthy woman who wore all black and had endless energy for gossip, but she knew she had not only married her husband, but his whole family; this was all too clear when Stavros introduced his mother to his wife-to-be. He had stood there with his arm around Eidothea's shoulder as she beamed with adoration into his eyes; it was obvious she idolized her only son. She was the only woman who could draw Stavros's attention away from Dita, the one woman he dared not disrespect—until the day she pushed him too far.

The first night Dita and he were to spend together as a wedded couple, his mother presented Dita with a white-embroidered bedsheet. Eidothea told Dita that in the morning she should hang the bloodstained sheet outside of the bedroom window for all to see what a good woman her son had chosen. Dita was horrified and began to shake uncontrollably. Stavros grabbed the bedsheet from his mother, threw it to the ground, and for the first time spoke back to her, telling her that his wife would not be subjected to such antiquated and ridiculous traditions. It was at that moment when Dita opened her heart to Stavros. Eidothea Mylopoulos, on the other hand, was in shock that her son would speak to her that way and disrespect her wishes. She took the bedsheet off the floor, wiped away spurious tears from her dry eyes, glared at Dita, and stomped away.

That night while Dita lay with her husband for the first time, she feigned pain when he entered her, but she suspected that he knew. If he did, he never said a word about it, and for that, Dita worked hard to please Stavros, even trying to be polite to his insufferable mother. She worked the fields and learned to cook; her hands grew coarse, her waist thickened. Famished in the evenings, she found solace in the warm bread that she had made with her own two hands. Those were the same hands that would rub her husband's shoulders when he told her about his day, and when Stavros would lie with this newly docile wife in bed, she showed him how much she cared, and something would happen. He held Dita and kissed her tenderly. Stavros told her about his hopes and dreams, and for this, she became endeared to him.

Dita accepted that her life had changed forever. She no longer changed oil on Jeeps. The only oil she worked with was the olive oil that she poured onto the deep red tomatoes that adorned her kitchen table.

8

Mid June, 2000

Feeling a bit melancholic, I decide to go for a walk. As I exit the blue door, I see the orange cat again. It looks at me perplexed and, like a dog, follows me down the hill. Every few steps, I glance over my shoulder; it is right there. It stops when I do and continues when I do—the whole thing seems crazy.

I stop at a little bench, half way down, to admire the view. The cat jumps onto the bench and starts rubbing itself against my thigh. While still staring forward, I rub its head as it gets closer and crawls right onto my lap. I have never been a cat person, but this furry animal is quickly entering my heart with its friendly ways.

"Okay, Tang, are you ready to start moving again?" I say, giving my new companion a name while gently lifting the cat up and setting it on the ground. It looks at me once more, and then disappears the other way. A smile covers my face, independent little fellow.

I pass a few houses and greet people as I snake my way down the hill. An old woman dressed completely in black, someone's yiayia I am certain, is sitting in the corner of a patio, crocheting a white-lace-something. The mama is probably in the kitchen cooking; the men of the house sit on the balcony drinking Ouzo even though it's only 10:00 a.m., their newspapers spread on the table. I can hear other family members scream at each other on the other side of the house, but it is clear that they are not fighting: it is just their form of communication. Then the man yells something to the lady of the house, and she brings out another tray with what looks like rusks, jelly, and butter. After she sets down the tray, she scurries back into the kitchen. The familiar, vociferous Greek clamor rings joyfully in my ears.

"*Kalimera,*" I say when the men look over in my direction. They return my good morning and ask me if I am Calliope Papadimitriou's niece from *America.* I say "*oxi,*" but I am Aphrodite Mylopoulos's granddaughter and, yes, from America. They act excited with my response though it's clear with their raised eyebrows and mumblings to one another that they don't know my grandmother. Yiayia lived on the other side of the village and kept to herself. The older, squat man stands and invites me up the few steps for an Ouzo, "*Ella!*" his hand waves in the air, gesticulating "Come!" But I politely decline, a bit too much noise for my quiet mood. Also, alcohol first thing in the morning is not my cup of tea. While leaning on the railing, he asks me more about my yiayia, and I am happy to oblige. Right here, right now, nothing gives me more pleasure than talking about my yiayia. While we are chatting, kids, so many, run up and down the stairs, jump on their bicycles, and then zoom off. Before my conversation with the men ends, the kids are back. They throw the bikes in the yard and run into the house. BAM! A door slams. They scream something to the mama who also screams back, then BAM! The door slams again. Jumping back on their bicycles, sans hat or sunscreen, only in their bathing suits, they wheel away once more. A toddler in the yard is playing with a dog, a situation that looks neither sanitary nor safe as the husky pet licks the child's face. I wave at the toddler, then the men, and make my exit.

Sitting in a café in the village's main square, I think about the family I just met and can't help but compare them to my own fractured Greek family and the quiet cottage that had been my sanctuary. Unlike our neighbors' homes that were filled with generation after generation of families, my yiayia's cottage was always quiet. When I was young, I believed my yiayia must have done something very bad to God because she had practically no family left. She would tell me: "Thair, when you find good man, you feed him good. You get to heart from stomach. He like your cooking, he marry you, and if you lucky, Theos bless you with many children. Children have children, and when you be a yiayia, you have lots of family, all everywhere."

So what did my yiayia do wrong? She had me, but I was just one grandchild—and I was a girl. I know she loved me, but sometimes words slipped from her mouth: "You lots of work, if you a boy, I no mind you stay out so late." I knew she really didn't mind my social life, but I knew a grandson could have helped her around the house, helped her fix things. In the handyman department, I was indeed worthless, and for that, I sometimes felt sad for her, for me. She tried to teach me, but I had no desire; books and pretty dresses drew my attention, not tools and toils.

With no man around to fix things, Yiayia had the Herculean task to keep everything working. Her skills were plentiful, but her bones were brittle and cracked just like the floorboards. Rust ate away at the wrought iron fence, exposing its innards; the shutters flapped in the wind, so hard to close, a constant thudding all night. The toilet's slight running sang through the wee hours of the morning, enchanting us like Odysseus's sirens; without beeswax in our ears, the cacophony of sounds actually lulled us to sleep and, like babies, we slept deep and peacefully. As the house became more decrepit, my romance with it grew. It was old and safe, just like my yiayia.

Our summer house was neither exploding at the seams with sniveling babies nor rambunctious adolescents, loud uncles nor demanding fathers, but we did have noise. Beautiful noise: Yiayia's continuous complaining, my constant chatter, our endless laughs. Every so often, though, I saw Yiayia stare at the neighbor's house, which was directly across from ours, but did not say a word. When she looked my way, I saw something in her eyes, but I did not know how to read her perplexed expression. I wondered if it made her sad or relieved to be just the two of us.

Even before my grandmother's death, my mother didn't like visiting Greece, saying it was a country that had suffocated her; unlike my mother, I came to life here. But, then again, I have always been so different from my mother. I always loved the heat of a summer in Greece. The humid afternoons sitting on the balcony watching Yiayia smoke her Karelia while she ignored me. After the third cigarette, Yiayia would go into the kitchen, get the vegetables that she had cut that morning from her garden, return to her chair, and begin to meticulously chop the cucumber, the green peppers, the onions, the tomatoes.

I always grabbed a tomato from the bowl and munched on it like an apple. "Stop," she would say, "that for dinner," as if there was some shortage of her red, delicious tomatoes. As I wiped the juice off my face with the back of my hand, I started conversations with her; sometimes she responded with short answers, sometimes my words just hung in the air with the silence. Then, finally, she would say: "I tell you about Italian soldier who got macaroni stuck up his *kolo*?"

"Yes," I would reply, "but tell me again." I had only heard the joke fifty-eight times, almost once a day for the months of summer, but if it gave her such pleasure to tell me about the guy who got spaghetti stuck up his butt, I would gladly listen. The next day I heard it again and laughed again, and again, then again. But there was a genuine payoff for me: her laugh. Just to hear that throaty, deep, heartfelt laugh made it all worthwhile.

I usually arrived pale, chubby, and unhappy, and left tan, trim, and rested. I didn't want to go back to the US; I never did, but I had no choice. The summer always came to an end, and I needed to go back *home*. At twenty-one, I had so many dreams. I had one more year to get my bachelor's degree, and then I planned to move to Greece *forever*.

So many plans, yet nothing happened like I had imagined. Yiayia died. I pursued a higher education and made a down payment on a condo with the sale of Yiayia's beloved Kythnos house. By twenty-five, I was an adjunct professor and a homeowner of a small place by the beach. A big step away from the suburbs, no more cohabitating with Mom, no more land-locked living, just miles and miles of sand and ocean, I finally had a breath of fresh air. And a place to call my own.

But I still felt unsettled.

I shared none of this with my mother, who believed her daughter was successful and happy. After years of a difficult marriage, I didn't want to burden Mama because for the first time in my life, I saw *her* happy.

I think about Mama and how different her life is now from when she was married to "the American"—as Yiayia called my father.

After my grandfather died, Mama sent Yiayia enough money to maintain her apartment in Athens and her summer cottage on the island, but after the divorce from the American, Yiayia had to choose: either the winter or summer house. Yiayia chose to keep the latter. It was her haven. Winters on Kythnos were brutal: sharp winds, low temperatures even for the Mediterranean, but she couldn't bear the thought of getting rid of her sweet, white house with its luscious garden.

Yiayia was only forty-seven when Papou died; the following year, a tragic accident killed her only son. She was a tough woman, and though I could still make her laugh, my mother used to say that after Theo Sotiris's passing, death lived in her eyes. Yiayia would repeatedly state: "No Papou, no Sotiris, no daughters," her daughters, not dead, but worthless in her mind. "*Doxa to Theo,*" thank God! She used to say, she had me. Even though I was a handful (and a girl!), I knew I meant the world to her. With every Sandro, Nikos, Andreas story, I brought color to her mundane existence. I was the red in her tomatoes. The young lady who arrived every summer and grew up before her tired eyes, the girl who talked incessantly, Dita's granddaughter: the storyteller. I knew she also had stories to tell, and the day she gave me the gold band and her fragmented tale was one of the happiest— and saddest—days of my life.

I'm playing with the gold band on the table, twisting it around my index finger. Hadley's initials are barely visible, worn with time, not with wear. Finally, I open my wallet and put it in the side with the small zipper, the place it has been living since Yiayia gave it to me. I pay my bill and decide it's time to head back, too much reminiscing. But before I do, I want to give Rick a call from the local kiosk. I am hungry for a friendly voice from home and want to temporarily escape all the haunting memories. After several attempts, I finally get my buddy on the line. I tell him about the last few weeks, and he gives me an update on my condo. He and Frank are staying at my place on the weekends to enjoy the swimming pool and have the beach close by. He tells me that a grumpy neighbor complained to the Homeowner's Association about these "strange men that have been frequenting the pool area and that it's bad for the children." I tell Rick that I will call the HOA, but he says that it's already under control. He also mentions that he has talked to Phaedra, and she was upset that I hadn't called in *so long*. He emphasizes these words, and I can hear my mom's voice in my head. We laugh about this; thirty-one and I still need to check in with my mother every few days. It's a short call because of cost, but I feel much better as I walk up the hill to my place. When I get to the front door, Tang is there, waiting to greet me.

9

From the breakfast nook in the kitchen, I have a perfect view of the electric Aegean. I have been taking my daily swims in the cove below, about a fifteen-minute walk down a steep hill. I came to Greece feeling "heavy," as the ancient Greek philosopher Parmenides would say, though lately, a jaunty insouciance penetrates my days for hours at a time. There have been days when I am so relaxed, I almost forget to eat. I drink my Greek coffee and turn the cup over in the sink. By the time I put on my bathing suit, the sandy grounds have dried, and I read my own fortune, a little bit of witchery passed down from my yiayia. Ah, I see lots of hearts around the rim. *Today will be a good day.* Today I will be surrounded by love.

As silly as it sounds, I do feel loved. Certainly, there has been no love from a man, but for the last month, Mother Earth has sure worked her magic on me. I wake up to the trills of birds; the heat from the sun sneaks its way through the shutters and onto my sleeping body; I taste the sweet, humid air and see the clear blue water below. There really is no love greater than this. I can't help but wonder why I fail to see these things when I am living in sunny San Diego. It's probably that ridiculous (but true?) saying: "the grass is always greener on the other side." But how long can this tranquility last? Better yet, how can I learn to recapture this feeling when I am home, trapped by routine, bored with grading, dissatisfied with life? I am not *afraid* to be alone, but I can't help the loneliness that sucks me dry when I am "home."

And now, for the first time in my life, I am happy with the silence. Have I changed or is it just the surroundings? I don't feel like I have to go out to meet anyone; in fact, I haven't had a real conversation in weeks. I do go to a café and have an afternoon Nescafe frappé every few days and people-watch; otherwise it's just me and Tang, my little pal who waits for his milk bowl every morning.

———

It's another perfect day, so I drink my coffee, put on my pink bikini, a quick flip of my coffee mug, practice my daily sorcery, then take off. I walk down the hill to take a quick dip and am back in about an hour, just before I begin to get a bit shaky from not having eaten anything.

My stomach is growling. I push the unlocked door open, walk into the kitchen, and grab the cucumber and feta cheese from the fridge. From a hanging basket, I get a sweet red onion and two tomatoes. As I cut up the first blood red tomato, my mind begins to wander. I have so many lingering questions about my grandmother's story, so after my snack, I get dressed and anxiously make my way down the hill to the local telephone kiosk.

"*Yasou*, Mama."

"Hi, sweetheart, what a nice surprise! I was just telling Greta that I hadn't gotten a call in about a week, and I was getting worried."

"Mama, you know there's no reason to worry. I gave you the neighbor's number, so *if* anything were to happen, someone would call."

"I know, but it's sad for me to think of you there all by yourself."

Cutting her off, knowing that each word is costing me a pretty penny, I ask: "Mama, how long were Yiayia and Papou married and what exactly happened to Theo Sotiris?"

"Thair, these are strange questions to be asking now and—"

"Mama, please, just answer. Just to be back here where Yiayia . . ." I can't say the words. "Mama, can you please humor me and answer?"

"Well, let me think. Yiayia was married to Papou for about . . . um . . . about thirty years when he died. You know, your grandmother used to say that he died because of me. Because I broke his heart. Isn't that awful?"

"Yes, Mom." I say as my chest heaves. "I remember that part of the story. But it was a heart attack, right?" *Just like my poor yiayia*, but I don't say that part out loud.

"Yes. But, I have to admit, I do feel a bit guilty. I should never have betrayed my father—but then again, if I didn't, I wouldn't have you!" When she says this, I can picture a smile on her face through the phone lines. My mother. The ultimate optimist, a woman who sees the glass overflowing, never just half full; she's so different than me.

"What about Theo Sotiris? He died young, right?" I used to ask Yiayia the same questions, but she never wanted to talk about him.

My mother's voice softens, "Yes, he was a good kid. Never really book smart, so he worked construction, and they told Yiayia he died when a beam fell on him." I can hear her pause. "Gosh, it was so sad, such a horrible death. Oh, Thair, please don't ask me anymore right now . . . Oh, I just remembered. I have some wonderful news! Aunt Lena will be visiting next month. She has a few weeks off from the London Philharmonic and will come to San Diego. Isn't that exciting?" When she says this, her voice goes up an octave. Mama adores and admires her older sister, another tough cookie, who pursued music when everyone told her that she had to get married and make babies.

"That's great, Mama. It's been . . . three or has it been four years since her last visit?"

"It's been four. Too long. Too, too long! I'm *so* thrilled! She is even going to stay the entire two weeks here with me!"

Mama beams whenever she sees her sister. They act like teenage

girls, staying up all night, talking and laughing into the wee hours of
the morning. It is always sad when she leaves; Mama never knows
when Thea Lena will come back. I tell my mother she should go visit
her in London, but she has no desire to go anywhere.

"I look forward to seeing her, too." I add.

It's the truth. I am usually busy teaching, but Thea Lena's visits are
always intellectually stimulating and her manner delightfully quirky,
so I try to make time. When I was a teenager, I had asked her why she
wasn't married. *Thair, darling,* she had responded, *my compositions are
my friends, my concerts are my home, and my cello is my lover!* Then
she laughed with a deep, throaty laugh that reminded me of Yiayia's.

"Mama, can I ask you something else?"

"Okay, I guess."

"Can you tell me about Papou?"

"What do you want to know?"

"Anything. Anything about him, about how he was with Yiayia."

"Okay." She pauses, and I see the phone clicker moving rapidly, but
money is not important right now. "Well, your grandfather was a tall
man with thick grey hair, a soft voice, and sensitive hands . . . but he
had a hard heart. Thair, he really was a good man. And I was—surprisingly—his favorite. When I left, he was heartbroken, but he was
also very, very angry. It's just that at the time, a respectable Greek girl
did not leave her family to go off and marry an *American*."

When she says "American," her intonation reminds me of the
neighbor's that day when he asked if I was the *American* niece. What
is it about America that makes some people say it in such a distasteful
way?

"Thair, Thair . . . are you still there?"

"Sorry, yes, Mama, please continue."

"Well, when you were born, your papou was furious that he had
not met his first grandchild. And yet he didn't want me to come back
to Greece to visit. I tried to call him through the years, but he forever

closed his heart to me, would never even speak to me on the phone. It was really a sad situation, especially for your grandmother, who was in between the two of us."

"Mama, why didn't you come back for your brother's or father's funeral?"

"Oh, Thair. Must I respond now?"

I hear the phone crack or is it my mother's voice?

"Please, Mama . . . "

"I just couldn't. Oh, Thair, I couldn't. Please understand. Please. Honey. Please . . . I can't talk—"

As I stand here holding the phone line, I don't quite understand, but I know when it's time to switch subjects. It hurts me to hear her so upset, and my questions are the cause of her angst.

"Okay, Mama. Thanks. Now let me tell you about this orange cat that has befriended me."

After a few minutes of light conversation, I hang up and pull out the equivalent of sixty dollars from my wallet. The woman in the kiosk gladly counts each thousand drachma bill then nods.

When I walk home, I think about our conversation. I remember Yiayia always wearing black, saying it was out of respect for her dead husband and son, but she never said more about them. Mama told me that when Papou died, she called her mother every day. But Yiayia did not want to speak to anyone. According to the neighbor, Yiayia sat in her room, stared out of the window, and did absolutely nothing. After the required forty days of mourning, she got up and continued with her life: she went to the market, cooked, and watched hours and hours of movies while smoking packs and packs of cigarettes.

Aphrodite's Story

Athens, Greece
August 14th, 1946

Their first child was staying with a neighbor because Dita knew the new one would be coming any day. Dita could not relax, tossing, turning, her huge belly twice the size compared to last time.

"Are you okay?" Stavros asked his very pregnant wife.

"Yes, fine, please sleep."

But he could not sleep, the days were long, working all day, studying all night, supporting his wife, his little girl, and now—so soon after the first—they were having another. It was not his work, his studies, or his responsibilities that were keeping him up that night, but sheer excitement. He was going to have a baby, and this time it would be a boy. A son!

Dita could feel her husband beside her, his breathing heavy, pulling the covers, and then turning towards her, "Dita, are you still awake?"

"Yes."

"Are you okay?"

She rolled over, slowly, every move taxing on her heavy body. "Yes, don't worry. The baby will be fine."

"Dita, I am not worried about the baby. I am thinking about you," he said wide-awake while looking at her.

"I'm okay."

"Dita, I know I am not home a lot, but you are a good wife, and I want you to know that."

"Thank you, Stavros, but you do not need to say these things." Dita liked it in Athens and didn't care that their families were far away. She had a lot of responsibilities but knew when Stavros completed his degree life would be easier for them.

Moving to Athens had been a godsend. The first three years on Kythnos were backbreaking. She had to accompany her mother-in-law everywhere without complaining while learning the trades of Stavros's people. From wheat to goats to figs, from picking, to cooking, to cleaning—there was never a free moment. And it only got tougher when Dita got pregnant right away and had to still do everything with a protruding belly, swollen feet, and endless nausea. When a family friend offered their small apartment, rent free, in Athens, Stavros was able to return to the mainland and continue his studies—and his wife was finally afforded a moment to breathe. His family did not understand why he wanted to attend university but supported him nonetheless; he had left them once before when he was a teenager to go to high school in Athens since no secondary schools on the island existed. His voracious desire to study troubled the villagers, but Stavros's gentle, yet persuasive, manner allowed him to garner the support of his family time and time again.

When he told them he was bringing home a Greek girl from Egypt to marry, they were not happy because they had already chosen a local girl for him. But he knew how to apply his oratory skills on his unlearned family, and so his new wife received a warm-enough welcome when she arrived. And he had chosen well. Dita was strong, willing, womanly, and though he greatly desired her, his tempered personality normally kept his passion at bay. But not that night.

Lying there close to her, looking at the mother of his first child, who was now carrying his son, he felt vulnerable, his love transparent.

"Dita, life will get better for us. You will not have to mend other people's clothes, and one day we will be able to go back to

Kythnos for the holidays. Maybe we will even have two houses! A nice apartment here in Athens and a summer house on the island. Just you, me, Lena, and our new son! It will be wonderful."

Through the darkness, he almost illuminated the room with his pride; his delight secondary only to anticipation. He had been talking about this unborn son now for several months; not normally superstitious, he had believed his mother when she had told him: "*Agori! Agori!*"

Dita's mother-in-law had come to Athens from the island for a short visit, and one evening, in front of her son, she pulled a long hair from Dita's head, asked for her wedding ring and slipped the hair through it. Then she hung it over Dita's round belly and waited for it to start moving. Slowly, but surely, it did move, and when the gold band circled to the right, her mother-in-law was ecstatic. It was a boy! The baby would be a boy because circling to the left would have meant a female, another little girl. It was this ritual that left Stavros with a deep sense of satisfaction that his family would soon be complete. And his excitement was contagious; his utter joy that night made him look at his wife with such intense emotion that something in her stirred. *God, she said, please let it be a boy.*

Under the covers, with his fingers perfectly intertwined in hers, she felt so close to her husband. Dita felt something so strange. Was this love? Was this what it felt like to be completely content in the world?

But the feeling did not last. The next thing she felt literally took her breath away: a sharp pain traveled through her as she yelled with all her might. Then the bed was soaked. It was time.

Twenty-three hours and seventeen minutes later, Dita held her baby. A baby girl. She looked at the perfect little thing in her arms and felt nauseated. She had never feared her husband; in the last four years, he had been nothing but good to her. He had not romanced her, never brought her anything, never told her she was beautiful, but he provided food at the table, was a good father, and made love to her regularly. He often talked to her and even kissed her tenderly. But as she held this child, for the first time since their wedding night, she was nervous because Stavros wanted a boy so much. He loved baby Lena, but a son would be his greatest accomplishment. He had said that over and over since that ill-fated night with his mother. Why had that stupid village woman put such an idea into Stavros's head?

She was a stunning baby, jet black hair and eyes; eyes that were wide open, too open, too expressive, too alive for a newborn. Dita held her tight, irked that this child was not a boy, yet loved her more because she wasn't.

Stavros walked into the room with the force of an army, moved toward the child with heavy footsteps. Though weak, Dita's first instinct was to hold the baby tightly to her chest, not wanting her husband to touch or see her. Stavros's face was pale, his fists drawn.

"Let me see the child!"

"Stavros, please. She's innocent. Please, we can try again."

"Let me see *it*."

Where had the gentle husband she had gotten to know for the last four years gone? Who was this man standing before her? Was he Chronos, the father of the gods, the beast who would devour his own children?

She feared for her baby girl.

"No! I will not let you have her . . ."

He pushed his way towards her, grabbing the child from Dita's embrace.

"Stavros!"

He held the baby in his shaking arms and pulled the blanket off to look at the genitals. It was indeed a girl. He was ready to throw the baby back to her mother when something entirely unexpected happened. The baby looked at him, deep into his eyes with her ebony stare, and he seemed to be momentarily mesmerized. Not gently, but mechanically, still in a haze, he rewrapped the blanket around the baby and gave her back to Dita.

He said only these words before he left: "The next one will be a boy."

He walked out of the hospital that day and continued to provide for his wife and daughters—and son, the one who was born two years later. He got his coveted son, a premature baby who had feminine features and was always a bit sickly; Stavros got his degree, became an engineer who owned two houses, one in Athens, one on the island; and he remained married to a woman who was strong and self-sufficient until death did them part.

But the illuminated man who lay beside Dita the day before Phaedra's birth never returned.

10

Every cobbled path, every olive tree, and every red tomato on Kythnos made me think of the woman who had raised me every summer for seven consecutive years. Yiayia was a complicated woman, not understood by many. She rarely hugged me, never told me she loved me, but actions do speak louder than words. On my summer visits, she would labor endlessly in her garden to serve me fresh vegetables; she would wink at the passing fisherman, and we would always end up with at least two fresh fish for lunch. We were two women living together harmoniously for three months of the year. From September until the following summer she lived alone, smoked her cigarettes, and watched American soap operas and the Greek news. She had occasional visits from neighbors, but she was not a social woman. At least she was not a social *old* woman. I think she missed her daughters, but she would never admit it, not to me, not to them.

The summer I was twenty, my mama finally decided to go to Greece with me. I had never seen my grandmother cry, but the tears she shed when she saw her daughter after so many years, I will never forget. Even my mother broke down, the two sobbing, holding each other tight. But it was a brief lapse into sentimentality. The rest of the time, Yiayia and my mother were constantly bickering—and not in the loving, Greek way. First it was light: Yiayia's food was too salty, Mama's skorts were too short, then:

Life was tough.
             Why you divorce if you love American so much?
Dad should have forgiven me.
             You should reach to your Babba more.
This place is falling apart.
             Me, Thair, love this house.

When Mama finally left, I sensed Yiayia was sad but relieved; I saw the same emotion on my mama's face when bidding adieu to her mother. Neither realized that they would never see each other again.

I think about all this while I make my way down to the cove below on my rented moped. As I lie on the beach rereading Kundera's *Slowness*, two little girls start playing in the sand in front of me, both topless, with sunburned bellies and bright red cheeks. They can't be more than two years old and look like twins. I listen to their precious voices; they are at that tender age when they have just started talking, squeaky voices with long pauses between words. I watch them for a few minutes. Behind me, I see a woman wearing dark sunglasses. She keeps wiping her eyes. I assume they are watering because she's sweating, but then a hirsute, bloated-bellied man walks over and throws himself beside her. The conversation becomes too loud and too personal: the mistress, the drinking, the mistress again. I try not to listen and refocus on my book, but her voice is too hurt, his too strong, and my quiet is disturbed, so I get up and leave.

I hop on the scooter and gas it up the hill. When I arrive, I see Tang waiting for me. He rubs himself on my leg. I bend down and wrap him in my arms, bringing him inside. I grab a piece of ham from the fridge and feed it to him as his raspy tongue licks my fingers. When he's done, I set him on the floor. I take a plastic chair and my fluffy towel and go outside on the balcony.

I am trying not to think about the conversation I heard at the beach, too reminiscent of a time in my life I don't want to remember. The man's angry words ring in my ears, her tearful sobs cut into me, and suddenly I am no longer thinking about two strangers fighting; instead, I am back in my mother's home. I'm listening to my parents' vicious voices as they resonate throughout the house. And I am seventeen all over again.

Lying on my rosy comforter, feet stretched out, I gazed up at my frilly canopy. My eyes darted around my bedroom. The pink curtains, the pastel prints, the Pink Panther—after years of cotton candy bedrooms, I learned to hate the color pink.

I swung my feet off the side of the bed, peeked out from my room, and saw my father stumble down the hallway, women's perfume encapsulating him. A coffee mug flew across the room, my mother hurling it at him with intense passion. Her mascara tears complemented the brown stains on the wall. I closed my bedroom door, placed my fingers on the volume button, cranked up the stereo; Depeche Mode's "Blasphemous Rumors" attempted to drown out my mother's high-pitched wailing.

"Just leave, why don't you? Just leave!" she yelled. Then her sobbing started again. I couldn't stand to hear my mother cry, so I did what most troubled teenagers (who are lucky enough to own a car) do: I grabbed my keys and fled suburban hell. In my black Honda, with the wind blowing in my hair, I was free. With one hand on the steering wheel, my other hand searched through my purse. I found my menthol Virginia Slims, pulled out the pack and lit one. Tightly forming my mouth around the filter, I inhaled all the impurities that made me feel so good.

My father used to tell me when I was a little girl that if I concentrated hard enough, the world would become a land with sugar mountains and lollipop trees. He said that there would be a chocolate ocean with peanut butter at its very depths.

Just thinking about Gordon Wright's words, even today, I get angrier and angrier. My heart races now like it did then. I remember speeding around corners, heading towards the beach. I couldn't handle another minute of the land-locked suburb, mountains all around me, suffocating me, and I loved the beach, the infinite expanse of blue. Being by the coast reconnected me to my other life. My Greece. My sanctuary. My yiayia. Every summer when school was out, I would quit my part-time job, buy a ticket, and go visit my grandmother. For those glorious months I would reconnect to my roots, reconnect to a stronger, healthier version of myself.

———

I pull out my laptop and read everything I have written. Did Yiayia ever really love Papou? For that, I never got a clear answer. *Agape* was a word she avoided. The day she told me about her Englishman was the same day she told me about her engagement and about her life on Kythnos. *But he a good man, Thair.* I asked her repeatedly if she was "happily married." Her answer was always the same: *Yiayia gets married, have children, and now cooks fish for you. Finish.*

So, her story ends there. I guess I will never know exactly how she felt, about the Englishman, about the South African man who, she said, *took something special from secret pocket of your yiayia.* I think I have concluded that she was a product of her time. In my mind, she was a feminist without knowing it, a woman who did not have the support of the movement to grant her choices but did the best she could. My only hope is that she did have moments, months, maybe even years of core happiness, though I will never be certain if she did. And I will never know if these moments were because of, or in spite of, my grandfather. Because she told me so little over the years, her tales always forced, always in fragments, I filled in the gaps with my imagination. How close had I gotten to her real story?

I reread the last part again: *But the illuminated man who lay beside Dita that day never returned.* Yiayia told me that with the birth of my mother, her life with my grandfather *was finish.* "What do you mean it ended, Yiayia?" *It finish, you no understand? Just like story now: it finish!* And she refused to say more.

I close my eyes and see her so clearly—it's as if my yiayia has come back to life and is here with me. I can hear her voice, her laugh; smell her scent; sense her stubbornness. It's a mix of emotions, but after ten long years, I wrote Yiayia's story as I know it. Now I will begin my mother's. And this one will certainly be more difficult.

Phaedra's Story

Athens, Greece
Mid June, 1964

The Hilton had just been built. From the balcony of Phaedra's home in Nea Smirni, she could see the Parthenon—but she never went outside to look at it. Instead, she walked ten minutes in the humid summer weather, paid less than one drachma, squashed herself into a bus with sweaty, foul-smelling old men and women, and rode standing up for twenty minutes to go and visit the Athens Hilton. When she reached the modern structure with its fourteen floors surrounded by hills of grass amidst a city of cement, she always lost her breath for a few seconds.

After neatly rewrapping her thick black hair under the round hat that was perched on top of her head, she looked directly at the doorman. With an air of confidence, she glided through the entrance, immediately reveling in the air-conditioning. Because of her chic Jackie Kennedy look, from matching black pumps to handbag and hat, she was allowed to linger in the lobby without being questioned. There was an area to the left that had large, comfortable couches and, to the right, a small bar.

"Hello," she said to the bartender in polished English that she had learned in school.

"*Yasou*, Phaedra." He always responded in Greek. He knew her name. She never had to tell him because Greek men always knew the names of young, pretty girls.

"A Nescafe, sweet with milk," she said without looking into his dirty eyes. She made her way over to the couches, slid her hands behind her bottom to make sure her skirt didn't wrinkle. Crossing her long, slender legs, she reached over and grabbed a magazine and began to flip through it. Despite her eyes facing down, she was completely aware of everything and everybody around her.

An ancient woman ambled over and sat next to Phaedra. She looked about seventy, so, so wrinkled. She was wearing hot pink, an outfit much like Phaedra's, except Phaedra's wasn't an obscene color. A respectable Greek woman would never wear pink. She must be an American, Phaedra thought. In America you can do whatever you want. The woman dug into her miniature purse and pulled out a silver lipstick case. She popped it open, her hands shaking. There was a mirror on one side. She looked into it, smacked her dry lips together, then proceeded to cautiously apply the lipstick to her cracked lips, smacking them every time she put on a layer. The outer parts of her lips were covered in fuchsia, a pitiful attempt, Phaedra thought, at trying to make her thin lips look luscious. Smiling at Phaedra, she acknowledged her presence. Phaedra smiled back. An elderly man came from the elevator and walked over to them.

"Ready darlin'?"

He grabbed the woman's elbow to help her up as she gently, lovingly, hit him on the arm, but took his help anyway. They looked at each other with a warm exchange and moved away, her arm wrapped through his.

Phaedra could see Dimitri across the lobby. He was the day manager. In three months, she had met all the managers, all the assistants, anyone who mattered. They were all men. They were all married. And they all had tried to bed her. She played the coy game, let them sit on the couch with her, put their nasty hands on her thigh, stare at her with lustful eyes. She usually told them she was bored with Daddy's money and wanted to work. They sat closer, leaned in further, reeking of heavy coffee and cigarette breath, slightly brushing her chest when they reached over to get their drink from the table beside her. Phaedra would just smile sweetly. After a few visits and making the necessary connections, she was finally hired as a receptionist. It was not the position she desired, but it was a step in the right direction. She was tired of studying Ancient Greek and mythology. No more Homer, Socrates, Hera, and Zeus for her. She wanted air-conditioning, not ceiling fans; carpeting, not parquet. She wanted rock and roll, not bouzoukia. To toast champagne glasses, not to throw plates. She wanted big cars, diamonds, Hollywood. And most of all, a big house with air-conditioning.

⌒‿⌒

After a few months of working at the Hilton, Phaedra was even more certain of what she didn't want. She didn't want the German businessman who would only take her across a few European borders, the Arab sheik who would stick her in his harem, or the wealthy Greek tycoon who would move her from Nea Smirni to Voula. She wanted to cross the Atlantic. She wanted to go to America.

From a young age, Phaedra had been dragged to the movies with her mother. *Gidget*, *An Affair to Remember*, *Jailhouse Rock*; from California to New York to everything in between, Dita's hobby slowly turned into Phaedra's obsession. Her mother may have been satisfied to see America only in the movies, but Phaedra had grander aspirations.

At the Hilton, most of the American visitors arrived with their wives; the single ones were either old and disgusting or young and ill-mannered. But they all had one thing in common: they wanted sex. Phaedra, a virgin, was saving herself for the perfect American—the one who was young, wealthy, and well-mannered—but she was starting to think that he didn't exist.

The other receptionists had been talking about a new American guest. Phaedra hadn't seen him yet, but she was certain she would be disappointed again. The girls at the check-in said that this one was rich, good-looking, *and* single. Rumor had it that he was spending most of his evenings at Syngrou Boulevard, the place where men found plenty of women to pass the night away. Although they said he was extremely attractive, he was offering something even better than himself. He had a Polaroid camera. None of these Greek girls had ever seen one, but they heard that it was a camera that not only made color photos but delivered them instantly. The girls said that the American was offering a date or a photo to the more attractive hotel employees. With Phaedra's seductive dark eyes and voluptuous Marilyn Monroe body, she was hopeful she would also receive the offer.

When she rode the bus home that evening, the other

passengers' putrid body odors did not intrude on her dreams. Maybe he was The One. She contemplated saying "yes" to the date if it were offered. Maybe she would fall in love. Maybe he would take her to America.

Phaedra was jarred back into reality when the bus driver yelled at her to get off because they had reached the final destination. She had missed her stop and had to walk the five extra blocks home because of her daydreaming. When she saw her almost-one-hundred-year-old decrepit building, she looked up and cursed the three flights of stairs that led to her home. With heavy footsteps, she finally got to her floor. The front door was open, but no breeze entered. She saw her plump mother hunched over the sink, cleaning the green beans that would be the family's dinner. Her pepper-gray hair was pulled back, falling sloppily from her bun. Phaedra's mother wore all black out of respect for her own father, who had died six years before—only her soiled flower apron gave any color to her appearance.

As Phaedra walked through the kitchen, her mother, engrossed in her duties, did not notice her. Phaedra neither admired nor appreciated her mother's indefatigable nature. Dita was a symbol of what Phaedra refused to become: dependent, overweight, and slovenly. Phaedra had never met the Dita who wore tight dresses and bright lipstick. That woman lived only in a few black and white photos kept in an album deep in a wooden chest.

Phaedra's father was sitting in the living room, smoking a pipe, and reading the newspaper.

"*Fere mou ena Ouzo!*" He yelled as her mother scurried to fix him his drink. Phaedra walked right by him, retreated into her bedroom. Not *her* bedroom really, just a room she shared with her sister and brother, a room suffocating with three beds twelve centimeters away from each other. For almost eighteen years, she had lived in the confines of these walls, and she knew her only salvation would be marriage. Her father had already begun advertising her sexy physique and good teeth, hoping to find her a husband and save her from old maidhood. But she was not going to marry just anyone.

Kicking off her square-toed pumps and tearing away her sticky clothes, Phaedra fell onto her bed. She had a hard time relaxing; beads of sweat on her temples and between her breasts made her wish the fan above did more than just blow the dust around. As she watched the twirling wings, her thoughts drifted back to the American. A photograph or a date? She knew a date would be precisely that: one single date with a vulgar American trying to bed her. If he was as good-looking as the others had said, then an instant photo could prove more exciting. Phaedra could tell her girlfriends that he was her rich fiancé from America. She would say they had met at the hotel, had an affair, but because he was with his dying wife, he could not declare their love, but would send for her when the woman passed away. Phaedra could always say later that the wife had never died because the brilliant American doctors had found some cure, but she would have the photo to prove her story. And from what she heard, it was like no other photo. It re-created all the colors right before one's eyes, an image appearing instantly. It sounded so odd and so wonderful; after considering and reconsidering her choices, she decided she would choose the photo. She attempted to convince herself that America wasn't that great after all. Anyway, how could she live in a country where people cut their food with the side of a fork? It would definitely be the photo. She should probably also quit the Hilton and go back to Georgios.

The following day, Phaedra was on the phone at the reception desk when she saw him walk through the baroque archway that led from the elevators to the main lobby. He headed directly for her desk and leaned his Rolex-and-diamond-covered arm on the counter, parallel to her eyes.

Looking up, batting her eyelashes, she asked: "Can I help you?"

"Hi, beautiful. I was wondering if you could tell me where I could find a good, authentic place to eat around here."

She didn't answer him right away, trying to decide if he looked more like Elvis Presley or James Dean. He was wearing a business suit, not jeans and a black leather jacket as she had envisioned her American, but he did have thick sideburns and the most perfect baby curl hugging his forehead. Elvis or James, either way, he looked like an actor. And his voice, with a bit of a drawl, was so sexy. His hands were smooth and manicured. On his pinky he wore a diamond ring, and on his wedding finger, nothing. A few seconds passed. He cleared his throat and repeated his question more slowly as though Phaedra did not understand English that well.

"Honey, you look . . . like a Greek goddess. Want picture? With Polaroid camera? Hell, have dinner with me and I can look at you all night long."

Phaedra's mind was reeling. Dinner? Photo? Dinner? Photo? Dinner?

Dinner?

America.

Phaedra sat up, her back erect: "Yes, I understand, and, yes, I would like dinner, Mr. . . . ?"

"Well, lookee here, she speaks. Gordon's the name. And you, pretty missus?"

"Phaedra."

"Well, Phaedra, it's set. How about I meet you in the lobby when your shift is over?"

At dinner Phaedra spoke about Homer and Delphi, about

the unbearable heat in Athens in August. Gordon told her about Las Vegas, Studebakers, and Sears, told her how they all had air-conditioning.

On their second date, she took him to the Acropolis, and then in a fancy store in Plaka, he bought her a gold bracelet.

On their third date, with no ring, but with words, he proposed.

Phaedra told her family that she was going to marry the American. Her brother said she was crazy, her sister's eyes showed disgust, her mother remained silent, and her father said he would disown her. But she didn't care. She was young, beautiful, and going to America.

11

I find myself drifting more and more, thinking about James—and Zeus. I *was* stuck, and if it were not for James leaving me, I still may have been living a half-life with him. That Sunday afternoon, what he had said jarred me out of my complacency. He had said clearly what I couldn't. We hadn't found The One. With all our intellectual musings, we had agreed that such a thing was ridiculous, but on that sad day in May, he discarded all our philosophies when he said *Thair, we deserve more, and who knows, maybe there is such a thing as The One. We are cheating ourselves because we both know we haven't found it with each other.* I couldn't believe he was using those words: "The One." I was furious. My God! After five years with James, I had finally managed to reprogram my heart with logic, finally killing my mother's stories. There is no such thing as The Other Half! Zeus did *not* separate us at the beginning of time. Soccer ball people with two faces, one heart, and one mind! How ridiculous! We simply find good partners, and then we settle down. The End.

So why am I still searching? God damn it. Maybe I could have convinced James to stay and have been happy. Well, happy *enough*. Just thinking about him and our breakup makes me feel empty. Again.

I find myself spending more time on my coffee reading, more time swimming, more time preparing lunch. And less time writing.

I came here to write, not to meet people, but there's a part of me that thinks it would be healthy to go to the local bar once in a while. Talk to people. Socialize. But I know how I am. This is my only opportunity. I need to go on.

I look at the basket of fruit on the table and the delicious tomatoes. As I begin sinking my teeth into one, my thoughts drift again to a person who has caught my attention here on the island.

Every afternoon, when the local villagers take their naps, she emerges. From my balcony, I have a perfect view of the cove below and a perfect view of her. In the afternoon, the tide comes in, and the beach becomes closed off with water on either side. She comes through the water, around the boulder that provides perfect seclusion to a small stretch of beach. She lifts her long, white skirt to her waist and glides through the still water. Letting down her skirt when she reaches the sand, she continues to walk all the way to the other side of the cove, where a sharp cliff creates a barrier to the outside world—a barrier for all except me. My rental is perfectly perched, providing an unobstructed view from up above.

She takes off her dripping skirt and lays it on the sand. She's not wearing any underwear. She slips off her tank top and reveals two tiny, perky breasts. From where I sit, her visibility is a bit blurry, but I can still make out bright pink, erect nipples. Her body resembles that of a young boy: slender hips, a flat stomach, and strong, well-defined legs. When she walks naked back into the sea, her long, wavy hair reclaims her femininity. I watch her for an entire hour, always fearful that she will look up and see me. But she never does. I'm always angry at the hour I waste watching her but rationalize that she may turn into a character for a book I may write one day, so this is actually research. Every day I find myself looking up at the clock, waiting for two o'clock, so this woman can appear. I even find myself looking for her when I take short day trips on my moped to nearby villages. But I've never seen her anywhere but in this cove, not in the main square, nowhere, and I wouldn't dare ask anybody about her—not yet anyway. I scold myself for wasting my time. Today, I decide: No distractions. No distractions.

———

It's another hot day. I have already had my morning swim and am back and famished. I make myself a breakfast sandwich, put the fan right in front of me, and grab my laptop. I reread the last few pages and picture this young Greek girl who had so many dreams; this Phaedra is starting to dance before my eyes. I know my mom would hate how I have depicted her; *no*, she would say, I can just hear her, *I was not desperate like that*. But these stories all came from her—the air-conditioning, the Polaroid, the description of a young Gordon— and, ultimately, it's my story, so I just need to keep writing.

It's already 1:30 p.m. I can't believe the time has slipped by so quickly. Fingers on the keys, I keep looking up at the clock.

At 1:45 p.m. I am antsy and sweating. I'm wearing jean cut-offs that I've had since the '80s and a floral bra. From noon to four, the heat becomes almost unbearable. I get up, grab a tomato from the fridge, refill my water glass, and go out to the balcony to hopefully encounter a breeze. The shorts have cut into my legs from the four hours I was glued to the chair; they feel damp and tight. I unzip them, stand up, and watch them drop to my heels. I step out of them and simply walk away as they lie on the floor. I would never do this in my own home; neatness doesn't matter here. I lay my towel over a chair and sit down. Stretching my legs over the metal railing, I can feel it burn my skin. The heat radiates into my calves; the sensation feels slightly painful, mostly good. Peering down at the secluded beach, I consider going and taking another dip, but my hair is washed, and for the next hour, the beach will be hers.

At 1:55 p.m. I look at the clock, then the tomato. I haven't bitten into it yet. I begin rolling it up and down my thigh. I roll it from my knee, up over my protruding hip bone, up the side of my stomach, over my left breast, my neck and just before it reaches my mouth, I pull it away. I tease it around my face. It's as if my hand and brain aren't connected: I put it up to my face and when it's close enough to bite, my hand pulls it away. I'm pretending my hand won't give up the tomato. "Tomato! Tomato! Give me Tomato!" I say in a small, squeaky voice. Another deeper voice replies: "No tomato for you! You are a bad girl!"

Silence. I haven't spoken to a real live person in nine days. I figure it's time I venture into town to buy more supplies and see humanity.

I take the tomato and bring it slowly, calmly, methodically, up to my mouth and bite into it. Some of the juice drips down from my mouth. I don't wipe it, just letting it drip onto my chest. Taking my index finger, I slide it between my breasts, mixing the sweat with the tomato juice. Putting my finger in my mouth, I taste the sweet saltiness. I glance at the clock—1:59 p.m.—one more minute.

Two o'clock. Perfect clockwork. I see her coming from the side of the boulder. The tide is a bit higher today; the water reaches well above her waist. She holds her skirt higher, but most of it is in the water, drenched. Today she walks more slowly than usual, stopping every few steps and just looking deep into the sea. Finally, she makes her way onto the sand and disrobes. She lies down on her skirt, face down this time.

I imagine going down to the beach. Pretending that I don't know she's there. Walking over to her, kneeling down beside her. Running my fingers through her long hair. (*What? Did I just think that?*) But I can't control my thoughts. I imagine my hand going down her spine, lightly touching her lower back. I imagine her arching, lifting her pelvis when I do this, slipping her hand under herself as she spreads her legs wider.

I think I'm horny, but that's no excuse. Watching a stranger—a woman no less—and imagining these things, feels so dirty, so wrong. Where are these crazy thoughts coming from? I have never been attracted to a woman before. What is happening to me? But I can't take my eyes off her. Today she seems so different, like a grief-stricken Eurydice waiting to be saved. Her shoulders are shaking. She rolls over and sits up. With her head in her arms, I can see that she's sobbing. Something deep inside me turns and burns. I pull the chair up closer to the burning rail and cross my underarms on the metal. So hot.

At 3:00 p.m. exactly, she stands up and slowly disappears back into the water. I sit there for another hour staring at the blue sky, watching the seagulls fly, feeling strangely sad.

Late July, 2000

I am on the edge of a swimming pool, but there is no water. I am looking into the bottomless pit, getting ready to dive. No, says logic, there is no water. But my feet prepare to jump. I can't stop myself; I plunge forward.

I wake up startled, sweating. My heart is pounding. I lie there without moving, eyes wide open. I see the numbers on the digital clock. It's 4:02 a.m. I can't go back to sleep, so I get up, go to the four-foot fridge and from the top, grab some bread. It's stale. I make a mental note that tomorrow I will have to venture into town again. Sitting outside on the porch, I watch the small waves form below. There's a half moon in the sky and the stars are especially bright. It's warm despite the time. Maria, the owner of the "mom and pop" store where I get my supplies, said that it's hotter than previous summers. Tonight, though humid, it's not uncomfortable; in fact, it feels nice. I look at my tan, shapely legs. Lots of water, tomatoes, and feta, I guess this is the miracle diet. Looking down at my stomach, I can see how flat it's gotten, making my breasts look fuller. I think about masturbating, but it feels like too much work right now, so I sit like this for about an hour until sleep finally calls again, and then I go back to bed.

Rolling over, I see the alarm clock. It's already 12:56 p.m.! I know I need to go into town for supplies, but I figure I can make it to the store and be back by two. When I don't want to drive the seven kilometers to reach the big, air-conditioned supermarket on the other side of the island, I get everything I need from Maria's store.

It's cooler today. As I ride my moped downhill, I enjoy the wind in my hair, the sun on my face. I drive slowly and take in all the sights: the still blue water, the gold beach, the white-washed houses.

"*Kalimera*," I say to Maria, the round sixty-something Greek woman behind the counter, when I enter. I come about twice a week for milk, mostly for Tang, and for fresh bread and feta. She knows me now and always greets me warmly.

"*Kalimera, koukla*," she responds. On rare occasions Yiayia used to call me that, *koukla*, her "doll." It's a faint memory, but still so powerful. Hearing that word again makes me feel protected, like someone alive and real actually cares about me.

I grab a little red basket, slip it under my arm, and walk down the first aisle where the coffee and jams are. I grab Bravo, the grainy Greek coffee I drink in the morning, Nescafe, my afternoon pick-me-upper, and a strawberry jam. Crouching on my hamstrings, I glance at the other spreads. Deciding to splurge and buy some Nutella instead, I suddenly feel someone brush past me and stop. While I'm still looking down, the first thing I see is a long floral skirt and tan toes in leather sandals. She stands above me, also looking at the jams. I hesitate. My hands are perspiring; the jar almost slips out of my grip. I set my basket down and steadily run my eyes from her fuchsia-colored toenails to the slender ankles, the skirt, and up the side of her leg to her round butt. A curve I know so well. I've seen this body—naked—on a daily basis now for almost two months. My eyes wrap around her waist, drown into the two inches of her stomach that teasingly peek through between her top and skirt. I finally look up as she says in perfect English: "Is that jam good?"

"Uh, yeah . . . yes."

She smiles widely and for the first time I can admire her face. A sharp jaw, deep dimples, full red lips, a petite nose, and bamboo-colored eyes.

She takes the jar off the shelf, smiles again, and goes to the register to pay. I'm still crouched down, unable to move. I watch as Maria, with a stern look, puts the jar and a few other items in a plastic bag, never looking the woman in the eye. When she opens her wallet, I hear Maria say something under her breath, grab the money, open the cash register, and throw the change on the counter while simultaneously turning away. The woman gently picks up the coins and puts them away, one by one. When she turns sideways, I can finally see her striking face once more, but all I see now are sad eyes. Not the eyes that a few moments ago looked into mine with such deep intensity. She glides out of the store and never looks my way again.

I finally stand up and stretch out my sore legs. Walking to the front, I anxiously look out the door for her, but she's not there. The silence breaks when I hear, "*Etimi*?" Maria is smiling, asking me if I am ready. I barely hear her, still in a trance when she repeats herself.

"*Ne, ne, etimi*," I tell her and then without thinking, I ask about the woman.

Maria suddenly becomes serious, "*Ugh . . . kakos anthropos!*"

A bad person? What does *that* mean? I don't feel like I can question Maria too much, so instead I ask, simply, if the woman is from Kythnos.

She hesitates, then tells me that the woman used to have a small private school in town and that she got too close, *too close* she repeated, to some of the female teachers. I know a part of Maria loves the gossip, but another part seems genuinely repulsed.

She begins to waddle away, huffing and puffing, having decided she will tell me no more. I pay and leave, but I can't concentrate on anything. I keep seeing the woman's face in my mind. Questions fill my head. *Too close?* Am I letting my imagination run wild or could it be what I'm thinking?

———

In my kitchen I cut up a cucumber, an onion, and three tomatoes. I douse them with olive oil and throw a big slab of feta on top. I pull out a jar of oregano from the cupboard. Sprinkling some oregano on top of the cheese, I look at the salad as my stomach growls.

At 1:55 p.m. I start moving a bit more quickly; I cover the feta and put it back in the fridge, feeling the artificial coolness envelop my body when the door opens. Cover the oregano, back in the cupboard; open the fridge, get a bottle of water; throw everything onto a tray; grab a napkin and a towel. I set everything down on the wooden table on the porch, cover the chair with the towel, slip out of my sundress, and sit down. Finally, I take a deep breath.

Tang is perched on the widest part of the railing, looking into the horizon. He turns his head slightly and acknowledges me, and then faces the direction of the cove once more—almost as if he, too, is taking part in this daily voyeurism.

1:58 p.m. Here she comes. Two minutes early.

3:00 p.m. Exactly. Gone.

3:15 p.m. Time to get back to work.

3:49 p.m. Time to get back to work.

4:17 p.m. Time to get back to work.

Phaedra's Story

Rancho Fierno, Ca
July 4th, 1988

After more than twenty years in the US, Phaedra spoke English like an American, with a slight accent, but no more strange looks from people, no more asking where she was from. Once in a while, she still mixed up an idiomatic expression, and this gave Gordon the opportunity to put her in her place. "It's not play it by 'year'! It's play it by *ear*!" He loved to point out her errors when they were with business associates and their blonde wives, loved to tell people that he had saved her from marrying a villager and picking olives all her life. He made these remarks, and the Americans at the table laughed at her expense, but Phaedra just held her head up high and pretended to laugh with them. Twenty-three years of marriage, and Gordon still treated her like a second-class citizen. The only time he acted interested in her life was when he wanted something, for her to host a party or to accompany him on a business trip. Phaedra's exotic charm and good looks always earned him points with clients. In front of other people, he mocked her, then said, "Ain't my Phaedra beautiful?" as if she were not present. At home he mostly just ignored her, usually came in late, took his dinner, went into the living room, watched television, and sat in the air-conditioning. After dinner, he ordered a scotch on the rocks, and asked about his daughter, who was already fast asleep.

Sometimes he came home drunk, his beard smelling of women's juices. His only explanation was that he had been working late. Phaedra swore at him in his native tongue, but her words were a cacophony of fumbled expletives that seemed to carry little weight. Phaedra's words meant nothing to him, and despite all her yelling and wailing, she had few choices. She had never worked in the United States, and she could not return to her country. Her father had told her not to marry the American, but she had not listened.

At precisely 6:18 p.m. on the day of America's independence, she sat on the corner of her big bed and decided she would no longer be Gordon's property. Mr. Wright had been so wrong for her, but because of Thair and tradition, she had stayed. Her daughter was nineteen and going to the local university. It was time. She could feel her heart palpitate, palms clammy as she gripped them tighter and tighter. She knew that this was the end. She caught her suppressed smile reflected in the mirror. She would be free—finally free! But then her reflection told her the truth: she was no longer young. She was forty-one and tired. Her once curvaceous body was now thin and out of shape, her long black hair was cut short; her eyes, dull. She glanced up to a Polaroid photo that was wedged in the corner of the mirror—a Polariod that had lost almost all its color—Phaedra and Gordon in front of the Parthenon more than twenty years ago. She stood up and moved closer to the photo, focused on the man and the girl: his smile seemed too perfect, and she looked like a child. Suddenly, a chill ran up her thighs and into her stomach—the air conditioner blasted air into her big, cold bedroom.

There's a breeze in the room; a slight wind picks up and keeps blowing the white curtain into my laptop. I don't want to move because Tang is sprawled on my lap, but I want to close the window. I gently lift him up, set him on the bed, and close the window, leaving it barely cracked open. I need water but need to continue more.

Phaedra's Story

Late June, 1989

The divorce was final, the house was hers, but as she sat with the calculator, it just would not add up. Gordon had made several bad business decisions and had been out of work for more than a year, so she walked away without any sort of future alimony agreement. Phaedra needed a job, but what could she do?

Thair, apart from studying full-time, had been waiting tables for a few years, and Phaedra saw that her daughter made fast money, but there were no benefits, and Phaedra was getting older. She needed a job with some security, but she had no skills—well, no skills past cooking, cleaning, and gardening. She thought of opening up a business, but with so little savings, it was too big of a risk. So she filled out several applications for the local grocery stores because she heard that medical benefits would be included. Phaedra knew it would not be easy work, but this was the choice she had made. She needed enough money to pay the mortgage, the bills, and help out her mother. And she refused to ask her daughter to pay rent. A good Greek mother would never ask for money from her child. Thair did help out when she could, but the university was not cheap.

Phaedra just hoped that she would land a job because, at almost forty-two years old, she hadn't worked outside the home since her receptionist position at the Hilton. How would others view her? Would she even be considered? Doubts haunted her as she put on her glasses and continued to look over the application. Work experience? What could she write? Hostess? Gardener? Housewife? She sat there nervously biting the nail on her index finger when Thair walked in wearing an apron and smelling of burritos.

"Hi, Mama."

"Hi, baby."

"Another application?"

"Yeah, hey, do you have any suggestions what I should write for work experience?"

"Hmm . . . How about domestic engineer? Head of the purchasing department? Carpool navigation specialist? Or, simply, Greek goddess?"

Both mother and daughter laughed.

"Thair, I'm pathetic."

Thair walked over to where her mother sat at the kitchen counter. "No, Mom, you're not. You are an amazing mother who has dedicated her life to a wonderful daughter." She laughed then continued in a more serious tone, "And I have no doubt when you walk in for the interview, everyone will be smitten with your smile and attitude, and you'll get the job."

"Oh, honey, you're too kind. Do you think so?"

"I am certain. Come on, Mom, seriously, you are a hard worker and if they hire teenagers to bag groceries, why wouldn't they hire you? I can see it now, week six: employee of the month. Month three: cashier. Year one: supervisor!"

"Thair, you know what . . . that's exactly what I needed. You'll see. You will be proud of me. I'll get the job, and we will both be fine."

"Mama, we *already* are fine. I'm proud of you."

Thair was not usually very touchy with her mother, but on that day, she sat beside her and leaned her head on Phaedra's shoulder. Her mother kissed her forehead and then continued to fill out the empty boxes.

12

It's been about a week since I've gone to the store and although I'm not out of supplies, I debate making a trip just so that I can talk to Maria again. I've been watching the woman with the sad eyes every day, and the desire to know more about her has become a strange obsession that pulls me away from my writing. I am working on my mother's story, but I keep drifting, a bizarre energy drawing me to this woman. I am plundered by memories of my worst English class taught by the dreaded Dr. Sibald. "Memorize, I tell you! Memorize! If you want to pass this class, you must memorize at least ten full-length poems!" The words of one poem won't leave me; almost like a mantra, they keep repeating themselves in my head:

> *I have not had one word from her*
> *Frankly I wish I were dead*
> *When she left, she wept*
> *a great deal; she said to me,*
> *"This parting must be endured . . ."*

I find myself reciting this part of Sappho's poem over and over as if in a trance. Who is this woman? I came here for clarity, and now I'm finding that I'm less focused than ever.

71

1:59 p.m. I watch her come across the rocks. Then something persuades me to get up. I grab the towel that's hanging over the railing and walk away from the sight that has intruded into my life. I jump on my moped and ride down the hill to the beach in just my bikini with the towel wrapped around my waist. I leave the towel on the motorbike, slowly walk into the cool water, and without hesitation, swim toward her spot. I'm not thinking. All I can hear is the rapid beating of my heart. I keep swimming, deeper, deeper, past the rocks, and finally I see her. She's lying face down and doesn't seem to hear me. I tell myself to turn around, but my arms keep pulling me toward the shore. The water reaches my waist, then knees, ankles, toes; I'm walking out onto the beach. *Turn around. Leave.* But my legs won't listen.

This is her time, her space, but now it's the two of us in this secluded cove.

I walk over to where the woman is lying. She rolls over, looks up—not startled, not embarrassed—and smiles. Almost as if she has been expecting me. "Hello," she says.

She's lying sideways now, her head perched in her bent arm. I can see her small breasts, her naked flesh. I catch myself staring. I'm the one who's embarrassed and doesn't know what to say. She pats the ground gently, motions for me to come sit beside her.

I am still standing when she repeats, this time with words, "Come," she says. "Sit."

I place myself beside her, and she rolls over completely. She's lying on her back now, with her arms crossed under her head, totally relaxed. I stare forward, then quickly glance over at her; her eyes are closed. I begin to drink in her body. Imbibe her smell. We sit like this for what seems like hours, but is probably only about five minutes. Then, she takes her left hand and rests it beside my thigh. I'm frozen. Then she takes the same hand and puts it on mine, lifts my hand and puts it on her stomach.

"Don't be nervous," she whispers.

Her hand slips away. I watch my hand as it begins to have a life of its own. It begins to caress her. My index finger makes circles around her belly button. I watch as it moves up to her breast, and the area between my legs pulsates. With my index finger on her nipple, I hear her let out a little whimper, lightly squeezing it, watching as her body squirms every time I do this. I hate my nipples being touched, and yet I am doing this to another woman; an insane pleasure fills me.

My hand continues to explore her body, touching areas that feel so different than when they are on one's own body. She takes my exploring hand and puts it in her mouth, licking every finger slowly, tenderly. Still holding my hand, she slowly sits up. Facing me, she brushes a stray hair away from my face; her pupils drive into my eyes, through my face, down my stomach, and another surge of wetness escapes from between my legs. Still with her piercing, hungry eyes, she continues to stare without reserve. It surprisingly makes me feel comfortable, relaxed. I have never felt so desired by another human being.

She motions for me to take off my bikini, and I do. We touch and caress every inch of each other's body; tasting, kissing, and just looking. I am sacrificing my every inhibition to something that I cannot define. Almost instinctively, I know I am there to make Love. No white-bearded God in the sky has formed this union for procreation—the act is for pleasure's sake alone. But it is not just sex. I have seen a few Hollywood films where there's girl-on-girl action, and it's always so highly sexualized, not about love unless it's a lesbian movie. This feels like love. But I know I am not a lesbian. I have been fiercely attracted only to men all my life. For a moment—just a fleeting moment—I want to stop. It's almost too much to take in, but when I look at her, my anxiety dissipates once more. Our parts fit together, not like a puzzle, but harmoniously. She is part angel, part enchantress. At moments I expect her long, dark-blonde locks to turn into snakes, but she remains gentle, amorous, with such longing in her eyes. After more than an hour of love-making, she gets up to leave. I have yet to speak a word. Though it feels right, something inside me needs to question her; a silent part of me is screaming out: *Who are you? Where do you live? When will I see you again?*

But there are no good-byes. She just kisses me on the top of my head, turns toward the sea and walks into it without looking back. I lay there, not knowing what to do, what to think. After about fifteen minutes, I jump to my feet.

It is twenty-four hours later, but I can still feel her hands on me. I decide I will stay away and just watch today. I know I don't have to be close to feel her. Maybe I wasn't an intruder all these weeks, instead, her silent companion. She must have known I was here, up above, watching. *Had she been waiting for me?*

1:58 p.m. For almost two months she has been my pesky fairy, my Muse of Distraction. But she has also given me a new energy. I am done with my grandmother's story and my mother's. I am ready to write *my* story now.

1:59 p.m. My heart is racing.

2:00 p.m. I watch.

2:01 p.m. Where is she? Calm, be calm. But she has *never* been late before.

2:08 p.m. Something must be wrong. I stand up. Walk in circles. Where is she? Is she okay? I'm angry, worried.

2:19 p.m. Empty.

2:30 p.m. Angry again. I feel as though I have drunk acid. My insides are on fire. Where is she?

After three days of hopelessly waiting and waiting and waiting, I go into town. I don't care what people think. *Maria, tell me, who is she? Where is she? Where has she gone?* Maria does not tell me anything. She just keeps repeating: "*Kakos anthropos! Kakos anthropos!*" Bad person, bad person. Then Maria walks in the back and does not come out again until the bell rings when I exit her store. Tempted to go back in, I'm weak, worn, so my visit into town only leaves me with more unanswered questions.

Exactly fourteen days later and not a single word, not a single sighting. I am dissolving. I have no appetite. My jeans won't even stay on my body. I sit in front of my laptop day after day and not one miserable word spills out. So many thoughts, so much uncertainty, nothing makes sense, and I can't seem to write anything. I'm plagued with images that I can't articulate. Who am I? *What* am I?

I am leaving in a few days, so I need to try to find her one more time. I will go into town, make one final attempt, maybe this time I can get something out of Maria. When I enter the store, I see a handsome, twenty-something man stocking shelves. Maria's son. She had introduced me to him months ago when he was home for the weekend. He's got a law degree and works at a British bank in Athens, his English immaculate. He must be home for *Dekapentavgoustos,* the 15ᵗʰ of August, one of the most important religious holidays in Greece.

My gods are finally aligned because he is here, and Maria is not.

"*Yasou*, Yianni," I remember his name.

"*Yasou*, um . . ."

"Thair."

I then continue in English. I want to make sure and be clear, my imperfect Greek feeling even more fractured now.

"Can I ask you a question?"

But instead he responds with, "Are you okay? You do not look well."

"*Thanks*," I say with too much sarcasm and watch him recoil. "No, I'm fine." Then I add, not knowing why because I could really give a fuck that I look awful, "I think I may have a summer cold. Anyway, I was wondering if you could help me out."

I sense a bit of discomfort coming from him, but I don't stop. "There's this woman, your mother knows her. I guess she used to have a school here—some kind of *frondistirio*—anyway, I was wondering if you could tell me where I could find her."

"Listen, Thair . . . if you can't find her, she doesn't want to be found."

Who is this cocky bastard? The God of Pathetic Quotes!

"I'm sorry, that is not the answer I was looking for." Trying to calm down and muster as much sickly sweetness as possible, I continue, "I'm sorry, you must have misunderstood. I met her in town. I borrowed a book from her, and now I want to return it because I am leaving in a few days. I just want to know where she lives. Where I can find her . . . to return *the book*."

"Okay, I will tell you what I know. She rents a house here that is owned by a foreigner; it's inland, in a small village. She comes every few years, but we never know when or how long she will stay. She loves this island, but had . . . how can I say? *Inappropriate relationships*. She lost so much business because of . . . *koutsobolia* . . . you understand? Too much gossip, so she finally had to leave. She moved her business to Sweden where people are more open-minded. That's where her mother is from; her father, a Greek, is dead."

Sweden? "So what is the name of the village here where she is staying?"

"It doesn't really matter. She left weeks ago."

My heart drops. "And how do you know this?"

"I just *know*. She is a beautiful woman. Magnetic, *irresistible* . . . and she doesn't just have relationships with—"

I cut him off. I do not want to hear more. *"Efharisto poli."* Though my words say, "thank you very much," my tone is one of disgust. I can feel my face heat up; I push through the door and jump on my moped. I gas it up the steep hill, going faster and faster; my vision blurs; my eyes sting, like brooches have been thrust into them. Oedipus did not want to see the horror he had committed, and I don't want to think about what I have done. The guilt and the rejection, both are overwhelming. But so is the beauty. I try not to see her, feel her hands on me, imagine my hands in her. It was wrong. *Or was it?* I wipe away my wretched tears and drive more slowly. I don't want to be blind, but these last few months on Kythnos have created more questions than answers.

August 19ᵗʰ, 2000

I've packed my last bag. I've already talked to the neighbor about Tang, and she said not to worry; he comes by her place and she always feeds him, too. I take a final look around the house to see if I forgot anything. On the checkered white and blue tablecloth sits a bowl. The bowl is empty, save for one rotten tomato. I grab it, throw it in the trash, and lock the door behind me. Tang is sitting on the front porch. I bend down and rub his head as he purrs wildly in a way that he hasn't before. I can't take the intense emotion, my heart lacerated with each of his cries, so I stand up and don't look back at him.

Encinitas, California

I don't call my mom to pick me up from the airport. I look awful. I am deathly skinny, never been so thin in my life. My eyes are puffy, and my chest is deflated. My thighs swim in my jeans. I must have lost twenty pounds. The first ten were fine since I have always been a bit curvy, the second ten make me perfect for Hollywood.

My suitcase is sitting by the front door, so little energy to unpack. I make my way over to the TV. Oprah is on. I don't know what the topic is. Oprah has just walked over to a table, and she is pointing to a real uterus that sits on the counter. She's talking about the size. It looks so small, shriveled up. I touch my stomach, get up, and turn off the TV.

Falling onto my bed, I lie there for hours.

The telephone rings. I listen to it ring and ring and ring. I forgot to turn on the answering machine. I know I need to get the phone, probably my mom, probably worried. Instead I turn on the answering machine. The minute it's on, the phone rings again. Third ring, then my mother's voice: "Thair, are you home yet?" I can hear panic. I'm a grown woman, but I still need to check in with Mom. "Honey, call me." She is about ready to hang up, silence, and then she continues, "Honey . . . are you in the shower? Can you hear me? Call me. I want to know that you are home safe and sound. You know, I could have picked you up! You didn't have to spend money on a shuttle! And I want to see you . . . okay, okay, call me. Love you, baby."

13

I am driving to suburbia hell for the first time since I got back from Greece. My mom visits me every weekend for a coffee, a lunch, or an over-nighter, but it is she who always comes to me. She drives to the coast. I hate being inland. I haven't told her anything about my trip, and she hasn't asked. She did make a comment that it must have been hard for me to be there without my yiayia, and I just nodded. There is so much more to it; I just could never tell her.

Since I have been back, I have been questioning my sexuality. Am I a lesbian? Is this why I have always been searching? I don't feel like a lesbian; in fact, lately I feel absolutely asexual. It's not like I'm interested in women now. I have no desire to date men *or* women.

I started teaching a unit on gender studies in my English 200 course. I am curious what young people of today feel about homosexuals . . . bisexuals. Most students love to talk about anything that has to do with sex, but so many have surprisingly strong feelings regarding gay rights. A military man in one of my classes stayed after to tell me that he was dropping because he found the content of my course "disgusting." For the first time in my life, I felt personally attacked for my sexuality, like I had a dirty little secret. But my experience wasn't dirty. So I smiled curtly and said, "Where is your

79

drop card? I will happily sign it." He grimaced and said something under his breath about all these college classes getting corrupted by all these liberals. I could feel the blood rush to my face, making my cheeks bright red.

———

Today I am not thinking about all this, though. I am just thinking that it's nice to be with my mama. Sometimes she drives me nuts, but today I am thriving on her company. She's setting the table for two. Just for her and me. A whole turkey sits between us, sweet potatoes, green beans with Durkee French-fried onions—very American—and a Greek salad on the side. The tomatoes in the salad aren't red, instead an awful pink color. And tasteless.

"Mom, I want to ask you something,"

"Yes, honey."

"I remember when I was in my twenties, you told me, and I don't remember why, that you never really loved Dad . . . is that true?"

"Thair, I'm sorry. I should never have told you that. I did care for your father, but 'love,' that's something else entirely." She pauses. I lean into her story, waiting, "Well, there was a boy . . . in Athens, from my high school. We dated for about a year before I met your father. He was kind-hearted. But I thought he wasn't good enough, couldn't take me where I wanted to go."

"Where did you want to go?"

She stops, pokes the turkey, looks down as if she is traveling down a dark wormhole, then looks at me directly in my eyes and says, "I don't know. Gosh, I don't know."

I swallow my food hard. She looks down again and adjusts herself in her chair. "What was the boy's name, Mama?"

A smile crosses her face. "Georgios. He was from a poor family. We saw each other mostly at school and at beach parties. In those days we would gather at the beach, someone would bring a radio or a guitar, and we would sing and dance with the light of the stars."

"Mama, I want to ask you something personal, okay?"

"Okay . . ."

"Were you a virgin when you married Dad?"

She doesn't blush. She looks up blankly, "Yes. I was."

I want to ask her more. Her eyes glistening, "Thair, I was really young. I made a lot of mistakes. But I am happy that I married your father. I have you. You have the same nose as him, the same inquisitive green eyes, the same drive. He is an intelligent man; he was just . . . I don't really know . . . some of the things he did were not good. Too much money and power make men do stupid things. But I always believed he had a good heart."

I know my mom has dated since her divorce, but there has never been anyone special. One gentleman was a permanent fixture for a few months, but it seemed to end subtly without heartbreak for either.

My mom is still very attractive, petite, with a thick dark bob, and an inviting smile. Her spirit comes to life through her smile. She never complains. Our visits at my place are mostly pleasant. She does continue to pester me about meeting Mr. PerfectMan, says I am too picky, but I just can't tell her what I am feeling. *I* don't even know what I am feeling.

"So what happened with Georgios?"

A wide smile wraps around her head. "He's fine."

"He *is* fine. Mom! You are using present tense! Do you still know him?"

Her eyes shine, "Yes, we are *friends*."

"What do you mean FRIENDS?"

"Well, after my divorce, the year I went with you to Greece for the summer, we saw each other again. He had heard from the island's gossip mill, of course, that I had divorced, so he wanted to see me."

"Why didn't you ever tell me?"

"Because there's not much to tell."

"What do you mean, *not much to tell*?"

"Well, we decided to meet in Athens, in a café in Plaka. We couldn't meet in Kythnos."

My pulse quickens.

"I remember waiting, drinking my coffee, and then a man walked in. I almost didn't recognize him because he looked so old. He had a beard, all grey, and his body was so . . . so frail."

He was dying! I couldn't believe it. Mom was going to finally find happiness and—damn it—he was dying!

She continues, "But his eyes. Oh, those eyes. They spoke to me the same way, like when I was a girl."

"What happened?"

"He came over, greeted me, and then we talked about the last twenty-five years."

"So what was going on?" I try to sound gentle, wondering about his health, but then remember that she had started the conversation saying, 'he *is* fine.' My heart is fluttering. He is *alive*!

"We talked about our spouses—"

Cutting her off, "He was still married?"

"Yes, but his wife was not well. She had cancer. He loved her very much. I held his hands as he cried; he told me that he didn't know how he could live without her. Their three children would be devastated. She was only in her early forties."

"What about *you*? How did he feel about you?" I know I am being so selfish. The woman was dying, and all I care about is did he still love my mother?

She is just about to continue when the phone rings. She jumps up as if she just got ejected from an F14.

"Hello?" in English first, then switching to Greek: "*Yasou!*"

A phone call from Greece? No, it can't be.

She takes the cordless phone and slowly, nonchalantly, walks into her bedroom and closes the door. I can hear her laughing and laughing. I have never heard her so playful. I make my way to the bedroom and, like a child, stick my ear to the door. She opens it suddenly and walks out, shaking her head.

"*Hronia Polla, na su zisune . . . ne, ne k'ego . . . endaxi, endaxi.*" Another set of laughter: "*Filakia*," then, she hangs up.

"Mom that was him! Why didn't you ever tell me?"

"Tell you what?" she said with a sly look on her face. "Honey, like I said, honestly, there's really not much to tell."

A short pause. I stare, eyebrows lifted. Waiting.

"Okay, okay. After Georgios's wife died, he started calling me on my birthday, at Easter, on Christmas, but, really, that's it."

"But Mom, do you *love* him?" Before she can answer, "Why don't you move to Greece? Be with the love of your life!"

"Who said he was the love of my life?"

"Okay then, tell me. Please. Tell me about him, about you. I *need* to know." What I need to know is who is my mom? What were the reasons for her decisions? Did I really know her story? And if this Georgios wasn't the love of her life, did she ever have one? And, if not, why?

While these questions pervade my mind, I realize one thing. Are my questions really about *me?* Am I trying to figure out why I am the way I am? Has she ever been truly happy? Will *I* ever be happy?

Like an ungrateful child, frustration swells, and an unknown pain fills my gut. My mother's voice softens, "Honey, again, there's not much to tell. He is a wonderful man. Now he's a widower, still lives on Kythnos, and continues to run his restaurant with one of his daughters."

"But do you *love* him?"

"Thair, he's a good man. But I don't want to live in Greece and surely not on an island. That's why I left. I got out of there. I don't want to go back."

There? She was talking about the place that I adored.

Were her choices really all about a country? Of course, I wrote it that way in "Phaedra's Story," but I assumed I had exaggerated my mom's feelings of "wanting to go to America." My stories were ultimately fiction, colored with creativity. But could the "Phaedra" in my story really be a closer representation of my mom than what I had imagined?

I pursued with exasperation, "But, Mama, forget Greece and moving, just answer one question: do you *love* him?"

She finally answered, "No, not that way."

Damn. So my mother never loved anyone?

"Mama, I'm sorry, but I don't understand. Did you *ever* love Georgios?"

"Sure, I loved him, with a wonderful, exciting teenage love. And I enjoy talking to him now. We talk about the beach parties. Elvis. Gidget. Vougiouklaki, Theodorakis . . . dancing all night long with sand in our toes. But I didn't, and *I don't* want a life with him."

"So, if you never really loved Dad, you didn't love Georgios, do you ever feel sad that you have never experienced crazy, amazing, undeniable *true* love?" If a student had written a list of adjectives like this, I would have put a nice long pencil mark through all the words, but now I need to load my noun. I mean, the noun is *Love*.

Instead of answering my question, she holds onto another word: "*Sad?* Why would I feel sad?" She almost laughs but refrains when she looks at me.

"I have a lovely home, good friends, and a daughter who loves me very much, right?" She's playful and teasing, her mood very different from mine.

"Mother, of course I love you. But is that enough? You are only fifty-four years old. You look great. You have more energy than I do. Don't you want to be *in love*?"

"Thair, who doesn't want to be *in love*? Yes, it would be nice to have a man in my life, but right now, I can tell you this with all honesty, I love my life. I have no one to answer to. I come and go as I want. I rent a movie, or I read a book. I cook, or I don't. I see my friends for a coffee, or I have dinner with them. I visit my friends who are also divorced, or I get invited to homes where my friends are surrounded by kids and grandkids. Thair, I can do whatever I want. I have freedom. And that makes me happy." I know she wants to say more, her voice sounding a bit defensive, but my mind is already wandering. It doesn't sound liberating to me, sounds kind of lonely. But she does seem to be speaking from the heart, and I *do* believe her. I just can't imagine my life without a man. Or without a partner. I am just not so sure about the man part anymore.

I don't want her life. I want love. I want what she promised me with the story of Zeus. Just like Aristophanes explained: we were cut in two, and I want to find my other half. All that bullshit, and I still believe it. I still want it.

What a softie, my tears can no longer stay behind their walls. As they pour out, my mama takes her hand and puts it on top of mine. "I'm sorry, baby, what's wrong?" Chest heaving, I am becoming unbearable, even to myself. I can't articulate my sadness out loud because it is too pathetic. People are starving, diseased, missing limbs, losing children, and I am unhappy because I haven't found true love.

I am ready to let the conversation end when my mother surprises me. "Okay, Thair, I will tell you something else . . . I don't know how you will take it, but here goes: when your father first bought this house, you were just a baby. At that point, I did want to leave him because I found out I was not the only woman in his life. But, frankly, I had nowhere to go. I would have been a disgrace to Papou. To go back to Greece, divorced and with a baby, I would have been ridiculed, the talk of the town. And what could I have offered you in Athens? We would have lived in a small apartment with my mother and father; instead, you were raised in a beautiful house in the best country in the world. I was able to give you a life that was close to perfect."

Perfect? She is so wrong. I hated Rancho Fierno. A *Truman Show* existence with cookie-cutter houses, people perpetually smiling, snobs at school, a sun that shone so consistently that it didn't seem real, but also a home where vicious fighting forced me into my bedroom, made me go under my putrid pink comforter, and cry myself to sleep. How can I tell her that listening to her scream, then whimper, tore me up inside? How can I tell my dear mama that my life is far from perfect? Especially after all she sacrificed.

Lost in thought, I hear her say, "Thair, I'll admit, since you are persisting, there's more. I *was* happy. I loved my home. I loved my life . . . but I did love someone."

"What do you mean loved *someone?*"

"Are you sure you want to hear this?"

My mind is reeling. Is *my* mother gay? Did she have a woman lover? If I, a woman who never even thought about women in a sexual way, fell in love with one, then anything seems possible.

"Yes. Please tell me everything." I take a deep breath.

"Do you remember your father's colleague, Charles?"

"You mean the British gay man that Dad called 'Flamer Charles'?" The hideous names my dad called people suddenly became a list in my mind: Jungle Bunny, Wetback, Bra-Burner, Faggot, Flamer . . .

"Yes, Charles. But, you know, honey, he wasn't gay. He is a dear, dear man who had . . ." such a long pause " . . . *has* your mother's heart."

"You must be kidding! Charles?" I say with such disbelief that I can tell it temporarily injures her. "Sorry," my voice lowers. "I just always thought he was, in fact, gay."

In a quiet, almost inaudible, voice, she continues: "He is such a good man. So generous and gentle." I see her travel in time, eyes downward, inward. "*He* was the love of my life."

Charles? I started riffling through my memory's Rolodex of all the scenes where Charles is present. Coming over to the house. Bringing an envelope from the office. Sitting at the counter when I came home from school. Leaving suddenly. A Saturday when my mom got dropped off by Charles, saying my dad was staying longer at the work BBQ. Then I remember, as clear as if it were yesterday. My God! The day I walked in on them with lips locked. How could I have forgotten? How old was I? Five? Six? It all starts adding up. How could I have not seen it? Remembered it?

I sit there for a few moments engrossed in my own thoughts, "So what happened?"

"Not much. He wanted to marry me, but I wouldn't leave your father."

"Why?" my voice rising.

"Because it wasn't right."

"What wasn't *right*?"

"Honey, please, don't push me. You can't understand. You have a career, your own home, but things were different for me. I didn't want to take the chance of losing it all. I didn't want to give up my home, my family, my life."

I am exasperated. I move in my chair, lean into the table, "But you didn't have to give anything up! You could have divorced Dad, married Charles. I would have understood." How can I tell my mom that I would have been so much better off if I had known she was happy?

"Where is Charles now? What about after your divorce? Why didn't you look for him? Do you still love him? Does he still love you?" I had a thousand more questions.

"I haven't seen Charles since he got married. I remember your father got him a box of illegal Cuban cigars. He showed them to me so proud: *Got these for Flamer Charles. Can you believe it, Phaedra? Who would have known? I still think the guy is gay, just a cover-up. But shit! What a beauty he got himself!*"

"Was it a cover-up? I mean, not gay, but was he marrying her to get back at you?"

"No . . . and this is the hardest part," she says while choking on her words.

"Mama, only if you want—" but of course I want her to finish.

"Charles finally left me. He said it was too hard, all the lies, all the hiding. You know, Thair, I loved . . . *love* him so much. That sort of love is permanent even if you can't be with the person. It feels like yesterday when he told me that he would not see me anymore. No one has ever made me feel like he did. It's unexplainable. Remember the story I used to tell you when you were a little girl about Zeus and how—"

"Yes, Mother, of course I remember." It's the single childhood story that has screwed me up for life. Always looking for that *other half*.

"Well, Thair, I think Charles was my perfect half. I found it and I let it get away," her voice cracking as she speaks.

We stay like this, sitting at the table, a big uneaten turkey between us, cold bean casserole, with silence, her lugubrious love story hanging heavy in the air. Finally, I take her hand, and she continues, "I think once he decided to close his heart to mine, it allowed him to love again. I met his wife years later, an accidental encounter. She had no idea who I was, of course. She talked about him with such admiration; such intense love shone in her eyes when she talked about 'her husband.' She couldn't have been pretending. I know Charles got the one thing I didn't. He got to fall in love again."

"Is he still married?

"Yes, with three kids and a new baby granddaughter."

"So you still talk to him?"

"No," a sudden sadness sweeps over her face. "Your father sends me his annual Christmas letter, and in it, he usually writes a few lines about all our old friends."

My first thought is *I don't get these letters.* My second response is shock. "You and Dad *still* communicate?"

"Well, not often. You father always liked to write. That was how he romanced me in the first place, with these long, seductive letters, at least one arriving weekly when we were apart, the months before our wedding."

My father a writer? I didn't know that about him. The truth was, I knew very little about him since he was never around, and I know even less now. He lives in Florida with a new wife and her two children. He visits about once a year, but our time together is always a bit awkward, a bit forced. He usually comes with his wife; they stay in a hotel, and while his wife shops or takes her boys to Disneyland, we have breakfast or lunch. I have never been open to meeting my stepbrothers; I'm not jealous or angry, just indifferent. But there are things I do care about. Oftentimes I want to ask about his bad behavior, his infidelities, but I just don't know what it would solve. And it's not like I hate him—well, not anymore. He's sort of a non-entity. I guess since he was never present, his absence once more is not surprising.

I know popular psychology would blame my father—the lack of a solid male figure in my life—for my failed relationships, my desperate search for true love, but I don't believe that crap. I have one solid parent who loves me unconditionally, more than most people in this world have, so when I hear of those sorry cases, people who blame all their problems on "not having my dad around," I have little mercy. There's a Greek proverb that says: *to pedi then orfanevi apo patera, orfanevi apo mitera*—"Children do not become orphans because they lack a father; they are orphans if they are without a mother." As a modern thinker, I think the definition can be extended to one good *parent*—I don't think gender really matters. What children need is love, love from at least one good mother or father or grandparent or adopted parent or guardian.

And I am lucky to have that one parent. And despite everything my father did, my mother never says one bad word about him. If she can be civil to him, then so can I.

"Mama. Thanks."

"For what?"

"Just thanks. And I am really sorry about Charles."

"Me, too."

We go back to eating our cold Christmas Eve dinner.

14

South Coast Community College, California
April, 2001

"I am tired of your bullshit. The way women like you are so damn homophobic. I was going to drop the class without saying a thing to you, but, shit, I really liked you." She says this to me after our class, in an empty room, while shaking her head back and forth, long peppered dreadlocks gathered at her nape with an elastic band. "The first few essays, you really got me to think. The first fucking teacher who appreciated my writing. You even said my writing was *brilliant*, but I can't stand to hear your damn homophobic opinions anymore." I stand there speechless while this statuesque black woman rambles on. My first instinct is to call security, but I always liked Angela, trusted her commentary. She is a good student, probably in her early forties; a strong, articulate woman who *does* write brilliantly.

I keep looking into her eyes, not wavering; for some reason, despite the plethora of expletives, I am not nervous. She must have a reason to berate me so. But what was going on? I knew she became quiet once the section on gender studies began, so I thought the material may have been a bit too controversial for her. She wears a little gold cross around her neck, and when I taught this section of the class last semester, the religious fanatics in my class either shut down or became combative. Had I read her phlegmatic disposition incorrectly?

What is she saying to me? Homophobic? I am anything but homophobic. Has my Socratic questioning regarding these issues been misinterpreted? What have I said that makes her think I am against gay people? Was it when I pointed to students as they sat in the circle and said: "Okay, statistically speaking, you, you, you, you, you, not gay. You," as I pointed straight at a muscular, white guy: "Gay." Everyone in the class roared with laughter. I smiled, too. But wasn't laughter the first step in discussing issues that make people uncomfortable? Then I continued, "You, you, you, you, you, not gay. You—gay." This time it was a thin Filipina, a little less laughter. My point was that we don't know who is gay. There may be more people who are gay, or others who see themselves somewhere else on the sexuality continuum rather than at one hundred percent heterosexual. You can't just look at someone and say that the very masculine man or that the feminine woman you see is straight. One never knows. And it's okay. My final point was supposed to be about compassion and acceptance, equality, but where had my little class experiment gone so wrong?

Angela continues to yell at me: "And you know what? I'm gonna tell you something. It's not easy living in the world as a female. In that respect, you know what I am talking about. But being black is hard. And it's a whole lot fucking harder to be black *and* a lesbian. So when you try to make a point and get the whole class laughing at gay people, I take great offense because you have *no idea* how it is!"

I have no idea? She's right in one respect. I don't know what it is like to be black, but gay? Or more accurately: not straight? I do know *something*. I'm a woman who has been dreaming about my one-day-woman-lover incessantly. It's almost been a year, and I can't get her face out of my mind. So when she says *I* have no idea, inside I'm screaming: no. *You* have no idea.

I have not told anyone about my experience—not Rick or Frank, not even Emily, my best friend of twenty years. It is my secret. But today I want to share it. I *have* to share it.

"Angela, please calm down." Her shoulders lift, visually tighten, in response to my words. "Can we please go to the cafeteria and grab a cup of coffee and chat for a bit? Please." I think she sees the desperation in my eyes, hears the weakness in my voice.

After she cools off a bit, her voice lowers to a normal decibel, "Okay, but I am still gonna drop your class."

We walk without talking; once we sit down, I sense that she is curious as to what could possibly temper the situation. The blood moves through my veins, and I am actually relieved to finally share my story, knowing she will understand. At least I hope she will.

The details pour out. How I watched her for hours, for weeks, for months. How I finally went to her. I tell Angela that the woman and I made love. How it made me feel. Angela sits there speechless. Finally, she whispers, "I'm sorry."

"It's okay. Really."

Then, without realizing it, I am crying. I got something off my chest that I have been carrying for so many months. It feels good to tell another human soul of my experience, about how confused I am. How I haven't dated or even looked at another man or woman because I don't know *what* I am. I feel like a fake. That's why I have been talking about gender in class because on a purely academic level, I can separate myself while trying to learn. I went to Greece to figure out who I am and returned more confused than ever.

As we sit in the cafeteria, I tell Angela about James. I explain that I have always been a heterosexual woman, and my experience was not a reaction to weak or bad men in my life. Of that I am certain. And it wasn't just exploration. I had opportunities in college to experiment if I had wanted, a cute, drunk girl saying: "Hey, let's kiss to get that guy's attention," but I was never interested, never curious. What I experienced with that woman on the beach was so different. It felt like love. I tell Angela all my feelings as if she were my closest friend, forgetting that she is still my student. The poor woman sits there listening, not interrupting, only nodding her head, her body slanted into mine, making me feel like it's okay to take so much of her time. Her gentle manner allows me to talk for what feels like hours.

Finally, she speaks, "Professor Wright, I ain't no therapist or nothing but, honey, I don't think you are gay. Of course, I would love to say you are because I have a lotta girlfriends that I am sure would like to *get to know* you, if you know what I mean"—I can't help laughing—"but I think you are just confused. I think you may not be as straight as you thought you were, and yeah, maybe you could love a woman, but I think you just got a chance to experience something special. You got to love a person. Not because she was a woman necessarily. *She* could have been a man who came every day into that magical cove and disrobed in front of you. It could have been a man who sat there and entered your life. It could have been a man that you made love to. It just happened to be a woman. What you got was the chance to love a person from afar, then up close. And you got to understand what a lot of people on this earth never get to know, and that it doesn't really matter. Man or woman. No preconceived stereotypes rammed down your throat. No society dictating what's right and what's wrong. Honey, you got to *love*. You didn't see color, race, religion. Or even gender. It was visceral, instinctual, pure, natural. If only others were more open, then they would see that there are a helluva lot of people out there to love."

As I sit and listen to this powerful woman, a sense of ease encompasses me. She is slowly nursing me back from the sexual dead. "Can I give you some advice?" she asks.

"Sure."

"Don't be afraid. Just let yourself go. You have to date again. You can't sit home every weekend and watch old movies and just meet friends for coffee. That's not *living*."

That's not living. That's not living. That's not living. I can't get that phrase out of my mind. But what choice do I have? Start going to bars? Join a dating service? I hear there is this new thing that is happening, spreading like wildfire: online dating. But none of it is for me. I do have hobbies. I love to hike, travel, go to art shows, poetry readings, the theatre, but lately I haven't met anyone. The truth is I haven't been open to that stranger's smile or the comment of, "So, what did you think of that piece?" I am closed, and it is time to open up. Maybe I will even start writing again.

Part II

Growth

15

I've spent the last few weeks, after finishing the semester, rereading the two stories I wrote about Yiayia and Mama to help me decide where I could start mine. At eighteen years old, they were both at the threshold of marriage; at eighteen, I was still a child. Maybe they were, too, but times were different, and they had so few choices. Today it seems we have so many choices that we are juggling rather than achieving balance, and usually something, or someone, gets dropped.

Maybe others have felt the same confusion or emptiness when a partner walks away; maybe they have felt the pressure from our parents' generation to get married, make babies. I'm hoping my stories can entertain, maybe even help, but, mostly, my desire to write has always been to understand. And just like Foucault stated, "I write precisely because I don't know yet what to think about a subject that attracts my interest." And understanding women—their choices, my choices—has always been important to me. I think what we are all looking for, ultimately, is a way to feel *at home* within our skin.

My odyssey has been a quest to answer this question: can we only feel complete in the arms of our soul mate or can we find this wholeness alone? Or is mere *contentment* with someone the solution for loneliness? Even with Circe and Calypso—gorgeous goddesses who tempt Odysseus and with whom he has extended affairs—he just wants to go home. He feels right and good only in the arms of Penelope; he is at peace *only* with her. These myths of love, these elusive Other Halves, have been my focus, but something strange has happened in the last year.

I genuinely feel at peace without anyone by my side. Sappho said that above "war, children, and family," the most superior feeling on this "black earth . . . is what you love." And from Oprah and Gloria, I learned that one must love—above all else—oneself. As corny as it sounds, I think it's true: a love for oneself is the most difficult thing to achieve, yet the most important.

So as I sit here, contemplating words of Sappho, Steinem, Homer, and Foucault, I decide that I will write using a third-person perspective; calling myself "Thair," instead of "I" will allow me to go deeper. And that's ultimately the whole point: to uncover, peel back the layers, and make sense of my role in this world. Unlike Aristophanes, I can't roam the streets of Plaka to discuss the importance of life and love with other writers, but I do have the privilege of time, so with a few months off from teaching, it's time to finally commit my own story to paper.

Thair's Story

Rancho Fierno
Late August, 2001

Standing at her mother's entrance, Thair searched for the keys in her purse, found the one for the front door, and slipped it into the lock slowly, every action taking so much effort. As soon as she had the door open just a crack, a cold blast of air seized her neck and shoulders. It was about ninety-eight degrees here in suburbia; very little would have made her drive inland, except that her mother had called and sounded a bit desperate.

"Honey, do you think you could come over after your morning class to do me a small favor?" Thair's mother was being a bit mysterious; maybe she had bought Thair something for her condo. She loved surprises, or maybe she had scheduled another *chance* meeting for her daughter. A few years ago, when she was still dating James, her mother had invited Thair over for dinner. A surprise sat in Phaedra's living room: the surprise being a six-foot man, her mother's idea of Prince Charming. Phaedra said Rick just happened to stop by, a handsome man indeed, a real estate agent. A chatty man, he had asked Thair if she thought of selling her condo since it was probably worth a lot more since she had bought it. Then, they dove into conversations about sunlight versus artificial light. They had chemistry and the conversation flowed. He asked Thair if she liked Coke or margaritas with Mexican food, if she liked driving a sports utility vehicle, a sports car, or sedan. She told him she liked sunlight, Pepsi with fish tacos, and that she had a Jeep she was selling since she had just purchased a Miata. They laughed and shared stories. Thair's mother had stayed in the kitchen and when she looked over at Thair, she smiled and mouthed: "I knew you would like him."

After dinner, they set up a date for the following week. Phaedra tried to hide her excitement when she saw them exchange numbers. She thought it was a romantic exchange, but in reality, Rick was going to show Thair houses in her neighborhood in case she wanted to buy up. Even though she was broke, it sounded like a nice diversion for a Saturday afternoon. Thair did like him, and she knew Rick also liked her, and that they would be fast friends even if she never bought a house from him.

From the smile plastered on Phaedra's face, Thair knew her mother could already hear the wedding bells; Thair decided she wouldn't tell her that one of the things Rick shared during their lively conversations was that he was gay and lived with his life partner. Happily ever after. They were high school sweethearts. Who would have known? Certainly not Phaedra.

Phaedra was a traditional woman with traditional values, and though she had no outward ill feelings towards gay people, she just "didn't get it" as she had told Thair on several occasions when they happened to catch a "coming out" show on TV. With Rick's masculine build and deep voice, she had no inkling that Rick was unavailable for her daughter, in more ways than one. Rick and Thair did end up having a relationship, a strong friendship; in fact, Thair had gotten even closer to Rick after her return from her last summer vacation. He and his partner were a couple that Thair could count on any time, day or night, either to share a glass of wine and laugh uncontrollably or to provide two sets of strong shoulders for Thair to cry on.

This time, though, Thair didn't think that her mother's request for a visit was for some surprise guest or present, Phaedra's voice sounded different, anxious. And Thair's first reaction was worry.

"Mama, are you okay?"

"Yes, honey, I'm fine. I just need some help with . . . um . . . something."

"What sort of *something*?" Thair asked suspiciously.

"I'll tell you when you get here, okay?"

So there she was, in the middle of suburbia, with the unbearable heat, trying to open the front door. She could hardly breathe. From the cooker to the freezer, she went from a burning hell into her mother's icy heaven. She felt a chill travel up and down her spine.

"Mom! What temperature do you have the air on? It's freezing in here!" she yelled while still entering.

Her mother didn't answer, just ambled from the hallway into the living room where she greeted her daughter with a kiss on each cheek (Greek style) and then a hug (American style). Phaedra looked radiant. Ever since the divorce from Thair's father, thirteen years before, Phaedra seemed so vibrant, so alive. Phaedra absolutely captured the essence of *joie de vivre* in her forever-smiling face. Nothing brought her down, a resilient woman, strong and proud despite her tumultuous life. Thair admired these qualities in her mother, and sometimes wished she were more like her—a stronger woman.

For the last decade, Thair was an adjunct professor (colloquially called a "freeway flier") at several community colleges in San Diego County, and every year she was becoming more disgruntled with her job. No job security, no benefits, so much work and so little recognition. To make a decent salary, she had to teach several classes at several campuses all around the county, much of her day spent in a car "flying" from one campus to another, colleges as far as fifty miles apart. The only thing she really loved about the job was her students. Jane, the seventy-eight-year-old great-grandmother who decided she wanted to return to school to finally finish her degree after two husbands, five kids, nine grandchildren, and one great-grandchild, always stood out in Thair's mind. There was also John, an African-American man who wanted to begin a degree at the age of fifty-six, his life's goal to graduate from a university. There were others: the mature, ambitious students; the young, lazy ones; the surfers; the princesses; the jocks; the pot smokers. They all had a story, all had something to share. Thair loved learning as much as she loved teaching. Her students were what brought her back to the classroom semester after semester, year after year. Of course, the other thing she loved about her job was June, July, and August. It was during those months that she got to rest and recharge her teacher's battery. Every May, she said it would be her last year teaching, but by August, she was excited to go back into the classroom.

During the long summer holiday, Thair got to relax, visit friends, and occasionally travel. The year before, she got to return to Greece. It was a tough visit for Thair, retracing cobble-stoned streets that she had known intimately as a teenager. Upon returning, she saw very little had changed. Kythnos was still a sleepy island with few tourists. Thair had spent the three months of her summer holiday on the magical island, renting a small summer house, and writing her grandmother's and mother's stories. The overall experience was irreplaceable: bright sunny mornings, warm afternoon winds, long days, endless reflections. Encountering a beautiful woman with sad eyes. It was a bitter-sweet memory now. It didn't hurt to remember, but it was a dull feeling that lived with her every moment of every day. She felt sort of like Blue Man Group, like a bucket of paint was poured on her; she was no longer the same color, no longer the same person. She had this coat of another color, yet—unlike the Blue Man—she was the only one who could see it, feel it. This new color was part of her, not something she could just wash away. It was a summer she would never forget. It had marked her forever.

Standing in her mother's living room, Thair looked up and saw a small painting of Santorini. It was a painting she had always admired, but she was careful during her years with James not to hang other artists' work in the condo.

Her mother approached her, "You know it's yours if you want it."

"I know, Mama, thanks, but it looks really good on this wall. I would hate to take it from you."

"Like I said, honey, you can have it if you want it." Her mother loved to repeat herself. Though Thair loved the painting, she knew it would serve as a constant reminder of her summer affair, and that was probably not the best thing for her, at least not yet.

"So, Mom, why did you want me to come by today?"

"Thair, I don't want you to worry, but Dr. Chung's assistant called and said that I should come in today. She said the doctor wanted to see me about my mammogram and suggested that I may want to bring a family member with me." When she said these words, in a very nonchalant manner, Thair's heart started beating furiously.

"What did she say was the problem?"

"I don't know, honey, that's why I wanted you with me. I'm sure I'm fine. I just wanted you to come along since you understand medical mumbo-jumbo better than I do."

"But . . . but . . . are you okay?" Thair's face grew pale and her eyes widened.

"Yes! Of course, I am! Don't look so crazy-worried."

"Mom, this is serious! How can you be so lighthearted?"

"Well, how can you be so dramatic? We don't know anything yet, so let's just get going because you are being silly."

Thair didn't feel silly. Assistants did not tell patients to bring in support unless there was something wrong. Thair could already picture donning a pink ribbon, walking the Susan G.

Komen three-day; she would hold her mother's hand with each injection of chemo, and she would stand by her since there was no one else. Tears filled Thair's eyes, how could this be happening? Her mother was so healthy, walking every day, eating wholesome food, leading a relatively carefree life. How? How? Thair started thinking about her own life. It was just the two of them in this world. Phaedra had never remarried; Thair had never married. And even worse, Thair had never given her beloved mother the grandchild she had yearned for. God, where were all these thoughts coming from? Thair didn't even want kids. She had come to this decision in her late twenties, just never had the guts to tell her mother because she knew how badly Phaedra wanted to be a yiayia.

These thoughts tore at her while they drove in silence to the doctor's office. Thair screamed in her head: God, why would you do this to such a good woman? Such a good mother? Damn it, it's not fair! Thair couldn't believe that she was even talking to God. She was not really religious, but now she found herself swearing, then praying to this God of her Greek Orthodox upbringing. *Jesus, sweet Jesus*, Thair pleaded, *please let my mother be okay. Please don't let her have cancer. Please. Don't make her suffer.* She continued to pray as the quiet in the car was overbearing. Her mother took her hand and said, "Baby, it will be okay. Really. Whatever happens, it will be okay." As she turned and looked out the window, Thair thought she saw a flash of terror cross her mother's face; when her mother turned around again and looked at Thair, a radiant smiled appeared.

The doctor's office was freezing. They had the damn air-conditioning up so high. Goose bumps covered Thair's body; sitting there shivering, she put on the sweater that she carried with her everywhere. Phaedra sat there with her long, thin legs crossed at the ankles, wearing nothing but a beige sundress. No goose bumps, she was perfectly happy in this environment. Her mother grabbed a *People* magazine off the table and started to read the first article about another celebrity supposedly cheating on his wife. Thair, on the other hand, grabbed several magazines and riffled through them, one after the other, throwing them back on the table without reading them. Every few minutes, she looked up at the clock hanging on the wall then at her watch.

Finally, she jumped out of her plastic chair and stormed the reception desk. "Excuse me," in a brusque tone, "my mother had an appointment at 1:45 and it's already 2:00 p.m. When will the doctor be seeing her?"

"I'm sorry, Dr. Chung is running a bit behind today. It shouldn't be more than fifteen minutes."

Fifteen minutes! It seemed like she was hanging on the end of Dali's clock watching it melt in slow motion. At 2:15 p.m., she got up again. "Excuse me, it's already 2:15 p.m., you said that . . ."

"Okay, the doctor is ready for you," she said with an acrid smile, getting up and opening the heavy door that allowed patients into the sacred back room where destinies were delivered.

Thair and her mother were led into the doctor's office. Phaedra sat in a chair in the corner of the room, her daughter in another across from the doctor's desk.

"Mama, come closer."

"No, I'm fine here." It was as if the farther away she was from the doctor, the further away she was from the truth.

"Mama, please let me bring you closer."

"Okay, geez, you never let me be," she said teasingly with a smirk.

Thair felt her face redden. How could her mother be so light-hearted? From irritation to sorrow, from anger to grief, she jumped off the swing of emotions, stood up, walked over, motioned for her mother to get up, then lifted the chair and brought it closer to the doctor's desk. Thair's sweaty hand soiled her grey dress pants; her other hand gripped her mother's. Everything that bothered Thair about Phaedra was amplified that day. Her mother never seemed to take anything seriously. She was so darn content with her little life in her little home in her little town.

Phaedra crossed her legs, pulled her hand away, calmly placed her elbows on the desk, fingers interlaced, tilted her head, and smiled—yet again. She looked like she was posing for a portrait, and why so many toothy smiles at a moment like this? How could she be so fearless? Suddenly Thair was overwhelmed with a different feeling, one of pride. Everything she admired about her mother was also present in that room. Her resilience. Her upbeat attitude. She would sit in that cold room and receive any news with grace and dignity.

"Hello," the doctor said as he walked in, not greeting either of them by name despite the fact that he held Phaedra's chart. He sat at the desk across from Phaedra and her daughter, flipping through pages that were in a manila folder.

A few moments later, he looked up at Phaedra and said, in one breath, "So, you have Stage 1 breast cancer, and these are your choices."

There was no hesitation, no preparation for the news they were about to receive. He could have been ordering take-out food as he rattled off "choices" for a few minutes while looking through her.

For a college-educated woman, Thair felt like he was speaking Pig Latin. She understood some things, but it was in a code she could not decipher. Yes, her mother did have cancer, but it was all "mumbo-jumbo," just as her mother had anticipated. Nothing was clear, and the choices did not seem like choices at all.

Phaedra did not utter a word as Thair began an attack of questions.

"What does Stage 1 mean? Where is the cancer exactly? Is there a lot of it? Can you please explain what a lumpectomy exactly consists of? And is it better to remove the whole breast as a preventive measure? And if she elects the entire breast could or would she have immediate reconstruction? And is radiation painful or dangerous? And what are the side effects? And can she really go without chemo? And what about . . . ?"

The doctor handed Thair a stack of literature, told her to look it over so that her mother could select one of the following: chop off some of the breast, all of it, or maybe both breasts for the price of one.

"I know you have a lot of questions, so why don't you read these pamphlets and make an appointment with the oncologist. He will be able to further direct you." He said this as he started walking out of his office and finished with, "Good luck."

Good luck? Had Thair just heard the words *good luck*? Was this some damn soccer game that they were trying to win? Good luck! Thair kept saying the words in her mind as she looked down at the pile of papers on her lap. Where was Phaedra's personal case in this stack of cold literature? Thair was irate: she is not just another patient. She is my mother. She could be anyone's mother. A precious mother. How could he treat her that way?

Phaedra seemed tense as Thair pushed the chair and stood up with the force of Atlas. She had forgotten completely about her mother but finally noticed her, sitting a little more slumped than when they had entered.

"Mama, are you okay?" Thair said with gentle eyes, mustering courage for her mother.

"I'm fine, baby. I am sure it will all be okay." She seemed tranquil, as if the grim reaper had not just knocked on her door.

A mix of anger, frustration, and sadness overwhelmed Thair. She wanted her mom to stand up and fight, but Phaedra just sat

in the chair, patiently, quietly, looking at a photo on the desk—
Dr. Chung and his family, a slim Asian woman and two picture-
perfect children.

The entire doctor's visit took seven minutes. In and out. It
took longer to get a hamburger than to receive this news.

It was hard to relive that day. My mother decided to get a lumpectomy
and radiation. Hopefully that would be all; hopefully they had found
the cancer early enough. The months ahead would be challenging
and, all of a sudden, looking for love just did not seem that important
anymore.

16

Encinitas, California
October, 2001

"Is that book any good?"

What a bad line, but he's cute, so I answer: "It's fantastic, actually. So good that I want to get back to it." *Shoot, why did I say that?*

"I guess a guy should know when he's being intrusive, but . . . I really wanted to buy it, just not sure if it was worth spending the money since it's still only in hardcover."

Great, a cute cheap guy, but I hear myself saying as my lips turn into a smile, "Listen, I am not particularly attached to bestsellers, so when I'm done, I can leave it here at Pannikin with your name on it. I figure I will be done with it by next week. I usually come here every Saturday, so just ask for it any day after that."

"I know you are here every Saturday," he says.

What do I say to that? Okay cute, cheap guy, you are a bit creepy since you know my schedule, but I have never seen you. I don't respond immediately, thinking that his handsome (Indian?) face with his gargantuan nose reminds me of a few of my Greek lovers from when I was younger. His strong features, including a strangely-sexy unibrow and dark skin, also make me think of where we are as a country and how discrimination is running rampant with anyone who is not perfectly porcelain. It seems that

111

I am not the only one a mess—as a country we are all suffering. It may be these thoughts of compassion or just that he is damn sexy, but my phlegmatic disposition changes, and instead, surprisingly, I hear myself say, "So, you come here regularly? I don't think I have ever seen you before."

He replies with a smirk, "I don't know how you would have seen me since you always have your nose stuck in a book or you're . . . grading a pile of papers?" He states the last part more as a question, but I'm not ready to reveal too much information yet.

This man strikes me as witty and incredibly attractive, despite the cliché, and I am pretty sure he's flirting with me.

"Can I buy you another coffee?"

I look down at mine and there's only about a sip left.

"Sure."

"What would you like?"

"Just a regular house coffee with a bit of milk. No sugar." It sounds like I am ordering a coffee from a waiter. Then I hear a voice in my head: *That's not living.* Angela, my student, had said what I already knew. I have to be more open. "Thanks, that will be great."

"Okay. I'll be right back," he says while grabbing my cup.

I look into his honey-brown eyes with a genuine smile.

Looking down at my book, I try to keep reading, but the words become blurry, so I lean forward and peek into Pannikin's entrance. Indian-man is in line, holding my empty mug. I guess buying me a cup of coffee means getting me a $.50 refill.

His black hair shines. He must be about my age, maybe six foot, with a strong back. He's wearing a long-sleeved T-shirt and a plaid short-sleeved shirt on top, a sort of skater-boy look. His jeans hang nicely on his slender hips, his legs, straight and strong.

I stop staring and shut my book. I close my eyes for a moment, tilting my head upwards, feeling the autumn sun on my face.

"Here you go," he says as he juggles two cups of coffee.

"I'm sorry," I say. "I didn't catch your name."

"You didn't catch it because I didn't throw it," he says with a big grin.

"Ha. Ha." I say aloud. I find myself liking this guy more and more. Silly humor works for me. "So, what's your name?"

"Ravi. Ravi Ghafur," he says while putting out his hand. I shake it and think that it does sound Indian. "And yours?"

"Thair." I don't give him a surname, not yet.

"What an interesting name. Does it mean something?" he says this while sidling up beside me on the marble bench.

"Well, kind of. It's a made-up name. My mom is Greek and as a young girl she loved the beach—the Greek word for beach is *thalassa*— and she has also always had this penchant for air-conditioning. She loved the way they both made her relax. She told my dad that when she had a child, boy or girl, she would name the baby Thair. Thank goodness she had a girl. I always teased my mom that a boy named Thair sounds like 'A Boy Named Sue.' Do you know that Johnny Cash song?"

"No," he says abruptly, but then leans in, "can we get back to your name?"

"Well, she took the beginning of the Greek word for beach and ended it with 'air' for air-conditioning and *voilà*: Thair."

"Oh, you speak French, too?" he teases.

I like his jokes. And he makes me feel comfortable, a feeling I haven't experienced in quite a while.

"So, Thair, do you have a middle name?"

"Yes, it sounds a bit strange in English, but I like it. It's Aphrodite, named after my Greek grandmother. But they called her Dita for short."

"Aphrodite . . . a Greek goddess, right?"

"Yes, the goddess of love . . . beauty, among other things," I blush when I say this.

"It's a really pretty name. Are you like your grandmother?" A man saying my name is pretty and asking about my yiayia. One brick is removed.

I tell him briefly about my grandmother, but then bring back the conversation to names. I want to clarify that I also, legally, use my mother's maiden name, not just my father's, so I state—with pride—my complete name.

"So it's Thair Aphrodite My . . . lo . . . pou . . . los Wright. That's quite a mouthful! Wow, your name will be even longer once you add your husband's name!"

So many presumptions in that statement and just when I was enjoying his company . . . I tell him that I won't be taking anyone's name if I do ever marry, *and* my forever-partner may not be a 'husband.' The brick is being pushed back into the wall, but instead I hear a mantra in my head: *living, living!* I decide to ask: "What about you? Tell me about your heritage. I am sure 'Ravi' means something."

He indulges me: "The name is of Sanskrit origin. It means 'the sun.' My mom wanted to give me a name from her native country, and she is a fan of the Indian musician Ravi Shankar."

"So, your parents are from India?"

"Yes, but the States is home. They have been here since the sixties, the story of most immigrants, coming here for a better life. I was born in India but have only been back once. What about you? You said your parents are Greek?"

"No, just my mom. My dad is from Georgia, a good old American boy with blue eyes and blonde hair. I took my mom's olive complexion and dark hair. Not complaining though, I can stay out in the sun for hours without being burned."

"So you love the beach like your mom?" He remembers what I said about my mom. Score: point number two.

"Yeah. What about you?" I say while thinking he has a lean surfer body.

"It's okay. To be honest, I love the cold. The mountains, the snow, skiing, but I also like a toasty fire and hot chocolate."

Sitting in front of a fireplace with hot chocolate sounds good, but I hate the snow. Hate the cold. Well, can't win them all.

We talk for more than an hour and then exchange numbers. Ravi works at his father's printing company part-time and is pursuing his PhD in engineering. Cute guy is smart, too. I am certain Mother would find him *presentable*. As he walks out of the café in front of me, I catch another glimpse of his strong V-shaped back, very, very sexy. He turns around and catches me looking. I giggle like a school girl. Despite a few awkward moments, he seems nice and I do hope he calls.

I wake up feeling just a bit lighter today. When I hear the phone ring, I jump up, excited, hoping.

"Hi, baby."

"Oh . . . hi, Mom."

"I'm sorry, honey, were you sleeping?"

"No, that's okay." Instantaneously, I feel heavier. "How are *you* feeling?"

"I'm good. Really." As she says this, I can hear her trying to sound optimistic. "I just wanted to know if you could come tomorrow to take me to my radiation appointment. I hate to ask you, but last time after my session, I felt a bit light-headed. I was going to ask Greta to drive me, but with the recent passing of her husband, I know she has enough on her own plate."

"Mom, you know I would *happily* take you to your appointment. I thought this was your week off; that's why I hadn't called. Please, Mama, always ask me, you know I want to be with you through . . .

this." I still have a hard time saying the "c" word out loud. If I don't say "cancer," then it's not real.

"I know, baby, but it's just such a far drive, and I know you are so busy."

"Mom," I reply a bit irritated, "*First,* it's only a thirty-minute drive to your place and, *second,* I am not so busy that I can't be with my mother. Of course, I will be there. Now, what time did you say?"

"The appointment is at 2:15 p.m.; if you could be here a little before 2:00 p.m. that would be wonderful."

The following morning, on my way to school, I hear the phone ring. I don't have time to pick it up because I am running late but stand above the answering machine in case it's my mom and there's been a change of plans.

My voice ends, "Please leave a message at the beep."

Beep.

"Hi, Thair. It's Ravi. Um . . . I think I got the right number since I can hear your voice. Hey, I just wanted to say it was really nice meeting you the other day . . . I was wondering if you are free this weekend, maybe we could go out for dinner? Okay. I guess I'll call back later and ask you in person . . . well . . . ha ha . . . over the phone, that is. Have a great day. Oh, you have my number if you want to call me back. I'll be in after 8:00 p.m. Okay. Bye."

Click.

I smile from ear to ear, and I am off. I'll call him back tonight when I get home.

Later that night when I return, I take a long, scalding shower, visualizing the photos in my mind: Yiayia, Papou, and my mom's yiayia and papou. Mom and I even came across a picture of her sitting behind the reception desk at the hotel, a Polaroid picture. It was a day full of retrospection. Then I remember Ravi's phone call. I want to call him back, but my spirits are a bit low, so I'll call him tomorrow. Instead of going to bed, I go into my office and turn on my computer.

Thair's Story

Rancho Fierno
October, 2001

"What are you doing, Mama?" Thair asked when she walked into Phaedra's house and saw her mother sitting on her living room floor, her legs spread wide, back perfectly straight, a pile of photos and albums placed between her thighs. Flexible and as youthful as ever.

"Just looking at some old photos."

"Of whom?"

"My yiayia and papou."

Thair bent down and sat next to her mother while her knees cracked.

"Wow, these photos are incredible. Where is this?"

"It's in Egypt. Where your yiayia was raised."

"You know, Mom, I never understood why Yiayia was in Egypt. I know you told me that her family was from the Greek island of Imbros, but Yiayia always talked about Egypt as her home."

"Well, that's because Yiayia spent most of her early life there. Your yiayia loved Egypt."

"Why did her parents leave Imbros in the first place?"

"I can't remember the year, but the Turks took over the island, and it was a good time to immigrate to Egypt. There was a lot of trade with Egypt; many Greeks went to Alexandria, the port city, and stayed there. Some went to Cairo. But few returned to Imbros. In fact, today it's a Turkish island with few Greeks still there. You know, Thair, I really have little desire to go to Greece, but maybe you and I could go to Imbros one day to see where your yiayia was born."

"That would be nice, Mama." Thair looked down at a picture of her grandmother and thought of all the stories that were lost. She knew a little about her grandmother's life from that one summer when she finally opened up. Dita told her bits and pieces about her life in Egypt, about the war, the Allies, her gentleman callers. She had even implied that she was not a virgin when she married Thair's grandfather with her bedsheet story. Those stories lived inside Thair, vivid, real—almost like memories—and now they were colored by her imagination and committed to ink. "Yiayia's Story" started in Egypt because, when it came to Imbros, Dita's life before Alexandria, Thair knew nothing.

"Why do you think Yiayia didn't ever want to talk about her life on Imbros?"

"I think she was sensitive to her parents' feelings; they never wanted to leave. They were forced out of their home because of the Greek-Turkish war. I think your yiayia just sort of cut out that part of her life. And the only reason I know a few things about their life on Imbros was because of my yiayia."

"Couldn't they return to Imbros after the Turkish people took over?"

"No, not really. The island was just not the same. Of course, your papou's parents were from Kythnos, so through her marriage, my mama's parents had a new island to claim as home after World War II was over."

Phaedra picks up a green-brown photo, "Look. These are your grandfather's parents."

Thair looked down at the photo, tattered at the edges, incredible. So many stories trapped in this image. A small, hunched over woman dressed all in black stood beside a tall man with a Groucho Marx mustache.

"And what happened to Papou's parents?"

"They worked hard tending their land in Kythnos. Your grandfather had always wanted to study, a very determined man, so he went to Athens, but when the war broke out, it was pure chaos at the university, so he got a job with a shipping company that went back and forth to Egypt. There was a lot of opportunity for strong men, and once he was immersed in the Greek community in Alexandria, he learned about your yiayia. She was quite a beauty, a strong-willed girl who was said to be a bit wild. I guess this piqued your grandfather's interest. From your yiayia's seventeenth birthday, her parents were looking for a good Greek for her to marry, and your papou was happy to oblige. Of course, they were delighted with the match since your papou was an excellent catch, from a decent family who owned lots of land.

"You know, Thair, life is funny. I see these photographs, and it's as if these people are still alive, still with us. I picture your yiayia and papou, and how happy they were every summer when we would go to Kythnos. Your grandfather was so proud that he had achieved his dream. A large apartment in Athens and his own summer house on Kythnos. He talked about the awful days on the ship during the war, yet every summer he hung up his shirt and tie, and once more became a fisherman. Our table was adorned with fresh fish and vegetables every afternoon. Those were good summers."

"Wow, Mama. I didn't know you had such fond memories of Kythnos, too."

"Of course, Thair. Do you think you were the only one your yiayia called a *poutana*?" She laughed.

She continued to finger the photos as her voice softened once more, "I know they all look so old, but I can still hear their voices, smell their scents . . . my father's when he returned from the harbor, my mother's when she sat on the balcony . . . the smell of fish on my father's shirt, the smoke seeped into my mother's apron. Funny thing is, these smells used to bother me, and now I think of them with such fondness." She said all this with long pauses in between, her mind seemingly light-years away.

Thair sat quietly listening to her mother, thinking of Chanel No 5. Thair could not smell that perfume without thinking of her mother. She never liked this particular perfume; it was too strong, overpowering, yet, she wondered, would there be a day when she, too, would yearn for the smell?

These thoughts were too much for Thair, too much nostalgia.

Watching her intently, Thair's eyes couldn't help falling onto her mama's breasts. Phaedra was left with one perfect breast, the other was deformed and burned. Selfishly, Thair wondered: who was more traumatized? She or her mother? Surely her mother; she would be the one who would have to see herself every day in the mirror for the rest of her life. But she wasn't sure. Phaedra was so tough. Thair, so weak.

Phaedra continued to sit on the floor, lifting the photos, one at a time. Thair wanted to tell her mother that it was time to go, but the words would not escape her lips. Time was precious, and Phaedra seemed so taken in the moment.

Thair and her mom sat on the ground, opening album after album, talking, pointing, laughing, then giggling when they saw the picture of Thair with a horrible big pink bow on her head.

Finally, after about an hour, Thair said, "Mom, I think we missed your appointment."

A dull, "Yes," was the response. "I'm sorry, baby, I just didn't have it in me today. Sorry for bringing you all the way here."

"Are you okay?" Thair said tenderly, putting her hand on her mom's thigh while still sitting on the floor.

A tear sprang in Phaedra's eye. It was the first sign of vulnerability that Thair had seen since Dr. Chung had first mentioned the cancer.

"Um . . . yes, I guess I am."

Thair took her mother's shoulders and wrapped her arms around them, so Phaedra could not see Thair's tears streaming down her face.

This time it was Thair's turn to say, "Mama, it will be okay. You'll see."

"Yeah, it will be okay." Her mother repeated. Then Phaedra hopped up with the agility of a teenage girl and said, "Let's go out for some ice cream! What do you say? I'm treating!"

Thair smiled through her tears. Her mother was the strongest woman she had ever met.

I reread these pages through wet eyes. I turn off my computer and make myself a jasmine green tea.

17

"Happy New Year!" hundreds of voices yell in unison.

Ravi grabs me close and says, "Happy New Year, Thair," then a long, passionate kiss follows. Ravi and I have undeniable chemistry; kissing him, making love to him, it doesn't get much better. His sweet sweat encapsulates his body as we sway amongst the people. For a moment, I feel like I could stay like this forever. Our bodies pressed against each other, Ravi's arms wrapped around my waist.

Accidentally, a twenty-something drunk girl in a yellow, rudely short mini-skirt bumps into us. "Ooops, sooorry." My hackles rise and Ravi smiles, not one aggressive bone in his body. He then twirls me around on the dance floor and gives me one more kiss.

"Let's go back to Emily and her date." He says this, but he is already walking me off the dance floor, pulling me through the throng of people.

The Violent Femme's "Blister in the Sun" blasts out of the speaker beside us. "Ravi, let's dance this one, please! I love this song."

"Aww, come on, Thair, let's sit this one out."

"Okay." I show my disappointment with lips turned upward, but he still tugs me away.

"Hey, you two," I say when we reach the corner table with bar

122

stools where Emily sits with Mark, an ex-convict who now works in social services. I can't stop staring at the Roman numerals tattooed on his four fingers.

"Hey, Mark, can I ask you, what do those numbers signify?" Ravi looks at me sideways as if I shouldn't have asked.

Mark stares directly at me, "It was the number of my jail cell: 1251."

Emily gives me a dirty look while Ravi changes the subject, "Thair, do you want another Guinness?"

"That's interesting, Mark," I say, ignoring Ravi, all my energy focused on this strange man. As an English teacher, I can't help but notice symbols—especially permanent markings on one's body—and analyze their greater significance, but I really just want to know more about this former delinquent who is my best friend's date, so I continue: "Is it sort of a reminder of where you never want to be again?"

Feeling a bit tipsy, I am saying what's on my mind without really thinking. Ravi and Emily stare me down. Mark notices that our dates are not happy but relieves the tension when he replies in a jocular way, "Actually, Thair, I was stone cold drunk when I got it, so I have no idea of the significance."

We all laugh though I'm not sure why. I have been put in my place, but then he continues, surprisingly more serious. "To be honest, I did do it without thinking, but I am sure deep down it was something like what you said. Those five years were the worst and, oddly enough, the best of my life. I know without my incarceration, I wouldn't be here today, be the man that I am today. And with all you lovely folk to boot. So, yes, it does serve as a reminder of where I was. Where I will never go again."

My eyes are glued on this interesting man, an ex-con who uses diction such as *lovely folk* and *to boot*, a man whose chiseled biceps could certainly do some damage to my waifish Indian boyfriend.

"And, by the way, thanks for asking. A lot of people skirt the issue that I was in jail, and, actually, I am proud to talk about it. Not too many people make a complete turn and, though I have some regrets, I have learned to accept and appreciate my journey because the destination has been sweet." He looks over warmly at Emily; she seems so happy.

My English teacher mind never turns off: he's speaking in metaphor, a bit cliché, but I like it. I guess I like him, too. From my inebriated bubble, I glance at Emily, giving her a thumbs-up with my eyes. Then I remember the words Angela had said, *No preconceived stereotypes rammed down your throat. No society dictating what's right and what's wrong . . . If only others were more open, then they would see that there are a helluva lot of people out there to love.*

I thought of those words now, and how badly I reacted when Emily had told me about her New Year's date, just hours earlier when we were getting ready at my place.

———

"So, you like this guy?"

"Yeah . . . um . . . I think so."

"Why the hesitation?"

She stops putting on mascara, peers at me, "There's one thing that is kind of bothering me. And I don't want to tell you."

My interest is suddenly piqued. "Come on, tell me!"

A heavy silence fills the bathroom.

"Okay, let me guess: he's got a good job, but they don't pay spousal benefits," I tease. "Or he has got four crazy sisters . . . or . . . he is sweet but only has a two-incher."

"Stop it, Thair!" she exclaims, then laughs. "Now you are making me feel bad. I guess it's not that big of a deal, but it just feels weird."

"Okay, spit it out."

"He was in . . . jail."

"Jail? You're kidding!"

"NO, I am not kidding. But he got out four years ago. He took some classes from a particular program and then got a job at the Department of Social Services."

"What did he do? Kill someone?"

"Geez, Thair, you are always so dramatic. No, he didn't kill anyone. He was in for five years after getting in a . . . fight and . . . um . . . stabbing someone."

"*What?* So, he *is* violent!"

"There's more to the story."

"What more could there be? Damn, Emily, you sure know how to pick them."

Emily turns around, back towards me, and I instantly feel awful for what I said.

"I'm sorry, Emily. I didn't mean that."

"Yes, you did, Miss I-get-every-perfect-guy-to-fall-in-love-with-me."

"Hey, that's not nice."

"Well, what you said wasn't nice either."

I couldn't believe we were fighting like school girls. This is how Emily and I had gone back and forth over our twenty-year friendship. We were the best of friends, but we were often cruel, attacking each other with words, then feeling guilty after. At almost thirty-two, I had finally learned when it was time to back down.

"I'm sorry, Em, really. I guess I expected you to say that he was in for selling pot or a DUI. Stabbing someone makes me think that he is . . . well . . . kind of dangerous."

"You know, he may have been, but I really feel like he's one of those that change. That *really* change. He is smart and funny. And open. We can talk for hours on end. I also respect the fact that he helps so many, every day, with the work he does. You know, he started as a simple office assistant, and now he runs seminars for teenagers because the psychologist he works with saw his potential."

"Well, good then, if you are happy, then I am happy, and I will try not to judge him. Okay?" I say this while still being worried about my best friend, *stabbing someone?*

———————

"So do you want another Guinness or not?"

"Oh, I'm sorry, honey. Yes, please."

"Can I get anything for you two?" Ravi asks our friends.

Mark sees Emily's full drink, "No, we're good, thanks." Mark is drinking Coke.

After another Guinness, I want to move again. "Ravi, let's go dance." His nose scrunches up like he has just sucked on a lemon.

"Naaah. Go with Emily if you want." Ravi doesn't really like to dance. He likes to excel at all he does, and it seems as if God, or Shiva, gave him two left feet. But I don't care. My partner could be John Travolta, Justin Timberlake, or Roger Rabbit; it doesn't matter. I just want someone who loves to be on the dance floor as much as I do, to feel the music, to feel the thrill of just letting go; to shake, move, rattle, roll, do whatever. But Ravi prefers to sit on the sidelines and watch. Once in a while, he dances, but I know he only does it to make me happy.

Just as AC/DC's "You Shook Me All Night Long," blasts through the speakers Ravi says, "Ready to go, Thair?"

"Can we dance this one first? Pleeease?"

Another scrunched-up face, "Okay, but after, let's go, okay?"

"Yay!" I say as I sashay onto the dance floor and begin to jump up and down like a teenager.

Ravi is moving his hips slightly to the left and right, laughing at my enthusiasm but a bit embarrassed that his mature girlfriend is jumping up and down. He looks a bit awkward, not sure how to move, but it's sweet. I think I really like this guy. It's too soon for love, but in the last few months, he has certainly made me happy.

Early November, 2002

Ravi and I have just made love, slow, rhythmic. I get up to put on a pot of coffee, and when I walk back in the room, Ravi has a serious look on his face. Oh no, I recognize that look.

"Thair, can we talk?"

I tie my silky robe tighter around my waist and sit on the corner of the bed.

Ravi is leaning against the headboard, pillows propping up his body. His sculpted chest is exposed; under the sheets he is still naked. I wish we didn't have to talk, but for the last few weeks, I've had a feeling this was coming. The stares have gotten longer, deeper. When he holds my hand, it's anxious, not relaxed.

"You know how much I care about you, right?"

"Yes," I state hesitantly.

"Every time I bring up marriage or children you always change subjects. I want to talk about it. All the way this time."

My shoulders sag, my robe opens slightly, my breast—my heart—no longer concealed. Of one thing I am certain: I don't want to marry Ravi. The worst part is I don't know why. It has nothing to do with him. It has everything to do with me. Something, just something, isn't *right*. I can't hide it anymore. I *was* giving this relationship a chance, but something has always been a bit off. I am not going to allow myself to slip down a hole and become isolated again, but this relationship is starting to make me feel uncomfortable, my discordant view of love, intolerable, even to me. I *do* like being with Ravi. I just don't want to marry him. Not now. Maybe one day? I don't know. I'm just not sure.

"All the way, Thair. We need to talk."

I sit on the on the corner of the bed as he continues.

"You've known since we met that I want to get married. I want to have kids. I want a family. I am thirty-nine years old and I still live at home. No one in America lives with their parents until they are almost forty. I'm graduating next month, I already have a good job lined up, and I want to start a real life."

Real life? I think to myself. What has the last year been? A fake life?

"Thair, I have a ring and a date. And I have two names on that ring. You are the first name, but I am ready. I *will* be married by this time next year."

All I hear is the "two names" part. A slight jab in the heart. "Two names?" I say out loud. I should be furious, but mostly I am confused.

"Thair, I have never cheated on you. But there is another woman. I don't want her, but I want to get married. I want to be a father. And damn it, it's you I want. He pauses then adds, "You are the love of my life. Undoubtedly. Unequivocally." *The love of my life.* I repeat the words in my head. He has never spoken with such passion before. The words "I love you" slipped out of his mouth after we had been dating for only four months and had one too many Cadillac Margaritas. I was a bit surprised to hear the "L" word so soon but responded in kind, though my "I love you" was more like a "Yes, I like you a lot, too." I didn't feel it in my heart, but it made me happy to see him happy. And those three silly words would always make him beam.

"Thair, there is a family in India that my mother has been in contact with over the years, and they have a daughter who has always been the one chosen for me. I know it sounds ridiculous, someone *chosen* in this day and age, but it's true. I never thought that I would marry her. I was always waiting for my Thair. And now that I found her, I just don't understand why she is so distant at times."

Slumping, I am again on the verge of tears. I don't want to disappoint this good, good man.

"What's wrong? Please. Please talk to me."

"I don't know. It's this dumb thing about Zeus," I hear myself say.

"What?" His voice raises, the blood adding crimson to his altered face, "What the hell are you talking about?"

"I don't know how to explain it . . ."

In a quiet voice, I hear myself say: "I do care about you, but I . . . I'm sorry . . . *you* are not the love of my life. Maybe there is no such thing for me. But there's also a part of me that is so stupid, such a damn romantic, that I still believe when I find it, I will just *know*."

It doesn't make sense, not even to me. Ravi is ideal . . . and I am not getting any younger. I'm already thirty-three. What am I thinking?

After Ravi leaves, I figure that I will never see him again. Surprisingly, I don't cry, but I am suffering nonetheless. He knew how I felt about children but thought he could change my mind. I did enjoy his company—I just couldn't make a commitment *for life*.

Thair's Story

Encinitas
December, 2002

Thair didn't want to go to Emily's annual Christmas party, too many people and too many questions. Last year she was there with her new boyfriend, Ravi, and this year she was alone—again. In her thirties, never married, never engaged. Apart from her recent breakup, life was moving along just fine. Thair was assigned classes regularly at the local community colleges, she had just remodeled her condo with hardwood floors, and the best thing was that her mother was cancer free, six months and counting!

The last two years were the worst and best of her life. On one hand, she had met a decent man who really seemed to understand her. Ravi was so patient, so helpful when it came to Phaedra. When Thair could not accompany Phaedra to an appointment, Ravi always stepped in. He was filling the shoes of a son-in-law with ease, not going because he had to, but because he wanted to. After only a few months of dating, Ravi had invited Phaedra and Thair over to his parents' house for a fabulous Indian dinner. Ravi's mother had cooked lamb rogan josh and chicken tikka masala, vegetable biryani, and there were all sorts of goodies on the side: samosas, chaat, and mutter paneer—a total feast. Lots of Johnny Walker Blue was poured that marked it as a night of true celebration.

From the moment they met, the mothers adored each other. They shared similar stories, similar lives: both were foreigners who had left their countries, making the US their home. And they both loved it here. Neither had any desire to return to their native country. More than lacking the desire to return, they no longer felt close to their country, saying that their lives before the US seemed so foreign, a distant memory, part of their past. Though Ravi's parents were quite modern, they held on to certain traditions and were against the relationship initially. They learned to accept Thair, and the invitation for dinner with Thair's mother was their way of telling Ravi that they would, begrudgingly, support his choice.

Ravi's mother had chosen another woman for her son, but after meeting Phaedra, she decided Thair was, indeed, suitable wife material. It did not really matter what Thair thought; after the delightful dinner, she was convinced Thair was the one for her son and agreed with Ravi that he had found a good woman. She planned to write a letter to the other Indian family, saying that her son had chosen his own wife, a Greek-American woman, a woman with strong values. Both mothers planned Ravi and Thair's wedding in their heads; it was a match made in Orthodox and Hindi heaven. Even though Thair's mother was going through radiation, she was happier than she had ever been. Her daughter had met Mr. Right. Mr. Presentable. Mr. Happily-Ever-After. He had a solid family, was finishing his PhD, and wanted to start a family right away. It was all so perfect. At least that's the way it looked to Phaedra.

There was a part of Thair that hoped over time she might fall deeply in love with Ravi, so she shielded her mother from the truth: that deep down she always knew Ravi was not "The One."

It made Phaedra so happy to hear stories about the two of them. While Thair and her mom waited in the radiation clinic for each session, Phaedra would say enthusiastically, "Tell me, Thair, how is Ravi?"

"He's well, Mama. Last night, we went and saw a production at the Old Globe Theatre. It was fantastic. We saw *The Taming of the Shrew*; it's a Shakespearean play, the one about—"

"That's nice, honey, so did you and Ravi do anything after?" As always, Thair's mother had very little interest in the Arts. All she was interested in was the love story—the one where her daughter meets Mr. Right, the one where he proposes, the one where two kids are born, the one where Phaedra can finally be a yiayia. And everyone can live happily ever after.

If Phaedra was not in such a vulnerable state, Thair would have been flustered at being cut off, but during those times, Thair's mama could do little wrong. Thair feared for her mother, and though her chances looked good, one never knew. Being in the hospital Monday through Friday made life, all of a sudden, seem so fragile.

The removal of part of Phaedra's breast had been successful. She did not want any reconstruction and instead had two lopsided breasts; one, a full C, the other, barely a B cup. But Phaedra didn't care. She dressed in front of Thair as if her body was in no way disfigured. She still exuded confidence and spirit. She acted like nothing in her life had changed. Thair pondered, could this be possible? Was her mom really that strong? Even when the skin turned bright purple and was obviously sensitive, Phaedra still wore a perpetual smile, one that wrapped all around her head.

With each session of radiation, Phaedra seemed stronger while her breast grew redder; she was more positive, her breast more damaged. Scratchy, dark scabs covered the entire surface of the lopsided breast. After thirty-three sessions of radiation, Thair found her mother cheerful while she was depleted. Ravi had come to about ten of the sessions, his schedule being much more flexible. And after each "visit" with Ravi, Thair's mother was certain that her dream for her daughter was coming true, the cancer being nothing more than a temporary obstacle in her life. For Thair it was the opposite. The cancer was everything. It was something that had the power to take away her beloved mother. Her relationship with Ravi was something, but it was not everything. Early on in their relationship, she had known this in her heart, but she would not allow her brain to accept it. And now, after causing more heartbreak, for herself and for others, Thair didn't know how to feel.

18

Encinitas, California

It's Valentine's Day. I can't believe I am going over to a couple's house instead of wallowing in my wine by myself. Rick called a few minutes ago, "Thair, what are you doing?"

"I just opened a bottle of wine," I grumbled.

"With whom will you be having this wine, Mademoiselle Thair?"

"With my three favorite guests: me, myself, and I." I say this as a joke because I am trying not to feel sorry for myself, but this damn holiday is the worst. Wherever you go, there is all this red. Red roses, red stuffed animals, red boxes of chocolates. I know it's just another day, but all this romantic crap everywhere makes me feel lonelier than ever.

"Thair, just hop in your car, and come on over!" he said.

"Are you sure? I mean it is Valentine's Day and you two . . ."

"Thair, I'm hanging up. We'll see you soon, okay?"

"Okay." I finally replied.

Thank God for Rick and Frank. Emily and Mark are celebrating some anniversary, and when I called my mom, she was already in bed. The truth is, I really don't want to be alone tonight. I put the cork back into the bottle of $9 Costco wine and go into my room to change. It takes me about twenty minutes to get to Hillcrest, and when I see the coral house, I already feel better.

"Hi, sweetie!" Rick says as he opens the door before I can even ring the doorbell. I stand there with a dozen red roses for the lovers (what the hell!) and a bottle of Pinot Noir, a '97 Calera Reed. It was expensive, and I was saving it for a special occasion, but on the way out of my house, I decided tonight is special enough. Sticking both my offerings out as soon as Rick opens the door, I hand him the wine and flowers. He juggles them while simultaneously giving me a kiss on the cheek. Frank is sprawled out on the big purple couch, the "Tinky Winky" couch, as they call it. They named it that after some religious zealot cautioned parents that one of the Teletubbies subtly depicts homosexuality because it is purple with a triangle on his head; the pink triangle being a gay pride symbol, a symbol that was used by Nazis to shame homosexuals but now is embraced by the gay community. The fanatic spread fear, saying that Tinky Winky subconsciously enters the minds of toddlers and introduces them to a "gay lifestyle." My first reaction was *how absurd*, but after reading the ridiculous rant in the the *New York Times*, I never did see Tinky Winky—with its high-pitched voice and red purse—the same way again. Now I loved Tinky Winky more.

As Frank is happily lying on his purple couch, I stand there thinking: it's unfortunate the measures crazies take to breed ignorance rather than compassion. And so what if Tinky Winky is gay? In fact, yay! Let's see more types of people—or creatures!—represented in our media. Frank sees me standing there pensive, puts down his magazine, and slides his legs to the side of the couch.

"Don't get up," I say while making my way over to him. *What a gorgeous man*, a naughty thought crosses my mind. I know I must be sex-deprived when I start to fantasize about one of my closest friends and his partner. Frank is wearing a Travolta-tight white T-shirt and Levi's. I know he is more than one hundred percent gay based on the Kinsey scale *and* absolutely taken, but it's hard not to notice his physical beauty.

I have learned a lot from these two, all about a world I didn't know existed. At one point, Frank was offered an excellent job in Panama but was not able to take it because after Rick's visitor visa would expire, he would have to leave. The company, because of the country's laws, could not support same-sex couples. Rick and Frank had made me aware of so many issues that I had rarely thought about as a hetero-sexual woman.

But now I, too, am *different*, not part of the norm, trapped some-where on the sexual spectrum, neither gay nor completely straight. I love men, my attraction to them visceral, but now I *notice* women— not just their physical beauty, but their humor, their intelligence, their movements—in a way I hadn't before. And sometimes I imag-ine having sex with them. The attractive girl at Nordstrom, the way she touched my arm when she came around the corner to hand me my shopping bag. How would she be in bed? Or I thought about the rough-looking girl with the piercings who works at the gas station. Would sex with her be wild, with black leather straps and handcuffs? Or the pretty, plump woman with the sensitive eyes who is a secretary at my school. Would sex with her be soft, comfortable? My God, is this how men thought? Is every walking-talking female a possible screw?

Of course, I am *not* attracted to everyone, but now there are so many more *possibilities*. I am not attracted to all men, just like I am not attracted to all women. But it goes beyond sex. I actually imag-ine relationships with these women. How would daily life be? What obstacles would we face? Would I be completely satisfied?

But I am not yet comfortable with the word "bisexual." Bisexuals seem to get a bad rap, as if they are just "curious" sexually. What ever happened to love? Ever since Denise Richards and Neve Campbell kissed in *Wild Things*, then Jennifer Aniston and Winona Ryder kissed on *Friends*, and Samantha sucked face and other body parts in *Sex in the City*, bisexuality has seemed like a fad. Girls kissing girls is fun; it's light, not taken seriously. Rick told me girls who look like me (feminine) and are with other girly-girls are called "lipstick lesbians," and lipstick lesbians, *bisexuals* in general, are considered dangerous. They don't know what they want and are not completely accepted by *real* lesbians because they have heterosexual privilege; in other words, they can always go back to men if they find the "lesbian lifestyle" too challenging. Lipstick lesbian. Bisexual. Queer. I hate labels. My one experience with a woman was unforgettable. But I still love men. I am just more open to the possibilities now.

And lately there is another woman who I find myself becoming increasingly attracted to. I try not to stereotype, but when I first saw her, I did think that she is gay. Tall, strong, she always wears pants, button-down shirts, has short hair and walks with determination.

———————

"Would you like red or white?" Frank says, interrupting my thoughts.

"On Valentine's Day? Red, of course, dahhhling. Serve me up some of that Pinot Noir, *por favor*, if you don't mind opening it."

"Of course not! It must be a special occasion for you to bring this over!" he says while examining the bottle.

I take a seat on the floor and prop up a few big, maroon velvet pillows behind my back. After a few glasses of wine, the conversation turns to Ravi.

"Does he still call?" Rick asks.

"No, I haven't heard from him since Christmas. He called to wish me and my mother happy holidays. Mom drove me nuts after the call. *Thair, I can't believe you got rid of him,* she whined. I told her that I didn't *get rid of him.* You get rid of an old couch, not a person. But I know she's still upset. She just doesn't understand."

"To be honest, Thair," Rick says, his voice taking on the I want-to-say-something-but-don't-bite-off-my-head tone, "Ravi is a great guy. We really thought you two were so well-suited. You seemed really happy when you were with him."

"I *was* happy. Just like I was happy with James, too." I hate hearing myself talk. I seem so spoiled, like a child who is never satisfied; the new entitled woman, who is grateful for the work of feminists, but who is now simply drowning.

I really don't feel like getting into this again, so I change the subject. "Instead of Ravi, can we talk about something else, okay? Maybe *someone* else . . ." I say this with a smirk, trying to tantalize them, "So there's this woman at work—"

"A woman?" Rick cuts me off and sits up a bit straighter. He had been trying to tell me that maybe I need to be with another female again, that my one-time lesbian experience wasn't sufficient to really understand myself. But then Ravi came into the picture, and Rick really liked him, so he had given up the idea that we would be two happy, gay couples.

"Okay, so tell us about *this woman.*"

"Her name is Jessica. Ms. Jessica Langstrom, and she's what you two call a Certified Capital *L* Lesbian. Unlike me, she's not a confused hetero-lipstick-lesbian-bisexual." Both men laugh as I continue. "She teaches next door to me on Monday nights, a sociology class with a women's studies emphasis. It started off with a 'hello,' then I bumped into her at the cafeteria one evening before class, and she sat with me while I had some dinner."

"Really? Do tell more," Frank says.

"Well, she's really fascinating. I almost feel embarrassed to call myself a feminist in front of her because her knowledge is so extensive; she's so well-versed, clear, and to be honest, though she looks nothing like Gloria Steinem, she's got the same powerful, yet delicate, presence. She does look a bit tough on the outside but seems so gentle inside."

"Go on," says Rick, leaning into my story.

"I guess you could say she felt my *energy* because the following week, after class, she was waiting for me."

"Waiting for you?"

"Yes," I pause. Both men are sitting on the edge of Tinky Winky, looking much more alert than they had only a half hour earlier.

"So, what happened?"

"Well, she asked if she could walk me to my car."

"And then?" Frank asks anxiously.

"And then Thair asked her good friend Frank for another glass of wine . . ." I say while holding out my glass.

"Thair! You're terrible!" exclaims Rick. "Hurry, babe, please get her a refill, so she can continue."

Frank gets up and opens another bottle while he peeks over the counter from the kitchen, so I continue, "Well, I naturally—"

"Naturally?"

"Stop it, Frank, don't interrupt. Please, continue, Thair."

"As I was saying, I *naturally* said 'yes.' I felt comfortable, and it was dark, so I usually look for someone to walk with me to my car anyway. As we were walking, we were talking and laughing, teasing and . . . kind of . . . flirting. By the time we got to the car, it was obvious that we both felt something. We ended up talking for more than an hour, neither wanting to end the night. But it was getting late. So, she asked me if I was interested in going out for a drink next weekend."

"What did you say?"

"I said yes . . . and then . . . she kissed me."

"What? She kissed you! How forward!" Then in the same breath: "How was it?"

"It was nice. It wasn't the exhilarating feeling like it was with Sappho-girl, but it was *really* nice."

"So if you like this woman, why the hell are you alone tonight?"

"She's away, visiting her family in Boston this weekend. But if she wasn't, I don't think I would be with her anyway. She hates commercial holidays; she was very clear about this. She also told me she is agnostic, doesn't have a spiritual excuse for the shit that happens in this world, and doesn't celebrate anything—Valentine's Day, most obviously, included."

"Wow, she seems a bit angry."

I laugh rather than get defensive because my first impression was the same, but after a few minutes of talking to her, her warmth and sincerity are what become most apparent. In the few conversations we've had, a soft and vulnerable side emerged. So, I respond, "Well, maybe she's a bit radical with some issues, but it doesn't bother me. I find her intriguing. The few times we chatted, I found myself enjoying her company immensely."

"Sounds like a basis for a good *friendship*," Frank comments.

I add, "And there's this chemistry. When we are close, I don't know . . . it's electric. Feels like a lot more than just friends."

"And what about Mama Phaedra? I think a non-believer will be tough for her, but a lesbian may push the little lady over the cliff." Rick says this with a mix of seriousness and facetiousness. Phaedra, though fond of Rick, has never welcomed Frank into her home.

"I think you are jumping a bit ahead of yourself. I don't know that she will ever meet my mother!" I laugh out loud, imagining introducing my lesbian date to my traditional mother. "I think I will cross that bridge when or *if* I come to it. For now, I am excited—and nervous—about our date."

After a few hours and too many glasses of wine, I retreat to their guest bedroom because I know I cannot drive. Brushing my teeth with a disposable toothbrush from Rick's "over night kit" for friends like me, I cuddle up on the queen-sized bed, and start to think not about Jessica, but about Ravi. I still have feelings for him and wonder whether I made a huge mistake. After tossing and turning for half hour, I slide my legs off the side of the bed and pull out a notebook from my purse. I always carry it with me, a place to relocate my tangled thoughts when they won't leave my mind. In my queasy, drunken stupor, I do the only thing that settles me.

Thair's Story

Though her relationship with Ravi was over, and she accepted that he was not the one for her, Thair still missed his touch and his laugh, but mostly she felt guilty. She couldn't commit, not if it didn't feel *right*. Maybe that's why a ring on her finger seemed like a noose around her neck. Her last two relationships were good. Relationships like that just didn't come around that often. Ravi was educated, kind, always made her morning coffee and brought it to bed while her eyes had yet to meet the morning light. When Thair rubbed his shoulders, she loved hearing his soft purring sounds. Her friends thought she was insane, telling her, "Thair, you can't let this one get away." But she did let him get away. When he started talking marriage, babies, her feathers rose and she flew the opposite direction. Why could she not be more like the yellow warbler: find a partner and stay with him (or her?) until you die? Be forever monogamous, not the serial monogamist like she was. Was it time to stop looking for Mr. Right and just settle for Mr. Almost-Right? Statistically speaking, women over thirty should just not be that picky because thirty is close to forty, and everyone knows forty is the beginning of the end. Just like that article she read as a teenager in *Newsweek* saying that women over forty have a greater chance of being killed by a terrorist than getting married! That *fact* in the article was later debunked, but the message certainly wasn't. It *felt* true. Her mom divorced at forty-plus, and she was still alone.

And the children part, that was always something Ravi had been very clear about, telling Thair he pictured her pregnant as soon as the vows were exchanged. Thair had thought a lot about children, but she lacked a maternal urge. If she had wanted kids, maybe Ravi would have been the ideal match, but not wanting them allowed her to continue to pursue The One without her body's pressure. When she was young, she loved to hold, squeeze, and caress babies, but in her twenties, she learned something: she had choices. And the simple desire she had had to hold babies was completely gone. At a barbeque, she would rather have a glass of wine in her hand and socialize than carry someone's baby. She could not imagine reading *Goodnight Moon* over and over when she just desired time to reread *Jane Eyre*.

Thair rarely told others that she didn't want children because people around her still expected women to become mothers. Some male colleagues would tell her: "Having kids is the best thing this world has to offer." Their remarks seemed genuine and, at times, she wondered if God had accidentally misplaced her maternal urge in them. And the mothers, with angst all over their faces, told her: "Thair, you really *must* have children. You will never really know the beauty of true, unconditional love!" Even Emily would say, "Oh, Thair, aren't you worried about missing out on something that is essential to being a woman—being *a mother?*"

None of these opinions changed how she felt. Thair had no desire to have children, and unlike women who yearn for motherhood, Thair was not worried about her eggs drying up, her follicles becoming fewer. Her decisions were not dictated by a biological clock. The only clock was Phaedra's: she wanted Thair to marry and make her a yiayia. But for Thair, there was no rush. No rush in settling down with someone if her heart, soul, and mind were not in agreement.

There were odd moments when she had thought: maybe what I do need is a child. Maybe then I won't be so caught up with my desire to find personal fulfillment and can live for another. What is it about these new independent women, herself included, that made them feel "entitled"? Entitled to complete fulfillment that included not only confidence, career, financial and emotional stability, but also a faithful, loving partner; a partner who was not chosen for his ability to pay the bills or to be an excellent father, but chosen just because he complemented this strong, independent woman. Thair certainly yearned for complete happiness. No more of Mick Jagger's "Can't Get No Satisfaction," she needed it, not only in the bedroom, but also in her heart, mind, and soul. Thair wanting this fairy tale, this myth that her mama had persuaded her young mind into believing was a true story, led to Ravi's walking out the door. She was not willing to compromise—become a wife because her choices would become fewer the older she got. Become a mother just to fulfill society's standards. No, Thair wanted that elusive happiness, and she still harbored hope that it existed somewhere . . . maybe alone . . . maybe even with that other half.

I've just finished revising what I wrote last night when I stayed at Rick and Frank's. I took the eight pages of muddled notes that were a bit hard to read and typed them into my computer. Though *I* am this woman, she seems at times so foreign. What prompted me to write about Ravi? And why was I still contemplating the children issue?

19

Encinitas, California
February 21st, 2003

I have a pile of jeans on my bed: Levi's, Calvin's, Tommy's. A pile of dresses also adorns my bedspread: a simple black one, a low-cut red one, a feminine, flowery one. Nothing looks right. How does one girl dress to go out with another girl? And to a lesbian bar no less? I have been to gay male bars a few times, but I was always with Rick and Frank. And it was always an afterthought, going with them for a drink after work and then going home early because I always felt a bit out of place. But this is different. I am going to a lesbian bar, and I have a lesbian date. My God, what would my mother think? What would my students think? I feel naughty, like I am living on the periphery of my own life, watching as I do things that normally would be abnormal for me, but simultaneously feel so natural.

I sit languidly on the corner of the bed, wearing only my black lace thong and a simple black bra. I can't decide what to wear, so I move to the bathroom and start to put on my makeup. I choose an olive-colored eyeliner that brings out the green in my eyes since they sometimes lean towards hazel. Squinting into the mirror while applying my mascara, I make a mental note that maybe I do need to finally buy some glasses. I notice a few new lines on my forehead and how my cheeks and the area around my mouth seem saggier than yesterday. I comb my long, thick hair and am pleased to have inherited it from my mother, whose dark locks still hang heavy on her shoulders.

Back in the bedroom, staring at the pile of clothes, I grab a denim miniskirt with tattered edges and a white T-shirt with a rose design on the front. Simple, and the skirt shows off my long, slender legs—something else I inherited from my mother. When I zip up my black-leather, knee-high boots the look feels complete: sweet and a bit sexy.

The doorbell rings. I had asked Jessica to meet me at my place but said I would drive. A second ring. I make my way to the door, nervous, anxious, and open it as my heart pitter-patters. Jessica is standing in front of me, and I almost don't recognize her. It's not that she's dressed so differently from when I see her on campus, but tonight *really* looking at her, I am stunned by her beauty. Her thin arms are ripped like Madonna's, sinewy, but strong. Her jaw is angular, her teeth so big and so white. When she smiles, I see a bit of Hilary Swank in her face. It's a beautiful face.

I am imbibing her when she says, "Hi, Thair, so are you going to invite me in?"

"Hi! Yes, of course. Sorry . . ."

She gives me a little unexpected peck on my lips and walks into my living room. "Wow, what a great place." She says this and stops in front of my bookcase . . . admiring? Or wondering? Overall, I have an eclectic collection, but at eye level, three whole rows are filled with all of Gabriel García Márquez's books, all of Milan Kundera's, and all of Raymond Carver's, three of my favorite authors. Other authors whose books cover the most accessible shelves are Shakespeare, Orwell, Steinbeck, Hemingway—all of a sudden, I find myself self-conscious. These are the books that I usually teach; that's why they are at arm's reach. Mostly all white males, not one woman in the bunch. What does that say about me? That I think men are better writers or that the traditional canon affected me more than I even realize? When Jessica glances down, I feel a sense of relief when she sees my Brontë, Austen, Morrison, Murdoch, Joyce

Carol Oates collections. I do adore the words of these women, but it's the men I take to bed at night. They are the ones with whom I curl up in the evenings, the ones who have left the strongest impressions on me. I love the magical realities in García Márquez's writing. When I spend time with him, I am tossed into strange worlds where western reason often becomes obsolete. My nights with Kundera often leave me restless and weak; the things he writes resonate deep into my soul, so much that I lose sleep and find myself sitting up in bed writing notes about my own *unbearable heaviness*. Evenings with Carver, though, are probably my favorite. I love his minimalist style, the way his simple words captivate me, how his stories of relationships gone bad make me laugh, then cry, so much catharsis. His drunk, depressed characters usually make my life feel much lighter.

But Jane will always have my heart, my all-time favorite heroine and novel, a love story like no other. Had Zeus separated Jane and Edward, too?

I am thinking about all this when Jessica slides a book off the shelf and reads the back cover.

"So, what did you think of this?" I see she is holding *Manifesta*, my comprehensive guide to feminism.

"I loved it. I know some stuff about feminism, but I thought it was very insightful. I think for many women the idea that there are waves of feminism gets kind of confusing. One thing for sure, this book made me grateful for *all* feminists, how they worked and continue to work to get us to where we are today, to where we can be tomorrow. It's too bad that many people have such an aversion to the word *feminist*; almost as if it's a dirty word when really it's feminists that we should thank for all that we, women, have today in regard to choices."

I see Jessica looking at me. I can't tell if it is a pensive or blank expression.

"I'm sorry, Jessica. You probably already know all this. I am sure you have a lot of interesting conversations in class about these issues."

She doesn't respond, just says, "Hey, would you mind calling me Jess?"

"Sure . . . Jess."

"So, ready to go?" she asks while slipping the book back onto the shelf beside my collection of Wonder Woman comics. When she looks my way, I instantly feel safe. With men there was always a sense of worry what will happen at the end of a date. Will they expect a goodnight kiss, a make-out session? Sex? Maybe it's the same way with women, with Jessica, but for some reason, there's a sense of comfort. But still excitement.

We walk out my blue door and take the elevator down to the indoor garage. The conversation flows easily. I have decided to drive tonight, so I won't go over my one-drink limit because I really want to be lucid for this date.

After I unlock the car with the automatic alarm, I walk over to her side of the car, and open her door. She laughs, "What a lady you are," she says, sort of teasing, as my *chivalrous* gesture does not go unnoticed. Once we are in the car, I find myself sharing my ideology of the importance of still opening car doors. I have probably said this speech to countless men, but it's really weird to say it to a woman.

"I don't mean to seem old-fashioned, but there is a part of me that loves tradition."

For years, I have had a hard time dealing with mixed emotions I would feel on first dates. I *did* want the guy to pay, and I *did* want him to open the door, but did that make me a hypocrite? Of course, I believed that women and men should have the same rights, so why were these gestures still important to me? I pretended to be someone I wasn't. It's only lately that I am finally coming to understand and accept myself, realizing that these seemingly contradictive ideals—wanting equality while still wanting to be treated "like a lady"—really aren't contradictions at all. It's okay for modern women to be an amalgamation of ideals; we just need to be clear regarding what we *really* want. Because when it comes down to it, we don't all want the same thing, or necessarily want to be treated the same way.

As I pull out of the garage, we are talking about a variety of topics. I end up sharing my Greek girl story and admit that I have never been with a woman before except for that one isolated experience.

There are a few moments of quiet, and I start to think about all kinds of strange things. I am a girly woman, admittedly, and have always relied on men to do chores like take out the garbage and change light bulbs. If Jessica and I start dating, who will do these tasks? I kind of like the duties-divided scenario, but I'm sure things will be different.

Suddenly I catch myself: I just recently met this woman, and I am already thinking about a *relationship*. Is it because I really like her, or am I just kind of lonely? It's only been a few months since Ravi and I broke up, and maybe what I need is to be by myself for a while. Become Oprah-healthy. Complete on my own.

Jessica starts to tell me about her life and how difficult it was for her to come out. I listen intently to her story, my heart opening as she speaks. She tells me about prominent figures and how they are trying to change marriage laws, about the marches she attends, and about the lives of gay authors. Then, suddenly, I'm anxious, like a little girl, almost like a student. I know very little about the gay and lesbian world. Do I even capitalize "lesbian"? I mean the island of Lesbos is a proper noun, and "lesbian" is a derivative, so should the "L" be capitalized? Like the island of Fiji; if you are from there, you are Fijian—capital "F." I feel like I am treading in murky water. Capital letters may not be an issue. What if someone asks me *what* I am? What will I say? "Bisexual" doesn't feel right. "Fluid" seems too sexually charged. Maybe I will just say Confused; oh, and with a capital "C." Truth is, I'm not that confused though I do feel a bit stressed. My hands are sweating, so I turn on the air-conditioning even though it's cool outside.

Jessica is staring at me, her intense eyes tilted downward, watching me. I have no idea what she is thinking. She takes her hand and gently puts it on my thigh, "Thair, will you do me a favor?"

"Yes," I manage to squeak in a pathetic voice.

"Will you, please, just relax?"

A nervous laugh escapes me. *Am I that obvious?* Then a deep sigh, "Okay." I guess I am completely transparent. "So, tell me more about this place where we're going."

"Well, this is a place I frequent a lot. There are not too many lesbian bars in the city that I really like, and this one has great music, the ambience is relaxing, and I know some of the bartenders quite well. It just doesn't feel like the typical pick-up joint, though I have to say," she states with a smirk, "it's probably the best place to hook up with a girl."

Hook up with a girl? Gosh, all of a sudden, this conversation sounds cheap. I guess I thought a woman, an educated woman no less, would be above talking about "hook-ups," but I am soon realizing that lesbian, gay, straight, bisexual, transgender, transsexual, whatever label people use nowadays, it's all the same shit. Going to a bar, looking for a "hook-up." I find myself getting unnecessarily irritated. So we are going to a girl bar where she *knows* a lot of people. How well does she know these women? Will we be meeting her ex "hook-ups"? And why is she taking me *there*? My inner voices start tormenting me.

I glance over at her, now looking straight ahead, I see her strong jaw line and her soft skin; such a strange contradiction of a woman, strong, a bit masculine with fleeting moments of girlishness when she smiles. I need to calm down. Why does any of it matter really? Who cares if we meet her exes? She obviously has no problem introducing me to people she knows, so maybe I am someone significant to her. But then I think, maybe this isn't a date after all. Maybe I am just a friend? A bit of incomprehensible jealousy and insecurity envelops me. Then a little voice unsettles me: maybe I'm just a *hook-up*? I thought dating a woman would be simpler, but all of a sudden, it seems the rules of engagement are even more confusing. This is a whole new world for me, and somehow, I don't think I like it any better. I can't help but wonder: how would I have felt if a guy took me to a bar on our first date? I *know* I would not have liked it. BUT if I were with a man, and we had chemistry, our choices for a first date would be limitless. With a woman, it is so different. What if we went to a nice restaurant, what if we shared a bottle of wine, would we be able to reach over the table and hold hands, give each other a kiss? The answer is clear. Two women in a restaurant sharing a kiss would still cause a bit of scene here in conservative San Diego. Even in somewhat-liberal California, people still stare when they see two women together.

Jessica, physically, has a hard edge, and I am such a girly-girl, so would people look at us holding hands and think, *oh what a sweet couple, look at how in love they look.* I don't think so. If two women want to be together and show some affection, where do they go? I guess we could have stayed at my place or hers and just had dinner and wine, but I also know where that probably would have led. And the truth is, I don't think I am ready for that yet.

Thoughts swirling in my head, reaching a vortex, I hear her words, sucking me out: "Thair, are you okay going to The Burn? If you want, we can go somewhere else. There are a lot of cafés and restaurants in Hillcrest where I think . . . you might feel comfortable."

Again, I hear that softness and real concern in her voice as if she is reading my mind, so in tune with my uncertainties.

"No, I think The Burn sounds fun. Let's stick with the original plan."

"Okay, good." She squeezes my leg, gives me a big smile, and looks forward.

After parking, we walk a few blocks to a club that has a large red-orange neon sign in front. Outside The Burn, a handful of women are talking, some smoking, some kissing; an overweight woman stands in the doorway.

"Hey, Jess," she says as she gives, I decide, my *date* a warm hug. "Two tonight?"

"Yes, please," Jess puts her hand in her back pocket and pulls out a small black wallet. I reach for my purse at the same time, though I know I am just going through the motions. I do want her to pay. I want to feel like she is taking *me* out.

"Don't worry about it. I got it."

As we walk in the door, she takes a hold of my hand, our fingers interlaced. I'm a bit nervous in this place but love the fact that she is in control. Funny. With a man, I hated it when they felt like they owned me, but with a woman, the control feels good. No patriarchal archetype dictates who is going to be "boss," just two women together, one taking the role of being more dominant (at least in this situation) than the other.

I overhear someone make a comment about the "lipstick lesbian and her dyke." It doesn't come across as nice. Jess is greeting someone and doesn't hear the woman's comment. I guess from the outside, with my long hair, miniskirt, and high-heeled boots, I look quite feminine. Jessica fits the description of "dyke," so I guess I'm "lipstick." Great. I can't help but wonder, why categorize at all? Why label? Isn't it this type of categorization that has caused so many problems in the world in the first place?

Then the questions start again. *What was I? Who am I? What am I doing in a lesbian bar with a woman?* Who am I fooling? It feels god-awful, weird. It feels weird, but not wrong. Part of me wants to leave the place screaming, but a larger part of me feels stuck to the chair, and the part that feels the strangest, the part that I cannot ignore, is that I am hugely drawn to Jessica, in a way that I never was to James or Ravi.

"Hey, Thair, where are you?"

"Sorry. I guess, I am just taking in the surroundings."

"Do you want to leave?"

Here's my opportunity.

"No, let's stay. Can we get a drink?"

"Sure, what would you like?"

"Do they have Tanqueray?"

"Yeah, I'm sure they do."

"With tonic and twist of lime, please."

"Sure, I'll be right back."

I open my purse and pull out a $20. This time the gesture is genuine. I hold it out to her as she smiles and says, "Save it. The next date can be on you."

When I hear these words, my heart leaps a bit. So, it is a *date*, and she expects a second one. A lightness encapsulates me. Then I wonder, how would I feel if a man had said that, *expecting* a second date?

I have to stop! Stop comparing. Stop analyzing. Just relax.

Jessica walks up to the bar, says something to a ravishing redhead bartender; then she leans over and they kiss on the cheek. My stomach burns. Gosh, am I jealous? Are lesbian relationships even more challenging than straight ones?

I have been telling myself that the last few months I have been growing and changing, learning to be genuinely content in my own skin, but tonight my growth seems stunted. I am uncomfortable, jealous, and insecure. I also feel though that I am stretching. Maybe discomfort will be good for me? My thoughts vacillate from negative to positive, from confused to content.

Jess notices my quiet and asks me again if I want to leave. But I don't. After my gin and tonic, I relax. To get closer to the dance floor and music, Jessica and I move from a table to the bar. There we chat a bit with Tawny, the bartender. Turns out, Tawny was one of Jessica's star students. She's a striking woman, probably in her mid-twenties with piercing turquoise eyes that offset her flaming red hair. Scissors are tattooed on her neck, and a tiny diamond nose stud decorates her face. I want to ask Jessica if she ever went to bed with her, but I know it is really none of my business. "Sweet Child O' Mine" comes on, so I grab Jessica's hand as we head over to the dance floor. Amidst a bunch of women, we sway our bodies to Guns N' Roses. For the first time all night, I am not thinking, just having a great time. We stay on the floor when AC/DC follows with "Highway to Hell." We dance for at least an hour and then go back to the bar, take a short break, then dance again. When we finally sit down, I look at my watch, and it is almost 1:00 a.m. The music is loud and it's hard to talk, so I ask her if she's ready to go.

Back at my place, I invite Jessica in. I am not ready for her to leave, and since I only had one drink all night, I'd like a glass of wine. She follows me in and sits down on the couch, making herself comfortable as she slips off her shoes and crosses her legs. I sit down on the otto-man and unzip my boots, my feet killing me. We must have danced at least a couple of hours, and she likes shaking as much as I do. I had told my mother just weeks before, *Mama, I decided I will not be in a relationship again if the person doesn't dance. Who cares about degree or job or intellect or humor? My next partner needs to love dancing!* Of course, part of what I said was in jest, intellect and humor will always matter. I remember my mother's reaction, just a simple *humph.*

I wonder what she would have thought if she saw me shaking flirtatiously with another woman, now entertaining that same woman in my home—a woman who I was certain would soon be my lover.

After I take off my boots, I wiggle my toes, jump to my feet, and grab a bottle of wine from my bar. "Would you like a glass of Cab, Merlot, or Pinot Noir? Sorry, don't have any white wine. I have Corona if you prefer a beer."

"A glass of Cabernet sounds excellent."

After I open the bottle, I pour it in my Riedel decanter to aerate while lighting the many candles in my living room. Then I take the decanter, set it on the coffee table, kneel on the floor, and begin to pour the wine into the glasses. I love watching the way the deep red falls into the crystal. Swirling it a bit and tilting it to one side, I watch the tears stream down. I don't know that much about wine, though I did take a class at one time, but mostly I just love the ritual of wine. Opening the bottle. Smelling the cork. Watching it fall into the decanter. I bought this decanter a few years ago, a bit pricey, a superfluous purchase. It's hard to clean because of the sediment that gets trapped at the bottom, but worth every cent for its beauty. This is one of the rituals that provides me with a sense of calm, a sense of joy. I think many must encounter this feeling when they enter a church, yet I find it in pouring, smelling, and drinking a good glass of wine. It's almost like I make love to each bottle of wine I open, often giving this ceremony more attention than I did the men in my life. I am thinking about all this as I swirl the glass one final time and take a good swig. The liquid rests in my mouth for a second; then I move it around, feeling it on my tongue, in my cheeks.

I stand up and make my way to the fridge and get some Trader Joe's truffles, set them out on another crystal dish, and bring them over on a tray with two glasses of water. I know trays seem so out of fashion—too ladylike, too much a reminder of the '50s housewife—but I love them. I often buy my trays from craft fairs. My latest tray is made from a Duran Duran album cover that has lots of acrylic poured over it, slippery and wet to the touch, but very useable.

As I set the tray on the table and see John Taylor smiling at me with his sultry eyes, I am sixteen again, screaming uncontrollably at a Duran Duran concert. Now, I feel a bit silly as I put it down and Jessica sees it.

Jessica sits quietly, taking in her surroundings. Beside the couch are a rustic side table and the book I am currently reading, some mindless bestseller, a tool for escape. She picks it up and a photograph falls out—*shoot*, a black and white picture of me and Ravi at the Del Mar Fair from one of those photo booths. I have been using it as a bookmark, and since I still feel a lot of warmth for him, it serves its purpose with little emotional turmoil connected. Just a picture of a man I once kinda loved.

"So, who is this? If you don't mind me asking."

"He's my ex-boyfriend, a nice guy I dated for a little more than a year."

"Handsome fellow. What happened?"

"Well, it's kind of complicated."

"Isn't it always?"

"Yeah, I guess." I look into my wine, not sure if I really have it in me to talk about Ravi.

Sensing my silence, Jess says, "Sorry, I shouldn't have asked, but I'll admit I'm a bit threatened to see that photo in your book. If your heart is still somewhere else, and I know this sounds forward, but I would like to know."

I get up from the floor, where I am sitting, and as if I am watching a movie, I see myself moving towards the couch, sitting beside Jessica, and looking at her deep in the eyes. "No, the only place I want to be is right here with you." I take my hands and place them on either side of her cheeks and kiss her long and tenderly.

20

Jessica is still in my bed on this early Saturday morning. The last three months have flown by. Every Friday, after our three-hour classes, Jess and I go for lunch, then to The Burn for a happy hour drink; we celebrate another week of teaching done, one week closer to summer break. One week I drive, the next she does, depending on who will be designated driver. We unwind and dance for a few hours, then always end up back at my place. Jess shares a big house with two roommates, and we just like our privacy so much more, so our place of weekend habitat has been my condo. Saturdays, like today, she usually sleeps in. I can never sleep past 8:00 a.m., but Jess can sleep until noon. And she sleeps so deep—it drives me a bit nuts. I wake up at 7:00 a.m., thinking about all the papers I have to grade, all the things I need to do around the house. There are bills to be paid, furniture to be dusted, and more papers to grade. My head is full of lists, lists, and more lists. But she sleeps and sleeps. A slight puffing, whirring, and snore escapes her every so often, not like Ravi's snoring that kept me awake. Hers is somewhat delicate, almost lovable. Jessica usually stays the weekend, leaving Sunday afternoon, so she can get some grading done and prepare for the week ahead. I like the company, but today I'm uneasy. I can't lie in bed any longer, so at 7:43 a.m. I put on a pot of coffee and turn on my computer.

Thair's Story

Thair met a woman at work, and for the first time since her brief encounter on holiday, she was once more enamored with a woman. The sex certainly was great. Thair likened sex with a woman to chai tea. It was sweet, smooth, went down easy. Sex with men was like a bold cup of java. Stronger, thicker, a bit bitter to the taste, but the pleasure it gave, unequivocally addictive. With Jessica the sex was delicious. Light snoring, no rolling over, just warm, soft flesh. So much touching, so much time spent looking into each other's eyes, talking, laughing; sex was endless, never a rush. Of course, there were times when she and Jessica got a bit wild, a bit aggressive, but mostly, the way she climaxed with a woman was certainly different. Was it better? No, she could not say it was. It was just different. And there had been so many other differences in the months that Thair had been dating a woman. Some differences were simply inconvenient (Jess expected Thair to take out her own garbage and change her own light bulbs), others were more serious (only a few districts in San Diego where they could go to avoid lascivious or disgusted stares and feel genuinely comfortable), and some differences were downright frightening (two white men with a confederate flag on their monster Ford truck had yelled out the window: "You fucking bitches need some cock to set you straight! CUNTS!").

The "c" word still rang in her head weeks later. Challenges existed that had never crossed Thair's mind when she was in a heterosexual relationship. When dating men, there were unlimited excellent restaurants to explore, places they could share a bottle of wine and be romantic. She had never felt harassed. In fact, quite the opposite. With James and Ravi, Thair often heard:

you two make such a nice couple! In the months that she and Jess had been dating, no one had ever complimented their coupledom. Instead, old ladies stared if they were to give a quick peck in a restaurant. Their husbands usually looked on lustfully with one hand on their penises under the table. The stares, hoots, and hollers Thair could ignore, but the men in the pickup had truly frightened her. So much so that she wanted to call the police, but Jessica calmed her down. "Honey, try to relax. We don't have a license plate number, and even if we did, and the police could find them, it's really hard to book someone for a comment we *supposedly* heard. It would be their word against ours. Do you really want to start something with two uneducated, possibly violent assholes?" Thair was surprised that Jess, who had seemed so polemically inclined towards issues she believed in, would allow such an event to slide so easily. Couldn't a verbal assault be considered a hate crime?

These things had caused Thair to reflect on the difference of being in a lesbian relationship compared to a straight one, but none of this was bothering her this morning. It was something else.

It was what Jessica had said the night before.

It had all started with a conversation about exes. "Thair, tell me a little more about Ravi."

"Why? I've told you several times that it's over, totally over." Thair said in a petulant manner.

"I'm sorry, Thair, you know this isn't about trust. I just want to hear more about what happened. I don't often wear my heart on my sleeve, but I don't want to do whatever the poor bloke did and lose my sweet Thair forever."

Thair smiled. She loved it when Jess used this voice, one of protectiveness, one that also sounded a bit possessive. Jessica continued: "I know we both have friends that are ex-lovers, but

I guess when we see mine, it feels transparent. When you see Tawny, you can tell that we are friends and nothing more. But, when we saw Ravi last week at Panniken, the warmth in your eyes was unmistakable. And, okay, I am a bit jealous."

Thair was playing with her wine glass, swirling the liquid in circles as she listened to Jess. She honestly did not want Jess to feel insecure. She had few romantic feelings for Ravi, but it was true, she did still feel a certain physical pull to him. And, yes, there was a part of her that would jump in bed with him again if she were single . . . ah, those slim hips and wide shoulders. But there was a big "but." She was not *in love* with Ravi. Of that, she was certain. But how did Thair feel about Jessica? Was she in love? Or at least, was she falling in love? With Jessica everything was really good. Jess never held back her feelings; an open book, from politics to love, she made no excuses for anything, for anyone. She stood behind her beliefs but knew when to back down, knew when a few steps back actually meant a few steps forward. Thair loved that about her even if she didn't always agree with her decisions.

They had open communication: they debated so many things, but their differences of opinions only brought them closer because after every feisty conversation, they would simply agree to disagree, then laugh and make ravenous love. And there was never any residual resentment. With men, if there was a difference of opinion, Thair found herself the next day trying to baby the man's bruised ego. With Thair and Jess it was simply good old-fashioned discourse; she imagined this was the way Aristophanes and Eryximachus argued that fateful day when they talked about the superhuman race and the creation of love. They stated their ideas, asked questions, spewed opinions, didn't necessarily agree, and when all was said and done, like Thair and Jess, they kissed and made up.

It was a solid relationship, exciting too. Jess knew Thair's body like a map. There was not one unexplored continent, not one mole-of-an-island that hadn't been tenderly kissed or caressed. Jessica would spend hours exploring every crevice, every peak, every flatland.

And Jess had this deep, raspy laugh that was so genuine, came from the heart, it kind of reminded Thair of her grandmother's laugh. Jessica was an extraordinary person and a fantastic lover.

But she was also a woman who hungered to be a mother.

Jess continued to probe, "Thair, tell me, even *I* can see how sexy and intelligent Ravi is." Taking Thair's hand gently, "Can you tell me what happened? I really want to understand."

Gosh, where to begin? Thair, on a whim, decided to tell her the story of the hand and the heart. "I guess I have always seen relationships in terms of pictures, images, symbols . . ."

Jessica squinted a bit but didn't interrupt.

"I know this sounds silly, but I feel like there is this hand that is connected to my brain, and it travels down my throat and stops just before my heart; this is my hand of logic. Then there's another hand that starts at my heart that is desperately reaching up to grab a hold of the hand that is dangling its fingers in my throat. The problem is, the logic-hand never wants to reach down far enough to hold onto the heart-hand. It's as if my heart wants to stretch, but the other hand always pulls back. I guess I imagine when I meet my . . . my . . . I can't believe I am going to say this— my other half, The One who is truly meant for me, the heart-hand will stretch out and hold onto the logic-hand. And I will *just know*."

As she finished talking, Thair realized that she sounded a bit loony. Brain/logic-hand? Heart-hand? This love thing was making her certifiably insane. The beauty was, through all of this, Jessica was listening intently.

There was a long pause, so Thair remarked: "I can't believe I told you about my brain and heart-hand theory. You must think I am crazy!" Thair said this as she tried to purge a nervous laugh.

"Thair, no, you're not crazy. Thank you so much for sharing that. Really. In fact, I think you've described what I am feeling. I could almost feel these hands enter me, one holding onto the other tightly. I know it's only been a few months, but I am sure you know how much I . . . I love you. I don't just love your humor, intelligence, and beauty, I am *so* in love with you. Using your analogy, if I may, my logic-hand and heart-hand are completely intertwined, completely connected."

After her admission, Jessica sat there calmly, another of her strengths, to open herself up, become totally vulnerable, unafraid of the consequences. Instead of meeting Jessica's gaze, Thair looked down, a burning sensation in her throat.

Taking Thair's hands gently in hers, Jessica, in an almost whisper-like voice, questioned: "Sweetie, I do feel compelled to ask, what about you? Where are these hands in relation to us for you?"

Silence again. Thair moved in her chair a bit, brows furrowed, finally she spoke, "Jess, God. I . . . I . . . don't—"

But before Thair could complete her answer Jessica remarked, "Thair, I'm sorry. Please don't answer yet. I don't want to push you. I certainly don't want to push you away. So let's just enjoy our wine and

I feel Jessica kissing me on the neck, so I drop the screen to my laptop and swivel around.

"What are you writing, babe?"

"Just those silly stories I told you about."

"I'm sure they aren't so silly. When do I get to read them?"

I let out a deep sigh. "I don't know. I'm not sure I'll ever really want to share them . . ."

Jessica's eyes drop, with feigned sadness she states, "Okay. But you know I would love to read them if you ever change your mind."

"I know. And for that you are so sweet, and I love you." *Oh shit!* What did I just say? I meant it in a very casual way, but I cannot ignore the expression on Jessica's face.

"Thank you. I needed that. I love you, too. I thought after last night I may have frightened you away. You know, talking about babies and . . . hands and all!" With that she lets out one of her deep laughs. Then she looks more serious, "Thair, I know that we haven't been together long, but when you know, you know? Right? Isn't that what you said? I knew, probably from our first kiss, that you are the woman I would love to spend my life with. And I have always been honest with you from the beginning. I have a complete life, but I also want to be a mother. I have *always* wanted to be a mother, and now it just feels like all the pieces of the puzzle are in place."

I look deep into her. I *do* love her. I *am* in love. But can I go back on everything I believe and become a parent? Share a child, be part of a two-mother household? I admire her character, just the way she is; it's as if an aura of positive energy surrounds her. And with her I feel so *light*, so happy. The way she throws her shoulders back, how she makes clever comments, how she astounds me with her knowledge of almost anything. While these thoughts cross my mind, she gets up and faces the sliding door, dressed in a simple white T-shirt, looking outside, at what I am not sure. She reminds me of Artemis as she stands there, the sexy tomboy diety who was known as Goddess of the Hunt, but a goddess who also loved children and who later took on Eileithyia's role in aiding childbirth. Like Artemis, my lover's strengths are two-fold: physically powerful and utterly compassionate.

My cheeks radiate love. A strong pull at the hands in me, maybe my heart–hand and brain-hand will finally clasp fingers?

Then I notice her touching her stomach in a motherly way. My enigmatic brain-hand shortens. What is she thinking? What am *I* thinking? I don't want to be a parent. I hear myself say out loud, "Jess, we do need to have that conversation again. But not today. Okay? I really just want to have some fun. Is that okay with you?"

"Of course, my princess." She is now towering above me with her hand gently resting on my shoulder. "It's just that my biological clock is ticking at light speed. Shit! I'm almost forty-one, so I do need to know how you feel about kids."

"Jess, please. Not today. Please. Not today. I just don't have it in me." God, I love this woman, but I am certain of what I don't want. Yet . . . Phaedra wants to be a grandmother so badly.

"Sorry, sorry." She says this as she lightly kisses my neck again. "You're right, let's not talk today. Instead . . ." she kisses me on the shoulder, "I have an idea," another kiss, "how about you turn off that computer," her hand slip between my legs, "and I'll show you—" before she can finish her sentence, I turn around and we are kissing passionately. She has both her hands on the computer chair, then moves down on her knees as I spread my legs, anxious to have this woman use her talents on me.

The phone is ringing and ringing and ringing, but I ignore it. Then I hear my mother almost yelling into the machine, "Thair, Thaaaaaair, are you there? Okay. Call me. It's your mama. Everything is okay, just wanted to talk. Okay. Bye, honey."

Click.

⌒‾‾‾‾‾‾

It's late Sunday and Jessica has just left. No sooner than I kiss her good-bye, the phone rings again. I pick it up immediately since I know it's my mother.

"Hi, Thair!" My mom says with enthusiasm in her voice. "I got your message Saturday afternoon, but I couldn't call back because I got in late."

"No problem. Jessica and I were out anyway. We went to a movie."

"Nice girl that Jessica? You two have really become good friends, huh? It seems you are together all the time."

"Yep." I haven't told my mom about my relationship, but I also haven't lied about anything. Jessica has answered my phone and they have chatted, but they have yet to meet. I tell my mother that Jessica stays over all the time, and that I met her at the college, that she's also a professor. My mom hasn't asked any questions, so it's the good ol' "don't ask, don't tell" policy in action. Part of me believes she knows something; the other part of me believes that there is no way in hell she even imagines that "this Jessica," as she puts it, could be my lover. I know Jessica wants me to tell her, wants to meet her. I'm just not ready, especially now after the kid conversation.

"So, Thair, I wanted to know if you could come and feed my cat next weekend."

Suddenly my interest is piqued, "And where are you going, Ms. Phaedra?"

I can instantly feel my mom's coyness penetrate the phone lines.

"Well, I met this really nice gentleman, and he wants to go on a road trip to San Francisco for a week, and I thought it would be fun."

"*This gentleman?* Where did you meet him? And how long have you known him?" From being interested, I am instantly worried, "And are you sure he's safe, I mean to be traveling with him?"

"If you stop asking questions for just a minute, I'll answer you."

"Okay, sorry."

"His name is Robert, and I met him through Greta. He and Wade were friends before Wade passed away."

"So, did Greta set you up?"

My mom laughs. "No, of course not, you know I won't get set up anymore, way too old for that." I know my mom is anything but old with her lively eyes and cute, slim figure.

"So how did you meet him?"

"He came by to see Greta, and I was doing yard work. Well, the three of us started chatting, and then he invited the two of us out to lunch. I declined, but I guess he got my number from Greta and invited me out to the movies. I went because he seemed like a nice enough man. And then we went to dinner the following week. You know how these things work. Anyway, he has invited me to accompany him to San Francisco, and it sounds like a lot of fun. *So* can you feed my cat?"

"Sure. But . . . can I meet him? I mean, will I meet him before this trip? And I want his full name and info, and—"

"Do you also want his social security number? Thair, relax. I'll give you his phone number, but I don't think you'll get a chance to meet him since we are leaving on Thursday." She says Thursday with a little squeal, and I can hear the excitement in her voice.

We chat for another half hour about this *gentleman*, all the while I'm thinking, *I can't remember the last time I heard my mama so happy.*

21

Costamar College, California
May, 2003

We are almost at the end of the semester, and as I look around at the students' faces, melancholy fills my chair. This is a memorable group. English 200, the highest course I can teach at a community college, the course that offers me students who are on their way to a four-year university, students who are intelligent and simply a lot of fun. I love teaching, always have; it's the endless grading that I abhor, but with every job, one must take the good with the bad.

I put them in groups today and as I do this, I find myself reflecting on this mixed bunch. There is Freddie, a man in his mid-forties who just lost his wife from a tragic accident, an eccentric man, an oddball, my most adamant crasher in all my years of teaching. I told him several times that I would not add him to the course, but he kept coming back. I could have called campus police, but he struck me as witty; still, I was at full capacity: "Freddie, I will not add you." I stated coldly.

"Yes, you will. You'll see. You know that just before the cut-off, a ton of students will drop, and then you'll be happy to add me to keep your numbers up." He said this with an ostentatious smirk.

"I will not add you."

"Okay. But you'll see, by week three, you will."

I added him by week two.

Then there is Cynthia, a mom of four rambunctious boys. *They are finally all in school,* she told me, exasperated, relieved, happy; the youngest in pre-school, so she could return to community college, thankful her forty-five units had not expired. Soon enough she would be able to transfer and get her coveted degree. Cynthia is a dirty blonde and compact with a great chest, a bit of extra skin around her waist from four pregnancies, but, mostly, a certified sexpot. Voluptuous figure with eerie gold eyes and eyelashes that go on forever. She loves to get fixed up for class. She told me that this class, once a week, is the only time she interacts with the adult human. At twenty-nine years old, she is a wife, a mother, but really just a girl. I can see her flirt with the young boys, boys still in their teens; they look at her hungrily, I've heard them call her a "MILF." When I asked them to explain, they all laughed. Google gave me the answer, but Cynthia has brains, not just booty.

Cynthia's personality is really the showstopper. When she speaks, in her smooth, sultry Southern voice, we are all spellbound. She makes the most articulate comments while accompanying her critiques with personal anecdotes that are both interesting and directly connected to what we are discussing. I can see Freddie also has the hots for her, but she tends to gravitate to the younger ones. There are two twins in the class, Chris and Kyle, eighteen-year-old studmuffin surfers; handsome young men with perpetual sunburns and excited eyes, not the sharpest tools in the shed, but certainly welcome additions to the class. They make us all laugh with their off-the-wall comments and bizarre insights. I always see them nestle themselves close to Cynthia, each one sitting on either side of her. And she adores the attention.

In the corner of the room is another young man, Jeffrey, painfully shy, who does not talk to anyone. He only speaks when I call on him. He is not strange, by any means, not one of those students that you are afraid will show up to class and blow everyone's brains to oblivion, just a quiet, pensive lad. When Jeffrey arrives to class, he opens a book and reads silently; he tells me he loves Tolkien, and this is his fourth time reading *The Hobbit*. The rest of the students enter noisily, and I hear comments such as "So what did you think about the reading?" Or "Did you get the revision of the paper done?" Or "What? I didn't know we had to turn that in today!" Other times the comments are more personal, comments such as "How was your weekend?" Or "No! He did not do that to you!" Even if it's not class related, as I take roll, I always allow them the first five minutes of class to catch up. Build community. Bonding time. At least that's what the professor at the conference said, and it has proven to work.

Today, as with most days, they are actively engaged, answering questions from the reading. I see Cynthia asking Jeffrey what he thinks. She is always kind and conscientious of who is in her group. In another corner of the room, Kyle has been assigned group leader, and he takes a deep breath and tries to make sure everyone is involved. He looks over at me, with pleading eyes, wanting to know if I approve of his leadership skills. In the same group, Freddie is writing away. He has been assigned the role of "The Scribe"; I made him the notetaker today, one way to make sure he doesn't always overpower the younger folk in the class with his strong personality and never-ending opinions. He's a good soul, tends to get frustrated with ignorance, but overall keeps me on my toes.

There are a lot of tough parts about being an adjunct community college professor, but these faces make it all worthwhile. I am feeling sentimental today, first taking my English 100 class, then (save for Freddie, who is new) taking the 200 class together. For the last two semesters, I have seen them change and grow, and I will miss them. Knowing that this is my penultimate class is making this day a bit emotional.

All of a sudden, Leah, a somewhat rebellious young lady, who has tattoos on her arms and neck, bright purple hair, and has missed too many classes, looks up and says, "Hey, Thair." Even though I have told my students they can call me by my first name, the way she says it sounds almost disrespectful with the "hey" attached.

"Yes?" I walk over to her group, assuming she has a question about the reading. She has been a bit challenging as a student, always takes the opposite position to the majority of class, often debates passionately with me. I don't mind though because her written work is astute, so I always give her room to express herself. Nevertheless, she does sometimes push my buttons. When I see her haughty expression, I can't help but wonder what she will say today.

Turning from the group, she says loudly, "I think I saw you in Hillcrest on Friday night. Outside The Burn." Not everyone knows what or where The Burn is, but the name itself creates a stir in the class.

Then silence. I don't know what to say. I am a fairly private teacher, an open book when it comes to my opinions of politics and the world in general, but details about my romantic life, I rarely share with my students. And now that I am dating a woman, I am more tight-lipped than ever.

Her comment takes me aback, not knowing how to respond, I reply, "Maybe." And "so what?" The way I say it comes out immature, too aggressive, too defensive, almost as if I am challenging her. At this point, the students pretend to be working, but their ears are as big as the Big Bad Wolf's.

Leah continues, "And? Nothing. I was just asking if it was you."

"Leah," I say with a sugary smile, "you know I don't like to talk about my private life. I don't ask *you* all what you do on the weekend."

Cynthia, to my surprise, pipes up, "Thair, you don't ask us what we do on the weekends, but you do probe into our lives. Through class discussion and your 101 questions, we all know that Chris and Kyle's parents are divorced, that I have a drunk for a husband and four sniveling boys; Jennifer told us the first day of class she is a pot-smoker. Freddie recently lost his wife. We've all shared with you bits and pieces of our life. So why are you so averse to telling Leah if that was you at . . ."

"The Burn," Leah states loudly.

"The Burn—whatever . . . " Cynthia says, and then looks away as if she has maybe said too much.

I cannot believe that my beloved student, Cynthia, is putting me on the spot like this. She is right though, why am I so unwilling to talk about going to a club? When I was in heterosexual relationships, I *did* share odd details about my romantic life, but now that I am dating a woman, I have become so secretive. And I think I know why. I am not gay. I am not a lesbian. Not one hundred percent anyway. I am one of those who are stuck somewhere, not somewhere in between, just stuck. I am still in the process of figuring out who I am. After thirty-four years on this earth, I don't know how to describe myself. I wish I could just say *bisexual*, but that label seems too negatively charged. Bisexuality seems synonymous with nymphomania, or it's a fad: girls kissing girls because they are curious, girls kissing girls to turn on boys. Many of Jessica's friends think bisexuals are just confused. Or, worse, they are traitors. They have relationships with women but then go back to men. From my limited experience, neither gays nor hetero-sexuals readily accept bisexuals. Just like the prefix "bi," I live on the periphery of both, but not part of either.

When I started dating Jessica, I wasn't curious (maybe just a little bit?), but I certainly wasn't playing with anyone's heart. I was just *open to the possibilities*. Then I came across the term "pansexual," and it was like Oprah's "ah-ha" moment.

Pansexuality. It doesn't just mean that a person is attracted to both sexes; it just means that gender is irrelevant when looking for love, almost as if pansexuals are gender-blind. Like the Greek prefix "pan," it means "all, whole, all-inclusive." Just like love should be. Of course, to those who care little about linguistics, or who simply stereotype, it's really the same thing: pansexual or bisexual. It's a group of people who are still marginalized. I've felt discriminated against, just in the few months I have been with Jessica. But what I have learned since that summer in Greece is that I am ultimately attracted to *individuals*, probably even to a certain body type, but above all to intellect and humor. It took years to adopt the word "feminist" and not to fear it, and maybe one day I'll feel the same way about "bisexual." And, in a way, I'm still not sure "pansexual" feels right either; the word choice, though it has a perfect definition for what I am feeling, reminds me of people who say *humanist* or *womanist* instead of "feminist" because they don't want to own up to a label that comes with so many stereotypes and baggage. Bisexual, pansexual—either way, now my heterosexual privilege has been tampered with. I'm changing and growing and relearning to be comfortable with *me*.

How hard it must be for people of a certain religion, race, creed, or orientation have their family expect them to fall in love and marry a particular person. A woman has to marry a man. A Mormon should marry a Mormon. A Catholic, a Catholic. A Muslim another Muslim. A Korean boy needs to find a Korean girl. A Chinese girl, a Chinese boy. An Italian another Italian. White with white. A good friend, an African-American woman, once told me, "I will only marry an educated, African-American, Christian man." She is still single and pushing forty.

How hard it must be for a boy to be raised in a macho Latino family and realize that he likes boys instead of girls. Whenever I see Ricky Martin, I wait for him to come out of the closet. But I can't help wondering if he is more like me. Maybe he does feel passion towards women; it's just that he could also find love with a man. Maybe if he could be more open to love, and not be afraid to be pigeonholed, he could tell the world who he really loves—and it wouldn't really matter.

Or does it?

These are all theories that I have been thinking about as I come to terms with who I am. But as the class stares at me, I don't know what to say. Freddie is sitting up tall, his interest much too piqued for my liking. Thoughts are scrambling through my mind. Part of me realizes my students have no right to be questioning me, and I can just change subjects or not answer. Or it would be simple enough to say that, yes, I have a girlfriend and leave it at that, but many of my returning students had met Ravi since he had picked me up from class on numerous occasions. I could just hear the jokes, *oh now our English prof is swinging both ways.* I want to scream out loud: *it's not like that. It's so much more complicated!* And, yet, as I think about so many things in those interminable minutes, I come to an amazing realization. In an ironic twist of fate, things *aren't* complicated; in fact, everything is so much simpler now for me. I am free to love. Just like Angela said: *No society dictating what's right and what's wrong.* I can fall in love with a woman, a man, black, white, a Christian, a Muslim, a younger person or an older one, a poor person or a rich one. There are no restrictions—finding love can be just about that—finding love; nothing to hold me back.

So, finally, I say out loud, "Cynthia, you do make a point. I do probe during class discussions to get you all to relate to what we are reading through your own personal lives, and I apologize if I have not met you all half way." I look at Leah straight in the eyes: "Yes, that was me at The Burn. I was there with my partner, Jessica."

Right away I see Kyle poke Chris in the chest both making deep, gorilla guttural sounds while huge smiles tweak their faces. Even Jeffrey says, without thinking, "Right on!"

Right on? What the hell was that? Am I now material for masturbation? Have I just opened Pandora's box? I wait for the salvo of questions. They probably want to know when I came out of the closet. Maybe they want to know more about Jessica. God, I hope they don't ask questions about our sex life. Of course, I won't answer. What if they ask me how long we have been dating and how serious we are? What if . . .

Then suddenly, something remarkable happens. They all turn around and go back to discussing the reading. They *don't care*. What a strange world this is, and why was I so worried?

22

I walk by the swimming pool, past the bougainvillea, down the stone
path; then open the gate to my condo's quaint porch. I take out my
house key and slip it into the sliding door's lock and enter my home.
I catch my reflection in the mirror and smile. I love being in my own
home. It's one of those days: I woke up and everything seems right
in the universe, a fantastic workout at the gym, a great day in class,
everyone smiling in Trader Joe's when I pushed my cart down the
narrow aisles.

Before I make myself a yummy salad with all the hearty ingre-
dients I just bought, I'll call my mom because I have not spoken to
her for a few days. It has been good talking to her again even if our
conversations are a bit guarded and we avoid certain issues. I am just
so relieved to have my mother back because the last few months were
so painful.

"Hello?"

"Hi, Mama," I say with enthusiasm when she answers the phone.

"Hi . . . sweetie." My heart drops immediately. The pause in her
voice tells me something is wrong. I know she visited the doctor last
week for her bi-yearly checkup. Could the results be positive? She has
been cancer free for almost a year and a half and checkups were just

that, *checkups*. I have tried to stop worrying that the cancer would come back, but now all my fears resurface. I suddenly feel queasy. Grabbing the barstool, I lean against it.

Just a simple "Hello, sweetie," and I know to my core something is wrong. I have been feeling so secure and strong lately that my mother's health has not been on the forefront of my mind. I sit down on the barstool and when my mouth has once more gathered some words, I ask, "Are you okay, Mama?"

"Mmmmmm, yes, I am fine," her voice still sounds down.

"Mama, what's wrong? You don't sound fine."

"I'm okay, really."

But I am not convinced.

"Did you get back the results from your mammogram? Is everything okay?"

Now she can hear the desperation in my voice.

"Oh, honey, I'm sorry. I didn't mean to worry you. Yes, I got back the results, and everything is fine."

Immediately relieved, but needing more reassurance, I continue: "So everything with your pap, mammogram, blood work came back well?"

"Yes, honey." Now her tone is starting to become a bit irritated. She hates it when I worry about her health.

"So the doctor said everything is normal?"

"Yes! I am fine!"

I know I shouldn't pursue, but it's my job to nag, just like she always nags me! "Mom, something is wrong. I can tell." Then with a gentler voice, "Please, tell me."

I hear what I think is a slight sob on the other end, and my heart breaks just a little.

"Mama, what's wrong?"

"Oh, Thair, I feel *so* silly."

"What do you mean?"

"At my age, can you believe it, at my age, I am acting like this?"

"Acting like what?"

"Like a silly . . . fool."

"Mom, is this about . . . Robert?"

Her voice cracks, followed by a soft, "Yes."

"What happened? I thought you two had a great time in San Francisco and have been dating regularly since then."

"Oh, Thair. I don't know why I get myself into these things. I was so happy before all this started. I have my home, my hobbies, my friends. Why did I even bother?"

Now I am getting a bit angry because I want to know what that jerk did to make my mom so sad but am simultaneously irritated with *her* since she is not answering my questions.

"So, Mom, what happened?"

"Well, we went to San Francisco and had a wonderful time." I already knew this.

"Yes, then?"

"Well, when we were there we got . . . you know . . . we got intimate." Great. Not sure I want to hear this. And still not going anywhere with the story of why she is sad, "So, what happened *next*?"

She hears the impatience in my voice and responds equally. "Do you want me to tell you or not?"

"Yes," I try to be patient.

"Well, we dated about once a week and then, all of a sudden, a few days ago he stopped calling. From one day to the next. No more calls. Finally, I called him, and he told me he is thinking of getting back together with his ex-girlfriend. Can you believe that? At my age, having an old fart leave me to go back to his ex-girlfriend! I hate it. I hate this dating stuff at my age. I should never have gone out with him in the first place."

Now she is on a roll, and I can't stop her. Sadness is replaced with aggravation.

"Can you believe that? Sixty-nine years old, fifteen years older than me, and can't decide between two women? So silly. So stupid. I'm so stupid. I can't believe I gave myself to this man."

My mom talking about sex, regardless of how liberated and modern I am, always makes me feel a bit awkward. "But, Mom, at least you had a nice time with him these last few months. Right?"

"Wrong!" I almost could not believe the fury in her voice. "I wish I had just stayed at home. I did not need to be lifted out of my comfortable home, romanced, and then dumped. I was perfectly happy the way things were!" Then another unexpected sob.

"I'm sorry, Mama," I say sympathetically, knowing how hard love can be, the highs, the lows.

"It's okay, honey. It really is all very, very silly. I can't believe the way I am acting."

"Mom, it's normal to be sad when a relationship ends even if it was just a few months. I understand and, really, it doesn't mean that—"

"Did I tell you that Greta got a new cat?" It is an obvious non-sequitur, and knowing my mom, she is done talking about things that matter.

After we hang up, I go to my office.

―――――――

Although I was upset to hear my mom so sad, I am happy that we are talking again. I hadn't written another chapter in "Thair's Story" because it had been too painful. My mother's anger towards me the last few months had broken my heart.

Thair's Story

Rancho Fierno
May, 2003

A day before Phaedra's road trip, Thair visited her, anxious to hear more about this man she would be traveling with to San Francisco. Thair sat on the corner of her mother's king-sized bed while Phaedra complained about the gigantic thing in her bedroom that her ex-husband had chosen with such zeal. Phaedra hated the size, too big for one 110-pound woman. Thair's father bought it a year before the divorce, just another symbol of Phaedra's failed marriage. When they were shopping for a bed, Phaedra asked Gordon, "Do you think we can get a queen-sized bed this time?"

"No."

A one-word response. That's how Thair's father communicated. Phaedra admitted it was partly her fault; she usually never stood up to that man, not until it came to signing the house papers. Thair could still hear her father's voice as she hid in her bedroom: "If you want this divorce so god damn bad, Phaedra, we're selling the house and splitting the money."

Like the transformation of a hummingbird who feels attacked, Phaedra's chest inflated, her wings spread, her claws unleashed, "We are NOT selling the house. Where do you expect me and Thair to live?" He had huffed and puffed, but he was no match for Thair's mother during these unexpected moments of power. All Phaedra wanted was the house. No alimony, no child support. But she wanted her home. It was her sanctuary, the one place in the world where she was happy, serene. It was her little piece of paradise.

Phaedra had been divorced now for fifteen years, and the emptiness she expressed initially was quickly replaced with strength and clarity. She loved her daughter, her hobbies, her home, her solitude. Not much could shake her.

As they lay side by side on the king-sized bed, Phaedra told Thair in detail all about the day she had met Robert. "It was an early Saturday morning, and I had just taken my morning swim." Thair could picture it, her mom's twenty laps, done in twenty minutes in her modest pool. Phaedra was no professional swimmer, and her head-out-of-the-water freestyle was not necessarily a stroke to be admired, but her morning ritual kept her in good shape and gave her endless energy.

"So after my swim, I put on my ratty jeans, my favorite pink T-shirt from the Susan G. Koman five-mile walk that we did, and my large straw hat." She told Thair how she had picked at some weeds, planted a new rose bush, trimmed her orange tree, pruned her lemon tree, cut down her browning bougainvillea so that new, burgundy flowers could bloom. Thair knew her mother loved being outside, in the sun, in her garden, pampering her own personal Eden.

While crouched on a knee pad, she explained, she heard Greta outside talking to an elderly gentleman. She looked up, waved, and went back to her gardening. "I was so engrossed in my task that I didn't even notice when Greta and the man came over. Anyway, his name is Robert, and he and Greta's husband used to work together at General Engineering."

Phaedra said she took off her gloves, wiped her somewhat sweaty hand on her jeans, and stuck it out. "I was going to apologize for the way I looked but thought: what the heck!" She laughed while saying this. Phaedra continued talking excitedly, describing the man as trim, nicely dressed, and clean-shaven, a bit old but a real gentleman who drove a Mercedes and opened doors for women.

"So, Greta told me that they were trying to decide where to go for lunch, and Robert said he had a craving for Greek food. Greta thought I may have a restaurant to recommend. Of course, I told them about The Acropolis Garden." Thair hated that place. "Anyway, he called the next day and you know the rest."

It had been ages since Phaedra had gone on a date, partly because she was so picky. Phaedra had been introduced to an affluent lifestyle with "The American," and though she would rarely admit it, money still mattered. Five years before, she had casually dated a simple man, Peter, a plumber, ten years her junior. He had become smitten with Phaedra right from the first date, and though she liked him too, when Thair asked how it was going, it was already over. Phaedra had ended it before it had even started because "he wasn't really presentable." His long, mousey hair and forever-plaid shirt did not meet Phaedra's standards. Ironically, he did have money and took her to nice places, but he just didn't fit the bill even if he could pay for it.

Instead of romance, for the last few years Phaedra had been painting, crocheting, gardening. Normally a bit miserly, on a whim, she took out some money from savings, money that she had been saving for Thair's inheritance, and decided to remodel her home, excited to see parquet again. Ripping out old carpet, laying down wood. How funny, Thair thought, in her mother's middle age she was making a full circle back, returning to the things she had tried to escape from as a young girl growing up in Greece. Phaedra had hated her family home with dusty, wooden floors, yearning for floor-to-floor carpeting, carpeting like the one that warmed the Hilton's hallway. Even the air conditioner that Phaedra had yearned for was no longer a priority. It had broken down the year before; between not wanting to spend the money to get it fixed and telling her daughter that her aging bones desired warmth rather than cold, it became another superfluous extravagance, a symbol of her American dream that had dissipated. Phaedra had a new dream, one of quiet, of serenity, of peace. The only piece of the puzzle still missing, she would tell her daughter relentlessly, was for Thair to get married and have children. Then her life would be complete. So as Phaedra effused about Robert, Thair was thrilled that her mom was finally interested in someone again—and would focus less on her daughter's life.

It was about a month later when Phaedra was working in her garden that a car pulled up. The happiness shone on her face when she saw Thair's Miata. The visit was quite unexpected: Thair rarely drove inland on weekends. So excited to see her daughter, Phaedra jumped to her feet and waved. When Jessica got out of the car, Phaedra's face dropped.

"Hi, Mom," Thair said as she simultaneously gave her mom a hug and a kiss on the cheek.

"Hi, Thair," Phaedra responded in a monotonous voice.

"Mom, this is Jessica."

Trying to muster a smile from somewhere, "Of course, we have spoken on the phone a few times."

"Hi!" Jessica said with enthusiasm, almost knocking Phaedra off her feet while giving her an unsolicited hug. Though Jessica was only 5'10", she looked like a giant beside Thair's petite mother.

Once Phaedra had collected herself, she said, "So what brings you girls this way?"

"We were just out driving, and decided since it was such a

nice day, we would come visit you. Maybe sit by the pool, have a drink."

"That sounds like fun . . . um, why didn't you call?"

"Call?" Thair felt affronted. "Since when do I have to call?"

Jessica seemed suddenly uncomfortable, looking away, but then Phaedra responded, "No, honey, that's not what I meant. I'm just glad I'm home. I would have hated to have missed you."

She continued to stare at Jessica, but then replaced her curious gaze with her winning smile. "Come on, girls, let's go in the house. I just bought some excellent margarita mix!"

Jessica beamed. The visit was indeed unexpected. Jess had no idea that they were on their way to Thair's mother's house; they had planned on going to the beach, but a sudden turn onto the freeway led them to Rancho Fierno. Jessica had been asking Thair for the last few months when she would get to meet Phaedra, but Thair would always make excuses. The truth was, and Jessica knew this, that Thair was petrified. How would Thair's mother react, and was Thair truly prepared for all the different possibilities?

So far, Thair was pleased. So far, so good, she thought. She invited them in even if her initial reaction was less than welcoming.

As they walked in, Jess affectionately touched Thair's shoulder. Thair instantly jumped, then looked back at her partner with scolding eyes, eyes that screamed: no touching!

Upon entering, Thair immediately felt a bit suffocated; the heat in Rancho Fierno was unbearable. Outside there was a slight breeze, but inside not even a molecule of dust stirred.

"Mom, why don't you have the air-conditioning on?"

"I haven't had a chance to fix it yet, and I guess I don't really miss it." Thair laughed at the irony; she used to hate air-conditioning and her mom loved it. She realized things *do change*.

Phaedra took off her hat and looked quite disheveled, but with her huge smile, her face lit up. Thair thought her mother looked absolutely lovely. *Maybe she will be okay with my relationship after all,* Thair wondered.

"Girls, just give me a moment to get cleaned up, and I'll be right out."

As Jess paced the living room, picking up frames, admiring photos of Thair and Phaedra, Thair looked at her lover from behind. Jess was so masculine, from her mannerisms to her walk, to her tight almost-boyish butt, to her long, strong legs. What a different type of woman than her one-time Sappho-girl. Jess was like a bull in a china shop; every time she set down a picture frame, Thair could literally see the shelf shake.

"Thair, just so I know, since you didn't prepare me, are we going to tell her? Am I here just as your friend? Am I allowed to show you any affection?" Jess was always up front, and Thair normally loved that about her. She always communicated clearly what she thought, what she felt. The problem was Thair hadn't thought any of this through. Driving to her mother's house was a spur-of-the-moment decision, no premeditation, no idea what she was doing. She didn't have a plan. If she told Jessica that they were here as "friends," she knew she would hurt Jessica's feelings, and she certainly didn't want to do that, but if she told her mother about Jessica, she took the chance of hurting the other person whom she loved more than anyone in this world.

Thoughts raced through Thair's mind: What does one do? Mom, sit down, I want to tell you about my sex life. I have sex with a woman. This is the woman. Oh, and by the way, I love her, too. Why did it have to be so complicated? If she had shown up with a handsome gent, it would have been clear to Phaedra that there was a romantic connection, so why did she even have to explain anything to Phaedra? Why did it have to be different?

But Thair knew it was different. If she had come with a man, and they were sitting by the pool, and the man put his hand on Thair's or gave her a little peck, Phaedra would not have reacted. She would have thought it normal, probably Thair's new boyfriend. She would have known the person was someone Thair obviously really liked because she had brought him home to meet Phaedra, The Mother. But now, the rules had all changed. What to say, what to do?

"Jess, I'm sorry. I haven't thought about it. Can we hold off on the physical affection? But I will not say you are just my friend because you are so, so much more." As Thair said this to Jessica, she touched her cheek, but quickly dropped her hand when she heard Phaedra's bedroom door opening and her mother approaching.

Phaedra appeared dressed in a one-piece black swimsuit and a white, jean skort. Her tan legs looked like those of a teenager and did not match the face of a woman in her fifties. Still, she looked adorable, almost bouncy. When she walked into the kitchen, she seemed to be in a fabulous mood. Was this the ostrich sticking its head deep in the hole?

"So, Jessica—"

"Please, call me Jess."

"Okay, Jess . . . actually, do you mind if I call you Jessica. It's such a pretty name, so feminine."

Thair had no idea what her mother was thinking, implying, what she was doing, but Jess, always agreeable in sticky situations replied, "Sure. My mom calls me Jessica, too."

"Okay, great, so Jessica it is. That is, if you *really* don't mind." Thair's mother feigned politeness, but she was obviously pleased to have gotten her way.

"No, that's fine, really."

"Okay, Jessica, an important question . . ." Thair's heart was beating fast. "How do you like your margaritas?"

Jessica happily responded, "On the rocks would be great, but only one because I am the designated driver today."

"Okay. Honey, what about you?"

"The same, Mama. Do you have any Grand Marnier?"

"I just bought some! It was on sale at CVS, another of my splurges." She giggled in a childish way, "Can you get it for me? It's in the liquor cabinet."

"Sure. Hey, Jess, do you want to put on your bathing suit?" Thair asked.

"Sure. It's so nice outside. A dip sounds refreshing."

"If you go down the hallway, on the left, you will see my old room. You won't be able to miss it. It's a piece of pink heaven." Thair said this sarcastically, wanting to say pink hell but decided, why ruin the mood?

"Okay," Jess replied as she disappeared into the back of the house.

Thair got the Grand Marnier for her mother, "I think I'll go change, too."

Thair noticed her mother's body twitch a bit, "Thair, you can use my room if you want."

"That's okay," she said with a mix of courage and rebellion.

Thair opened the door to her childhood cell and saw the pink canopy bed. Who even had canopy beds anymore? She could not believe that her mother had left her bedroom the same, untouched, for the last fifteen years. Thair saw her Pink Panther on the bed, looking a bit tired and old, but with the same stupid grin on his face. Jess, a bit startled when Thair opened the door, instantly relaxed when she saw her girlfriend there with her beach bag.

Before Thair could say anything, Jessica grabbed her and started to kiss her passionately as her hands traveled everywhere.

"Stop!" Thair said with a smirk. "We'll get caught!"

"And if we do?" Jess said between kisses.

"You are very, very naughty," Thair said, controlling her giggles. She indeed did feel naughty. The last time she tried to keep this quiet in her room was when she snuck her seventeen-year-old boyfriend in through the window to spend the night. Those were her rebellious days. Now though, she felt that same sense of naughtiness and intense excitement.

"Want a quickie?" Jess said as she began moving down on Thair's body with kisses.

"NO! Behave yourself, young lady!" Thair said in her teacherly voice as she motioned for Jessica to get up. "I just came to change. And I can see you are already dressed, so I think it's time for you to go," her tone playful.

With an affected pout, Jessica opened the door and walked out in her very boyish board shorts. Again, so different than Greek-girl, Thair thought, but equally beautiful—in an absolutely opposing way.

When Thair came out in her Brazilian, almost X-rated black bathing suit, she could feel Jessica's eyes hungrily eating her up. A slight crimson flushed her cheeks when she took the first sip of her Cadillac Margarita. Thair knew she would be having a few of these today. The tension in her shoulders was intense, but certainly no massages in front of Mother.

"So, tell me, Jessica, how long have you been teaching?"

"Gosh, it must be about twenty years now. I started at the ripe age of twenty-two."

Thair sat back with her eyes closed, allowing the sun to burn her face and warm her body. After a while it was as if the TV was on, but the volume was off. She watched her mother's and lover's mouths move, but she didn't hear the words. She became a bit too relaxed with the sun and the margarita.

Jessica and Phaedra continued to talk and laugh and were getting along so well. The afternoon was gorgeous, the swimming pool sparkled invitingly, and the drinks expelled all the tension from Thair's body. Jessica had stopped after one margarita, Phaedra was a lightweight at two, and Thair was well into her fourth. She was so pleased that the visit was going so well, she didn't realize how much she was drinking. When she got up to go to the bathroom, she was quite dizzy. Upon returning, without thinking, she stood for a while behind Jessica, resting her hand on Jess's shoulder. It could have been a meaningless gesture between two friends, but when Phaedra saw her daughter's hand lying on the shoulder of this woman, her face went blank.

Thair sensed her mother's discomfort and lifted her hand. Then, without planning it, and without knowing exactly why, she reacted. (Was she still that rebellious girl? Did she want to bring her mother fast forward into the year 2003? Was she irritated by her mother's reaction from just a hand on the shoulder? Or was she just a bit drunk and throwing inhibition into the wind? Whatever it was, it was certainly done with little thought of the consequences.) She took her hand off of Jessica's shoulder then leaned down and gave her lover a passionate kiss on the lips. Jessica pulled away, but it was too late. The deed was already done. Nonchalantly Thair plopped down into the poolside recliner and again shut her eyes, feeling very lightheaded.

Phaedra rose to her feet, looking a bit unstable, "Excuse me," she said in a polite, proper, and *presentable* manner.

She walked into the house and went straight into her bedroom.

Jessica looked at Thair and said, "Baby, I don't think that was such a good idea. I think you need to go talk to your mother."

Thair harrumphed and got to her feet as they wobbled below her.

Jessica jumped up and stabilized her while gently turning her towards the house. "Thair, go speak to her. Please, be gentle. I know you've had quite a bit to drink, so please, try to be kind."

"ME? *Me* be kind?" The alcohol was making its devilish head apparent.

"Thair, maybe I should go talk to her."

"Are you crazy?"

Jessica could have felt attacked, but instead said, "Sweetie, maybe we should just leave."

Instantly, Thair calmed down. Jessica's loving voice had this effect on her.

"I'm okay. Really. Sorry. I didn't mean to speak to you that way. I'll be back. It'll be okay."

Thair saw that her mom's bedroom door was shut, but without asking, opened it quietly. She did not see her mother initially. Walking in slowly, towards the master bathroom, she found Phaedra sitting on the closed toilet seat, tears falling from her eyes.

"Oh, Thair," she said as if someone had died.

"Mama," Thair replied, hunched down, squashed between the wall and the toilet. "Mama, I wanted to—"

Before Thair could say anymore, her mom pulled her shoulders back, wiped her tears away, equalized her voice, and said, "Thair, I think you and *your friend* need to leave."

"Mama, please, can I—"

"Thair, I will not ask you again. I want you and . . . that woman . . . to leave now."

With that she got up and pushed against her daughter to get

out of the tight quarters. Turning on the TV in her bedroom, she propped herself up with a couple of pillows and stared at the screen.

Thair stood at the foot of her mother's gigantic bed.

Looking at her daughter with wet eyes, she screamed much too loudly, "Thair! Please leave! Take that woman now and leave!"

Thair's eyes were glued on her mother, and for the first time in her life, she could not speak. No words formed in her mouth. Judge Judy blared from the TV, the volume on full blast. Thair continued to stare at her mother as her heart broke into a million pieces and fell onto the parquet floor.

But Phaedra had escaped into the TV. Even though the tears continued to fall down her cheeks, her mother's face was so angry, so ugly.

"Mama . . ." one last attempt from Thair was swiftly silenced with a look that Thair had never seen before. Or maybe she had seen it before. It was the same look she had seen on Phaedra's face the night she finally told Thair's father to leave, the night he came home a little drunk, smelling of women's juices. It was a look that she had never forgotten. Eyes like Othello's when he believed his wife to be unfaithful. Eyes that were filled with so much disappointment and anger. It was the look of hate. And now this look was directed to her.

Thair lost her balance, feeling so small, so insignificant. The woman who spoke to Thair was a stranger, not the mother who had loved her unconditionally and nurtured her for the last thirty-four years of her life. Suddenly, there were no more tears, just Lyssa, the Goddess of Rage, sat on the bed, a being so unearthly and foreign. "Leave! I will not tell you again. LEAVE!"

Weakly moving away, she walked out of her mother's bedroom and shut the door lightly as if she were a teenager in trouble. She had done something so bad, so wrong, and her mother was utterly disappointed. There was nothing on this earth that hurt Thair more than disappointing her mother. But this time, she wasn't a teenager, and god damn it, she hadn't done anything wrong! She was looking for love, and she had found it in the most unlikely place, but she found it. How could her mother not relate? She had forsaken her family and moved to the US to follow her dreams. Why could she not understand her daughter, even just a little bit? Given her just a little bit of acceptance?

Jessica had already changed and gathered their belongings and was waiting in the living room.

"Are you okay?"

Thair held on to Jessica and began sobbing uncontrollably. She knew her mother could hear her, but she didn't care. In fact, she wanted her to hear. Why was she consciously hurting her daughter this way?

23

Encinitas, California
Late April, 2004

"Jess, I would really like to go to Greece this summer. What do you think? Want to go?"

Jessica doesn't answer, just lies beside me in bed, still half asleep.

"Hmmmm . . . I don't know."

"I was just thinking it would be great for the two of us to get away, and you would love the Greek islands."

Jessica rolls over, her expression suddenly serious. "Thair, money is kind of tight, and you know I'm saving for fertility treatments."

Shit. The baby talk again. I have fallen in love with Jessica. She is a fantastic partner, and we have a lot in common, but there is also one monumental issue that we do not see eye to eye on that causes continuous friction. Children. She talks about her plans to have one, and I tell her that it's not what I want. But neither of us leaves. Most days we are happy and in love, living in a fantasy world where one of us will change our minds; the problem is, it's a year later and neither is relenting.

I didn't think we would be having this conversation today, but our time spent together is getting heavier and heavier; Eris, the Goddess of Discord, is making her head apparent in our almost-perfect relationship. Maybe I should just say: "Okay, fine. I'll have a baby with you." But I just can't say those words. How can I plan to co-parent when it's one of the things I know, viscerally, I do not want?

If Narcissus had had a baby, would he have been less enamored with himself and found that living for another's happiness is more important—possibly, more fulfilling? I don't want to lose Jess, but as much as I try to talk myself into conceding, my gut tells me one should not bring children into this world if one is not one hundred percent ready to commit to a lifetime of loving unconditionally. And I do know it to be unconditional. *Thair, what about when you are old? You don't want to be alone.* I think that's a lousy reason to have a child. When children grow up, in my mind, the last thing they need or desire is an aging parent. I know I certainly love my mother with all my heart, but I will never love her with the same love she embraces (and often-times suffocates) me with. Still, is there any part of me that desires an itty-bitty, innocent baby in my arms to love unconditionally?

No.

I get up, my nude body a bit tan from the early San Diego sun, grab my silky robe, then turn around as I see Jessica languidly stretched on my bed. She has already fallen asleep again. She looks so peaceful. Tears fill my heart and I think: instead of a wonderful romantic summer in Greece, it has come to this.

Disheartened, I make a cup of coffee and go into the office and turn on my computer and get online, sitting there impatiently as it boots up. I log onto Yahoo and see an email from Bertha A. Woodson. Immediately, my mind accepts the name as a previous student, but I can't picture a face. My mental Rolodex of students' names begins flip-ping in my mind's eye; then it screeches to a halt. Of course! It's been years, and her email has her official name, not "Angela" as I know her. I haven't spoken to her since our class ended about three years ago.

I usually delete my mind's file of students' names after the semester is over, not for any malicious reason, but so that my aging brain has room to learn another one hundred plus names. It's the same story every semester, about one hundred and twenty new students all with new interesting names to learn. But Angela. How could I ever forget her name? She gave me the words that became my mantra for loving.

I wonder what she would think if she could see me now. I open the email and read:

Dear Thair,

I have thought about you over the years and have wanted to write. I am in the process of moving and have been throwing away all sorts of papers, and I came across a file with all the essays from our class. I had to laugh when I saw all your markings. I remember how angry I was when I got back my first essay and you gave me a B+. I had poured out my heart and soul into that personal essay! Ha! And a B+! I have to laugh about this now because I just reread it and it's awful! Anyway, I am really excited to tell you that I accomplished my goal and got my Bachelor's in English from UCSD! And, there's more! Crazy as it sounds, I am going right back to school (can you imagine, at my age!). Anyway, I just got accepted, including a very generous fellowship, to Columbia University!!!!! I will pursue a degree in Women's and Gender Studies. (I guess being a black lesbian woman has finally paid off!) Obviously, I am SO excited.

But with good always comes bad, I guess, that's been the story of my life. My partner of ten years doesn't want me to go. It's a once in a lifetime opportunity, and I will only be gone for a few years and planned to travel home frequently, but she doesn't understand. I think it's more than the distance. She doesn't want me to change.

I am not writing to unload all my personal issues on you. I actually wrote to see if you have time to have a quick lunch, just to say good-bye because, honestly, I don't know if I will come back to San Diego. At least, not for a long while. Let me know if you have time. I could meet you at one of the campuses you teach at if that makes it easier.

Warm regards,

Angela

I am so excited to see Angela's email that I respond immediately, setting up a time to meet. I sit quietly for a while thinking about this incredible woman and how she had, probably unknowingly, changed my life. I became more open to love, more open to life in general, after our conversation. She was such a talented writer, her essays always so articulate, her words so powerful. I laugh out loud thinking about her first essay and her complaint! I thought she had always got straight As from me. A fellowship from Columbia. Wow. I can't wait to hear all about it. Even though she is older than me, I feel like a proud parent. I jump to my feet and go into the bedroom because I want to share the exciting news.

Jessica is still sleeping, deep asleep. Deep, deep asleep. I stand above her a minute or so, then go into the kitchen to make some breakfast. I open the fridge, grab a few eggs, some washed spinach, and some feta cheese to make an omelet. I look in the fridge's drawer for a tomato and find one stuck in the corner behind the cucumber and apples. I take it out, but it is reddish-purple, mushy, and has white fungus growing on its side. I step on the pedal of the garbage can and dump the tomato in the trash. I hear a loud "thump" when it hits the bottom.

I am sitting in Thai's Tasty Cuisine, one of my favorite restaurants in Hillcrest. I found a cozy table outside and am looking over the menu, Pad Thai for sure and maybe a cucumber salad. After deciding on lunch, and since I arrived early, I start reading the book I brought.

I had gone to Borders yesterday to buy the assigned novel for my book club, a bestseller by Sebold, but instead stumbled on her memoir called *Lucky*. From the first few pages, I was captivated: a powerfully sad, but important story. I devoured the first half last night and now have it on my "All Women in America Should Read This Book" list. It's a good warning for young women regarding safety. Mostly, it reaffirms my belief that women (of all ages!) should always move in pairs and not be alone—especially in dark, lonesome, or secluded places—those places including fine university campuses.

While reading it, I find myself becoming irritated with the author's father and his reaction to her rape. I don't want to be grumpy when Angela arrives because of what I'm reading, and literature tends to affect my mood, so I stop and instead just watch the people walk by. I see two, round, jolly-looking fellows holding hands, then two young girls who are dressed in a Gothic style with eye, ear, and nose piercings. I enjoy seeing a variety of people, pleased that no one has a problem with anyone or anything that looks just a bit out of the norm. This is also probably the one area in San Diego where people who are not straight can be totally free. Even people who are expressive in their choice of style seem to be comfy here. Maybe there are other areas in San Diego that appreciate diversity, but I have yet to encounter them; here, though, there is such freedom in the air. And it makes me almost blissful.

Right then Angela walks up. I am a bit taken aback by her size, so painfully thin. She looks stressed with a long, drawn face, thin arms, boney chest, not the powerful Amazon-looking woman I remember. She sees me immediately, and right after a big "Hello!" and a warm hug, she begins to excuse the way she looks since I am sure she read my expression. I am genuinely worried by her frailness.

"I think with the move, the excitement . . . the breakup, the overall stress, I have lost a bit of weight, but I can tell you one thing: I am *hungry*! I could eat a horse today!" We both laugh.

Right away the ambiance is comfortable; though never a good friend, she has occupied a place in my heart that can't be replaced. She gave me words that I now live by, difficult as they may be at times. We spend the first hour just catching up about school, where she's going, what she will be studying, how she feels about giving up her nursing job. We touch briefly on her breakup, but I can see it's still a sensitive subject, and I don't want to probe, so the conversation turns to me. I tell her about Jessica and she is not surprised to hear that I have been in a lesbian relationship for more than a year. I also tell her about that dreadful day when Jess and I went to visit my mother.

"Wow. That must have been really tough. I guess I went through something similar with my family, but because they were all the way on the other side of the country, I never felt their wrath acutely. So, what happened after you left that day?"

"Well, I called my mother the next day and the answering machine got it. I was still really angry, but I wanted to talk. I called for three consecutive days, but no answer. Finally, I rung up her neighbor, Greta, because I was nervous that something may have happened to her. I guess I just have never seen her so angry . . . so cold."

"When did you finally talk to her?"

"Greta told me she hadn't seen my mom in a few days, so she would call her and go over if necessary. But she answered Greta's call immediately. Greta told her that I had been trying to get a hold of her and asked if everything was okay. My mother told Greta point blank that we *were having problems* and she *did not* want to talk to me." The sarcasm in my voice was the way I imagined my mother saying it. Greta had relayed the message as sweetly as she could, all the while, I am sure, feeling quite awkward.

Angela sits there quietly, obvious concern coming from her as she grips my hand as if to say, "I'm sorry." She knew how close my mother and I were. My voice still trembles when I talk about what happened that day.

"Finally, I knew if I wanted to see her, I would have to drive to her home. I waited a few weeks until I cooled down too, then drove to Rancho Fierno to confront her." I pause then continue, "Gosh, Angela, I can't believe how retelling this still hurts so much. I have been through two painful breakups, but this was so much worse. It was awful. Not talking to my mother for weeks was unimaginable. I would wake up every morning, and in the pit of my stomach, it would feel like someone had died. I remember those cruel words she said to me so clearly. It was so unlike her. I guess I was stubborn and thought if I waited long enough, she would call me and apologize. Was I ever wrong."

"I'm sorry to hear this, Thair."

"So, I finally went to see her, and when she answered the door, tears instantly sprung into both our eyes. I asked her if I could come in, and she opened the door, but very hesitantly. Then I saw her look over my shoulder, as if I would have brought Jessica with me! I was incensed, and that promptly fired her up, too. She began screaming at me, telling me I was her only child, that I ruined everything and that *she* will never be a grandmother!"

Then I told Angela how she said that she would never see me walk down the aisle in a stupid white dress on the arm of a *presentable* man. As I recount this part of the story, I can feel the blood boiling in my face: "She told me what I was doing with *that woman* was not normal, and I needed to grow up! I was so pissed." I continue, almost forgetting that we are in a public place, my voice getting a bit too loud, "What right had she to tell me how to live my life? And all her complaints had nothing to do with the quality of *my* life; they were all about *her*! What *she* wanted. Not what I wanted or what was good for me." Finally, I take it down an octave. "It was a disaster. She screamed, and I screamed, and then finally after an hour or so, I couldn't take it anymore, so I left, tires screeching behind me."

"Thair, how awful. So, have you talked to her since that day?"

"Well, we didn't speak for about three months after that, each too stubborn, hurt, and angry to call the other. It was terrible. Every day I woke with a growing sinkhole in my stomach. I had never gone so long without seeing or speaking to my mother. It also made me question unconditional love. My whole universe was upside down. If my mother didn't love and accept me, then what did I have in this world? During that time, ironically enough, Jessica and I became closer . . . she's such a supportive and loving woman." I pause for a moment because she is the most compatible partner I have ever had. *Yet. But.* Those damn coordinating conjunctions! Pushing those words away, I continue, "Finally, after months of no communication, my mother broke down and called me, asking me to come over for lunch. She was chilly on the phone, very matter-of-fact, seemingly impervious to my pain. I initially declined, but then, when her voice softened, and she asked me again, I accepted."

"It must have been good to see her after all that time?" Angela asks rather than states.

"Yeah, though I still felt hurt, I really needed to see her, but I was shocked when she opened the door. Her hair was all grey; I guess she hadn't dyed it for months. I couldn't remember the last time I saw her looking so old. Her face was pale, her eyes looked abnormally large, and her body so tiny. When I saw her like that, I couldn't help but worry about the cancer again, so all my anger instantly subsided as I stood there."

"Was she okay?"

"Thank God it wasn't the cancer. She told me she had lost weight because of our situation. We talked for hours, much more calmly than the first time, but every sentence was cautious. At one point, she told me that she didn't understand how I could be a 'ho-mo-sex-u-al'. . . it was almost ridiculous how she said the word, as if it were so disgusting, she had to separate it into five syllables just to get it out."

"Did you tell her you were really . . . bisexual?"

"No, I didn't respond. For me, at that moment, it was easier to let her believe that I'm gay than tell her I am some deviant human who does not care about gender." When I say that, I picture myself in some sort of futuristic space suit holding the hand of a being that has both a penis and a vagina—and two heads! I almost want to chuckle, but the image is a bit disturbing even to me.

"So, has there been any progress with your mom?"

"I guess a bit, kinda like the *progress* we made in our military. *Don't ask, don't tell.* She told me that she loved me and that would never change. But she didn't want to hear any more about *that woman.* Then she had the audacity to ask me if I could change; maybe we could pray together to ask for God's help! I tried to remain calm when she said that, but the entire visit was surreal. I have never prayed with my mother, let alone talked to God about my sexuality!"

I can see a twisted smile cross Angela's face. "It shouldn't be funny, but in a way, it is. Some people are still so ignorant. They think they can change their loved ones with prayer or a magic wand."

As Angela and I continue talking, she asks me more about Jessica, and immediately senses my turmoil. I tell her about Jess's desire to have children, and how I just really don't want to be a parent. I explain my theories on children, trying to be careful so as not to offend, because I know Angela has an adult child with her high school boyfriend. I remember our first conversation when she told me about her own "coming out" experience. Angela said she was certain she was always gay but did remember having crushes on boys and even loved her son's father very much—but in a very different way than she has loved women. She likened it to a familial, platonic love. She told me that she could never see herself with a man again, but as a teenager, her raging emotions were directed to the male population as well. Over the last few years, I have come to the conclusion that sexuality doesn't have to be monolithic; in fact, I am starting to believe that for many people it is fluid. It's society that makes us choose. In Kinsey's world, you don't have to choose.

"So how did you and Jessica weather that storm?"

"Angela, the irony of the entire situation with my mother is that while I was simultaneously trying to defend my relationship, I knew in my heart that Jessica and I are not going to make it. Even though we did get closer than ever during those months, I know Jessica and I are not meant for the long haul." After I say this, guilt seizes me. I feel awful, so, so awful. I have contemplated ending it with Jessica, but never allowed my thoughts to enter the world with real words spoken outside of my head. And here I am with Angela, an ex-student, an acquaintance, telling her something that I haven't even told the woman I love: that it's almost over. But there is something about this woman's powerful stare and consoling eyes that have once more gotten me to open up my soul and lay my heart on the table. I needed to talk to someone, to make it real. I know this feeling, and I can't put it off any longer.

Angela and I talk for hours, just like we did three years ago, not engaging in the light lunch banter I had imagined; profound conversations are eating up the minutes of time. When I glance at my watch, I realize that I have to rush to make it to class on time; thus, it's time to bid adieu to this amazing woman. As I give her a long, warm hug and wish her well, sadness overwhelms me. I am really going to miss her. Strange how people can come into one's life, even for brief moments, and change how one sees the world.

I get into my tiny Miata and am instantly suffocated. It feels too small; my books are everywhere, my school bag strewn open with papers and files falling from it, an extra jacket on the seat. I decide at that moment that I am done with this car. I want a normal-sized car, no SUV, but no two-seater either, a sensible car that will give me good gas mileage and afford me more space. I imagine telling Jessica that I want to sell my Miata; her reaction, I am sure, will be positive. She has been talking a lot about how we need a sedan for "the baby." I picture Jessica with a small round belly, and a sorrowful smile covers my face. Every moment I spend with her teaches me something about myself. It is one of the healthiest, happiest relationships I have ever been in, and yet, there's a pink elephant in the room with us every moment of every day.

Suddenly, I get another image of Jessica with two screaming—but gorgeous—toddlers at her feet. Something is tugging me, not kids at my feet; it is a tugging in the pit of my stomach. Then I feel something else. There is Zeus again poking me in the butt with his damn lightening sword!

24

Encinitas, California
Early June, 2005

Rick and I are lying on our backs in the sun, two towels on the hot cement with our legs bent at the knee, feet dangling in the cool water. The pool at the condo is quiet with kids still in school for another week or so, and the sun beating down on my face feels marvelous. Rick rolls over on his stomach, sits up on his elbows to get a better look at me.

Suddenly he's serious: "Thair, you are no longer a young pup. Almost everyone our age is married, some married a few times! Even though it's not legal for some of us," he adds with a "Humph." Then continues: "And most have a handful of kids. You need to start dating again!"

"No, I don't." I say this with an air of confidence. Ever since that "coming out" with my class, everything started to change for me again. I am no longer living in that metaphorical closet, no longer willing to live someone else's dreams, my mother's, not even Jess's. I needed to be true to myself.

Yes, I would love to fall in love again. I would love to meet my other half if s/he exists, but if I don't ever meet him or her, it's okay. For the first time, ironically enough, I kind of understand my mom. I have my own life, and I am fine. I am better than fine. I am *happy*. Settled. I write, teach, take long walks on the beach, and when I am home . . . I am *home*. I can do whatever I want, whenever I want.

Yes, there are moments of loneliness, times when it would be nice to have a partner, but my life is *good*. In four years I will be forty, but I am no longer dreading the BIG 4-0; in fact, I am excited. With age, I become wiser, kinder, and more compassionate. Since my separation from Jessica last year, I have taken up yoga and love it. I hike more, read more for pleasure, surround myself with positive people, and I am just genuinely content. And the strangest part of it is I have found happiness *alone*. What a novel idea: to be happy with only oneself as company! I am finally—after thirty-six long years—at peace. And damn, it feels good!

As Rick and I lay there soaking up the sun, I think to myself: I am living. *Really living*, gosh Angela would be proud of me.

"Want another one of my delicious drinks?"

"No, thanks. I'm already feeling a bit tipsy. Hey . . . Thair . . . ? "

"Yes?"

"Are you sure you want to go away for the whole summer? Frank and I will really miss you!"

"Oh, come on, you two will be just fine." Times have been tough for the two of them, and Rick and I are seeing each other more than usual. "I told you that you two are welcome to come anytime and stay in my place."

"Yeah, I know, but remember what happened last time? Your little, old conservative neighbors weren't too happy and complained to your HOA."

A small, layered giggle: "Maybe. But do you think I care? Seriously, if you two want to stay, I'll write to management ahead of time and inform them that you are taking care of my place. Then you can come whenever you want and take advantage of the pool and spa. Anyway, it will be good for the two of you to have somewhere to get away again, don't you think?"

"Yeah, Frank is still so down, and a getaway may be just what he needs. But . . . I would prefer to go with you to Greece! Ah,

Mykonos . . ." He is lost in thought, probably reliving the week he spent there with Frank in the late '90s, a gay man's paradise.

"You know, you are both certainly welcome to join me. I'm sure the real estate business won't fall apart any worse if you were to leave for a few weeks."

I see Rick's eyes flicker, but he and I both know he is not going anywhere. Since the death of Frank's mother, at the young age of fifty-seven, Frank has been really depressed. It's been frustrating for Rick because Frank has completely shut down. I just keep telling Rick, *give him time, sweetie. He is going through something really tough, and I guarantee you that he is not intentionally trying to push you away.*

Over the last year, since his mother's passing, Frank has become so different, so closed. I guess that's the difference between friends and partners. I don't live with Frank and can give him the occasional upbeat visit as he goes through this, but Rick suffers along and continues to be supportive. He comes home and finds Frank lying on Tinky Winky in the exact same spot he was when Rick left for work. Rick also told me Frank goes for days without showering, zones out in front of the TV, and is non-communicative. I knew Frank was a "momma's boy," but after a year, I am starting to wonder if he needs more help than Rick can give him. I know Frank and Rick have that connection that only comes along once in a lifetime (and never for others, I am starting to think), so I hope they will make it. They *have* to make it. I am still a hopeless romantic, and these two are (were?) my role models.

It's been thirteen months since Jessica and I have broken up, and I still think about her daily. I see her every week at the college, but my nights at The Burn have come to a close. Gay clubs, straight clubs, it doesn't matter. I don't like the bar scene at all, just not my thing. I prefer to stay at home or go out for a quiet dinner with friends. I do miss Jessica, and every time I see her, there is a shot of pain, but I'm okay.

As always, Rick is so intuitive, always seems to know what I'm thinking, "So tell me, how has it been seeing Jessica at the college this semester?"

"I can tell you, honestly, it hasn't been easy. I still find myself hugely attracted to her even with her five-month belly. In fact, she just glows, just like they say about pregnant women. It really is true. She looks more amazing than ever. *She just glows.*" I can't help repeating myself.

I am silent for a few minutes, processing, remembering, then I have this burning need to share with Rick something that I haven't told anyone. Without further thought, I begin talking, "I don't know if I ever told you, but after Jess started dating Tawny again, I did something really inappropriate. I went to her place one night, like a young foolish girl, and rang her bell. I knew she was alone because Tawny always works at The Burn on Fridays. Anyway, she was shocked to see me at her door . . . but also delighted. We hadn't spoken for months, not since the breakup, and I just had to see her. She offered me a cup of coffee, and we started talking about everything, everything except us. About school, classes, students we loved, others we didn't; we argued about that new website called Facebook, Jessica saying she already had an account, and me being so skeptical. She called me a Luddite, said I needed to move into the twenty-first century, and I argued that I preferred the '80s when technology didn't consume so much of our lives. We bantered happily back and forth about a variety of topics, and the feistier our conversation got, the more turned on I was. After my second cup of coffee, I had to go to the restroom, and when I came out, she wasn't in the living room. Instinctively, I went to her bedroom, and she was lying naked on her bed. It was one of the most breath-taking sights. Her long limbs, flat stomach, shapely arms, strong jaw, and that fantastic smile."

I look over and Rick is sitting straight up. I don't stop because in my mind's eye, I am already there in bed with her again.

"So, I made my way over the bed, turned around, bent over, took off my jeans, then my shirt. I lay down beside her with just my bra and panties; she got on top of me, straddled me. Then she took my face and kissed me passionately. I remember lying flat as she worked her way down, kissing my neck, then my belly button. When she reached—"

Suddenly, I am embarrassed, wetness between my legs, my heart racing. I have never been so explicit with Rick before. Having already crossed the invisible boundary set by friends, I try to make a joke, using the classic weak line utilized by soap operas and my students when they need to end their stories because they don't know where to go next: "And then I woke up and it was all a dream!" Of course, it wasn't, but Rick laughs and lightens the mood.

Before he can comment, I add, "Now let's get in the pool! I need to cool off!"

"Yes! Good idea, Ms. Thair!" Rick seems relieved.

We both jump in the chilly water as it instantly calms my hormones. I swim a few laps to warm up, and then make my way over to Rick, who is leaning against the wall, with water up to his waist.

"So, Thair, do you regret breaking up with her?"

"I do miss the times we shared, but it just wasn't right. She wanted a baby so badly, and you know me, God just didn't give me the baby gene. I couldn't take on the most important job in the world if I didn't believe in it heart and soul. I can admit that I was irritated to find out that she went back to Tawny right away, especially after all the conversations we had, all the times she told me that they were *just* friends. Now, though, it does make sense. Even though Tawny is about fifteen years younger, I know how much she adores Jessica. And I believe it runs much deeper than the ex-student-teacher attraction. I guess maybe I saw it all along, just didn't want to admit it."

"But does Jessica really *love* her?" Rick blurted.

"I don't know." I am looking down, staring at my feet that look distorted under the water. "I really don't know. Do we ever find that special person that loves us as much as we love him or her?" I say this while thinking Rick and Frank have found that sort of love but, based on what's been happening lately between the two of them, I can't help but wonder if Rick feels like he loves Frank more than Frank loves him right now.

Out loud, I bring it back to Jess and Tawny. "I guess I'm just trying not to judge their relationship, and I do sincerely hope that they are both happy. Tawny adores kids. I told you she has a three-year-old girl, right?"

"Yeah, you did."

"Anyway, Jess's kid will have an older sister, so I really hope it works out. Jessica is an exceptional woman."

"And what about that night? I assume Tawny never found out."

"Actually, Jess told Tawny the next day. Can you believe that? She also promised her that it was the last time she would ever be with me or another woman for that matter. A sort of final farewell to being single. Of course, Tawny was initially upset, but Jess ended up asking her to get married, to find a place where it's legal and make it official. Tawny was in heaven because Jess is always true to her word. I think being with me one more time solidified this for her, that she wanted to move on, close the chapter that was us. She made a choice. Above everything, career . . . me . . . she wanted to be a mother. She says that if she and Tawny are to share children, then she wants Tawny to be her wife. So now Jess is totally committed to Tawny, and we are simply colleagues again. End of Love Story #3 for Thair."

"Oh, sweet Thair . . . "

"It's okay. Really. It would have been nice to remain friends, but she made it clear that I am not welcome in her home or in her life. She said it would be too difficult for her."

"So, Thair . . . do you think Jessica could have been *The One*?"

I start moving the water around me, fingertips lightly touching the surface. It's not that I'm avoiding the question, it's just that for a moment, I don't know how to answer.

"Thair, you don't have to respond. It's a stupid question anyway."

"No, it's not a stupid question. I have actually been thinking about this a lot, and I guess the answer is 'no.' I figure if she were The One, I would still be with her, right? I think we had all the makings for a great long-term relationship, but we didn't fit together completely." As I say this, I grab Rick's hands. "Let me show you something. Take your hands and interlace your fingers." Rick does as I ask him, always a good sport. "Good. Now see how that feels. Feels good? Feels *right*? Now take your two index fingers and switch them. How does that feel?"

"Awkward."

"Good."

"Not good, Thair, I said awkward." I smile. Rick always plays along with me.

"Okay, see how it feels awkward, strange? Well that's me, and how I am in relationships. One minuscule thing is off kilter, and the whole thing feels damn uncomfortable. Simply not *right*."

We are still standing in the pool, the water keeping us cool from the waist down. The sun is burning my back, but it feels nice.

"I just don't think a person can want something so different from the other and expect to have a healthy, good relationship. With Jessica, yes, there was understanding, communication, and let's not forget the incredible sex," I say with a laugh, "but some fundamental goals did not match up. I think that's one problem with people today in regard to romance; we are fed all this bullshit that if you meet The One, any obstacle can be overcome. I just think that if I ever meet my other half, of course, if there is such a thing, there won't be any *real* obstacles. Or if there are, they will be minor issues not fundamental differences; in fact, I imagine I won't even see them as obstacles because the fit will be right. I assume there will be compromises to be made because nothing is perfect, but there won't be fundamental differences in what we want from each other, from life."

"So, my friend, you have everything figured out."

"Nah!" I say as I splash him. "I don't have anything figured out! Just me and my crazy philosophies!"

"Thair, I'm happy for you."

"Why?" I say with a smile.

"You seem happy, genuinely happy. I don't think I have ever seen you . . . this light. It's almost strange, no hot mama or sexy man in your life and, yet, you seem so radiant. And I'm happy just to be around you."

"That's so sweet," I reply.

Suddenly, Rick's face seems strained and sad. He probably wishes that Frank could have been with us, enjoying the pool, the sun, and the conversation. Then, changing the much-too-serious conversation to one more playful, I state, "Of course I am light and radiant! In three glorious days, I will by lying on a sandy beach in the Mediterranean! Are you sure you don't want to come with me?"

"Don't tempt me!" A huge splash comes my way, and a water war breaks out as we lose ourselves in the moment, acting like children, splashing, laughing, no worries in the world.

———

Twelve T-shirts, ten panties, five bikinis, four skirts, three bras, three pairs of jeans, three cute tops, two pairs of shorts, two sarongs, and one simple black dress. I have been packing for the last three hours, trying to get everything ready for my trip. I am so excited that I almost can't control myself. Then I start thinking about my mother. I want to finish packing, but my fingers are itching to write.

Thair's Story

Encinitas
Late May, 2005

"Thair, are you sure you want to spend the entire summer in Greece again?"

"Yes, Mother. I've told you that so many times already."

"But remember how you came back last time? So thin and unhappy. I just don't understand how a woman can travel alone for so long. It's just not healthy. It doesn't seem safe to me either."

"Mama, don't worry. I'll give you the name and number of the pension where I will be staying. I looked up the village online, and it's a quaint place right by the sea, just about two hours from Athens. It's called Kamena Vourla. Have you heard of it?"

"No, it doesn't sound familiar. Is it north or south?"

"It's north. I saw some pictures and it looks charming, a village that is nestled between the mountains and the sea. The website boasts over twenty cafés and restaurants right on the seashore."

"Thair, why do you have to go for so long? I just don't understand." For the last few years, she seemed to understand her daughter so little. Why did Thair want to go to Greece? Because she loved it there, even if her last visit was tumultuous, this time it would be different. She was different. Still, the third degree from her mother continued. "So where exactly will you be staying?"

"I rented a room with its own private bath and balcony in what seems to be an older woman's *polikatikia*. I spoke to her several times on the phone, and I have to say, she reminds me a lot of Yiayia. She was a bit short, grumbling in Greek, cutting me off a few times, but she did finally answer all my questions. She rents four rooms, but mine is the only one with a balcony that overlooks the town's beach. Nothing too fancy, she said, nothing like the islands, but she told me I could drive to a pebbled beach called 'Aspronairi' that was only a few kilometers away that had clear, blue water. Kyria Akrivi said that breakfast was included, and since I was alone, she wouldn't mind including me in her family's lunch for an extra charge. I told her that would be nice, and then I could get my dinners out if I need to."

"Thair, it sounds fine, but why do you have to go for more than two months! Can't you just go for a few weeks?" She said this with desperation in her voice.

"Mom! Why are you giving me such a hard time? In fact, why don't you come with—?" But before Thair could even finish the words, her mother said, "Thair, can I please say something else?"

"No."

But Phaedra continued anyway, "Thair, I just think two weeks, even a month is a vacation, but over two months is like you are escaping from something . . . from someone. It just seems that ever since you and . . . you and . . . well, since that thing with . . . that woman . . . ended, you always seem to be alone."

"Mom, that's a funny thing for you to say. I thought you, of all people, would understand that doing things alone can actually be quite fulfilling."

"Thair, please, don't compare me to you. I've had a good, full life. I just want you—"

"Mama, please stop. I am really looking forward to this trip and—"

"*Agape mou*," Mother. Daughter. Cutting each other off, each wanting to have the last word. But Thair had not heard her mother call her 'my love' since she was a child; it was the one phrase that took her words away, feeling like a little girl again. It was the same soothing phrase she had heard from her grandmother throughout the years in different situations. When she fell off her bicycle, gravel mixed with blood, puss pouring out of her leg, her yiayia held her, cleaning her injury and telling her gently, "*Agape mou*, not cry, you a big girl, fifteen, a woman." When she left Greece and hugged her yiayia at the airport, her grandmother used those words again "Ah, *agape mou*. You write to your yiayia, okay?" But Thair never wrote. She did call every so often, but during the long school year, she never wrote. It was one of the few regrets she had in her life.

Now her mother was using those tender words, and she knew she had to listen. Phaedra's voice remained placid, "*Agape mou*," repeating those words that tamed Thair, "I want you to go, to have a good time, but I am just worried that you may be escaping. When you were a teenager and unhappy, you always wanted to go to Kythnos. I think you persuaded yourself into believing that you could only be happy in Greece. Yes, most of the time you came back vibrant, but then you became sad so quickly. You can't escape your problems by going away. I am sorry, honey, but I have to tell you how I feel."

For some reason, Thair was not agitated with those final words; more so, she felt relieved. It was as if her mother had said something out loud that she had been thinking: she had told others, Rick and Emily and Angela, she was happy, but was she really escaping?

Suddenly, an uncontrollable lightness streamed through Thair's body. It was as if a dam had been broken, the little Dutch boy had pulled his finger out of the hole. A flood of emotions and words came out, "Mama—you need to hear this. First of all, 'that woman,' as you call her, is named Jessica. And, yes, when we broke up, I did spend a lot of time alone. Frankly, I was devastated; in fact, I was a bit devastated when Ravi and I separated as well as when James left me. In all three relationships,

I questioned myself, like I was just not meant to be loved. I did care for all three of those people in such different ways. But can I tell you something? And I am not saying this to make you feel guilty. Remember that story you used to tell me when I was a little girl about Zeus, and how he separated these ball figures, and how we now roam the world looking for our other half?"

A meek "Yes," came through on the other end.

"Well, I guess I took that story to heart. And just like the thousands of girls who grow up with this unrealistic image of Prince Charming, or the idea of a Soul Mate, or in my case, the Other Half that Zeus rudely separated from me, I have spent my adult life looking for this other person to complete me. I have always imagined meeting someone who will truly complement me and all I want from this life. James was a kind soul, and I learned so much from the time we spent together, talking about art, painters, ideologies, the concept of right and wrong. It was such a tranquil, positive relationship, made me learn so much about my career, made me a better teacher, a better human. But damn it the magic—I hate to use that word—was not there."

"Logos, ethos . . . pathos." Thair heard her mother say as if she were in her own world.

"Exactly, Mama, our relationship was too cerebral. A good guy, and two of three weren't bad, but he knew, even before I did, that we were not each other's Other Half."

"What about Ravi, Thair? He was such a handsome man with such a wonderful family . . ."

"Talk about pathos. The passion was intense. And I know you adored him and pictured us together with two kids and a house on the hill. You know, I saw him about a year ago, and I was drooling like a teenage girl. I still think he is gorgeous, and yes, another good one, but not for me. Did you know he wanted me to quit my job and be a full-time mom?"

"But, Thair, is that so bad? Do you think there's a chance—"

"*As* I was saying, I don't want a life with him. Can you please try to understand me?"

"I am trying, *agape mou*, but it's hard. I guess you and I are so different. All I want is for you to be happy." She hesitated, then asked, quite surprisingly, "The woman. Jessica. Do you still . . . care for her?"

Thair paused. Her mother had never asked about Jessica. Not since that terrible fight. Her heart swelled with love for her mother. Yes, they were different, but this was the first time in a long time that Phaedra was, at least, trying to understand her daughter. "I know this is hard for you, but, yes, I loved Jessica. Probably more than James and Ravi put together. We had so much in common, but, unfortunately, neither of us wanted to compromise on something very important, and this tore us apart."

Thair heard a gulp, then her mother said, "It was my . . . fault."

"Mama," Thair said more gently, "there were other issues." She didn't know if she had convinced her mother, but today was not the day to talk about children. Thair usually avoided the kid issue with Phaedra because she knew it was the one thing her mother still longed for—a grandchild. Thair wanted to have this conversation with her mother, be truthful, but she knew that days before her trip was not the right time.

Before her mother could say more, Thair added, "Okay, no more deep talk after this, but can I tell you the best part?"

"What?" another quiet response.

"I am happy to the core of my being. I guess I did not think that people who are single could really be content. And now I believe it. I think there is a different kind of happiness when one is in a good, loving relationship, but there can be genuine happiness in being alone, too. So, I just want to say thank you."

"Thank you for what, Thair?" Phaedra responded sounding confused.

"Thank you for asking me if you thought I was trying to escape. I didn't want to face that question because I, too, had wondered if I was returning to Greece to find something that I just can't find in the US. But because of your comment, now I am certain that I am going there as a whole woman."

"Oh, sweetie, *Doxa to Theo*," her mother said and sighed.

"Yes, Mama, thank God! Every day I give thanks for my health, my mama's," Thair thought she heard a slight sob but she was on a roll, "for my security, my pay check, and that I am an American woman who has choices. A woman who has a wonderful Greek mother who has also given me another country to call home."

"Baby, you're gonna make me cry."

But Thair couldn't stop, it was as if her entire adult life finally made sense: "Mama, Greece is a country that warms me, welcomes me. It's a place I can go to and relax; Greece is my sanctuary away from a hectic American lifestyle, but the US is where I belong . . . at least now. When people are comfortable with themselves, then anywhere can be home."

"Are you done, sweetheart?"

"Yes, Mama."

"Well, then I am happy for you, too."

I looked at what I wrote: "anywhere can be home." I don't know where those words came from, but I guess they are true. I do love my condo, but the feeling of comfort that has embraced me lately is not from a physical roof over my head for which I own the Title (though it certainly helps); the real sense of serenity has come from accepting who I am as a person—appreciating my strengths and forgiving my faults. This comfort has also stemmed from giving Zeus the boot, a relief to not be looking over my shoulder anymore. I know there will be days when I will long for a partner or some intimacy, but it is no longer a priority in my life.

I jump up from my swivel chair and, with a renewed energy, continue packing.

Part ~~III~~

Peace

25

Athens, Greece
Monday, June 6th, 2005

The airplane touches down at Venizelos Airport in Athens with a bunch of Greeks clapping their hands excitedly upon arrival. It makes me smile. I have been on countless international flights and only in Greece do passengers show their appreciation with hoots, hollers, while their hands pound together like Neanderthals when the tires hit the tarmac. Greeks are happy people, loud, opinionated; the older men are hirsute with a distinctive body odor; the yiayias round and love to gossip; the younger generation is so much different, still loud and loquacious but also svelte and sophisticated, and all of them— young and old—have a cigarette in their hand. As we slow down, I can see a few women dig in their purses, looking for their pack of Camels, making sure it's at the top and ready to be opened the moment they are out of the plane and in the airport. Men pat their pockets, ensuring that their cigarettes have not mysteriously disappeared on the twelve-hour flight from New York City.

While the airplane is still taxiing, a few elderly Greeks have already jumped out of their seats and are pulling down hand luggage from the compartments above as the flight attendant tells them to "sit down immediately." Her tone is just short of rude. She is Greek too, her strong accent giving her away. When they continue to stand, she switches to Greek and, in a harsh voice, commands them to sit down. The entire scene is almost comical. In the US, a flight attendant has to use sugary politeness even with boorish passengers for fear of being sued: here, anything goes. I love that about Greece and its people. They may seem a bit barbaric with their grand gesticulations and resounding voices, the way they communicate that makes it seem like they are arguing when in fact they are in total agreement. All this, ironically enough, gives me a sense of peace. They seem to be so in touch with their feelings: say what they mean, mean what they say. They lack falseness, pretense, something so pure and honest about these people, their culture. My culture. I *am* somewhere in between two cultures, somewhere in between two sexualities. I exist, just like Hamlet's "to be or not to be," and I choose to be. I am no longer trying to fit into one or the other; I finally learned to appreciate all aspects of my life and feel thankful that I was given this gift to be open. And as the saying goes, have an open heart, not just an open mind. No longer is the "grass greener on the other side"; sometimes it's damn yellow on both, but now I finally have the ability to appreciate, regardless of inadequacies. Taking in the good with the bad, the easy with the difficult, the beauty with the beast. Open. Truly open.

The pushing starts and there seems to be a race to get off the airplane. I sit calmly and watch the mayhem; again, the scene strikes me as a bit humorous. We are then crammed into a bus and brought to the terminal. I see a few individuals put the cigarettes in their mouths, and even though signs in the Greek airport say "No Smoking," almost everyone, including the tiny yiayia, has already lit up, and soon my lungs are gasping for air while the passengers puff in unison. I stand in the "FOREIGN" line and enter with my US passport, since I have never got a Greek one, so my allocated stay is for a maximum of three months. Years ago, I had tried to get a Greek passport but was told at immigration, "If Father is Greek, it take six months; your mama, need five years." I never pursued it since my Blue Magic Passport takes me almost anywhere I want to go.

Thinking about the conversation with the stinky man at immigration years ago still incenses me. Overt gender discrimination. That is one of the negative aspects of Greece: most women over forty still treat their husbands like kings, there for their every beck and call; men still seem to control the wife, the home, the bank account. Many married men have lovers, often swearing on their children's lives about their fidelity. But when there is proof, they better watch out! The wife will cry and shout and scream and beat him with a frying pan, (then serve him dinner a few hours later, made with that same pan!). Of course, these are all generalizations. Women now work outside their homes and demand more respect, but with employment comes more stress, more responsibilities, and more divorce. It is no longer acceptable for men to have their honey and money on the side. Men have to help with some household duties and they don't like it. It's not just the US where things are changing.

I talked about all this on the airplane with a Greek mother and daughter who sat beside me and became my drinking companions on the flight. As bottomless, free wine was poured into plastic glasses, our animated discussion drew a few casual glances, then downright stares, as we teasingly compared men to dogs.

"Just feed them, rub them where it counts, and they will be happy forever," Eleni said.

I chuckled and added, "I think the problem is women try to cram forty-eight hours of work into a twenty-four-hour day, and doggie doesn't get all the rubbing he wants, then doggie-not-so-happy. So doggie runs away and smells the neighbor dog's ass and humps it to be happy again."

The three of us were laughing hysterically as we talked about this—our comparisons mostly in jest, but laced with truth.

I was tired when I got onto the flight but with the animated conversation, I was soon wide-awake. It felt good to be speaking Greek again and in the company of a bright woman and her not-so-old-fashioned mother. Eleni is a podiatrist in Brooklyn, and her mother had been visiting from Larissa, a city with village-like attitudes. I told them that gender inequalities have always interested me, and I was toying with the idea of researching the changing roles of women in Greece and possibly writing some articles.

What I didn't tell Eleni and her mother was that I secretly wanted to finish my "stories" that I had started more than five years before. Despite my desire to write, I have already decided that there is not going to be any pressure on this trip. If I want to write, I will. If I don't, I won't. This trip is going to be all about "R and R" and certainly some sightseeing. Although I spent every summer of my life in Greece until I was twenty-two, I have seen very little of the mainland. There are so many places I have seen on documentaries or read about on the Internet that I decided this year to stay in a village on the coast and rent an economical car to go wherever I wanted, whenever I wanted.

Online I stumbled upon a site that had pictures and a description of a mountain town called Metsovo that sits at an altitude of 1,200 meters. Green landscapes with beige stone houses and red roofs made me think this village looked more like Switzerland than Greece. The website went on to say, "Metsovo promises to show life in Greece from another era." With that I was sold. On that road trip, I would also go see Meteora. Since I was a young girl, I have always wanted to see the remarkable churches that are perched high on mountain tops. When I bought my favorite band's latest CD, called *Meteora*, my interest to see the real Meteora was reawakened. For the last few years I have been playing the song "Somewhere I Belong" over and over again on my long drives to school and back. The lyrics have hauntingly spoken to me, words about healing and inner strength. I am finally healed, and I did it all by myself.

I am so excited to see this historic site, and I plan on rocking out to Linkin Park in my rented car as I drive the many hours to get there. I also read online that from Kamena Vourla I can easily drive to Delphi, too. I have been there once, but it was so many years ago.

While I'm standing in line, images of these places make a movie before my eyes, and instantly I am a child on her first trip to Disneyland. Despite my good mood, I am having a hard time breathing as clouds of cigarette smoke float around me. A bunch of people hover around an upright ashtray in the corner of the room, and when a chunky Greek woman in front of me reaches the man in the immigration box, she yells to the people in the back of the room while waving her arm frantically in the air, "*Ella! Ella!*" And now instead of one person in front of me, an entire Greek clan has gathered—all with blue passports. Normally this would irk me, but today nothing can get to me. I'm just so excited to get out of this airport and begin my adventure. As I stand there twiddling my fingers, shifting my feet back and forth, laced with this excitement is something relatively new in my life: a sense of peace.

One hour and counting, I finally make it through the lines to get my suitcase. When I exit, I see families kissing, tears streaming down faces, vigorous hugs, Greeks talking one over the other; absolute joy from all involved. No one is there to greet me. But it's okay. No jealousy, sadness, or emptiness courses through my veins, just adrenaline. I look around, trying to find a sign for taxis when Eleni comes over and gives me her business card, telling me that the phone number and address of her family's home is on the back, and if I want to see "real" village people, I should come visit. She says this with a hearty laugh (that reminds me a bit of Jessica), gives me a few kisses on the cheek and departs. Maybe I will visit, who knows? Slipping the card in my wallet, I go outside where I see several taxis lined up. Since I will stay put in Kamena Vourla for a while, I decide to save some money and get there by bus and rent a car later.

Within minutes, I am on my way to Liossion Station. I think about taking an airport bus to the main bus station—I read online it's about 3 euros—and seriously regret not doing it when the taxi driver tells me I owe him 35 euros for the short trip. Once I get out, I pull my heavy suitcase behind me, no gallant Greek to help, just atavistic men huddled like cavemen around an ashtray. I ask a few bystanders about tickets and, finally, a yiayia dressed in black from head to toe points me to a line. I stand in the queue, hoping that she was right, and I am not wasting time. After three people in front of me get tickets, I reach the woman behind the glass, a tired-looking woman about fifty-something with a cigarette hanging from her lip. She asks me where I want to go with such an attitude I instantly feel like I did something wrong. I respond that I want to go to Kamena Vourla. She yells the price, and I give her my money as she throws me a ticket. Before I can say anything, she says the equivalent to "NEXT!"

But I don't move. Now with a stronger, annoyed voice (Peace has temporarily deserted me) I tell her that the ticket says *Lamia* and I want to go *Kamena Vourla*. The rude, wrinkle-mouthed woman screams at me again, saying that the village, Kamena Vourla, will be about half an hour before the final destination of Lamia; I just need to keep my eyes open and listen to the man who yells the destinations and get off at the right time. *Great system.* Lugging my suitcase, I find bus #32 and see a line forming. An older man with chest hairs popping through his shirt grabs my suitcase and before I can ask what he is doing, he screams, "*Pou pas?*"

"Kamena Vourla," I reply. He does not look at me and throws my suitcase into the bottom of the bus in the luggage compartment. Then he hollers at another woman and I am reassured: he's not mad at me. Oh yeah, I am in Greece. No American niceties. Greeks are not rude: they are just *Greek*. Moving more slowly because I can feel the jetlag settling into my tired bones, I get onto the bus, find my seat, and plop down. Feeling totally exhausted, I think it's safe to sleep for a bit because Kamena Vourla is about two and a half hours away. The seat beside me is empty, so no fear of engaging in any conversations. Thank Zeus.

All of a sudden, the bus comes to a halting stop, and I am jarred back from my dream world, realizing that I don't know where I am or what time it is. It takes me a moment to get my bearings, ah, on the bus, in Greece, going to Kamena Vourla. I look out the window and see that we have stopped. I have no idea how long we have been on the bus. I ask a woman sitting in the row over how far to Kamena Vourla, worried that we have already passed it. She takes on a motherly tone when she hears my accent, telling me that we are still an hour away and this is a rest stop, but if I want to go get food or go to the bathroom, I had better move fast because once the bus driver is ready, he waits for no one. My stomach is growling and the *tyropita* that the little boy is munching on in the next seat over looks too good to pass up. I jump out of my seat, get off the bus, go to the bathroom first, then make it into the bakery-restaurant-corner-market thingy. The smells tickle my nose, a mixture of fresh bread mixed with deep olive oil. A slight hazelnut, Nutella scent tops it off (the boy in front of me has a moist chocolate croissant). There are still a few people from the bus in line, so I'm confident that I will not be left alone in the middle of what looks like nowhere.

Back in the bus, I am revitalized. Looking out the window excitedly, munching on my *tyropita* as flecks of crispy phyllo dough land on my jeans from the cheese pie, I sip my Coke and smile like a stupid American. A cute gent, a few seats away, catches my eye, but he turns quickly when he sees me. I realize he's probably in his early twenties, and as a woman in her thirties, I have to admit, I just don't attract them like I used to, don't have that mysterious, young foreign girl allure anymore. But it's okay. I still feel thrilled to be alive.

As the bus moves along, I stare out the window while the warm air blows my hair around, enjoying the country side, thinking it looks much different than the islands; mountains hover to the left and every so often, on a steep mountain turn, I can catch the blue of the Aegean coastline to my right. The houses are varied, some small wood homes, some stucco houses that remind me of Californian residences; other bigger, brick homes on the mountainside look more lavish. I see big warehouse-type buildings; some stretches of land, then a few more company buildings can be seen in the distance. Finally, the bus slows down and it seems we are entering the middle of a small town. The matronly woman on my left points to me and tells me we have arrived: "*Imaste sta Kamena Vourla, agape mou.*" *Agape mou.* My love. Instantly, I feel welcomed. She doesn't even know me. For as fierce, loud, and as rude Greeks come across, there is unequivocal warmth to them also.

"*Efharisto,*" I reply, thanking her as I pick up my purse and quickly collect my rubbish. Then a piercing, "KAMENA VOURLA!" is heard from the conductor-like man and a few people stand quickly, including the handsome lad. Before the bus comes to a full stop, people are pushing their way to the front. But no one seems offended; it's just their system. The young man is first in line, waiting anxiously, leaning on one foot then the other. From the window I see a girl, who looks barely fifteen, standing under the green awning wearing a bikini top and a miniskirt; a teeny-weeny, itsy-bitsy white miniskirt. Long, brown hair falls on tan, sleek shoulders and big, black bug-eye glasses sit on her perfect face. Her body swings nervously from side to side; every so often she stands on her tiptoes trying to look into the bus that has yet to open the doors. Whooooosh. The doors open, and the blazing heat is let in. I see the man-boy and girl staring excitedly at one another. He pushes past the conductor, hops off the bus; she runs to him, flings her arms around his neck, and gives him an (almost) indecent, tongue-filled kiss. I find myself hunched over, staring from the bus window, ah *young love.*

I can't say it warms my heart, but neither does it make me jealous. More than anything I think, gosh, how many times will she feel that way? That exhilarating anxiety, the endless minutes of not being able to wait to hold her lover. I also wonder how many times her heart will be broken. How many suitors will revert to frogs after those luscious kisses? My thoughts sound a bit negative, but I see myself more as a realist now. I almost (just almost) feel her pain when she realizes he's not The One (for whatever reason). But then I tell myself: she has to go through it. There is no other way. And then a remarkable thought enters my mind: What if he *is* The One? What happens when one is tender and young and innocent (okay maybe not so innocent with that long lizard-like kiss), and finds his or her perfect half? Do they recognize the other as being The One? And can everlasting love *really* be found at such a young age? Could they be that rare couple who fall in love before twenty, get married, have children, stay happily married for fifty years, and then die within six months of each other because neither can bear to be on this earth without the other? Hmm . . . ?

I don't think so.

Then I think . . . maybe?

Who knows?

This newfound tranquility makes me believe that anything is possible, and even if I haven't found my ideal, that doesn't mean bug-eyed girl won't find her misplaced half. They continue to embrace when I hear Mr. Conductor shouting at me: "*Kyria, PROHORA!*"

A woman behind me is pushing, and I realize I'm the one holding up the line, so lost in thought, eyes glued to the window. He screams again: Lady, MOVE! When I get to the bottom of the bus, I think: *shoot, my suitcase!* I look up at him, explaining that I need my suitcase, and he replies I should have been listening earlier because he asked if anyone had any luggage. I apologize, wondering if the bus will just drive away with all my belongings; a slight sense of fear momentarily takes over before I hear myself yell again in typical Greek fashion, "*E*

validsa mou PARAKALO!" My suitcase PLEASE! Almost pummeling
an old lady on the bus's stairs, he gets out, pulls out a magic key, pops
open the bottom of the bus, and yanks out my heavy suitcase and
throws it on the ground. Before I can thank him, he is back on the bus,
and it is pulling out of the makeshift station. The helpful woman on
the bus waves at me, and again, I am comforted. As I stand there with
my purse, a laptop bag, and my newly-scratched Samsonite, I see two
men that look about one hundred years old playing backgammon;
three others sit around them, drinking coffee in miniature cups that
look more like a child's tea set, and in their other hand, each one has a
cigarette. An ashtray, full of cigarette butts, decorates the table as does
a pile of newspapers. I walk up to their table, but am non-existent,
so I decide to go into the café where the bus has dropped me off and
inquire about my residence. The woman at the counter ignores me
too; I finally get her attention on the third "Excuse me!" I know cus-
tomer service is not Greece's specialty, but this is getting ridiculous. I
am now certifiably grumpy and tired, and I just want a bit of help.

With no more feigned politeness, I slam a piece of paper on the
counter and ask where I can find Kyria Akrivi's pension. She stops
putting chip bags away and finally shows me her yellow smile. She
tells me to take a seat, that she will call a taxi to take me to Kyria
Akrivi's place. I ask if it's that far and can I walk, but she just looks at
my suitcase and keeps dialing. Within a few minutes an elderly man
pulls up in a grey Mercedes. Great. Not a regular taxi, but a Mercedes!
They are already "grabbing my ass"—a Greek expression meaning to
take advantage of the stupid tourist. I don't feel like fighting, so I say
efharisto and get into the car. I later find out that *all* the taxis in town
are Mercedes because supposedly they are such solid cars and cheaper
to maintain, so my first assumption was wrong; they weren't trying to
take advantage of my derrière or my wallet. The driver takes me to,
what literally feels like around the corner, a beige five-story building
with a huge garden that overlooks a little bay. The setting is quaint. It's

about 5:30 p.m. and the beach is full of people. Yiayias with skinny legs and round bellies are taking a dip while men with equally round tummies sit together on the shoreline throwing stones into the water. Mothers stand in knee-high water as their toddlers, wearing inflatable arm rings, jump and float around them. The sun is still shining brightly, and it's hot, quite warm for the beginning of June.

Stelios, the taxi driver, stops and beeps his horn loudly as a woman comes out of the building. My heart drops through my rib cage and into my kneecaps. I cannot believe her resemblance to my very own, dear yiayia. She is wearing a flower apron over a black dress that tells me she is a widow. (I later learn that I was mistaken, and that she had lost her son to a tragic drinking and driving accident.) Her pepper-grey hair is pulled low in a bun at the nape of her neck. Her black shoes are soiled with mud; she is wiping her hands on her apron as she approaches the car. She says something brusquely to Stelios, but I can't make out the words because her back is turned to me. I go to pay him, and he says, "*Oxi*," gets in his taxi, and drives away. I later learn that Stelios is my keeper's first cousin through marriage, and there is no way she is paying him to drive me eight blocks to her house. I soon find out that everyone in this village is somehow related, and no one ever really expects to get paid. Uncle Yannis goes into his niece Maria's café, has a dessert and coffee, then leaves, having spent not a single euro, but knows that Maria's daughter will be in Yannis's sister's bar that night for a few free drinks. Dimitri's yiayia goes to the local grocery store and gets her milk for free, but then Dimitri knows the grocer's wife's next taxi ride is free. It's an interesting system, and I wonder how many disgruntled family members are out there, who never get an equal payback. But I guess it works. At least it did this time for Kyria Akrivi's guest since I didn't spend a dime or a drachma or a euro now.

After Stelios drives away, Kyria Akrivi does not greet me, just grabs some keys out of her apron pocket, and tells me to leave the suitcase; someone else will bring it up. I say that I can get it, but her look tells me I better leave it right where it's at. So I do. I follow her up black and white speckled marble steps. Kyria Akrivi huffs and puffs as she walks me up four flights; just when I think we are about to arrive, there is another set of stairs about half the size, metal, that circle dangerously to another floor, steps so small that my foot barely fits on them completely! At the top, there is a wooden door with the number "2" hanging on it, lopsided, so it looks more like a letter from the Greek alphabet. She instructs me how to open the door: a pull, she says, then stick in the key and turn, pull again, then a slight push with the hips. And another push if it doesn't open. While she is talking, a laugh escapes my lips. She looks at me angrily, instantly silencing me. *Great.* I guess I am not making the best first impression. From her point of view, I may seem rude, laughing at her door-opening system, so I apologize telling her I was thinking of something else, but she seems less than interested in what I have to say.

The door finally opens, and I see a tiny room with a huge balcony. The single bed is made of wood with a thin mattress on top; crisp white sheets adorn the bed, tightly tucked in at all corners, a ceiling fan swirls above, and a small desk with a thatched chair are squeezed into the corner of the room. I see a minuscule bathroom that looks incredibly white, as if Mr. Clean has just been there. A white shower curtain encloses a stand-up shower that is barely big enough for me even though I am only 5'6", and a small white toilet that looks almost child-sized sits in the corner. A long silver chain hangs from the ceiling, the way to flush I presume. I am already feeling a bit enclosed, so I walk out onto the balcony, and then—almost instantly and without knowing exactly why—a few tears come to my eyes. It is ideal. There is a large swing with sun-bleached blue pillows, a plastic table with four chairs, and the entire area hosts about fifty potted plants that make it look like a garden in the sky. Green everywhere, only a cold concrete floor peeks through. I realize it's not really a balcony, but a roof, my own private rooftop, complete with a large awning and a little Eden. It's perfect. I can see the sea below and feel a slight breeze. I could stay here forever.

"*Einai telio.*" I tell her how perfect it is, and she smiles sheepishly. Then like a drill sergeant, she tells me the rules:

1) Towels are washed twice a week, more than that and there will be an extra charge.

2) Bedsheets once a week. Every Monday it is my job to strip the bed and put them in a pile outside my door; otherwise it will be two weeks without fresh sheets. (I have the option to change them more than once a week, an extra charge *of course.*) She says a Bulgarian woman cleans the room every other day unless I say otherwise.

3) Breakfast is between 8:00 and 10:00 a.m. After that, too bad. Not even the option for an extra charge to get served later. She says she is out between 10:00 and 12:20 p.m. every day and cannot be reached. (Her shopping time? Daily swim? I know not to ask.)

4) Lunch (extra charge has already been discussed through correspondence) is at 2:00 p.m. Sharp. Not on Greek time, she tells me, British time. If I cannot make it, I need to tell her twenty-four hours in advance; otherwise I will be charged.

5) I can have my lunch in my room or in the family dining area with the other guests or her family. If I choose to take the food to my room on a tray, I will be responsible for bringing the tray and plates back to the kitchen.

5) I can come and go as I please, but NO GUESTS in the room after dark. (I dare not ask if there could be an extra charge if I want an overnight guest!)

6) I can drink and smoke cigarettes, but nothing illegal on the

premises. (I assure her that I am completely against any drugs, but she is already on number seven.)

7) Lastly, she says, and most importantly, she wants me to be comfortable (then she forces a smile), and if I need anything, just to let her know (there would be an extra charge I am certain).

I thank her warmly, and she exits the room without so much as an *adio*. Yes, she definitely reminds me of my grandmother.

I don't really feel that tired because of my catnap on the bus, so I want to change and go down for a dip, but my suitcase is still in the garden. I decide to go down for it, but before I can, I hear a light knock. I open the door, and a boy, about eleven or twelve years old stands there with my suitcase, sweating profusely. It looks almost as big as him. I feel guilty that I didn't bring it up myself and telling him to wait, I get a euro from my wallet. He seems pleased with his tip and skips away down the metal, twisty stairs.

I find my favorite daisy bikini that must be over a decade old and too small, but I fit my widening thirty-six-year-old booty into it. I look at the one and only mirror in the room that hangs above my bed, showing me from my waist up. I guess in all my tranquility, I still have an ego, so I jump on the bed, and turn around to see my backside. A few dimples here and there, a little muffin top, the skin much saggier than last time I was in Greece. I remember reading somewhere that the average woman in America has between twelve and sixty negative body-image thoughts per day, so I decide right there and then that every time I critique my puffy eyes, my wrinkles, or my fat, I will counteract the negative thought with a positive one. It's a novel idea. I just don't know how long it will last, but I'll try it. I smile at my reflection, grab my towel, work on the door for a few minutes to lock it, and head down my treacherous stairs.

26

Sitting outside with a towel on the plastic seat, I look out into the horizon and see the sun setting. It's a bit warm, but comfortable. I can't believe I have already been in Kamena Vourla for more than a month. Life has been quite perfect. I have my daily routine, a relatively healthy one at that. I get up around 7:30 a.m., splash my face with water, and still in my PJs (a matching purple Eeyore shorts and T-shirt set), I go downstairs. While Kyria Akrivi, my temporary landlady, makes me a Greek coffee—in a mug with lots of milk, "tourlou café" style, just like yiayia used to say—we chat briefly. I bring the coffee back upstairs, push the door open (rarely locking it because it is just too much effort) then throw down my yoga mat on the balcony, and do a few Sun Salutations. Before I left home, I started doing yoga at a local gym, and, on a whim, stuffed a mat in my suitcase. From a once-a-week workout, it has turned into an addictive daily practice.

After a few Downward Dogs, I stop and have a couple sips of my hot drink. Dripping with sweat, I slip into Pigeon Pose and after a few minutes, get up on my elbows and drink some more coffee while my leg is still wrapped under my torso. Drinking coffee while lost in the practice is not necessarily the yogi way, but it works for me. After about thirty to forty-five minutes of poses, I jump in the shower to cool off. Donning one of my five bikinis and a sundress, I head downstairs for breakfast. Usually after breakfast, it's a swim, then a catnap on the shore. I read, swim some more, lunch, another short nap on the balcony with the afternoon breeze. Later, in the early evening, I stroll into the center of town for an ice cream or a cold coffee at my favorite café. Walk some more. Then back to my room to read some more. It's a simple, pleasant existence.

Today I met some interesting characters that I keep thinking about, so for the first time since I have been here, I am inspired to write.

Thair's Story

Every week Thair had breakfast with different guests. Most of them were foreigners; sometimes they were Greeks. Only a few were unresponsive; most were friendly. Thair loved chatting and hearing about the adventures of the many travelers with whom she shared her meals.

But these relationships with this motley crowd of vacationers always remained at the morning table. Thair was not interested in getting to know anyone past breakfast. There were a few handsome travelers that turned her head when she saw them in the morning, so she smiled and chatted, but it never went any further.

As she opened the kitchen door one particular morning, Thair saw Kyria Akrivi standing over the stove, her husband sitting at the table reading the newspaper. A college-aged couple also sat at the table, voraciously eating all the bread that Kyria

Akrivi had set down. Thair could see that her keeper looked a bit disgruntled, but her advertisement did say "unlimited fresh bread for breakfast."

"*Kalimera*," Thair said, followed by, "Good morning."

"Hello," the boy said in a British accent.

"Hello," Thair repeated. The young girl looked over, but Thair was wondering if she could see her since the girl's eyes were so red and glazed. Both guests reeked of alcohol. Kyria Akrivi muttered something under her breath, threw down another basket of bread on the table, and walked away.

"I'm Thair," she said while pulling up a chair.

"I'm David and this is my girlfriend, Kelly." Kelly looked up again and nodded.

"So, have you been here long?" said the young man.

"Well . . . gosh . . ." Thair thought while calculating in her head, "It must be more than six weeks now."

"SIX WEEKS!" he exclaimed. "I mean this place has a few fun bars, but aren't you bored by now?"

No, she wasn't bored. She was far from bored. She loved waking early, doing her own form of yoga, taking a walk, a swim, a nap, reading a bit, going to the local Internet café to find out what was happening in the world, and her favorite pastime, sitting quietly in a café. In fact, she hadn't even been to a bar yet. And she hadn't felt lonely either. This was her time.

Thair didn't answer right away. Based on the look on his face, the young man may have thought he had offended her, so before she replied, he continued, "I'm sorry. Are you here with your kids? Your husband? I guess it's a nice place for families."

Yikes, for many women over thirty (who want to be married and yearn for children), he could be touching on a sore spot, but Thair didn't care. She was used to it. "No, actually I am alone. I just came for some rest and relaxation."

"Rest and relaxation? And all alone. That's wicked. I think it's cool that women like you can do these things without worrying about what people think," the chatty lad commented.

Thair smiled. She was just traveling alone, nothing revolutionary.

After a moment, the girl echoed: "Yeah, that's wicked."

"So, no crazy ex-husband you are trying to escape from? Hehe," the boy teased.

If Thair was not in such a good place emotionally, the last comment might have irked her. Spousal abuse was not something to be taken lightly. She almost wondered if youth gave people the right to say whatever idiotic thought came to mind. Nevertheless, something about him was authentic, not so innocent with those flaming eyes and still-drunk girlfriend, but Thair decided to engage in the conversation in a more meaningful way.

"Actually, I've never been married. My former partner, Jessica, and I broke up last year, and I'm just taking the time to enjoy being by myself." Thair's tone was gentle, inviting. The boy, and now the girl too, were certainly interested.

"Now that's cool!" David said while looking at her from head to toe.

All of a sudden Thair could feel this barely twenty-year-old sizing her up. Being feminine and loving a woman always seemed to make males think that it was an invitation for a ménage à trois.

Then Kelly piped up, "You don't look like a lesbian. Even my good friend at home in Hastings who is gay looks . . . I mean you can tell. I can't tell with you."

Thair sat there and wondered, what was she supposed to say to that? It was 2005, and yet one still seemed to have to choose: gay or straight. What about all the other parts of the LGBT+ abbreviation? Like bisexual and transgender? Or the varying sexualities the "+" signified?

Thair was not in the mood to discuss, lecture, or debate, so she decided to switch topics, "So what about you two? Do you go to uni?" Thair said 'uni' instead of university, trying out a bit of her British slang just for fun, but it sounded ridiculous after she said it.

"Yes, that's right! Kelly here is studying to be an architect, and I just don't know what I am doing!" He said this and laughed. "Just taking courses, hoping that something will come to me one day." Kelly continued to eat, face down, stuffing more bread into her tiny, geisha-shaped orifice.

"Well, you're in school, that's a start. I am sure something will interest you."

"So, what do you do?" the boy said between bites.

"I teach college. English."

"Cool. My favorite teacher was an English teacher."

Then switching topics again Thair said: "So how long will you two be staying in Kamena Vourla?"

"Just for a few days. We need to save some money and this place is cheap, so we decided to stay until Sunday then head to Ios." Then he let out a "Wooooo hooooooo, paaaarty! We hear that island is bloody wicked!"

"Yes, *wicked*," Thair repeated as all three laughed.

The boy then dug into the bread and jam and gulped down the coffee that was now, certainly, lukewarm.

Kelly looked up at Thair with her protruding eyeballs and said, "Tonight, David and I are going back to the bar we went to last night, and if you want, you can come with us." She said this thoughtfully, almost as if she felt sorry for Thair who had been alone for six weeks.

"Thanks, Kelly, but I like going to bed early."

"Aw, come on, Prof! It will be fun!" David chimed.

Thair smiled, cute kids, but, no, she wasn't interested.

"Thanks, really," then Thair dug into her own fresh bread and gulped her cold coffee.

It's about 9:00 p.m. and still bright outside. I seem to have a lot of energy tonight. I decide to go to my favorite hangout, Café Royal, and have a coffee and my newest find: a dessert called *ekmek*. It is probably the most delicious thing I have ever tasted in this world. It has shredded phyllo dough, is covered with syrup, then a layer of what tastes like fluffy vanilla pudding and finally a light layer of a fresh cream, simply divine. I go to my pint-sized closet and fish out my simple black dress. As I slip it over my shoulders, I find it falls heavy and doesn't stick to my hips like it used to. Since I have no scale and only half a mirror, my view has been mostly waist up for the last few weeks, and though I feel trim and tan, I didn't necessarily feel like I lost weight until I put on this dress. I hop on the bed and look at my derrière. Hmmmm? *Looks the same. Kinda lotta dimples despite the tan,* I start to think, but instantly cut myself off. No! Not a lot of cellulite for a woman who eats a dessert every night and is enjoying life. So instead I say: "You look good, baby!" then laugh. My face has a healthy color with pink cheeks and red lips. Even my tan toes look pretty with a cherry nail polish. But better than looking good, I *feel* good. The little bit of yoga every day has made me more flexible than I have been in years. Even the tension from my chronic back pain that started ten years ago from grading thousands of essays has dissipated. I am completely relaxed from head to toe, including everything in between. Yes. Everything in the universe seems right today.

I jump off the bed, grab my small purse, equipped with money, lipstick, and comb, and head for the door. For some reason, I decide to lock my door tonight. I walk carefully down the stairs and see the door of Kelly and David's room cracked open. The distinct smell of marijuana floats out, and I think to myself that they are not following

Rule Number Six. Naughty children. They are laughing uncontrollably as their voices are somewhat muted with what sounds like punk music in the background. I walk by quickly and after a shortcut, I'm on the main road in a few minutes. The road is bustling with people. It's a Friday night and almost all of the cafés are busy; some people are even spilling out onto the main road. I have heard that many people from Athens have beach houses here, and that's why it gets so busy on the weekends. I go to Café Royal, and Thanassis comes over immediately even though I can see that other people got here before me and have yet to be served.

"*Kalispera,* Thair!"

"*Kalispera,* Kyrie Thanassis." I try not to chitchat because I can see he's busy. I think Mr. Thanassis also feels a bit sorry for me, a woman traveling alone, staying alone, and even though I have told him I am perfectly happy, I know he doesn't believe it. How could he? He's been enculturated to believe that a woman must have a man by her side to be fulfilled.

After taking my order (although he already knows what I want), he returns with my *ekmek kadayifi* and a cold, Nescafe frappé. The people at the table beside me look a bit irritated because he has yet to even greet them. He puts down my dessert quickly, and a tear of sweat snakes down his temple. I watch him for a minute; instead it's me who feels bad for *him.* He must be well into his sixties. It doesn't seem right that anyone at that age should be a waiter or work so hard. He should be relaxing, retired, but he told me he made several poor business choices. Kyrie Thanassis said the best thing about his life is his three children, his five grandchildren, and his wife (I can't help but notice that he always lists his wife last). He has invited me on several occasions to his house for lunch, but I always decline. I know he likes me (and I'm sure my generous tips), but I just haven't had the urge to meet people.

I sit at my regular table by the street because it provides a great view of all the people walking by. During the day, I bring a book and sit at my other regular table, the one closer to the shore, but at night, I have to admit, it feels silly—even pretentious—to read. I still look a bit odd, sitting all by myself, but I really don't care. I finish my *ekmek* and just before I pay for the bill, two people plop down beside me, one on either side.

"Heeeeello, Prof!" I hear gregarious David say.

I can't help but laugh. "Hi, David. Hi, Kelly."

"So, what's Prof doing tonight?" David says while putting his finger in my plate and then licking off the fresh cream that I haven't finished.

"Not much. Just enjoying an excellent dessert called *ekmek kadayifi*. If you haven't tried it, you absolutely should." Kelly stares at me with unusually huge (surprisingly for being stoned) cerulean eyes. They are like a blue ocean slowly being drowned by the red sea. A pretty girl—tiny, tiny, with a big bobble head—she's wearing minuscule jean shorts and a halter top that reveals she is sans bra. I catch myself looking at her boobies, not in a sexual way, she's much too young, but they catch one's attention nevertheless. Even the old Greek lady, at the next table over, can't take her eyes off of Kelly's perky nipples, and I am quite sure she's not a closet lesbian or bisexual or curious (but then again, who knows?). I think this and laugh.

Then David and Kelly laugh too, though I am not sure why. (I have a nagging suspicion it's because of those happy herbs.)

Kelly squints and whines, "Pleeeese David, let's get one of those ecky mecky desserts. It sounds delish!"

"Whatever my girl wants she gets, right?"

Another round of laughter. I find myself laughing too; almost like they are my own private comedy act.

I call over Kyrie Thanassis and order one for them.

"Hey, Prof, shall we get a beer to toast our good luck of bumping into you?"

"I don't think *ekmek* really goes with beer. And I still have the wonderful sweet taste in my mouth."

"Oh, come on, Prof!"

I hesitate. "Okay." What? Did I just say *okay*?

"Wicked! A round for us all!"

The *ekmek* arrives and I imagine it tastes awful with the Heineken, but they wolf it down and order another one. Soon after, David orders another round of beer. Huge green bottles adorn the table, and I find myself refilling my glass as the cool yellow liquid travels much too easily down my throat. I can't remember the last time I had a beer let alone two.

After an hour of chatting about university and the other two islands they have been to, Corfu and Zakynthos, I see our table has six giant, green bottles on it. I can feel my head spinning, and I find myself giggling, stupidly, at whatever David is saying. Kelly is laughing too, and I can tell we are making a bit of a scene. I can also see that Kyrie Thanassis is uncomfortable. He comes over and says he can call one of his sons to take me home; both are taxi drivers. But I tease him and tell him I am a thirty-six-year-old woman and perfectly capable of taking care of myself. His look seems to disagree.

"Hey, Prof, let's go to a bar that's around the corner, what do you say?"

"Yes! Yes!" says Kelly though I am not sure why they would want the company of a woman almost twice their age.

"Come on, Prof, don't overthink it. One more drink. And there's a really good DJ with a small dance floor."

After a few beers, I am itching to move, and when he says there's a dance floor, that sells it for me. But I am still a bit surprised when I hear myself say, much too enthusiastically, "Okay. Let's go!"

In my slightly inebriated state, I am feeling rich, so I pick up the bill, their two *ekmeks* and our six Heinekens. (Maybe that's why they want my company? Don't overthink it, I tell myself. I want to treat, so I do.)

When we get to the bar, I can see a bunch of kids standing outside.

When I scrutinize the crowd a bit more, I can see a few people that look like Real Adults. People more my age. I even see a few men that look too old to be out and should be home with their families. Touché! I catch myself and edit my thoughts. I can't make assumptions about their lives because look at me: at a bar with two young, blonde, stoned Brits.

We find a vacant area at the bar and David orders us shots. I am not sure what's in them, but they are called *karpoosi* and I love watermelon. We slam the first ones down; it's really sweet and easy to swallow. By the time I look up, we have another three shots in front of us. Down the hatch they go. We are standing there when the bartender tells us that he is treating us to another round. A third, super sugary shot, my goodness, am in college again playing Quarters? Then I hear Bob Sinclair's "Love Generation" coming from the speakers and my feet *need* to move. I start making my way over to the dance floor, but suddenly David's hand pulls me, "Hey, Prof, what do you want to drink?"

"Nothing now, thanks."

"Aw, come on, Prof." He shines his cute smile.

"Um . . . okay, a beer," I say as I continue walking. Without a care in the world, I am in the middle of the dance floor swaying my body, and every so often, I remember to open my eyes. I am a bit drunk, and when the song ends, I feel like an inebriated silly woman when I notice some lewd stares from some older men. Feeling a bit embarrassed, I walk off the floor and think: *now* is the time to escape. Time to go home, Thair! But before I can let the thought of leaving process itself, there's Kelly tugging my wrist, saying, "Come on, Thair! Let's dance this one too! It's DJ Dero!" (Too? Was I not alone on the dance floor the first time?)

While techno beats blast through the stuffy room, I can feel her delicate hand still pulling me. Again, alcohol overpowers reason, and we are moving back towards the dance floor as she stumbles a few times. David passes me a Mythos and I take it, "Thanks" (I guess).

I am again swaying to the music, with a beer in my hand this time. Kelly is moving erratically, like a little bug on speed. She seems to have a disparate beat in her head. Her eyes are shut tight, and suddenly I'm more sober when I catch the lascivious older men (looking more closely, I see they are probably my age!) ogling my new, young friend. She is dancing with her back to them, shaking her tush uncontrollably, and from their barstools, they start saying rude things to her in Greek, then in broken English: *Hey, koukla, ella dance here with Babba.* Then they laugh insidiously. This is not fun anymore, and I want to leave so badly. Perverted men saying, "come dance with Daddy," my head spinning, my stomach nauseated, I hate what I am feeling.

Unexpectedly, David shows up, and gallantly puts himself between the men and his girl, winks at me and says, "I gotta keep my eye on Kelly. She just doesn't know how to handle her alcohol." Her alcohol and the pot and the *ekmek* all mixed together, I think. But I say nothing to this charming young man. Then, quite suddenly, I see Kelly hold her head with one hand while the other hand is on her mouth.

Oh shit. She's going to throw up. Now, suddenly completely sober, I pull her off the dance floor and lead her towards the women's restroom. A line of girls look at us angrily; I push past them and into a stall at the same moment a girl comes out of one. They don't know I speak Greek and are insulting the *poutana kori* and her *poutana mitera*! Geez, the whore daughter and the whore mother! I don't know whether I should laugh or cry; all I know is I need to take care of Kelly, so she doesn't vomit all over the Greek girls' pretty platform shoes.

I use one hand to keep her hair away from her face and with the other, I support her forehead, so it doesn't hit the toilet seat. Kelly lurches forward as puke comes spewing out. It splatters the side of the bowl, light yellow liquid dirtying her diaphanous top. The situation is surreal. Am I really here? Is this the life I imagined for myself? Instead of being married with kids, I am holding back a drunk girl's hair at a disco bar? The absurdity of it all makes me want to laugh. But I can't. I don't want to be here. God, I don't want to be here. As Kelly continues to dry heave, I picture myself with Jessica. Two blonde babes sit at our feet. Then I see Ravi, with two dark-haired kiddos now. Finally, a picture of James crosses my mind. Two old souls sitting close to a fireplace with a pile of books and paintings stacked beside us. I literally feel my body shiver. I shake just a bit, trying to erase these images. I am honestly glad that I didn't settle, and I am certainly happy that I don't have children, but I surely *do not* want this life either. I have been carving out a new life for myself that's mellow, but there are times when I want to drink, dance, or let loose; I just haven't figured out where that will be yet. One thing I know for sure: it's not here in this bar.

I wait until Kelly is all done, then I grab a wet paper towel and wipe off her face. She gets up, trips a bit, then looks at me with the eyes of a child: "Can we . . . (gulp) . . . go home?"

Home? I am not sure where home is for this young lass, but I will at least take her back to Kyria Akrivi's pension. When I leave the restroom, I scan the bar for David. The place is packed now, bodies pushing against each other. Finally, I see him in the corner, sitting with a few guys that look Greek. I walk over and ignore them all. Kelly looks like she will fall, so I let her sit down in an empty seat for a moment and then say in a mother-hen voice, "David, we need to go. We need to take Kelly back."

David doesn't look worried. He jumps to his feet with the oomph of the Energizer Bunny and says: "Amigos, we must go, but nice to meet you all. And . . . one more shot for Angelos Charisteas! May Greece once more win the European Cup!" With that, I see David and the guys at the table do a shot that looks lime green.

I stand there impatiently, ready to leave David with his drunk girlfriend, when one of the Greek guys looks at me and smiles warmly. He seems tall, though I can't be sure since he's sitting, with dark brown hair and huge, wolf-like teeth. He looks directly at me: "Hello," his English is heavy with a strong accent.

"*Yasou*," I say, even more irritated now. I respond in Greek, so he knows I am not just another drunk foreign woman. The man looks at me, a bit confused, then says, "Do you want a sit?"

"*Oxi, efharisto*," another laconic response from me. At this point, David is on his feet and has Kelly on hers too, asking me if I am ready, telling me I can stay if I want.

"No, I'm ready to go." Then a curt, polite, "*Yeisas,*" to the table of men, and I am already turning around when only one responds in Greek and the others begin to speak in what sounds like Spanish. The toothy gent who earlier asked me if I want a *sit* says *ciao*. Maybe he's not Greek after all, but I am too tired, buzzed, and annoyed to care, so I nod and just walk away.

The next morning, I sleep in until noon. I wake up groggy and feel a bit guilty for wasting my day but try to excuse myself. It was just one silly night. The room is so stuffy, Eeyore is stuck to me, I'm totally drenched, and my head is pounding. I see the yoga mat in the corner. That's where it will undoubtedly stay today. I didn't do anything wrong, so why do I feel this way? Guilty, trashy. What was I thinking getting drunk with those two kids? A hollow sensation fills my stomach. I *really* didn't do anything wrong, so again, I try to forgive myself, for what I am not sure.

While still in bed, I take off my PJ top and wipe down my chest. I throw it on the chair across the small room and look longingly at the bottle of water that is on the desk. I move my legs over to the side of the bed. Argggh. My head. Upper body on the bed, with my feet now touching the floor, I slowly lift my dead weight at a snail's pace, go to the Loutraki water bottle. I grab it and my toiletry bag and make my way back over to the bed. I set the water bottle down on the floor quickly, feeling like I will pass out, my skin cold and clammy. Lying down flat again, I close my eyes. I dare not open them. If I do, I know I will vomit. Suppress the urge. From some sort of instinct to not spin out of this world, I do open my eyes and see little circles swirling on the ceiling, a rainbow of colors. My stomach lurches; instead I swallow. For what feels like at least half an hour, I don't have the energy to sit up and drink the water though I know it will make all the difference. My dry mouth hungers for the liquid, but my body just can't respond.

Finally, I do sit up, place my fingers delicately around the bottle and take a small swig as the water travels down my throat. Then, I drink and drink and drink, almost a full liter in one shot. I open my bag, find a small bottle of Tylenol, pop two into my mouth; my head hits the pillow once more and I am out.

When I wake again, it's about 5:00 p.m. and I am starving, but I feel much better. I am still moving slowly as I shower, every movement taking great effort. In a bikini and sundress, I walk down the stairs and do not dare look in the direction of David and Kelly's room. Thankfully the door is shut, and there is no noise.

No one is in the kitchen and since I have already missed lunch, I go to a corner restaurant. No Greek eats at 5:00 p.m.; it's past lunch time and much too early for dinner, but I know several restaurants that stay open during siesta time to cater to the town's visitors.

The tables are all covered with checkered red and white table-cloths, and a papou-looking man sits on a chair, half asleep. I hear some noise in the kitchen and peek in. A round woman in her sixties brusquely asks if she can help me. In my most polite Greek, since my options are limited, I request some food: a Greek salad and a few *kalamakia*. The meat is out of the question, she mumbles; the grill is already turned off, but she has a homemade meatball dish. I pass on the home-cooked food (much too heavy for now) and ask for a *horiatiki* and some bread.

Within moments, the most magnificent salad is sitting on the table. Fresh crunchy cucumbers, white onion, and the largest, reddest tomatoes I think I have seen in years—almost as red as my own yiayia's. The entire salad is floating in olive oil and there is a slab of feta on top sprinkled with oregano. The bread is a bit stale, but after I saturate it with the olive oil, it's delicious. I am thoroughly enjoying my salad and just casually looking around when I see a group of guys walking on the other side of the street. I immediately recognize one of them as the seemingly-polite man from last night who had offered me a "sit." I can feel our eyes meet even though we are both wearing sunglasses. I quickly look down, pretending that I have not seen him, but it's too late. He says something to his buddies, they stop, sort of look over to where I am; then they are off, and he is crossing the street.

I am not in the mood to make small talk.

"*Hello*," he says with his deep Greek accent that puts all emphasis on the "H"—that hard "H" sound that comes from the epiglottis, the sound that English lacks, that "H" sound that makes one think the speaker is about to spit.

"*Hello*," he repeats.

"Oh . . . *Yasou*," I reply curtly.

"*How* are you today?" he asks.

"*Kala, efharisto*." I continue to speak in Greek, feeling that it gives me more credibility rather than being the single American woman on holiday. Maybe I have family here. Maybe I am not alone. I *love* being by myself, but I am getting tired of explaining myself. No, I am not married. No, I am not divorced. No, no kids. *Damn it, leave me alone!*

He chuckles then says, "Can I ask why you keep speaking to me in Greek? Do you think you know me from somewhere?" Though his accent is strong when he says this, I do notice his grammar is not bad.

I am a bit perplexed. He looks more than six feet (I can see now that he is, indeed, tall) with wide shoulders and a strong physique; the words *hale* and *hearty* come to mind. His hair is cut short, slicked back; chest hairs poke out of his T-shirt, and a cigarette floats in his hand. He must be Greek.

Finally, in English I say, "You aren't Greek?"

He smiles. "No," he says. "My name is Gabriel. I am from Peru."

Peru? I visualize a globe, spinning it with my mind's fingers. Stop. South America. But where exactly? I am starting to feel like the ignorant American because geography has never been my strong suit. And is this what Peruvians look like? My goodness, always teaching not to stereotype and listen to my thoughts! But the only pictures I have ever seen of Peruvians show them as short, dark people clad in brilliant colors surrounded by llamas.

He stands there in front of me, with perfect posture, ostentatious if not for his big smile; he leans over to an ashtray at the next table and puts out his smelly cigarette. I still haven't said anything, so he asks, "What is your name?"

I sit silently. Why should I tell him my name? I was having a nice lunch, and I really don't want to be disturbed. So, I say in one breath, "My name is Thair but, I'm sorry, I really just feel like being by myself."

It still comes out rude, but, frankly, I am happy to be discourteous on a day such as today.

I can see his eyes drop, and all too politely he states, "I am sorry. I did not mean to molest you."

Molest? I have to smile. I remember my two years of high school Spanish and the "Words Confused" lesson. Señora Rodriquez repeated over and over: "Do not say 'embarazada' for 'embarrassed' because embarazada in Spanish means *pregnant*, AND the Spanish verb 'molestar'—to bother someone—is not the same in English as 'molest,' because it means something entirely more serious in English."

He is walking away when I hear myself say, "Really, you are not *molesting* me; it's just that I am tired, and after last night, I just need some quiet time."

He still looks a bit rejected, but puts out his hand, "It is very nice to meet you . . . Thair. I will leave now."

Just when I think he is going to walk away, instead he says, "See this?" He points to the big mountain on his T-shirt. "If you can tell me what this is called, I will take you there one day."

Not that I want to go anywhere with this man, but shoot, what mountain range is it? It sure looks familiar. The majestic peak with all the stone formations around it. I cannot bring a name to mind and once more feel like an idiot. I like this guy less and less.

"I'm sorry. I guess I will never get to see it with you."

"It is okay. I will give you another chance later."

With that he bends down and steals a kiss from my cheek, "*Mucho gusto, pretty señorita.*" The words roll off his lips, sounding too sexy for me today.

Before I can say a word, he is off.

And I am disturbed.

After my swim, I return to my room, take a shower, put on a pair of shorts and a T-shirt and grab *Blonde*, a book I am enjoying immensely, a book that will allow me to escape. I walk out onto my concrete Eden-in-the-Sky and plop down on the swing. I prop the pillow on the arm rest, lay down with my feet hanging over on the other side and read for about fifteen minutes, but with the slight rocking of the swing, the gentle breeze, I can feel my eyes getting heavier. And heavier and heavier.

The sun has gone down, so it must be around nine-ish. I am drenched with sweat despite the fact that it is getting cool outside. I see the images flash in front of my eyes. My God, what a dream. It was so disturbing, so real that I can't help but relive it, frame by frame. My mother lying on a hospital bed, deathly pale and thin, her hands on top of the sheets, clasped together, fingers intertwined. She looked both peaceful and sad, as if that were possible. Jess, Ravi, James, and Yiayia were standing looking at her. And that guy, what was his name? Gabriel. He was in the corner, pointing to a blackboard with chalk in his hand. And then he wrote . . . yes . . . he wrote: "Machu Picchu." The mountain range with two peaks, the grass plains, the large stone walls. Of course! The famous Inca site in Peru. The picture that was on his T-shirt. In my dream, he smiled at me, but then my mother's bed started spinning, almost diabolically. My yiayia was wailing. And I began to vomit. What a strange and awful dream.

I wipe away the sweat that trickles down my temples, feeling dizzy and strangely sad. Today has not been a good day. I get dressed to go down to the corner kiosk to call my mama.

27

Sunday, July 24ᵗʰ

I woke with a lighter step today. I am out my door and in Kyria Akrivi's kitchen within minutes. As she makes me my morning coffee, I am tempted to ask about the Brits, whether they are still here, but I decide against it. They were a cute couple, and we did have a few good laughs despite the drama at the end of the night. Today I have no hard or icky feelings.

I am back in my room, doing Downward Dog and it feels so good. Deep breaths. Inhale. Exhale. My wrists crack when I lower myself to a plank; hovering for a few seconds, I'm happy to have gotten back my strength. Body and mind are aligned once more. I stretch for about ten minutes, then stop and sit in Half Lotus as I sip my coffee. When the top of my foot aches, I switch, then switch again. Coffee to the side, I do a few more Sun Salutations and after about fifty minutes, I am a sweaty mess. Instead of showering, I quickly slip on a bathing suit, grab my towel, my beach bag, head downstairs, cross the street, and walk onto the beach across from the pension. Kyria Akrivi always puts up a few umbrellas and lounge chairs for her guests (of course everyone uses them), but there is an implicit understanding that if a guest goes to the beach, the locals vacate. There is a French couple I met a few days ago lying on one set, and two Greek kids are happily playing on and under the other set; as soon as they see me, they flee.

I almost say: it's okay, you don't have to leave, but it's too late. They are already back in the water, and I do actually want a chair and an umbrella.

I set down my stuff on the chaise lounge and walk into the water without a second thought. It's absolutely refreshing. There are a few pebbles and some seaweed that don't bother me; it's not the sandy beach of the islands, but the water is still clear this time of the day, and I can see through to the bottom like a swimming pool. It's a simple beach. It feels friendly; not perfect, not dreamlike, just real. I swim for about half an hour, a bit of freestyle back and forth, some breaststroke, then tread water while looking up at the curtains of mountains that lie directly behind Kamena Vourla. It's an interesting village with lots of local Greeks, a lot of older people everywhere, but it's also a vibrant place with a plethora of teenagers and twenty-somethings; plenty of pubs and cafés line the streets, and these young people fill them at all hours of the day and night, playing backgammon, drinking frappés, smoking cigarettes.

From treading water, I start to scissor my legs until finally I'm spent. Time now to just relax, read my novel, soak up some sun. Mostly, I am so relieved to be over yesterday's awkward mood with that crazy dream and all.

Settling down on the chair, I close my eyes for a moment.

"Hello," I hear above me.

The sun is blinding, but instantly I know who it is—and my heart races. Damn it. How did he find me? I should be feeling stalked but through the glare, I see his warm smile and . . . well . . . he is simply very handsome. And seems genuine.

"Hi."

"Do you mind if I set down?"

"No, that's fine. How are you?" I ask as I set my book down and sit up a bit taller, so my tummy roll hopefully flattens out a bit.

"I am good. How are you?"

"I'm doing well, too." I respond.

"I did not see you last night at The Acropolis Bar." Then he adds, "I was hoping to see you there."

"No, I didn't go out. Actually, when I saw you and your friends that night, it was the first time I had been out to a bar here in Kamena Vourla."

"Really?" he sounds disbelieving.

"I actually came to Greece just to relax. And see a few sites. I just haven't gotten out of town yet because it's been so nice."

"How long have you been here?"

"A month plus eight days."

"More than a month!" another disbelieving tone. Then he continues with, "That's nice. That's very . . . very nice."

"What do you mean by 'very, very'?"

"I guess I am just tremendously tired and think it would be nice to stay in . . . one place for some time."

"Why are you *tremendously tired*?" (I try not to sound like I am teasing him, but I can't remember the last time I heard the words *tremendously* and *tired* put together.)

"Some friends and me traveled from Peru, where I live, of course, to Italia and spent twelve days in Napoli, Roma, Venezia, Firenze, and Milano." I love the way he uses the Italian names for these cities rather than bastardizing them with some English version. "Then we took the sheep to Kerkyra. We stay there for two days, magnificent, from there a bus to Athina. We saw Acropolis, of course, then we go to Mykonos, Ios, and Santotini, then back to Athina. My friend is a culture teacher . . . um . . . I think it's called social-something class. Anyway, he wants to see Delphi, so we go to Delphi, too, last week." When I hear Delphi, where I am planning to go, my interest is piqued, but I also start noticing more grammar issues when he speaks more quickly. "And now we are here for four days since this town is on the way back from Delphi—" *Just four days?* my heart begins asking—"to finally relax, then Skiathos, an island we heard is a big party, then back here for one night, and finally back to Athina and fly home again."

"My goodness, I can imagine how tired you are. I am tremendously tired just hearing it all! And all those Italian cities in just two weeks. Did you really get to *see* anything?"

"My friend, the teacher, had it all planned, and we just follow. But, yes, it was long, and I didn't like seeing Italia that way. I prefer to stay one week in Firenze and one week in Milano. Those are my favorite."

"Really? You liked Milan that much? I have never been to Italy, unfortunately, but I always imagined Rome and Venice would be my favorites."

"They are very nice, too, but in Roma my friend got his wallet pickpocket. That's how you say, right? And my other friend had his camera grabbed off him, so it left us with . . . how do you say? Alcohol taste in our mouth."

I laughed. I didn't mean to. "You mean a 'bad taste in your mouth'? What about Venice? I have always dreamed of going to Venice. I can just visualize the buildings that melt into the water. The photos I have seen are just simply breathtaking, just seems so romantic there . . . " I say while my mind travels with the countless images I have seen of that city.

"Yes, it is very beautiful, but there was too many people in July. So, *so* many people everywhere! I don't like too many people. It was not fun. I walk in the streets and there are people everywhere! We wait more than two hours in line just to enter the Palazzo Ducale. And then inside, more people. Oh my gosh!"

I find his expressions so sincere and adorable. "So, what did you like so much about Milano?" I decide now to add the "o."

"It was nice and clean, and," he smiles widely, "I love to shop. I spend hours in the Armani shop, the Hugo Boss shop. Of course, I don't buy anything . . . well one small thing," that he doesn't elaborate on, "but I imagine one day to come back with money and my wife and buy both of us something amazing."

Wife. Did he just mention a wife?

"So, you're married." I say as a matter of fact.

He laughs, "No! What I mean is *when* I marry, I will bring my wife."

I decide not to pursue the wife conversation and ask: "What else did you like about Milano?"

"There was this small street that looked like a 'V,' and at the end, were a few cafés. And a restaurant and they had a pizza that was yum-yum-so-good." As he says this, he licks his lips in a childlike way.

"What kind of pizza?"

"It called margarita."

"Isn't that without meat? Are you a vegetarian?"

This comment gets a loud roar of laughter from him.

"Me?" he says as he points to his chest, "NO WAY! I love meat. But the waiter said I should try, and I do not know it was no meat. But then it was just was SO good. After, I ate this pizza, NINE times while I was at Italia!" He is such an animated fellow that I find myself smiling inside.

There is a temporary pause in the conversation; then he asks me, "So what is your job, Thair?"

"I'm a teacher. Well, a community college professor."

His eyebrows lift.

I wonder if he's impressed or curious about the community part. I am not sure people around the world understand the concept of community college.

"I work at a school, too. At the American International School of Lima."

A teacher too? My heart flutters. Maybe he's a literature teacher and loves books as much as I do; maybe a language teacher and can help me work on my Spanish? Maybe a math teacher? Whatever subject, someone who will understand the wrath of grading student papers! I loved having that in common with Jessica, a lover but also a colleague who understood how challenging it is to be a teacher and that June, July, and August are necessary parts of the job. Most people think teachers are spoiled to have that much vacation, but what they don't realize is that those three months aren't a perk; they are essential. When a teacher is working, there is never a day off—weekends are for planning or grading. It's nine months of pure work. Ravi never understood this. He always demanded my time.

But why was I thinking all this? *Who cares if this Gabriel guy is a teacher*? He will soon leave Kamena Vourla, and I will never see him again.

"So what do you teach?" I decide to ask anyway.

He chuckles. "Oh, I am not a teacher. No way! I work in the office in the school. In the accounting area."

Perfect. Saved. Someone who certainly doesn't understand grading, someone who probably doesn't like to read. Someone certainly not for me.

"What about your friend? You said he was a teacher."

"Yeah, the two guys I travel with are teachers. Both American. I know them by playing soccer on Fridays at the school. Cool guys. Party guys."

Great. More partiers.

"So what about you? You like *to party*?" I say this with some sarcasm. I am so done with *partying*, especially after the other night.

He looks down sheepishly then says, "Actually, I really like to eat."
Eat?

"What I mean is I like to go and try restaurants, but my buddies like to spend their money on booze at night and museums at the day. To be honest, I really don't like museums. I prefer to see a few important things fast, then enjoy a nice restaurant. In Firenze, I took a bus alone to Toscana and had the most good lunch at a wine house."

"That sounds nice."

"Yeah, it was . . . okay-nice."

"Why just 'okay'?" I ask, wanting an explanation for his qualifier.

"Well," he chuckles again, "I guess I am too romantic. I was thinking it would be nice to share it with my wife."

Damn, that wife word again.

"Can I ask you a question: why do you keep referring to a wife? Couldn't you share it with, say, *someone special*?"

"Like a friend? No way!" he laughs.

"Not necessarily a friend, I mean . . . a romantic partner, but why does she have to be 'a wife'?"

He looks straight at me, swivels his legs to the side of the lounge chair, takes off his gold-rimmed Aviator glasses and says, somewhat seriously, but still with a smirk on his face. "I am not an easy guy. So when I meet a nice girl who I am sure, I will marry her, so she does not leave me."

My gosh, did he just say that? Should I laugh? Run?

I choose to laugh. "You're funny." I say.

"Thank you." He smiles, then his face drops, "But I am serious. I can be like the story, you know, Grumpy."

"What makes you 'grumpy'?"

"Lots of things. Loud kids in restaurants when parents don't make them polite. When someone says they call, and then don't. When I pay a lot for a movie and it is stupid. When I wake up and see my sister drink the juice that my mama made for me. You know, things like that."

"Wow! That sure is an interesting, comprehensive list. I guess it's good that you know what makes you grumpy." I say this so seriously that he feels the need to defend himself.

"But I am not always like that. I am more times happy. And even more happy when I am with someone I like." And then without reservation adds, "And I like you."

I find myself blushing and sweating, so I say, "I need to take a dip. Will you be here when I get back, or should we say good-bye now?"

"Good-bye? Why? Let's swim! I love the water." He jumps up, pulls off his T-Shirt (one without a mountain on it) and runs to the shore. "Come!"

I stand up a bit self-consciously, thinking about my soft thighs and dimpled derrière. I try to reprogram the negative body messages, but it's already too late. So, I stand up straight, choosing confidence over self-punishment; okay, Mr. Gabriel, here I come. I take off my sunglasses, put them back in their case, and strut into the water. Gabriel is already in the water splashing about. He's doing handstands and then starts swimming towards my direction, but before he reaches me, he takes a big breath and swims under me and blows bubbles. I find myself laughing.

When he resurfaces he says, "It's amazing, isn't it?

"Yes, it is."

"Can I tell you what I love about this place?"

"What?" I ask.

"I love the mountains are behind, like this place is closed to the world, the way you are in the water and feel like the mountains are right there." As he says this, he reaches his hand out, "Like you put your hand out and touch them." Then he sinks under the water, hand still straight up in the air.

When he resurfaces with a big smile, we begin to tread water, "So what brings you to Italy and Greece, specifically, I mean, from all the countries in the world?"

"It is always my dream to come to Greece; Italia was the choice of my friends. Most regular Peruvians can't afford Europe. The airline ticket only is about $2,000! But when my American friends say I can share the rooms with them, and they don't mind to pay a bit more, I save for this trip for more than a year. And it's been good." Suddenly serious, he adds, "But not perfect."

I decide not to question him.

We make our way to the water's edge, with the sea still up to our knees, continue to talk of other things. For some reason, I am no longer self-conscious in my too small, too old, sun-bleached bikini; instead, I am beyond comfortable in Gabriel's company.

Then I hear myself ask: "Why has your holiday not been perfect?" I imagine the sob story of a lost love, of an ex-girlfriend who he had imagined seeing these places with.

"Please, no laugh, I mean . . . don't laugh, okay?"

"Okay."

"So, I tell you that I save for this trip a long time, right? Well I save because it's my thirtieth birthday."

"Oh, happy birthday," I add genuinely.

"No," he smiles, "my birthday already pass, but *gracias*. It was when we were in Venezia. So I do reservations for a nice restaurant on the water for me and my two friends to bring in my birthday."

"*Bring in* your birthday? I'm sorry what does that mean?"

"Yes, in Peru we celebrate the night before until 12:00 a.m. then say *feliz cumpleaños* and *salud* the birthday person. So me and my friends go at 9:00 p.m. to have dinner. So pretty the place. With purple table clothes and candles. And the food. Yum-yum," he does his licking-lips thing again. I can't help but giggle. "So they eat fast, don't look at the view, only the girls that go by, and by 10:00 p.m. they have anxiety to leave. I buy one other round of drinks because I know this will keep them, so we drink until 11:00 p.m. but then they say, 'Man, come on! Let's go to the club!' I offer other round, but they want to leave. I have no choice, so I pay the bill. I offer since they will never eat in a restaurant like that. I use my credit card and we leave at 11:15 p.m. At 12 a.m. when it rings my thirtieth birthday, I am at a bar with three too tall Hungarian woman with too much red lipstick, and I don't understand what they say. My one friend is drunk trying to . . . you know . . . to get with one tall girl, and the other friend, I don't know. He is somewhere. So then, I think, *where is my wife?*"

The wife again. I am not sure what to think of his story. Is he one of those trapped between a boy's and a man's life? He seems like he wants to settle down. That's obvious, or is it really? Is he just one of those men or women who needs someone to feel complete? Gosh. I am so glad that I am not looking for a husband . . . or a wife . . . anymore.

"See, you don't say nothing? What you thinking, Thair?"

"Hmmm. A lot of things. I guess I was just thinking that I was in a similar place, like you are now, when I was in my early thirties."

"How old are you now?" blunt, to the point. I wonder about the etiquette of asking a woman her age in his country. But I respond, kind of enjoying the directness.

"I'm thirty-six."

"Really?" That look of unbelievability. Am I to think he finds me younger?

"I thought you were about thirty-four or thirty-five."

Is that a compliment? Slashing one or two years off a woman's age? My only thought is that I appreciate his honesty.

"So Thair, you have, what you say earlier, a *special someone?*"

"No, no, special someone."

"Good!" He exclaims. "Then, you will go to dinner with me tonight. Yes." He says this more as a statement than a question.

I find myself looking away, my eyes dropping to my toes, watching them wiggle under the water. I know I want to go. Everything in my heart tells me I would like to spend some more time with Gabriel, but shoot. It's that damn brain. My logos. He's only thirty years old. Here only one more day. Peruvian for god sake!

"Thair, why do you stop?" he says this with a high degree of sensitivity. There is a large part of me that is hesitant. He sounds too smooth. Almost like he's played this role before. Am I being a sucker for his good looks and love of food and shopping?

"Gabriel . . . I just don't know. I really don't think it's a good idea."

"Thair, why not a good idea? Tell me everything, what you

thinking?" Part of me thinks he's missing his helping verbs, and part of me thinks: don't go! Another part wants me to hear him say: it's just dinner, relax, it's *just* dinner. But instead he says, "You think it is not a good idea because you like me too much, after dinner we fall in love, and then you are sad, right?"

"Ha!" I say out loud. Cocky bastard! But could he be right? Am I afraid of a summer romance? A quick, deep affair that will inevitably come to an end?

"Ha!" he repeats, and smiles with those big, wide teeth. A good smile always defeats me. He continues: "Think, if we have a great dinner and fall in love, that will be excellent. If we have a bad dinner and don't fall in love, that will be good too since you live in America and me, in Peru."

"But the first one won't be good," I repeat, "and for the same reasons as the second scenario."

"Oh, Thair," he says, as his hairy chest heaves, "Please. Make me happy. I like you and you like me, right? Now let's eat some good food. You like to eat too, right?"

Me? I *love* to eat.

"I saw this restaurant called El Camino at the end of town. It has delicious Italian food. It is on the beach. I saw the food when Bob, Jake, and me were having a beer next door before going out last night."

Italian food in Greece? True, I have been living off of a diet of village salads and souvlakia, and pasta sounds like a nice change.

"Okay, Gabriel, but only if we go Dutch."

"Go Dutch? You have a Holland restaurant you want to try?"

I laugh again, so cute. "I mean, we'll pay for our own."

"Oh, Dutch is a saying?"

"Yes, it means we'll each pay for our own dinner."

"Oh, yes. I mean, no. Yes, I now understand expression. But you pay for your own? Why?"

"Why?" I find myself saying out loud what is in my head without editing my comments for diplomacy. "I want to be sensitive to your budget, and . . . let's just say, I like to take care of myself."

"You can take care every day when I am not here. Tonight, I pay, then next time . . . you pay! And we go to an even BETTER restaurant!" He laughs loudly.

I feign a smile. Hmmm? First time young hunk pays; next time old broad takes care of the more expensive bill? I don't like the sound of that either. Gosh, I'm so complicated.

Nonetheless, I hear myself say, "Fine," as if there will be a next time.

We walk out of the water and sit down again; he asks me if I mind if he lights a cigarette. I do mind, but I just nod my head and say: "Okay." We chat for about another hour; then it's time for lunch and I am ready to go. I've already spent too many hours with this guy, especially if I will be seeing him again tonight.

28

Monday, July 25th

It's about 10:00 a.m. and I just don't want to get up. I drank a lot of water last night, so I feel fine, except for an empty feeling in the pit of my stomach.

I watched Gabriel for about an hour last night, from my rooftop, after our date. When I first came in, after leaving Gabriel at the entrance of Kyria Akrivi's building, I washed my face, put on a long T-shirt to sleep in, but something was drawing me to go outside. I walked out onto my rooftop, and saw Gabriel still sitting on the lounge chair with his eyes wide open, hands behind his head, just staring up into the luminous sky. I was so tempted to go back down, but for the first time in my life, I did not want sex from a man I most definitely desired. Was I, Ms. Feminist, forward-thinking, gotta-break-down-years of enculturation in women's attitudes, acting in some traditional, subservient, Goody-Two-Shoes way? Did I think withholding sex from him would make him want me more? This is what my brain kept asking, but it was not that easy to rationalize. It just felt right *not* to sleep with him. Yes, I could still have wild nights and the occasional one-night stand, but my sex was sacred, and once in a while—like this certain full moon night in the little village of Kamena Vourla—I did want it to count for more than a romp in the sheets. I wanted to remember the kisses, the conversation, not a great orgasm.

The more I tried to analyze this strange shift of feelings, from liberalism to traditionalism, from freedom of body to appreciation of soul, the more I came back to the simple fact: it felt *right* to stop there.

As I lie here in bed, I can't stop thinking about him and our date last night, so I get up to find my faithful friend.

Thair's Story

Sunday, July 24th, 8 p.m.

Thair tried on the only nice thing she had brought: her favorite black slip dress. Simple, sophisticated, just below the knee, a dress that hugged her curves and was quite flattering, but it was also the same dress she was wearing the night Gabriel had first seen her, the night when she was slightly inebriated taking care of a young, drunk British girl. Would he remember? And did it even matter?

She put it on and looked in the mirror, but something just wasn't right. Taking it off she saw her jean skirt, also somewhat sophisticated because of the A-line cut, dark jean fabric, and just-above the knee length. Holding it up against her, she thought, no, it wasn't right either. Finally, she saw her faded 501 Levi's (the same brand she wore in high school) and put them on with a simple white Anne Klein V-neck T-shirt. This was it. It looked simple, relaxed. She slipped on a pair of platform espadrilles and large silver hoop earrings (she never got over this '80s fashion), and the outfit was complete.

Thair had told Gabriel that she would meet him at the restaurant. They had gone back and forth because he wanted to pick her up, but she flatly refused. When walking gaily through town, she heard "Thair! Thair!" Oh goodness, she thought, it was the Brits.

"Hey, Prof!" David said and wrapped his arms around Thair, giving her a big hug.

Kelly also hugged her in a tender, almost-daughterly way, "Thanks for the other night, and I'm sorry it was such a drag for you."

"No, it was fun." Thair could not believe she had just said that. Fun? Then she noticed that they both had their backpacks stuffed to the rim and that Kelly's, literally one half the size of her, sat beside a lamppost on the floor.

"So, Prof, we had a wicked time getting to know you, and if you are ever in London, do look us up. You can stay with us for free. We never did get to repay you for the other night."

"That's fine. It was nice getting to know you both, too." And she did mean it. They were happy souls, good people.

David handed her a piece of paper with what looked like two email addresses on it and said cheerfully, "Here's our contact info. Don't hesitate to write, okay?"

She grabbed the crumpled paper, and even though these two kind-hearted kids didn't really fit into her real world, she gave them her email address too. "So you two are off to Ios?"

"Actually, there's been a change of plans. Remember those Americans we met the other night? They say that Skiathos, an island that we can get to by taking a short ferry ride from the next town over, is raging cool, so we're heading there first, and we'll hook up with those guys tomorrow night."

Tomorrow night? Why was this information so surprisingly disheartening? Of course, Thair could care less about the

Americans, but Gabriel was going with them. 'Tomorrow night,' the words kept ringing in her ear. A fish was swimming in her gut. Where were these tumultuous emotions coming from? She had met this man less than forty-eight hours earlier, and he was already making her stomach do uncomfortable flips.

While Thair stood there thinking, David reached over and gave her another tight hug.

"Well, have a good time you two. David, take care of this precious lass. And not too many drinks for you, okay, Kelly?"

She batted her eyelashes, hugs were given all around again, and then they were gone. By tomorrow night, they would all be on a picturesque island, and she would be here with her beloved books, her yoga, her laptop, and her waiter, Kyrie Thanassis. Of course, she could go if she wanted to. She was sure Gabriel wouldn't mind; she had no lease, no obligations, but the more she thought about leaving her tranquil setting, the more she realized the last thing she wanted was to go *party*. Her crazy contemplations were really only about spending more time with Gabriel. With a physical shake, as if to shed her foolishness, she decided, no more thinking, just enjoy tonight.

After walking at a steady pace for about fifteen minutes, she reached the end of town and could see El Camino in the distance. The restaurant's structure was on the left side of the street, but like all cafés and restaurants on this main avenue, it had tables on the beach side. She imagined how tough it was for the waiters to have to cross the street for every order, especially on Friday and Saturday night when the road was bumper to bumper with cars. But they managed skillfully, trays adroitly balanced above their heads as they crossed, one hand extended telling the cars to stop as they practically walked right into the vehicles. But it seemed to work. Greek efficiency.

Her steps grew a little longer, her palms a bit sweatier, when she saw Gabriel at a table. She loved this feeling of excitement but feared it simultaneously because feelings of elation never lasted long for her.

Gabriel sat comfortably at the table looking out onto the water. He looked too handsome for words: a crisp white shirt with the sleeves rolled up, faded blue jeans and a black belt and shoes. He turned and saw her, standing up right away and kissing her on the cheek. Pulling out her chair, he waited until her bottom hit the seat, helped her with it, a final push, and she was close to the table.

"Hola, Thair."

"Hola, Gabriel," she responded practicing her Spanish.

"So how was your afternoon?"

"It was wonderful. Kyria Akrivi made stuffed tomatoes with ground beef and rice with oven-roasted potatoes on the side." As she said this, she could see him licking his lips like he always did when food was discussed. "Then I read a bit after lunch."

"Then what you did?"

"Well, I took a nap, then woke up and edited some stuff I had written."

"What is it that you write? A diary?"

A woman in her late thirties writing in a "diary," but it was more than a diary. These were her stories, reflections, a third-person quasi-memoir, maybe something to publish one day . . . and what better way to understand life? Foucault and Aristotle both agreed that writing is therapeutic.

But instead of explaining any of this to Gabriel, Thair simply responded with, "Yeah, I guess you could call it a diary."

"Tell me more about this diary." He seemed genuinely interested, so she continued.

"Well, the last time I was in Greece, five years ago, I started writing these stories. I started it with my yiayia's, my grandmother's, life and how she met my grandfather. I wrote it the way I remembered it, and then it's about my mom and dad. And now it's about me. Gosh, I am probably boring you—"

"No, please, please talk."

"Are you sure?" He nodded. "So the first two parts are done, now I'm finishing the part called *Thair's Story.*"

"So, what do you write in this diary?"

"Things about Zeus and how he's a really awful god," she said facetiously.

 Gabriel looked confused. "I do not understand."

"I'll explain some other time," Thair said though she never planned to tell him that horrific myth. But then added, "I guess I just write about life and relationships."

"It is about love?"

"Isn't everything?" Thair paused, then continued: "I want to finish it soon and release myself from this story because it's been haunting me for years. My goal is that by the end of the year, it will be done. Finished. *Finito.*"

The waiter had passed by several times not wanting to interrupt, but finally asked if they would like drinks to start. Gabriel handed Thair the wine list and asked if she wanted to share a bottle. Thair loved red wine, but on such a hot evening, Chardonnay would probably be better. But then Gabriel said, "We get red wine?"

"Sure. Why don't you choose?"

"Okay."

 He chose a red and when it was served, the bottle came to the table chilled. Normally Thair would hate red wine cold, but here it was perfect. Just perfect.

"Thair, you eat meat, yes?"

"Yes. In fact, the tenderloin with fettuccini looks yummy."

"No!" Gabriel says.

"No, I shouldn't order that?" She wondered if he didn't like the fact that it was the most expensive item on the menu.

Then another chuckle. "Oh no, I meant, that is what I will order, too. See Thair? We think the same."

"Should I get something different then, so we can share?" she asked.

"What about other meat dish with wine sauce and potatoes?" he responded.

"Sounds good to me. Rare?"

"That's not cooked a lot, right?" he replied.

"Yes."

"Good. I like it that way, too. And Thair, we must save space in our stomach because they have a dessert that is my favorite in all the world now. I got it to-go when I saw it that night."

Better than an *ekmek* she pondered. Couldn't be. "What is it?"

"It's called panna cotta. Have you ever try it before?"

"No, I don't think so."

"Okay, you will love it! You will see! Now *salud*!" The wine was poured, their hands were in the air when Gabriel said, "To pretty Thair, to *rica comida*, and . . . to us." While the word 'us' passed his lips, he winked.

Thair lifted her glass and said, "One more." Glasses were raised again, "And belated *feliz cumpleaños*, Gabriel!" she said with a horrible American accent.

Gabriel didn't drink. He just sat there and stared at her. His voice was low when he finally spoke, "Thair. *Gracias. . . gracias* for remembering. You are so nice. So, so nice." He just looked into her eyes without a single movement.

Thair did not expect Gabriel to be so moved. She almost regretted saying it, but the awkward silence finally passed with the clink of their glasses.

"So tell me about your family, Thair. You have a big family?"

"No, it's really just me and my mom. My mom has a sister that she loves dearly, but unfortunately, they hardly see each other since my aunt lives in London. She does visit San Diego once every few years."

"And you? Brothers? Sisters?"

"Nope. My mom lost a baby girl a few years after me in her fifth month of pregnancy. It would have been nice to have a sister, but it never happened. Just me and my mama."

"Your mother is Greek. I remember you say today at the beach."

"Yes, but for some reason, she has few ties to Greece, doesn't love it like I do." Then Thair told Gabriel all about her yiayia and the summers she spent on the island of Kythnos. She also, remarkably, told Gabriel about her father. Everything. How he left. How he called periodically. How she finally forgave him. How he continued to visit her a few times a year. That there were no ill feelings anymore, that it was what it was.

The more she talked, the better he listened; leaning in, eyebrows lifting, tilting his head, nodding, agreeing, sighing. It seemed he was hanging on her every word, laughing when needed, consoling eyes when she told him about her mother's cancer, a soft hand reaching across the table, holding hers tightly.

It might have been the two glasses of wine, but she could not stop talking. At one point, the expulsion of emotions was overwhelming; she needed to come up for air, "Gosh, I have been talking so much about myself. I'm sorry. Please. Tell me about your family. Do you have brothers? Sisters?"

A wide smile crossed his face. "Brothers? No, not one. But I wish. Sisters? Too many! Too many women in my life!" Then he laughed. Thair wondered what he meant by that, but he quickly explained. "I have four sisters, two grandmothers, and a mother who never leaves her *hijito* alone. And more tias than a guy should have. My dad is a quiet man. I guess he has to be with all this woman around!"

"So, are you the oldest, in the middle?"

"I am the baby of the family. I was an 'oooops,' I think you say in America. You know. Not planned. My one sister was married and gone when I born. My littlest sister was five when I born. She used to dress me up with dresses and put bows in my hair." He chuckled. No gender identity problem here, Thair thought. "I guess she believed I was her doll."

"How old were you when she did this to you?"

"For as long I can remember!" Another hearty laugh. "At least until I was seven. One day I answered the door with a . . . those feather things that wrap around your neck."

"A feather boa?"

"Yes, I think that is the name. One of those on me and with a pink skirt and heels. Oh, and some pink lip paint. My father heard from my mother what happened and came home and beat me with a belt and told my sisters to never do that again to me; otherwise they get the belt, too. I tried to tell him that I didn't mind, that we just playing, but he said I grow up to be a *maricon* if I didn't stop it." Thair assumed, rightly so, that *maricon* was a derogatory word like *faggot*.

"How silly, don't you think?" Gabriel continued. "A boy play-ing with dolls or dressing up will change and turn into a homo-sexual? I don't care what my dad say about this things. I have gay friends, you know. I just don't care."

Thair could not believe how open-minded this very mascu-line Latino man was. Was this for real? "So did your friends ever know that your sisters dressed you up?"

"Ha! Are you serious? No way! I would get my butt kicked if they know!" In between the laughter a moment of seriousness took over, "I just was making my sister happy. It was no big deal.

I think too many people make a big deal of things." Then he sat up tall, "I tell you something, but no laugh. Okay? When we were in Roma, I tell my buddies, I can't remember why, that my dad and I cuddle when I was in high school."

"Cuddle? What do you mean by cuddle?" Thair became skeptical.

"Yes, like lay on the bed together, watch TV, hug."

"Hug?"

"Thair! Now you are looking at me like Bob and Jake! That is what I mean! In my culture, you can be an adult and still show love to your parents. In America, you all think everything is weird."

"I'm sorry. I guess it does seem a bit strange to me. To imagine two grown men, lying on a bed together, *hugging*."

"But why? He is my father! I was telling you because I thought you would understand since you are Greek; Latinos are warm. But you are making big deal like them." His eyes dropped. Gabriel started eating and stopped talking. Was this a moment of grumpiness? As he started eating, his facial expression turned drawn and long.

Thair could see that this was not going well. Her culture had taught her that these things were weird, wrong (maybe even incestuous). For the first time in years, she felt like she was the student being pushed to be more open-minded. Was this how her students felt? Her comfort zones were being tested, and it was no fun. Maybe that's how her right-wing students felt when she pushed the lines of "normality" for them, talking about gay people being parents or wanting to get married legally.

Finally, after a few bites and too much silence, she apologized. "I'm sorry, Gabriel. I guess I do need to see this through another lens. I'm sorry. Really. Please, do tell me more about your sisters." She almost added: *Did Dad cuddle with them too*?

But decided against it since this entire discussion was challenging her limits of social behavior, and she really didn't want to continue to offend him.

Looking up from his food, his eyes were hesitant but genuine. "Okay."

Thair felt a tenderness like she never had before, almost as if she wanted to protect him. "I think it's lovely that your family is so close. Please, Gabriel, tell me more."

Thair leaned in, and with Gabriel's giant grin, it was clear that his mood had shifted, "So, my sisters, they are good woman. The oldest has two kids, so I am a *tio* and love it!" His face lit up, "They are tremendous kids. Her boy, Francisco, is seven and the girl, Daniela, is five. She is so cute," his eyes raised when he said their names and a new smile was born.

Thair's first thought was, *oh no, he loves kids.* And, then, what did he want from this life? And, most importantly, why was she allowing herself to think about such serious matters on what was, essentially, a first and final date?

Ensnared by her thoughts, she missed something he was saying, so trying to refocus: she heard: " . . . three sisters are professionals. Two are doctors. Mariela, the *pediatra*, is the one with the two kids. My other sister is a teacher at the school I work at and single, and the last one is an artist, so she lives everywhere. Right now, she is in New York with a Venezuelan boyfriend."

"It must be nice to have such a big family."

"It is, but it also makes it hard to find in love."

"Why?" She asked, thinking his English was sweet. "I would imagine you had a lot of women around your home, having four sisters and all their friends."

"Yes, but my sisters do not like anyone. And the ones they like. Well . . ." A snigger followed by: "They are not the kind of girls *I like*."

Thair didn't know what kind of girls he liked, but she left it at that.

———————

They continued to talk while eating dinner; the two of them ooohing and aaahing all through dinner as the succulent meat melted in their mouths. Thair shared her food, Gabriel shared his, and with every bite, every sip of wine, orgasmic sounds emerged from the two of them. She couldn't remember the last time she enjoyed a dinner so much, the food and company included.

As the evening progressed, more people emerged from their homes, and the sidewalk in front of the restaurant became busy with teenagers, couples, women with baby carriages, middle-aged men in groups, old people in hordes, all walking from one side of the town to the other. Lots of looky-loos eyed the food as they sauntered by, a few stopped for dinner, some went to the next café over for a frappé and dessert. Sometime during dinner, boisterous Bob and shifty Jake (Thair had already sized them up) stopped by with a couple of local girls to tell Gabriel where they would be and then to remind him, with a wink, not to stay out too late because the ship was leaving at 10:00 a.m. Thair heard those words, and reality hit her again, a lovely evening, but nothing more, one pleasant evening and then another good-bye.

The Americans told Gabriel and Thair that they should go to the bar later, but then again—wink—if they had better *things* to do, they would understand. Americans. She loved them. She was one of them after all. But they could be so crude and rude, often too forward, lacking tact. With every loaded comment to Gabriel, he pushed his sleeves up and looked away. It was obvious that he was uncomfortable, and his discomfort gave Thair comfort. She did not feel like this was a simple hook-up. She was special.

Even if it was for just a night.

⌒

After the Americans left, Gabriel and Thair continued their feast, with more bread served and more wine flowing, Thair's belly felt like it would explode, and then, the dessert arrived.

"Gabriel, if I eat another bite, I fear I will not live to see tomorrow."

"No rush. Let us enjoy our wine, but I want you to have one bite."

The conversation ensued while the dessert, a white mousse-looking pudding drizzled with some raspberry sauce, sat patiently on the table looking exquisite, even tempting. After a few minutes: "Ready?" Gabriel said this as he pierced the panna cotta with a fork and stuck a small bit out to her, fork lingering in front of her mouth. She opened wide as the soft texture hit her lips, then sat on her tongue, dissolving slowly, creamy and just sweet enough. She was in heaven. She thought there was no rival for her beloved *ekmek*, but now that she had met panna cotta, the war of desserts was established. It was obvious from the look on Thair's face that she loved the flavor, and because of her sheer delight, Gabriel was obviously pleased.

"See, this sweet is not from this world, like UFO, yes?"

"You're right. It is simply divine."

After a few quiet minutes, "How are you feeling?"

"Good, why?"

"I was wondering after dinner, if we take a walk? I really need to move this food," he said this as he put his hand on his belly, which did look a bit rounder under his white shirt. Thair had already unbuttoned her top jean button and would have to re-button it if they were going to stand up.

The check arrived, and without looking at it, he passed the man his Visa, and Thair did not try to argue. Taking her spoon and dipping it into the panna cotta again, Thair licked the utensil as Gabriel's eyes lit up again. "It is *so* good, isn't it?"

"It is indeed."

Thair could not believe that she was talking this much about a dessert with a man. Not even Jessica liked food that much. James and Ravi saw food as fuel. Dinners out were sparse, and they surely did not enjoy talking about the flavors of the dishes with endless enthusiasm. After another bite, he finished off the dessert, licked his lips happily while simultaneously rubbing his belly. His hand quickly moved to his face, covering his mouth as he suppressed a burp. If he wasn't that charming, Gabriel's boor-ish gestures might have resembled those of a pot-bellied King Frederick after finishing his fourteenth dessert.

"Are you ready?" he said while pushing his chair back.

"Yes, I think so." But as she got up, she realized in the almost three-hour sumptuous dinner, she hadn't gone to the bathroom.

"Actually, Gabriel, I need to go to the restroom. Can you wait here?"

"Sure." He pushed his chair in again, and she got to her wobbly feet, carefully crossing the street to the bathroom.

Half way to the other side, on impulse, she looked back and saw Gabriel staring at her. Not just looking, but staring, and when their eyes met, he didn't look away, but smiled openly.

Upon her return, he said, "Can I tell you something . . . a bit strong?"

"I am not sure. What do you mean?" Thair responded dubiously.

Another chuckle. "Actually . . . no, never mind, sorry. Let's just go."

Thair didn't push because she didn't know if she wanted to hear something *strong*. Whatever that meant.

As they started to walk through the town, past the cafés, past the bars, he took her hand ever so naturally, and she didn't resist. They continued to talk about different things from serious to frivolous topics. After about half an hour of walking and reaching the other side of the village, coming to the final small bar, he asked, "Would you like one more drink?"

"No, Gabriel. I don't think so. In fact, I should probably be getting back to my room." Why she said that she did not know.

"Your room? You must be joking! Will my Thair turn into a . . . *calabasa* . . . how do you say?"

"Pumpkin?"

"Yes, a pumpkin?"

"No, but it is already past midnight and—"

"I know, so why don't we go for a Nescafe instead?"

"Really, Gabriel, I don't think I could put another thing in my mouth."

"Okay, I have another idea. Let's go swimming!"

"You must be crazy!"

"No, it will be fun."

"I don't think so." She didn't want to sound boring, but she did not feel like swimming at 12:30 a.m. even if it was nice outside.

"Okay, I know, let us go to the beach; I take a dip and you see me, be sure I don't drown?"

"Oh, Gabriel. . ." She did not want the night to end, so Thair agreed with a slight revision. "I have a better idea. Let's just go sit on the lounge chairs for a bit, and then we'll say goodnight."

"Okay . . . but I take a dip later."

"Okay."

When they reached the chairs, they each sat down on one. Thair's hands dropped, again, so natural the separation, just like the connection. They both put their heads back, hands behind their heads, and looked up at the stars. It was another warm night, like most of the summer nights in Greece, unlike California, where the nights were always chilly and sitting on the beach was always more painful than romantic.

Gabriel then opened his legs, letting them drop to either side of the chair. He grabbed Thair's hand and ever so gently murmured, "Come, Thair. Come sit with me." Without a moment's hesitation, she stood up, a bit woozy, and sat cautiously on the chair with him. Her back was against his chest, her tailbone touching the most intimate part of him, her head resting on his shoulder. His arms were wrapped around her, holding her around the waist. She could feel his warm breath behind her, as he stroked his cheek on her soft, shiny hair. It would have been so easy at that moment to take him back to her room, screw Rule Number Five, but something inside wouldn't let her. Tonight, it would stop here. Her body yearned for him, her loins did, her pulsing legs, her warmth did, but her heart spoke differently.

Even logic, her brain, the one who drove her nuts, agreed this time: Thair tonight should end here. Following her heart had been easy; it was logos that always demanded more, instructing (deceiving?) her: women and men are equal. Independent women can have numerous sexual partners without feeling guilty. Women can have sex without love; sex can be a physical act without emotional baggage; women could be like men in this respect. This is what her mind and education had taught her. Long gone were the days when women were considered sluts because they wanted non-committal sex. Rationally, Thair believed this, but emotionally, she didn't. And tonight, even her brain agreed: Thair, wait. And since the two, heart and mind, were in alignment, she did not dare disagree.

She swiveled around, after about twenty minutes of quiet,

feet on the ground, halfway facing him and said, "Gabriel, I need to say goodnight."

"Do you want me to come to your room with you?" So blunt, so forward.

Her answer would remain: "No, not tonight."

"Okay," he said a bit disappointed, then looked at her as she sat sideways and whispered in her ear, "but I do want a goodnight kiss." Before she could respond, his lips were on hers and the kissing started. It was long and deep and wet. She felt her head spinning. She opened her eyes to catch her breath, but he kept on kissing her. She could not say how long they kissed for, minutes? Half hour? Finally, she pulled away though his kisses grew more desperate.

"You really must go?" he pleaded.

"Yes."

"Are you sure?"

"Yes, Gabriel. Please don't—"

"When will I see you again?"

"I don't know, Gabriel. I think this should be good-bye."

"No!" he sounded almost like a petulant child. "I return from Skiathos, then I have one day. I will be back here to see you. Okay?"

She didn't know if she believed him, but said, "Sure."

The next kiss she gave him was quick, afraid to get sucked in again; jumping to her feet, she stood above him.

"I will walk you to where you stay."

"No, it's right there," she said, pointing to a building across the street. "I'll be fine."

"Please."

"Gabriel, how about you just sit here and watch me walk away? You will see me enter the gate. Okay? I'll be fine." As Thair spoke these last words, she imagined this to be the end of her story, the end of a great love that was never realized. He was her Orpheus and she was Eurydice. But unlike Orpheus, he would be the one following with his eyes, and she would be the one who would not look back because if she did, he would be pulled back into the darkness forever, and this would undeniably be the end of their love story. She would not look back at Gabriel, not allow him to be pulled back into the depths of Hades. If there was a chance in a zillion for this to work, she would not be the one at fault.

"Just watch me walk away, okay?" she said again, a bit more teasingly though it sounded much too quixotic. Though he was not happy with her idea and wanted to cross the street and at least walk her to the building's entrance, she remained adamant, so he had to finally agree. He stood up beside her and held her close, very close. Thair could feel him press into her and was ready to say, *Screw it! Come back to my room*, when other words escaped her lips: "It was really nice meeting you, Gabriel. I do hope to see you in a few days. But, if not, do take care. And I hope you find . . . 'your wife' one day." The way she said this might have sounded facetious, but it was, in fact, genuine.

The next words out of his mouth were the most ridiculous of the entire night.

"Maybe I already have."

29

I need to get moving; otherwise I am tempted to go back to bed. I turn off my computer, but his face will not leave my mind. Gabriel is so different, yet so many things about him feel familiar. He is a little of all my loves rolled into one. He is a bit of James: compassionate, sensitive, someone who I could talk to for hours; a bit of Ravi: incredibly sexy, with a magnetism that was visceral and could not be qualified or quantified; and then he is a bit of my Jessica. The one who seemed to have it all. Would the one thing that kept me from Jessica be the one thing that Gabriel and I would also not agree upon? Would Gabriel tell me that he desired to have children one day? As I think about all this, I suddenly feel absolutely ridiculous. I just met this man for god sake! He is too young, lives too far away, and I will probably never see him again, so why am I torturing myself with these thoughts?

But last night, sitting quietly on a chair just to the side of a large plant, I watched him from my balcony while these and other tumultuous thoughts penetrated my mind. Finally, after about half an hour on the chaise lounge, he jumped up with an explosion of energy, took off his shirt, his jeans, was down to some tighty-whities, and took his dip after all. He swam a bit then just lay there, floating on his back in the water. With the light of the almost-full moon, I could see him perfectly. When he got out, I could tell he was a bit chilled. I was so tempted to go down and give him a towel, warm him with my embrace. At one point, *I* could feel him shiver. He put on his shirt, his jeans, looked up at the building, and I almost thought he saw me, but the blankness in his expression made me realize he hadn't. He shook his head, and then he was off. I couldn't sleep, so I spent hours remembering, reliving every detail of the night. Sleep finally claimed me in the early hours of the morning.

After eating a few crackers, drinking more water, looking at my yoga mat and thinking *forget it,* I move slowly to take a shower. My shoulders feel heavy, a Herculean numbness paradoxically weighs me down.

Gabriel and I had such fascinating conversation and intense chemistry, but a part of me wishes I had never met him. He seems too good to be true. I hate this feeling because it never lasts, yet something about him is so different. I finally force myself to stop this internal haranguing because my heart and mind are close to driving me insane. Just a month ago, I was telling Rick and my mom how satisfied I was with my life. Is today just a temporary low? How can I recapture my feelings of tranquility, confidence, security, and peace?

The room feels so small, and I need some fresh air. Despite my dark demeanor, it's another gorgeous day. I am lying on the chaise lounge, and the beach is still packed since people don't start leaving for lunch until around 2:00 p.m. I am trying to read my book but have read the same paragraph five times and still don't know what it says. I stop and watch the kids play for a bit. They're laughing. Happy.

I run my fingers over the white plastic chair. Just last night I was sitting on this chair with . . . words, an expression . . . crosses my mind that I dare not think. Push those words away. Those are the words of Zeus. Of fairy tales. Not of real life.

But I keep hearing those words that he said to me, those final words. Why would he say such a thing? Why would I even consider believing him? Did I not rebuff marriage a few times because it wasn't *right*? So why did his words make my insides feel like mush? When picturing his face, why do I smile when all I feel is disturbed?

I decide that it's time to get out of town, time to go see some of the sites that I had intended to visit. I go to the rental place at the end of town, and after some haggling, get myself a car. I want to leave tomorrow, but they don't have any economical vehicles until Wednesday. After waiting this long, I know one more day won't make a difference; I'm anxious and want to leave, need to move. But I will wait since there's no choice. The car is booked, and I leave in two days. I won't be here when Gabriel gets back to town; that is, even if he comes back this way. No more star-crossed lovers, I will go back to creating my own fun.

It's only 6:00 p.m. and I am still antsy. I go to the OTE to call my mom. I have been trying for more than a week, but I just keep getting the answering machine. Last time we spoke, gosh weeks ago now, she said she had a bad summer cold and was weak, so we spoke very briefly. I tend to worry, and almost four weeks without speaking normally would have concerned me, but the wonders of technology. I set her up with a Yahoo account and gave her my old computer, and since I have been getting emails from her every few days, I know there is no reason for alarm. She tells me she has been busy, gardening, running around with friends. It is a bit strange though, no concern or worry, just wishes for me to have a fabulous time.

On the other end, I hear the phone ringing and ringing, and when it's just her voice on the answering machine again, I let out a deep sigh. I really wanted to talk to her today.

I decide to take a walk into town and go have a frappé and an *ekmek*. Kyrie Thanassis is happy to see me. We chat for a bit as he tells me his eldest daughter, the nubile twenty-year-old from the picture in his wallet, just got engaged, so I congratulate him. When the dessert comes, I poke at it with my fork, one bite, then the fork rests on the plate, another poke. I know it's good but has nothing on the panna cotta from last night, and I really have no appetite, so I leave most of it on the plate to the chagrin of Kyrie Thanassis who comes over after a while, asking me if there is a problem. I explain that my stomach is not well, and he tells me I should not drink the coffee then either. He sounds more like a father than a waiter, but I do agree, so I leave both and ask him to just bring me some sparkling water. He doesn't want to charge me, but I leave him the money for the entire bill and a good tip, too. My book sits miserably on the table. Riffling through some pages, staring at the words, I tap my feet against the table; needing to move, I get up and start walking. I make my way to the end of town and turn around, stopping aimlessly at shops, looking at nothing really.

I am back in my room around 9:00 p.m. I have this aching sense of aloneness that sits heavy in my gut. I'm also starving, so I ravenously inhale the two souvlakis with gyros I got at the tavern around the corner from my building. I drink almost a full liter of water in one long swig, then sit on my swing for a bit, so tired but not sleepy, wanting to go to bed, wanting to lose this feeling. I stare straight ahead for about an hour, then go into my tiny room and do something unorthodox for me. I search my suitcase for the small icon my mother gave me when I was a teenager, a wooden one with a picture of Mary holding a baby Jesus, the one that accompanies me when I travel, the one I carry more out of habit than for any religious purpose. After finding it, I place it under my pillow, and in a mantra-like fashion, I start repeating a Greek prayer I had also learned when I was young. Curling up in fetal position with the cool sheet resting on my body, I finally fall asleep.

It's another day and I wake with a fresh disposition. I jump out of bed, splash my face with water, go downstairs, get my coffee, and, back in my room, stretch out my yoga mat. I start with Warrior poses today, then Tree. I stand; my hands are in prayer pose and my leg is making a "less than" symbol with my foot resting comfortably on my inner thigh. I decide to close my eyes. I wobble for a bit but am able to hold it for a few minutes, such a different pose with the eyes closed. Normally when I close my eyes in Tree, I fall over immediately, but not today. I switch legs, a small wiggle, and then I'm motionless like a statue; even with my eyes closed, I am balanced. After Tree, I move into Dancer, again, feeling so centered that all the poses take minimal effort and fill me with a sense of tranquility. After a few standing poses, I sit on the ground, cross my legs and roll out my shoulders. I stop, take a few sips of coffee, close my eyes, and just listen to the sounds. Everything sounds enchanting. I hear birds, the splashing of the sea, even the children's voices that echo up to my rooftop sound pleasant. While I have my eyes closed, an image of Gabriel places itself before my dropped eyelids. His face once more brings a smile to mine. I imagine him licking his lips after eating the panna cotta, and I almost giggle. I think about changing my road trip plans and staying a few extra days here, maybe I would get to see him again.

After my morning yoga, I walk over to the car rental place. I confirm my reservation for the following day, but ask, just ask, about the availability for the following week. The man says it's all set, but next week they will have cars, too. If I want to change the date, it won't be a problem.

I just stand there.

The man asks me again if I still want the car tomorrow, or if I want to change the date. "No, thank you. I am leaving tomorrow," my lips say.

Everything in me tells me I must not change the date. My heart and mind "hands" are connected, shaking in agreement: *don't change your plans.* So, I get maps and the gentleman shows me all the main roads, where it's nice to stop, where I can stay the night. I plan to drive to Meteora, spend the day there, then continue to a quaint town of Metsovo, stay two nights there, just relax and take a few day-hikes. The drive back will take me about four hours without stopping. I think that I'll come back to Kamena Vourla, maybe for a few nights, then leave again to see Delphi since they are not in the same direction. I thank the man and tell him I will be by tomorrow morning early, 7:15 a.m., to get the car. He tells me he can bring the car to me tonight and drop off the keys as Kyria Akrivi is his mom's cousin's aunt, so he knows where I am staying. "Perfect," I reply, thinking I won't have to cart my suitcase around town at some ungodly hour. It's all set, and I am excited, happy again.

This last week has certainly been tumultuous, from the adventure with the Brits to a fabulous first date. Meeting Gabriel was interesting, to say the least, but I am glad to be back to normal, thankful for the time we shared, but also resigned to leave it at that: one enchanting evening. I am grounded and light.

I eat an early lunch with Kyria Akrivi and her three new guests from Australia. A bit of small talk, then I head back to my room. I'm full and debate taking a nap, but decide to go down to the beach, read a bit, maybe nap on the chaise lounge.

It's really hot, so I have the umbrella all the way open and am wearing a big Audrey Hepburn-style black hat and large sunglasses. My knees are bent with my book propped up on my thighs. I am finally enjoying *Blonde* again despite my heavy eyes. I can feel them slowly falling, so I set my book down and travel to my peaceful dream world.

Thair's Story

Her eyes felt too heavy to open them, but she sensed someone had come and sat down beside her. She felt the presence stand up, bend over, and a kiss was placed on her cheek. Slowly opening her eyes, she saw everything blurry. Her hat hung low in her face, and her glasses were stained with sweat. The sun was bright, but even though she could not see him, his voice was unmistakable.

"Hello, pretty Thair."

Suddenly jolted, wide-awake, she took off her hat, peeled off her glasses, wiped the sweat from her eyes, and saw a figure that she wanted to recognize, but (because he was not supposed to be there) was not sure if what she saw was real.

So he spoke again, "How are you?"

"Gabriel?"

"Yes, Thair, it's me!" he said enthusiastically.

"What are you doing here?"

"I am back," he said proudly with his shoulders pulled back as if on a podium receiving the gold medal.

"But you are not supposed to be back for a few days."

"I know. But I should never left. I was on the boat the next day after our dinner, thinking: Gabriel, why did you leave? So as soon as I got there, I was so mad. I tried to leave the same night, but there were no more sheeps, so I stayed, and then this morning, first sheep back, I'm here!" Again, he said this with chest inflated. "I will see my friends in a few days in Athina, at the airport."

Then he added with a huge, confident smile: "I am yours until Saturday!"

Yours until Saturday?

Was this guy crazy? His reaction did seem young, totally pre-
sumptuous, but Thair actually loved his spontaneity.

She squinted her eyes, her brows furrowed, a zillion thoughts
zipping through her mind.

"Thair, say something." His eyes appeared a bit worried, the
life sucked out of them. "Are you not happy to see me?"

Thair eventually allowed a grin to appear, thinking this
couldn't be happening. "Of course, I am happy to see you . . . but
. . ."

Sad, bulldog eyes again, "Why you say 'but'?"

"Well, I had planned to leave Kamena Vourla for a few days.
I rented a car and am leaving tomorrow for Meteora. Remember
the monasteries I told you about that—"

Cutting her off, he exclaimed: "That is great! I go with you!"

Her stomach rolled, his excitement contagious. Did she, all
of a sudden, have a road trip partner? And was this what she
really wanted?

But before she could share his pleasure, he became deathly
serious. "Thair, you leave tomorrow for how many days?"

"For about three or four."

Silence. Dark, gloomy eyes, "You were not going to be *here*
when I get back! Why, Thair?"

Gosh, this was getting more complicated than she wanted.
This sudden change of mood, was this the grumpy side that he
had warned her about? Or did he have due cause to be upset?
How would she have felt if the tables were turned?

"Gabriel, I wasn't trying to *not* be here." (She didn't feel
like she was lying. She had really made these decisions on
gut instincts.) "I just felt listless. I couldn't imagine just sitting
around hoping you would come back. And then if you did, then
what? One more day together and you are off to Peru, and I go
back to the US? And now that you mention it, maybe it is not

such a great idea that you go with me. I don't know if we should spend more time together."

He bent down on the sand, eye level with her, thinking, just looking, then through the silence he asked: "Thair, why are you scared?"

"Gabriel, I am *not* afraid. I just don't see a future for us, and I don't think I am interested in a short summer fling just to feel heartbroken at the end of it all."

A half smile. "So, I can break your heart?" He always knew how to hold on to the words that counted.

Without wanting to, she was smiling. "Yes . . . I guess . . . you may be able to." Why was she allowing him to see her this vulnerable?

"I like that." A large grin.

"You like that you can, possibly, break my heart? That's not very nice."

"Thair, *I am* nice! And I am happy because I can only break your heart if you give it to me. And since you say I . . . maybe . . . can break it, then maybe one day, I will have it." Then he added, "But I will not break it. You will see."

Shakespeare's eloquence, his words often left Thair speechless, and now, these simple phrases, strangely enough, had the same powerful effect. She lay there lost for words. But he still had words, simple clear words: "So, I am happy. I forgive you for wanting to leave early. Now, trust me and let us have fun, yes?"

"Gabriel . . . shoot . . . okay. But I will go on record saying that this is probably not a good idea for either of us."

"You have a record?" This time, she knew he was teasing. "Really, Thair, do not say that. You do not know. Look, let us go see these mountain churches and then, if we like each other still, you come and see the mountain on my T-shirt." His face glowed and then he winked, "Remember, you still have one more chance to tell me the name."

"I already know the name," she replied matter-of-factly.

"Really?" He looked skeptical. "Then tell me what it is called."

"Hmmm . . . I don't know if I want to use my chance now. You said you would take me there if I could tell you the name. But what if I don't want to go there?" she said mischievously.

"Okay, no more talk of my Peruvian mountain. We go see Greek mountains together. At the end of our trip, if you still like me, you tell me the name; then we go to my mountain together. And you meet my four sisters. And my mother. *And* all my tias." He laughed out loud as did she.

They shook hands playfully. Then he leaned over and gave her a long kiss. It tasted like a mix of Marlboros and mints. She could not hold it together, every orifice in her body stimulated.

"Let's swim!" she said as she jumped to her feet and instantly got a head rush, "I need to cool off." He laughed, knowing entirely too well what she meant.

30

I reread the words I wrote last night, put my laptop in its pink case, and skip down the stairs. The Fiat Panda is parked in front of Kyria Akrivi's building. When I reach the bottom floor, I see Gabriel waiting for me by the car with a reasonably-sized suitcase. He greets me with a gentle peck on the lips while Kyria Akrivi stands at the door, watching without one ounce of discretion.

"You ready?"

"Yes!" Gabriel looks entirely too alert for 7:02 a.m. Last night was mellow, a souvlaki dinner, a few beers, a few kisses, more conversation, but I shooed him away before midnight because I wanted to pack, write, and sleep well.

"Would you like me to drive? Gabriel asks.

"I can start off, and then we switch later. How does that sound?"

"Great!" more enthusiasm. "I was wondering . . . I know it will be early for shops to be open, but I *h*eard that the first big city, Lamia, *h*as some good sales. Can we *h*ave a coffee and walk and look at windows for just a few minutes?"

All those hard, epiglottal "Hs," I must be smitten because everything out of Gabriel comes across as endearing.

"So, what you think?"

Shopping. Sure. A man after my own heart. "That sounds fine, but maybe no more than half hour because it will take us more than three hours to get to Meteora." I annoy myself with my teacherly tone.

Lamia is a city of concrete. It is far too hot at 7:45 a.m., and few souls stir in the town's center. We find, by smell, a bakery; fresh bread and croissants have just come out of the oven. I get a Nutella-filled croissant and Gabriel gets two *tyropitas,* a croissant with ham and cheese, two small boxes of juice, and a coffee. I have no idea where he will put all that food, but in less than fifteen minutes he devours it all, looking like a happy Boy Scout, rubbing his tummy and licking his lips. I take my hand, bring it to his face, and wipe away a piece of phyllo dough that is on his cheek as he gazes at me. There are no words, just comfort. We see a few shops, but nothing catches my attention, and Gabriel doesn't seem impressed either, so we are on our way again by 8:15 a.m.

When we get back in the car, he is wearing a devilish grin and staring at me.

"Why are you looking at me like that?"

He doesn't say anything but unzips his backpack and says: "I have a present for you." *A present?* I have never been good at receiving presents though I love to give them. What could it be? I am curious and, admittedly, excited. Looking all too pleased, he hands me a homemade CD. I open it and, on the cover, handwritten, it says: "For my Pretty Thair. To Mountains of Amor." I read the inscription again. "Mountains of Amor." He may be an accountant, but his way with words is poetic in its own right.

I lean over and give him a kiss. "When did you make this?"

"When I get stuck on Skiathos, I went to a music shop and asked them to burn a CD for me with my favorite Spanish songs . . . they couldn't find all I wanted, but . . . the ones they find, they remind me of you. I also added one that will be a surprise." He looks almost shy, but very pleased.

My insides are warm and disgustingly emotional. I can't help but remember the last time someone put music together for me, probably eighth grade when my first boyfriend made a cassette tape with my favorite songs. Now, more than twenty years later, a CD has been burned for me, and I am actually touched by the gesture.

I had asked for a car with a CD player, so I slide it in, and the first song starts. It is a dance song with an upbeat rhythm. I can kind of make out the words to the refrain, so I ask him about the lyrics.

"The song is called 'No Puedo Olvidarme de Ti.' It says something like: *I can't forget about you,*" he replies.

"Oh." I have no other comment. I just continue to listen intently. Another song plays that sounds entirely too sad, and as it blares from the speakers, he sings along in his sexy voice.

"What did she say there?"

He laughs. "I really like all these songs, but not all are perfect, yes?"

"So . . .?"

"The guy says to his lover that he must leave because his wife desires him back."

"Great." I respond.

"Thair, you so funny. I like the man's voice, the words are inadequate, but . . . sssssh . . . now listen, this one is important. This song I put because *you* will sing it to *me* one day," he says with a smirk while turning up the volume. I think I recognize the voice. I remember hearing this song somewhere . . . was it at Emily's wedding? I stop thinking and just listen to the words:

You are my heart, you are my soul,
take my heart with your hand,
hold it tight, don't let it go . . .

The words enter me. I don't think I have ever spoken such words to anyone and now, in this car, Gabriel thinks that I will be capable of saying these things to him one day. *Take my heart with your hand.* My brain-hand and heart-hand are reaching for each other . . . my God . . . are they connecting?

After the song is over, he places his hand on mine, and speaks quietly, "It is beautiful, don't you think?"

I have to agree. Tears well up in my eyes, tears for what I am not sure. I look away in embarrassment, feeling entirely too sentimental. I see a rest stop and pull over.

"Thair, are you okay? You look sad."

"Sad? No, I am fine!" Then wanting to break the all-too-serious moment, I shriek, "I just really need to pee!" I stop the engine and ask, "How about you?"

"No, I am good."

After a quick stop, back in the car, he asks me if I want to hear more of the CD. "Of course," I say hoping there are no more love songs because I'm already on the ledge. I hear more Spanish songs that are fun, dance rhythms, a pause, another song is about to start; he gets really excited and turns up the volume: "Now listen! This is also for you!"

I, honestly, don't think I can handle another song of adoration, but when I hear the first two beats, a huge smile pulls at my cheeks.

"You remembered!" I squeal.

"Of course! You said this was one of your favorite songs, makes you want to dance!" As "You Shook Me All Night Long" blasts out of the speakers, I put the volume on full, so now it's a bit scratchy, but still sounds much too good. I let loose with reckless abandon, scream-singing in my horrible voice while I bounce up and down in the seat. Gabriel looks over at me and chuckles. He, too, knows most of the words, so we are singing together and simply having a jolly time. After the song is over, he turns down the volume, "Thair, you are funny. You make me laugh."

"You make me laugh, too, Gabriel."

The next song makes him a bit serious again, "This one is for you

. . . but this is a song *I* will sing to you one day." It's in Spanish, but I don't ask him to translate. I do catch the words "quiero" and "amor" and "corazon." Words I do remember from my two years of Spanish. He asks me if he should translate; I tell him it's not necessary, so he just sings to me with his hand gently leaning on my leg. A part of me is curious, but I want to keep it real since the last few hours have been a bit too fairy tale-ish.

From the map and the directions the man at the rental place gave me, I can see we are on the long stretch of road between the cities of Lamia and Karditsa. The road reminds me of the road to Oz, flatlands lie to the left and right of the two-lane highway. One car whizzes by dangerously close, but then there isn't another car in sight for miles. I can see the long, straight stretch of road before me, about 40 km of pavement placed between wide-open fields, a very different landscape than one I have ever experienced in Greece.

"It is amazing," Gabriel says as he looks out the window.

"Yes, it is."

The CD ends, and we drive in a comfortable silence for a while. I tell him we should be reaching a small town called Karditsa in a bit, but because I am afraid that the monasteries may close early, we should make it a quick stop. At the *cafenio*, old men are playing backgammon and smoking cigarettes. The women are at a different table and one gets up and helps us. We get Nescafe frappés to-go and are back on our way.

After two more hours of driving we decide to stop for lunch in Trikala, a small city where cafés are right on a river, just half hour from Kalabaka, the town at the foot of Meteora. In the restaurant, a group of teenagers smoking packs and packs of cigarettes makes the ambiance stuffy and hard to breathe. I become crankier when Gabriel finishes his food and lights a cigarette. He hasn't asked to smoke in the car, but here he lights up as soon he is done eating. I am still poking at my food, deciding to be done when another puff of smoke reaches me.

"Gabriel, I need to go stand outside, okay? The smoke is killing me."

"I am sorry. I will put it out."

"No, it's okay. There is so much smoke in here anyway." While saying this, I look over at the table of teenagers. I can't help but wonder how all these people still continue to smoke. Do they not read the reports? Hear the ads? I don't like that Gabriel smokes, but it's strange—it should be a total turn off since I hate the smell of cigarettes, but on his kisses it is, I hate to admit, sexy. I haven't kissed a smoker since high school, and it kind of turns me on. Of course, I will not tell him any of this because I would by no means want to be in a long-term relationship with a smoker for a number of reasons that hugely outweigh my twisted perversity of tobacco-on-the-tongue stimulation.

"No, no, I put it out. I pay, you go get fresh air, okay?"

"Thanks."

I let him pay without argument since I filled up the car with gas. I figured the trip should be split, so it's his turn. I have not clarified any of the details with him, who will pay for what, where we will stay, how we will sleep; I guess I am just *going with the flow*, a first for my Type-A, hyper-organized personality.

Back in the car, Gabriel is driving, and I am getting really excited because I can see these enormous rocks coming out of the earth in all directions.

Even with the windows rolled all the way down, I can smell the cigarette on Gabriel. He leans over and kisses me tenderly on the cheek. My most private part pulsates. Everything about him has changed my previous rules of attraction: I used to be repulsed by chest hair; it irritated me to hear grammar errors; food in someone's teeth grossed me out; mood swings were a definite red light. Why is it that everything about him is tender, sexy, interesting—acceptable? Is this what it's like to be truly taken?

From the majestic scene outside, my eyes are again on Gabriel, staring at him while he's driving. Physically he is not as perfect as I thought. His nose is actually quite large, and his eyes, I remembered them being green, indeed bright and vibrant, but they are brown, as brown as brown can be. From his face, I make my way down his neck, not too long or too short, but I notice a bit of a double chin may be forming, too many croissants and chips. I love his strong shoulders, his chest; my eyes drop lower: I see a little Buddha belly starting to form. At only thirty, he will definitely have to be careful if he doesn't want a beer, or should I say, food belly. He knows I am staring at him, so he finally asks, "What are you thinking, Thair?"

The typical answer would be "nothing" but instead I reply, "I was just thinking that you are not as perfect as I remember from our first date." I don't say this to demean or dominate him; I just feel free to say everything that is on my mind, bad, good, regardless. But after I say it, I do realize it sounds not-so-nice.

Before I retract or at least clarify, he replies with certitude, "Thair, you are not perfect neither." I don't know if I like his response (or his grammar) but touché! Then he continues, "See, I am not perfect. You not. For sure! *Je je*. And that is why we are perfect for each other!" Another unrestrained laugh.

Why is it that Gabriel finds everything so simple, so clear? I have almost decided to teasingly pursue the subject regarding my lack of perfection when I see a sign that says "Kalabaka," and, in the distance, something that looks like a birdhouse perched on top of a mountain. I have read about Meteora over the years: how monasteries, built over six centuries ago, are suspended on the tops of mountains; how monks found refuge in these cavernous churches; how St. Athanasius, founder of the first one, had been carried up by an eagle (when, in fact, he probably scaled the wall and then lifted the long ladder when he got to the top); and how these Orthodox havens had been built to escape the chaos of the world.

As we drive up the sinuous roads to these monasteries in the sky,

I can't find words to express how I am feeling. We walk silently up the long path to The Great Meteoron and reach an entrance. Since I am wearing a jean skirt that reaches just above my knee, I have to wrap a long, somewhat scratchy piece of material around me; Gabriel, wearing shorts, has no problem entering the monasteries. I guess women's knees are more tempting than men's (humph!), but it is not a battle that I am willing to fight today. Some women in tank tops have to wrap their shoulders with the same pieces of material, but in my T-shirt with short sleeves, I am free to go in.

Once we are in the monastery, it does not look much different than a typical Greek church, and because of that fact alone, I find myself retreating to a position of subservience. No wonder people feel God in these churches. The saints that hang on the walls, enclosed in great silver frames and placed in every corner of the room, demand respect; elaborate frescoes decorate the roof, and the scent of *livani* lingers in the air, so powerful I can taste it. All this makes me humble, feeling closer to my God than I ever have before. I stop and face an elaborate gold podium with a large wooden cross behind it. Jesus is pinned to it, his head tilted with drops of blood on his temples, red paint on brown wood.

Gabriel and I walk around the church together, but when I sit down on a bench across from this Jesus, Gabriel decides he will wait outside. As a faithful Catholic, he says that he can admire these places, but has a hard time praying here since it is not his church. When he tells me this, I find my cheeks burning because it is all about one God anyway, right? Comments like Gabriel's are what turned me off to organized religion as a teenager.

On the drive here, Gabriel and I talked quite a bit about God, religion, faith. I told him that it wasn't until my early thirties when one day, for no explainable reason, I finally succumbed to a higher power. After many years of questioning, then criticizing hypocritical religious people who were less than Godly, pushing them in corners, quizzing their beliefs, their actions, their knowledge, I decided: no more trying to figure out God. I would just try to *feel* God—I wouldn't look for Him anymore. No more looking for anyone or anything.

Gabriel told me he was raised to just believe, and for the most part this worked well. So like him, now I just accept the good along with the bad and the ugly. And we both agreed that since there is nothing rational about God, and we cannot prove—nor disprove—that God exists, we choose to believe that there is something greater than us out there. As for a heaven, I told him, the verdict is still out, and I still tended to believe "dust to dust," and that nasty, little, crawly critters will eat away at my remains.

He laughed when I told him this, his voice still clear in my head, *Thair, tell me more about 'your' God.* As he drove, I continued, emphasizing the same possessive pronoun: "*My* God, having been raised Greek Orthodox, with images of Jesus and Mary hanging in every corner of our house, gave me a reason to try to do good. *Be* good. Jesus is the one I call to when I want to give thanks or ask for something. He is the one I visualize, but I also understand that the image, or archetype, will be different for people depending on where they were born and the religion of their culture or family." *Yes, with this, I agree*, he said. "Lately, I find myself buying sculptures of the jolly, fat Buddha." I commented. "Seeing his round little belly in my home makes me happy, and the fact that he is on a shelf, right beside an icon of the Virgin Mary, sits very well with me, not sacrilegious one bit. If there is a heaven, then Buddha and Jesus are probably buddies. Maybe they even share a beer from time to time. Or a glass of wine." *Je je*, he chuckled, *sounds good to me, but don't know word, 'sacri . . . something?'*

He made me want to talk more, so I explained, "For me, it came down to one thing: strive to do good in your life. And if prayer and icons help you in the process, then go for it. Hang a cross around your neck, wear a bracelet with saints on it, attach an angel to your dashboard, or stick a bumper sticker on your car. You aren't hurt-ing anyone. So why does it have to be so complicated?" *It doesn't*, he replied. *Nothing has to be complicated.*

But as I sit here, I recognize that religion may not be complicated anymore for me, but it makes me overly emotional. On the bench, in that monastery, shrouded in Frankincense, tears begin dropping down my cheeks. I have always felt overwhelmed in churches, not only in Greek Orthodox ones, but also in any church for that matter. I am not sure why, but the way a church fills my chest is so overpower-ing that I stay away from them because I cannot take that ride too often for fear of losing my rational self.

Gabriel comes in after a few minutes and lights a few candles. I watch him cross himself in a perfunctory manner. I am happy I found my religion, my own way to be spiritual, so comments like Gabriel's of not wanting to "pray" in "my" church, though still a bit irksome, are not deal breakers.

Before we leave the Great Meteoron, we go into its gift store, and I buy a bracelet that was (supposedly) made by a monk and has a prayer for its every knot. About thirty knots make up one bracelet. Then I see hundreds of these in baskets around the shop, and think, *the monks must be busy*, and pick up a few more as souvenirs for friends.

Before we leave Meteora, we decide to visit two more monaster-ies: Varlaam and St. Stephen, and in each one, I get weepy-eyed, and in each one, Gabriel carefully crosses himself. It's a somber afternoon, not much conversation; in the last monastery, Gabriel enters and sits on the bench with me and closes his eyes. Later I ask him about this, since he had said earlier that he doesn't pray in "other" churches, but he says he felt like coming in and being with me. I decide not to push the issue because it was nice to have him on the hard pew with me, holding my hand.

It is past 3:30 p.m. and the monasteries are closing; we are both tired, and we still need to drive for about an hour to reach Metsovo.

We walk back to the car, Gabriel opening my door and moving automatically into the driver's seat again.

Back on the road, I stretch my feet straight out onto the dashboard, bend my toes back and forth, open them up wide, good yogi toes, then peer out the window, watch as the large pine trees zip by, and feel like we are now in a California forest and no longer in Greece. Comfort has so quickly entered my life again. I'm so at home with Gabriel it is eerie, as if his presence is like an old friend, a long-time lover. There is a sense of excitement and newness, undoubtedly, but there is also a sense of utter calm.

We twist down a few roads, then come to a pass where I see hundreds of red-roofed houses covering a mountain side. Driving into the village, I see signs that say "Fresh Cheeze," "Room for Rent," "Good Café." We follow the tight roads, looking for the central square, and stop to ask directions from an elderly woman. The woman is dressed in an ornate outfit: polished black shoes, white hose, a silk dress with thick velvet at the bottom, a silver filigree belt, a gold-embroidered pattern at her neckline, and a long braid that falls over her shoulder as she leans into the car to speak to us. She has a strange Greek accent but is very happy to help us, and after our brief conversation, opens her hand.

After an awkward silence, the woman is still leaning into the car, so I grab my wallet and give her a euro. She smiles but doesn't move. A bit annoyed, I give her one more. Whatever happened to good ol' Greek hospitality? Gabriel is amused by the entire scene and pokes fun at my irritation.

After one more turn, we see the center square and the big sign on the side of a building: Hotel Galaxias. The man at the car place in Kamena Vourla recommended it; he said he has a daughter who lived in this village for a year while doing her teaching internship. He was surprised I had heard about Metsovo because this place is not necessarily a common stop for tourists, especially in the summer when there is little to do except drink homemade wine, eat good food, and take long walks.

Gabriel and I have yet to discuss the sleeping situation. I only booked one room, and he has not asked about our accommodations. Finally, when we pull up, he says most comfortably, "We stay in one room, yes? . . . Or no?"

He is giving me the opportunity to say "no," but I just lift my shoulders and let them drop. He smiles, "Thair, that means yes or no?"

"I don't know."

"If we stay in same room, you don't have to worry."

"Worry about what?" I ask.

"You know. 'Funny business' . . . is that not what they say in America?" I smile. He's been watching too much TV. He continues: "We spend the night doing nothing. Or we do what you want." With the last part, he adds a smirk. Yeah right, I think, in one room and nothing will happen, doesn't seem likely.

I imagine the evening, a bit of homemade wine in the garden restaurant; I'll be feeling a bit tipsy, very sexual, and having Gabriel in my room just to cuddle seems unrealistic. I would just be fooling myself. This is my moment of truth—either make him spend the seventy-eight euros on another room, and after a delightful evening, sleep separately, *or* throw caution into the mountainside and share a room with him. In the quiet of the car, I listen intently. What is my mind saying? Where is my heart?

They both are dead to the world.

Wake up! Help! What do I say? No response. No nagging brain, cautioning me that I may be making a mistake, no liberal mind, telling me it's not a big deal; no passionate heart pushing me into his arms. No gut reaction. All are deathly silent. Am I eager to stay with this man? Or would I prefer to be apart? All of a sudden, I am plagued with images of a Polaroid camera. Date or photo? Her choices had seemed so simple and yet, that one choice changed my mother's entire life. Could this choice also determine my future? Sex or separation?

Suddenly, the answer is clear.

No one or nothing has to persuade me. I know what I want. I want Gabriel.

I look at him, sitting patiently, letting me process this moment; he never seems to be in a rush, and I appreciate it more than he will ever know.

"Gabriel . . . "

"Yes, Thair?"

"I think we should just stay together . . . I mean, in one room."

"Okay, but you know that—"

Taking my finger, I put it on his lips, "Shhhhhh. Please. Let's not talk. No plans. Let's just enjoy ourselves." Then I laugh, "See? I'm learning. Isn't that what you told me the first night?"

"Yes." He murmurs as he gazes into my eyes, not looking away. It's too much, like the stuff of trashy novels. But I kind of like it.

"Hey, let's get moving!" I open the door with alacrity while Gabriel pops the trunk open and gets our suitcases. I try to help, but he always wants to carry everything, and I find myself sitting back, allowing this chivalrous man to take over as he struggles up the stairs with two suitcases and a backpack while I follow with a light gait, my purse flung over my shoulder.

The hotel is exactly the way the man described, rustic with an entirely wooden interior and a welcoming receptionist. She checks us in quickly and gives us a large gold key hanging on a piece of rope connected to a large piece of wood with a nondescript shape that says: "Room 8." We walk up the steps and easily open the door; the room has one double-sized bed (just as I had expected), a brick fireplace (that doesn't seem to work), a small wooden desk, a painting of an Alps setting, and a diminutive window. It's chilly here, hard to believe that it's the middle of summer in Greece. I always thought the entire country was sweltering during the months of July, August, and September. But not so. The cool air came through the car window right after a large tunnel that we passed through, and once more hit us when we stepped out of the car, and now, in this room, it feels nippy.

"Gabriel! Close the window, please!"

"Okay, but first come here. Look."

I walk over to the window and I wonder where I am. Below there is a traffic circle, and in the middle, a raised hill with benches to one side. Some old people in black sit on the bench and don't seem to be talking. They look ancient: snowy hair, frail limbs with rotund stomachs; the men, with moustaches that twist up on the ends, lean on canes. Across the center, the view is wide open all the way to the other side, and green mountains, miles away, make me feel like I am in Switzerland (even though I have never been there, this is what I imagine it is like). Simply breathtaking.

"Wow. It's beautiful." I swallow all the images then look over at Gabriel.

"Yes. It is. And you are beautiful. You have a tremendous smile." He takes my chin in *Casablanca* fashion and tilts it up. I stand on my toes because I am wearing tennis shoes and can't easily reach him. We begin to kiss, and before I know it we are lying on the bed, still kissing. I feel a chill and shiver from head to toe, so Gabriel gets up and closes the window that is still open. I also get up and pull back the duvet that looks like one a grandma would make, take off my tennis shoes, slip off my jeans and crawl under the covers. Gabriel doesn't say anything. He takes off his shirt, his jeans, and lies under the covers with me. We kiss again as we are facing each other; then he pulls me on top of him. I sit up for a moment, straddle him, taking off my top and bra. He smiles, outwardly, awkwardly, sits up, and kisses me where his lips reach. Falling to the bed once more, we disrobe completely, and then it happens slowly, yet quickly, every part of my body woven with his. There are moments of anxious hunger and moments of quiet connection.

Afterward, I feel strangely whole. It wasn't supposed to happen right away, but it did. And it felt right. We lie there for hours; I think we must have fallen asleep at one point because when we wake, I am starving. He's snoring deeply: it's not a sexy sound but endearing nevertheless. I get up slowly, take a shower with scalding hot water, and when I emerge, my chest is bright red. Gabriel's snoring is so loud that he sounds like a freight train. I decide to dress before waking him because I need food more than sex at this moment and fear that waking him with only a towel on will lead to another round of lovemaking.

In my tennies, jeans, T-shirt, and fleece jacket, I move him gently, "Gabriel, Gabriel." Nothing. With a final, strong push, "Gabriel!" I startle him awake.

"What?" he sits up, alert, worried. Not a very romantic waking on my part, but it seemed the only way.

"Sorry, I was trying to wake you up . . ."

"Oh," he plops back down on the pillow, opens one eye, looks over at me, "Thair, what are you doing? Why are you dressed?"

"Gabriel, I'm starving. Do you want to get up, so we can get something to eat?'

"Okay, but one kiss first."

This looks dangerous, but I go over and give him a quick peck. He chuckles, then hops up and walks to the bathroom. No modesty. I guess most men, regardless of size or weight, are much more comfortable than women with their naked bodies. "I will take a shower fast. Do you want to wait here or maybe go to the lobby and have a drink?"

I have read online about the local wine and can picture a glass. "Yeah, that sounds like a good idea. I'll go down. So I'll see you in a bit?"

"Yes, okay, Thair. I'll be about twenty minutes." He winks and then closes the bathroom door.

"Okay, Gabriel. I'm leaving the key here on the desk, okay?"

An echo from the bathroom, "*Si.*"

Down in the lobby, I see a small bar that is connected to the restaurant. There are about fifteen wooden tables in the restaurant with white linen tablecloths. I see an older, hirsute man behind the bar, a man so hairy he seems to be covered with fur. He's got a dense beard and looks like Dionysus reincarnate—the more stereotypical version, not the sensuous, androgynous youth. He approaches me with a huge grin, and I can see more hair coming out of his nose and ears. His jolly, festive attitude is contagious as he holds up a jug of wine. I inquire about it, so he brings me a glass. He pours me the house red, and it is very good, a bit sweeter than I normally like, but it goes down smoothly and has a wonderful berry aftertaste. While I am sipping my wine, I hear my stomach growl; I think the man hears it too because he disappears and returns with a basket of warm bread. I devour it, one piece after the other. Christo, the waiter, serves me another glass of wine without asking, and I happily accept. After another sip of this second glass of wine, Gabriel comes down the stairs wearing a black Columbia jacket and a huge grin.

"*Hola, amor,*" he says.

I am a bit taken aback with the word "amor" as I know it means love, but since it is not my language, I don't know the seriousness of it, so I simply respond, "*Hola,* Gabriel."

He pulls up a barstool, takes a sip of my wine, asking if it's okay with just his eyes, and then digs into the bread basket. His actions, at times, are a bit barbaric, not delicate at all. I find myself watching him, thinking a million thoughts a minute. Making love was intense; at one point I felt like he would eat me alive, Cronus in my bed. Then he would transform into Yogi Bear, a bit oafish, silly; heavy paws, but a tender heart. The one emotion I could not shake was the feeling of completeness. When we finished making love, I felt round.

"Mmmm good bread."

"Yeah, I know. I had three pieces already."

"Three pieces! Do you have space for dinner now?'

"For sure!" I say while flipping through the menu. I see some dishes that I don't recognize, so I ask for a suggestion from the waiter. He tells us that they have excellent *kontosouvli* and *kokoretsi*; I know Gabriel will probably love these rotisserie meat dishes, so I order one of each. The few times I had *kokoretsi*, I ate it greedily until I found out it's lamb meat wrapped in caul fat and yards of cleaned intestines. I have to admit, I still love the taste, but I just don't eat it the same way I used to.

We get a carafe of the house wine and sit outside. It's bit cool, but there is a heat lamp, and the view is spectacular. The hotel's restaurant is on a balcony overlooking a small park that is utterly green with colorful wild flowers. From our table we can see the village's center, and there's the bench with what looks like the same old people from hours ago. Happily glued in the same spot, none of them are talking, just sitting calmly, with not a worry in the world.

In the far distance, the mountains create a majestic lining to the horizon. It is quickly getting dark and cold, but the wine is keeping us warm. Gabriel takes the seat beside me, so although I can't look at him, his shoulder and leg are touching mine. As we eat, the discussion centers around the flavors that we are ingesting, the fabulous wine, and other light topics. After a very tranquil dinner, he leans back and puts his arm around my shoulder and asks a loaded question, "So Thair, why are you not married?" It should be a simple enough question and yet, for me, it's so entirely complicated.

Sitting here in this romantic village of Metsovo, beside a man to whom I have just made love, my independence is being tested once more. It is an uphill battle that I am quickly losing because hypocritical feelings are emerging. I find myself regressing to that girl of the Zeus stories, picturing myself marrying this stranger—not just living with this man, but *marrying* him. For the first time, I feel like I could dive headlong into this relationship and give *everything* of myself. And it scares the shit out of me. I should be so happy right now; instead I find myself overanalyzing, and the outcome seems less than rosy.

Despite my caustic thoughts, my intuition tells me something else. Maybe he is feeling the same way. We seem to have a lot in common. I can't remember ever laughing this much with a lover. He seems to have this incredible ease, a simplicity that is infectious. When we are together, there is no place I would rather be.

Doubt, as well as love, fills my heart as I sit next to this man and he calmly waits for a response, but I am not sure how to answer his question. I don't feel like telling him all about James or Ravi, or Jessica for that matter, but I know that the day will come to explain who I *really am* if I am ever to have anything serious with Gabriel. But is tonight the night to really put it all on the table? And how will he take my sexuality? Even though he seems open-minded and has gay friends, will he really understand since he is from a conservative country with conservative values?

"Thair, do you not want to answer?"

"It's not that, Gabriel. It's just that, for me, it is such a layered question, and I am not sure you want to hear the whole story."

"Yes, I want to hear! Please tell me. I am serious. We have all night. I want to *know* you."

He says this with such intensity that a floodgate of emotions, ideologies, and histories pour out onto our table. Just like our first dinner in Kamena Vourla, the more I talk, the better he listens. He questions my philosophies, agrees with some of my ideas, and disagrees openly with others. At one point, we start talking about kids, and I wonder if this will be our splitting core value. We go back and forth, and after an hour of intense kid-talk, the conversation does not get any lighter.

He asks about past loves but says he does not want details; that is, until I mention the name "Jessica."

"A *woman*, Thair?"

"Yes." A part of me is defensive, wondering how he will take this new information, if this will change how he feels about me, how he *sees* me.

"So was this . . . how you say . . . an experiment part of your life?"

I can feel the hairs rise on my arms, blood rushing to my face, sometimes I think being a lesbian would be easier, how to explain that gender does not matter without sounding like a nymphomaniac?

"Gabriel, it was *not* an experiment, and I am not a lesbian. Obviously. But I am not entirely . . . *straight* either." He's staring at me, waiting for more, so I continue: "I found out, quite surprisingly actually, that I could be attracted to women, in a very real and intimate way. And that it is not wrong. Or bad. Or weird. Or strange. I loved Jessica very much and when we separated, I was open to finding love with another woman, or if I loved a man, then that would be okay, too."

"So you love me?"

He listens closely and holds on to words that I say. I am giving him, with language, more than I want to.

"Gabriel, I did not say that. I just said I would be *open*. Anyway, how long have we known each other? Five days? Two, maybe three dates? How could I possibly *love* you?"

"Because love can happen right away . . . what they say . . . 'love at first vision'?"

"You mean 'love at first sight.' How about '*infatuation* at first sight'? Love is much more complicated."

"Thair, you make it complicated." He states calmly.

I am fidgeting now, the wine hitting my head. I ask if we can change topics. Instead, he says with a slight smile, he wants to know more about Jessica. And this makes me irritated, the alcohol making me too antagonistic. I begin firing a salvo of questions at him: "Why do you not want to hear more about James? More about Ravi? Why Jessica? Because she is a woman? And why should that matter? Why are you so interested?" But he is. And I know why.

I do recognize that, seemingly from the beginning of time, men have been fascinated to see women together (maybe because women's bodies are so beautiful?). I can just imagine two cavewomen bonding, falling into the throes of love, and a caveman sitting in the corner, whacking off while watching them. Ugly thoughts penetrate my mind, and the longer I sit here, the worse I feel.

Because I loved a woman, but also love men, what does he think? Sometimes I wish my sexuality were more defined, but it isn't. I could be anywhere on the Kinsey scale on any given day depending on with whom I am interacting. And if I am single. How can I make him understand that monogamy with the right person is more important to me than the sex of my partner?

"Gabriel. I really don't want to talk anymore about this. At least not tonight."

"Okay." I can tell from his voice that he is a bit perturbed that I cut the conversation.

"Do you want to take a walk?"

"Yes."

We gulp down an entire bottle of water, he pays for the bill, and we get up ever so slowly, moving through a thickness in the air. From the restaurant, we walk down some stairs and around the plaza. Some stores are still open, so we go in and browse, lots of souvenirs, lots of products made from wood. I see a key chain of a heart made with wood that says "Metsovo." I buy it while Gabriel watches.

"What you buy?"

"A key chain."

"Can I see?"

"Of course," I say and pull it out of the brown bag.

"It's nice," he says while he caresses it with his index finger and thumb.

I look at it: "Yes, it is nice, isn't it? It's for my mama; she collects key chains."

"Thair, it would make me happy to meet your mama."

I don't say anything, just put the key chain back in the bag, grab Gabriel's hand as we exit the shop, and walk around the center. It's cold, so I hold onto him tighter and with each embrace, security envelops me, and despite the very uncomfortable dinner conversation, I'm uncomfortably secure because no one should feel this safe in such an unstable world.

"Shall we go back?" I say.

"Are you cold?"

"Yes, what about you?"

"Yes. A bit," he responds.

We walk in silence and he stops for a moment. "Look at the moon."

I look up and it's a full moon, a dark sky, a few stars but a full moon is hanging treacherously close to us.

"Thair?"

"Yes?"

"Can I tell you something . . . strong?"

This time I am ready to hear a *strong* comment. Looking into Gabriel's eyes, I sense my life unfolding. Despite everything I shared tonight—not wanting kids, having loved a woman, all my philosophies—does he still want to pursue this 'thing' we have?

"Okay, tell me something *strong*."

"You have a great butt."

A laugh bursts from my mouth, but it's more from surprise because, when it comes down to it, what he said was not funny. Standing there in the moonlight of a terribly romantic night in Metsovo with a handsome man to whom I am losing my heart, the words I hear out of his mouth are not declarations of love and happily-ever-afters, or that we'll work it out despite our differences, but *you have a great butt*.

After my first explosive laugh, I stand there dumbfounded, with no reply, no expression. All my life I have wanted a lover to appreciate my curves (James never noticed, Ravi thought I was too thin, and

Jessica wanted me to work out more) and now that I seem to have one, I am conflicted. My heart is swelling with love, and my mind is doubtful. I choose to stand there and not say anything, and he seems to be fine with this. His strong arms wrapped around me, he continues to look up at the round, curvy moon, the moon that I presume reminds him of my ass.

After a few minutes, he asks me if we should go back to the room. I need to lighten up, so with a barely-there smile I respond, "Yes, let's go back. But I am really tired. I just want to sleep." The side note in that is clear: I do not feel like having sex.

As we walk back to the room, my embrace is still a bit frigid; finally, he stops and asks me, "Thair, something is wrong, yes?"

The easy answer is no. But instead I say, "Gabriel, I just don't know what *this* is. I met you a few days ago. And, yes, I have crazy-strong feelings for you. But . . . I have to admit . . . I doubt your sincerity at times. Then I believe you. Then I think you are going to tell me how much you care for me and instead you talk about my butt."

He laughs loudly. So much so that he lets go of my hand and holds his stomach for a minute.

"Ayyy, Thair, you are so funny. So *sensitiva*."

Funny? I don't feel funny. But, yes, I do feel sensitive.

"I am sorry that I think you have a tremendous ass. If you prefer, I will not tell you again how much I like it. Okay?"

"No, that's not okay. I *want* you to tell me that you like my body but . . . shit . . . shoot . . . I don't know. I guess I just didn't think that you were going to say that. I mean, right NOW." I drop my eyes, feeling foolish, unreasonable, looney-tunes: "You must think I am crazy."

"Yes. A little." A smile crosses his face. "But I also like you very . . . very much. So, I have a question for you." He stops and unzips his jacket. He is wearing his T-shirt of Machu Picchu. "This is your last chance." He chuckles. "Tell me what mountain this is, and I will take you there."

I can't help it, but my mouth is pulling towards my ears, and I want to smile, even laugh; he has this way of taking a touchy situation and making it light, making me happy. But first I say, "Are you sure you want me to answer? Especially after our conversations and what I think about *everything*?"

Without any hesitation he exclaims, "Yes, for sure! Because, you will see, we will work it all out. Now tell me what this is called, and I take you there!"

So I state very clearly, a bit too loudly for a silent night: "MACHU PICCHU!"

"BRAVO! Now tell me when will you come to Peru, so we can visit Machu Picchu . . . and you can meet my family?"

A huge smile and then a kiss, "We'll see, Gabriel . . . we'll see."

Back in the room, I disappear to wash my face and clear my head. Even though I am completely attracted to Gabriel, my body and mind are exhausted from a long day; we saw so much, said so much. I am hoping my new lover will not try to romance me because I can easily be tempted, but what I want more than anything is a warm embrace and a night of spooning. While in the bathroom, I hear a train pull in. I wonder whether I am tired enough or if Gabriel's snoring will keep me up. I put on my thick night cream, peek around the corner, and smile when I see him soundly asleep with what looks like a smirk on his face.

He is lying halfway under the covers, with one leg on top of the duvet. He is wearing white underwear that say Hugo Boss (his singular purchase from Italy) and a white T-shirt. He looks angelic save for the noise that is expelled from his nose that turns him from a cuddly cherub into a wild bear. I lie down beside him slowly, though it seems nothing can wake him, and pull the covers because I am starting to feel the chill again. Despite the heaviness of the night, I can't ignore what else I am feeling. He opens one eye, grins, and gives me a kiss, "*Buenas noches*, pretty Thair."

"*Kalinihta*, Gabriel." My soul feels light as a big heavy hand pins me to the bed, a loud snore, and the bear is back.

31

It's about 8:00 a.m. and I can't sleep anymore, so I get dressed, grab my notebook, pull out a piece of paper, and leave a note:

Kalimera Gabriel,
    Happy Peruvian Independence Day! (See? I was listening last night! ☺) I hope you slept well. I am in the restaurant having some coffee. Come down when you get up.
Filakia, Thair

I sit in the restaurant with a warm cup of coffee and begin to relive last night's conversation. So much was said, and though I'm at ease today, I need to see the words written to make sure I'm not hearing them the way I want.

Thair's Story

Thursday, 28th of July
At dinner the night before, even though Thair didn't know where to start, one thing she knew was that she wanted to talk about children with him, and sooner rather than later.

"So, Gabriel, tell me more about your niece and nephew. Do you get to spend a lot of time with them?"

"I wish I would spend more time, but it is hard. My sister lives on the other side of Lima, and I work long hours, so I don't see my nephews much."

"I thought you only had one nephew and one niece?"

"Yes, two nephews, Francisco and Daniela."

She finally realized that they were saying the same thing and decided to let the masculine overpower since it did in his language, and she was in no mood to correct him.

"So, are you close to them?"

"Close enough." He chuckled.

"What do you mean *close enough*?"

"They are kids, you know. We have, how do you say, not much common. They are cute. Daniela loves dolls and purple. So when I visit, she shows me her new babies, but, then, I don't know what else to say."

"And what about the boy? Do you do things with him? Play soccer?"

"Oh no, he has his own life. Usually, he says 'Hi Tio,' gives me a kiss, then he is gone. Most times, when I go to my sister's house, it is to see her and my brother-in-law. He is a real cool guy. I usually see them on weekends. We take the kids to the park, maybe go for a ceviche and Piscos. But during the week, I usually stay home. I get home late and am tired, watch TV, maybe play some sports, but mostly, just stay on the couch, watch the news, and relax."

"So who do you live with? Do you have roommates?"

He smiled. "No, I live at home . . . with my mom and dad."

Thair's first thought was with mom and dad? Thirty years old and still at home? But Thair knew life was different in other places of the world, with other cultures; even Ravi still lived with his parents last she heard. Not all children leave home at the ripe age of eighteen, as in the US. It was not too long ago that she, too, lived with her mother, up until she was twenty-five and bought her own place.

"That's nice." A diplomatic, but honest response. Living with her mom had been mostly nice for Thair, too. "Do you like still being at home?"

"I don't mind it. I like my mom, and we have a lot of fun together even if she makes me a bit *loco* some time."

"I know what you mean. I guess that's the role of being a kid, to drive our parents a bit crazy and then think that it's the other way around!" Thair was not sure if he grasped her humor, so she continued: "What about your dad?"

"He is a good guy, too. We play golf sometimes and . . . you know . . . he's the man of the house. When he is angry, we stay away." Then he laughed. "He gets grumpy like me! I think I got it from him!"

Thair wondered again about this "grumpiness." What she saw a few times wasn't bad, but did it get worse?

Gabriel continued, "I will like to have my own home one day, but in Peru, we don't leave our family house usually until we get married."

"Yes, I know what you mean. Most Greeks are the same way. I lived at my mom's until I bought my own place."

"I save money for an apartment, but everything is so expensive. When I saved some money, I changed and buy a new car. Then I save again, but Bob and Jake invite me to Europe, so now I have to start again."

"So how is life in Lima?"

"It's busy, very busy. The traffic is terrible. The food is great. The people are very nice. And what about you, Thair? Do you think you will always live in California?"

It didn't have to be a difficult question, but in a way, it was. Thair had always imagined moving to Greece one day, buying an apartment in Athens for the winter and a modest beach cottage on Kythnos for the summer. She always felt so at home in Greece that if she were ever to fall in love deeply and completely, she imagined it would have been with a Greek—never in her wildest imagination had she pictured a possible soul mate being from South America. But as she sat next to this Peruvian, she wondered how life had thrown her such a curve ball. She had only known Gabriel for a few days, but she was already sensing that this man had something special, that if she did not have him close, she would miss him greatly. In just a week, he had become her phantom limb.

She was anxious about the next topic, her weight shifting back and forth in her chair while one foot started tapping the table leg. So far, she knew that age, religion, country, nationality, may not be deal breakers, but this one would . . . could be.

"So, Gabriel, how do you feel about children?"

"They are okay." Then he took a big bite of food.

"What do you mean by *okay*?" Thair needed to push.

"I don't know. They are okay. I guess I never think about children."

"Really? I mean you are young . . . but not *that* young. I know you want 'a wife' but what about kids? You talk about 'this wife' but how many kids do you visualize with her? One? Two? Five?"

A strong laugh. "Five? No way! Maybe one . . . maybe two."

Thair just sat there. What did she expect? He was a Latino man. Of course, he would want to have children. And of course, Gabriel's family would want him to have kids. That was the way of the world, and for certain the way of Latino and Greek families.

"But, Thair, like I said, I never think about kids too much. What I want is *a wife*." He said this with great determination.

"A wife who will understand me. That is the number one thing I want. Kids? I don't know. Or if I care. What about you?"

"Well, Gabriel, I guess I do care. And a lot."

"Really? You want five? You want to start tonight?" Another roar of laughter, but Thair's seriousness cut him short.

"Actually, Gabriel, I am quite certain I do not want any. Zero. Zip. None. Not one."

Then a long, "*Really?*"

"Yes, really."

"And why? Are you okay?" concern seeping from his voice.

"Yes, I'm healthy. If that's what you are asking."

"Then . . . why no kids, Thair?" he asked, more serious than he had been all night.

"Well, when I was a child my mama used to tell me this story about Zeus—"

Cutting her off, he had a perplexed look: "About Zeus?"

"Yes, about Zeus." A short pause, then, "Anyway, it was a story about meeting your other half, a sort of fairy tale. Like the Prince Charming thing. One day, I would meet this perfect half and we would gallop off, or roll away, and live happily ever after."

Thair told him about the soccer ball people and Zeus's magic sword that cut these perfect people apart.

"So every time my mama told me this story, I always pictured this man I would one day fall in love with. Tall, handsome, someone with a good heart."

"Like me?" Gabriel said teasingly.

"Yes . . . like you." Thair said warmly. "But never once in that story did I see children. I imagined happiness connected to one single individual, not a family. I spent all my life looking for my Prince Charming. I mean, I knew that Prince Charming didn't exist, but I was looking for a person who would be that perfect half of me."

"Oh, okay, so you know that *Príncipe Azul* is not real. Thanks goodness."

"Well, now I do, but I wasted a lot of my life unfulfilled, waiting for this other person to come before I could be completely happy."

"Oh. That's sad, Thair. I want a wife, but I am happy now," he said with a grin.

"I'm glad, Gabriel, but I don't think it's always that simple for women since we are fed so many messages from a young age. To get that rock. To wear that white dress. To have babies."

"Rock?" he asks.

"Diamond. In the States there's so much hype about 'putting a rock on one's finger.' If I ever get married, I want a simple, gold band. A ring with no beginning, no end."

"Me, too." Gabriel said.

Thair told Gabriel all her theories as he sat patiently listening to her. "How is a woman supposed to do it all? Work a full-time job, be a chauffeur, housekeeper, a cook, and then—this is usually at the bottom of a wife's list—a sexual goddess! Who even has the energy and desire at night to have sex after such a long day?"

"Yes, but a couple must make time."

"I agree, but this new woman is expected to do it all. If I could have it my way, I would have women and men choose. Do it all, I would say, but not at the same time. Get a college degree. Then choose. Be a parent, then have a career. Or have a job and have the man or partner be the homemaker and in charge of the daily duties. Save money, buy fewer toys—"

"*Toys?*"

"I mean cars, clothes, jewelry, bikes, trailers, trips, technological gadgets; instead spend quality time with your family in simple and meaningful ways. We can't go on telling women that they can have it all and *at the same time* because it's not reason-able, and it leads to a lot of unhappy people."

"Thair, what you say makes the world seem not very good. Is this how you see life?"

"Yes, unfortunately. I think career women are still expected to do the majority of the child care: make the lunches, take the kids to school, pick them up, drop them off at soccer practice, drive them to a violin lesson; maybe there's a dentist appointment that day; maybe try to make a healthy dinner, too."

"But American women fight for this change."

"Yes, of course. I am a proud feminist, and there have been so many great changes, and I know there are a few awesome dads who help a lot at home and with the kids, but some things in our world just haven't gotten completely figured out yet. I think women try to do too much, and oftentimes something has got to give, and it's usually the marriage, for sure the sex. At least that's what I hear from disgruntled girlfriends and colleagues."

When Thair looked at Gabriel's tired eyes (and ears, she was certain), she felt a bit guilty, but Gabriel had to know. This was integrally who she was, what she believed.

And then, in typical Gabriel style, he responded: "So, please let me summarize. You don't want kids because they are too much work?"

Thair laughed at how Gabriel always simplified everything. "I guess, yes, that's part of it, but it goes deeper than that. I choose romantic love over kids. If I ever commit to someone forever, or even marry one day, I want that person to be my number one. My *numero uno*. I don't think I have it in me to divide my attention."

"I don't know if I agree with all this, but, okay, finish your kid story," he said while pushing his chair closer to the table.

"I know my choice will also, undoubtedly, have consequences.

But if I am lucky enough to spend my life with someone who truly complements me, and we laugh a lot and grow old together, then my decisions will have been the right ones for me."

"Thair," she had never heard him use that tone with her name before, "I think what you say is clear. I am glad that you tell me how you feel. I also think that you plan too much. What if I am that 'other half' that you talk about, but I want that one *bebito*? It would end here?"

"Yes, it would." He was sitting straighter, looking ahead, and his hand on her thigh was now on the table. "Gabriel, I can't apologize for how I feel. Please, tell me what you are thinking."

"I think you think too much," he said quietly.

"Gabriel, this is who I am at my core. I analyze everything. And at thirty-six years of age, I am not going to change, and I am not going to change my mind about children either. These are my choices." Thair gave a brief consolatory smile.

This finally made him loosen up a bit. "Okay, let us not talk about kids more tonight. Maybe I will see things like you, too. I just never think about it. I just don't know how someone can make such plans, say 'no' when a person never knows. But, well. Okay. If that is what you believe, that is what you believe." He paused, smirked, "I do like idea of being *numero uno* . . . but for now, no more talk about *bebitos*. Do you like dogs at least?" This made Thair laugh, but before she could answer (she didn't really like dogs either) he said: "Now, tell me more about your life in California. No details, *por favor*, but did you have a boyfriend, someone you

"What are you writing, your diary, Miss Wright?" he says while leaning down and giving me a peck on the lips.

"Yep." I smile with his silly pun, ignoring the fact that the word

"Miss" is outdated but who can pronounce Ms. anyway? Not to mention almost everything out of Gabriel's mouth sounds genial.

"So how is Thair in this story? Is she happy?" He beams and then points to himself, "Has she met tall, good man from Peru yet?"

I have to laugh.

"Have you eat anything yet?"

"No, just two cups of coffee."

"I am *so* hungry," Gabriel says while looking around.

"I'm not surprised."

There is a positive energy in the air this morning as I tease him, and he parrots my upbeat attitude with a loving poke to my tummy, "I am sure you are so hungry, too, *flaquita*."

I am not sure what *flaquita* means, but I assume it's something positive (at least I hope it is!). He sits across from me today, and for a moment I realize I am naked in the face. I thought about putting on a dash of mascara, or at least some lipstick before I left the room, but it didn't seem necessary with Gabriel's next words: "Thair, you look beautiful today."

Normally I would say *nah*, but instead I reply, "You make me feel beautiful." When I say this, I imagine Rick overhearing us, oh how he would laugh. This is as sappy as a tree gets.

"Thair, what you want to do today?"

"I asked the person at the reception desk, and he said there are some trails if we want to take a hike. Some are about five kilometers, others as long as seventeen."

I can see his eyebrows lift with enthusiasm, "That sounds very good. Maybe one not too long? It looks like a superior day!" *Yes, a superior day*, I think.

Friday, 29th of July

I wake to the sound of Gabriel. He looks so happy when he sleeps. So relaxed, so peaceful in this world, if he never wakes, he most certainly would go to heaven—that is if I were God; I would give him a VIP pass, enter without a line, right to the front. But I am not God, do not have the power of Zeus, have little power or control for what will happen to this amazing person, so instead I roll out of bed and do a few Downward Dogs to feel at peace as well and stretch my back that is a bit sore from yesterday's hike.

After a few Sun Salutations, while I am on the floor with my butt in the air again, I peek at Gabriel and his eyes are wide open.

"*Kalimera*," he says with a perfect Greek accent.

I jump forward, hands on the floor, slowly uncurling my back, one vertebra at a time, as I stand up erect. "*Kalimera*, Gabriel," I respond. "How did you sleep?"

"Great!"

"Are you sore at all from our hike?"

"No. You?"

"Yes, a bit. I don't think I have used those particular muscles in more than a month."

Sliding his legs to the side of the bed, he comes over to where I am standing and gives me a quick kiss. "I am going to have a shower," with that, he is in the bathroom and the door is closed. And I have some time. I finish writing the part about "Thair's" lovers and then continue.

Thair's Story

She picked up her watch off the little wooden desk. It was already 10:43 a.m. and she wanted to be on the road early to drive back to Kamena Vourla and have time to spend with Gabriel before she saw him off the following morning. He was planning to take the 7:00 a.m. bus from Kamena Vourla back to Athens Saturday morning, then from the bus station at Liossion, get to the airport well in time for his evening flight. Thair hadn't said anything yet, but she was debating renting the car for another day and taking him all the way to the airport. The thoughts she was having about this man were simply insane; she knew she might never see Gabriel again, yet she kept picturing those damn soccer balls. She even visualized herself stuck to Gabriel, back-to-back, rolling around together, laughing, playing. It was such a ridiculous image, but she finally admitted to herself, she was simply and completely in love.

But she had loved before, and she knew those initial feelings of excitement had been there with others, but something was, undeniably, different this time. If Gabriel did not desire children, she pictured an amazing life with him. He stimulated her mind, not with conversations of art and literature, but with conversations about life, values, politics, the world in general. He was smart, sexy, witty, and funny. He loved outdoor activities like she did; he loved food, and of course, he seemed to love shopping. There were other qualities that were almost indescribable, how he looked at her, touched her, made her feel. The way he laughed at her silliness. The way he wasn't afraid to disagree with her yet made life seem so uncomplicated. Yes, she pictured a long, good, exciting life with this man. But when? Where? How? Those parts were very unclear.

With a towel around his waist, he hovers above me, "Thair, are you ready to go or do you want to write more?"

"No, I'm ready. I just wanted to get some thoughts down, here, in this place, before we leave."

When I say the words: *before we leave*, I can see Gabriel's face look heavy, drawn.

"Thair, I am sad." Simple, to the point. Gabriel always says what he feels, no need to be macho, play the tough guy. There are still fleeting moments when I question his honesty; he seems too good to be true, but this is not the time for doubt, not our last full day together. So I ask, "Gabriel, why are you sad?"

"I love this place. I would buy a small house and live here forever with you."

I want to laugh, but I can't. "I feel the same way." I walk over to him and wrap my arms up and around his neck and we kiss, not long or lustfully, just a few short pecks, looking into each other's eyes in between. Tears are gathering in my throat: "Okay, time to go," I say while pulling away from him.

"Wait," he says. I can see him struggle for words. "You will visit me in Peru, yes? See my life. Meet my family?"

I say with an unreasonable amount of confidence, "Yes, if you still want me to once you go back, I will come."

"Of course, I will! When?" His one-word direct questions.

"Oh, Gabriel, I don't know. My first break will be Thanksgiving."

"But that is when?"

"The end of November."

"That's too long!"

"Gabriel, let's see how things go. I may have a holiday in October, but it's only a long weekend, and I can't imagine spending that much money for a few days."

"Okay, I can wait until November. I will wait for you, Thair."

When he says this, for some reason, I believe him.

———

Halfway back, we see a rest stop on the side of the road that has a mini-mart and a tavern on the other side. We pull up on the dirt road and park in front of a mom-and-pop restaurant that has blue and white tablecloths, a thatched roof with grape vines growing insanely in all directions that creates shade for the tables.

We sit down, order a few *souvlakia*, some *tzatziki*, and a *horiatiki*. A friendly black cat tickles my legs, begging for some love. I lower my hand and scratch his head with my nails as Gabriel takes out his cigarettes.

"Do you mind if I smoke?'

I pause. "I guess not."

"It molests you that I smoke, yes, Thair?"

"Honestly, yes, but I won't try to change you. I just wish you would read how awful it is for you, and . . . if we were to ever be together . . . I would not be okay with smoking in the house."

As I say this, he smiles. "So you imagine us in a house one day together?"

"Maybe . . . " In a non-sequitur manner, I ask, "So you had a good time?

"Yes, for sure, but let me ask you," he pauses and puffs, "tell me three of your favorite things about Greece. Then I will tell you what I think also."

"Okay, but you say one, then I'll say one." I reply.

"Yes, I will start . . . I really like the Acropolis and the Parthenon so much. The tour guide told us how all the pillars are a bit curving, but when people look at them, the pillars are straight, perfect from every side. Even if they are not really perfect," he says this while overtly looking at me up and down with a smirk.

"Ha ha. Good one. I agree; that is, with the Parthenon, but let me choose another. I really loved Meteora. By the way, have you heard of Linkin Park?'

"No, is it a president park in America?"

I giggle, "No, it's a band, my favorite actually. I'll send you a CD. One of their albums is called *Meteora*."

"How cool. Okay, so your choice is Meteora?"

I picture my three choices instantaneously, so I reply, "No, actually, I am going to change. My first will be the water in Greece. For me, the most beautiful places in Greece are the beaches on the islands with their clear, icy blue waters. There's a place in Kythnos too, about a half hour drive from where my yiayia had her summer house, where there is a little peninsula, and at certain times of the day, the water is so blue, it's almost unreal."

"Wow, that sounds amazing. I would love to see it one day . . ."

"Okay, your turn now."

"My second is Metsovo. I had no idea places like that existed in Greece. If it was not for my Thair, I would not have been there. I really liked it."

"That's sweet, Gabriel. I thought it was amazing too, and it's the first place we . . . never mind." I find myself getting a wee bit shy, "Okay, my second choice is the Greek tomato. In the US, I rarely eat tomatoes even the organic ones. They are just so tasteless. My yiayia grew the *most* delicious tomatoes; compared to tomatoes in other parts of the world, Greek tomatoes are so rich in flavor. So my second choice is the red, Greek tomato!" I say this as I stick my fork in the village salad and put a huge piece of the red fruit in my mouth! "Yum!"

Then Gabriel says, "That is *my* second choice!"

"The tomatoes?" I gurgle, trying to speak while eating.

"Well, no, not the tomatoes, but all the food. The *souvlakia* with *gyros*, the *tyropitas* with ham and cheese, the meat at El Camino, the *pastichio* we had last night, even the . . . how do you say? The *koko-ret-si*—it's all SO good!" He says this while rubbing his tummy. "I know, for sure, I put on at least five kilos this month! And it makes me very satisfied," he looks down and laughs, "but I need to go back to the gym when I get back to Peru! Okay, your turn now! Last one . . ."

I sit there and think; there are so many things I love about Greece, where to begin? But the truth is three things did pop in my mind when he asked the question, and the third is sickly romantic, but— what the hell! I look over at Gabriel, take his hand, "My third favorite thing is . . . *you*. You in Greece. Meeting you has definitely brought out all the things I love about this country. It just seems with you the blue of the water is clearer, the red in the tomatoes is deeper, and the light in my soul is whiter." After I say this, I almost make myself gag. It's so cheesy, but being so wrapped up in this genuine emotion, the words keep tumbling out. These must be the kinds of things people say when they are alone together and really in love. I just never believed I would be on one side of it.

Gabriel doesn't say anything; he just scoots his chair closer and gives me a long kiss. "That is my choice, too. You."

"Oh, come on," I tease, "that's not what you were going to say . . ."

"Okay, maybe not *exactly*." His eyebrows lifting, "I was going to say something *strong* . . ."

This time my heart doesn't start a romantic pitter-patter because I know Gabriel's strong comments usually imply something else.

"Can I say my strong comment?"

"Sure, why not?" I say with a half-smile, ready for anything.

"Okay my three favorite thing in Greece was waking up and seeing you on the floor doing that funny *dog* thing with your tremendous, beautiful butt in the air!"

We both laugh loudly as the cat meows.

We arrive in Kamena Vourla in the late afternoon and, despite being tired, I am imagining the wonderful evening we will have. I am looking forward to some fresh fish at one of the harborside restaurants and maybe a few drinks at the pub. Then a night of lovemaking, and I will tell him that I can drive him to Athens. A few more hours together, a few more stolen moments. I also have to figure out how to get him into my room since I'll be breaking Kyria Akrivi's Rule Number Five!

We barely pull up into the driveway when Kyria Akrivi runs out of the house and towards the car. *Oh shoot* she is going to tell me that Gabriel can't stay even before I get the chance to sneak him up into my room. Gabriel looks a bit uncomfortable, sitting a bit lower in his seat when she hurries toward us.

"Tell her I am helping you with your bags and then I leave."

"Don't worry." I place my hand on his thigh and smile inwardly, thinking the whole situation a bit infantile.

But then my world changes.

Just the look on her face tells me everything will no longer be right in my universe.

She speaks quickly, eating her words, using some village slang, but before I can digest all the information, she wraps her arms around me, holds me tightly, lovingly. But like a fish I am gutted; Amphitrite, goddess of the sea, has pierced me, taken out all my organs and thrown me on the shore.

"Thair, what is happening? Talk to me."

I am shaking all over, I feel faint, and my legs are liquid. Gabriel holds me up when Kyria Akrivi lets me go. She pulls up a chair that is close by and pushes me into it. My hands are gripping my thighs with such vigor that I don't notice what has happened: one of my fingernails has flipped back and my finger is bleeding. A pulsing sensation, but I can't locate where the pain is coming from. Maybe my heart? I can't see in front of me, my vision blurry, I think I am crying, but I am not sure.

The woman starts talking again, but this time the words are a bit clearer. "*Then ine pethameni akoma. I thea su ipe pou prepi na tin paris telefono amesos. Omos then ine pethameni. M'akous? Zi! Akoma zi!*" She says this with so much enthusiasm that all I can hold onto are the words, "Alive. She's *still* alive."

Gabriel, has bent down on his knees and looks absolutely desperate, wanting to soothe my suffering, but doesn't understand the cause. He does not understand that this woman has just told me that my mother is on her deathbed.

32

Saturday, July 30th

My flight is four hours earlier than his, but Gabriel goes through customs at the same time, so he can see me off. Yesterday I called the US and found my aunt there. My mother is barely conscious. My aunt was stoic and gave me a few details. Mama was frail when I left, but she told me she was still recovering from last year's shock because the situation with me and Jessica had taken a toll on her. I was certain she was trying to make me feel guilty by no longer dying her hair, staying thinner than normal. She had looked so weathered the last time I saw her, but I thought she was still silently punishing me for my last relationship, showing me how it had permanently aged her. I always asked about her checkups, and she always told me everything came back clean. Had she been blatantly lying to me? And why hadn't I asked to see the results? God how I hate myself at this moment.

And while I have been in Greece, the communication has gotten worse and worse. After the first week, she couldn't talk on the phone; a simple cold, she said, made it hard to talk. Then only short emails! It is now all falling into place. My God, how could I have been so blind?

Honey, go have a good time. Don't worry about me. The kind words. The tighter than usual hugs. I had not heard her voice for more than five weeks, but because I was so wrapped up in my own life, I hadn't tried to call again except once when *I* needed *her*. How I despise myself right now. And how long had Thea Lena been there? And how long had my mama known? But damn it! Why didn't she tell me? I would have never planned a trip to Greece if I had known she was sick again.

I would never have come to Greece. I would never have met Gabriel. My God, how could I even be thinking about my love life while my mother lay in her home, being eaten away by that god-awful disease. Tears fill my eyes again while a cacophony of diatribes against myself fills my head.

Gabriel is holding me tight as we sit at the gate, but, suddenly, I'm suffocating, so I wiggle out of his embrace. He looks like a hurt puppy. I could give a shit. My God, my mother is dying; I have no patience to baby this man.

"Gabriel, I need to say good-bye. I can't have you wait here until the last moment. It's too much for me right now."

Another hurt, desperate look. "Okay, Thair. I understand." *NO, you don't understand,* I want to scream at the top of my lungs. How could you even begin to understand? You have a mother! A father! Four sisters! You have a family! All I have is my mother! She is my family! She is my everything! My God, my God . . . I need space. I need to breathe . . . I can't see . . .

I am now lying across the seats and everyone is staring. I have a cool rag on my forehead and a foul-smelling piece of cotton stuffed under my nose. There are a few people in uniforms around me. I can hear a buzz of words. Gabriel tells them I am okay, just in a bit of shock, that I got some bad news, that I will be fine. *I will not be fine,* but I understand what he is doing: assure the flight attendants, allow me to fly.

After a few minutes, the crowd scatters and he is sitting beside me, holding the cotton close to my face. I slowly sit up and take it from him, "Thanks."

"Thair, I don't know what to say. I hurt to see you this way. I wish I could take away your pain. Please, tell me, what I can do?"

"Gabriel, there is nothing you can do. Thank you for being here. But I need you to go now." I look away as tears pool in my eyes. This time I am not crying my mother. I am crying for him. I want him. I need him. I know how to be alone. I know I am strong, capable, but, God, it would be so nice if I stumbled upon The One, the one to provide me support in times like this. But I am flying to my country, and he to his. He will not be there to hold my hand, carry me in my darkest hour; he will never meet my mama. My God, he will never meet my mother! The only one who has loved me my whole life. He will never see her dark eyes, her brilliant smile. And she will never watch me walk down the aisle, a dream that she has had for years that I could have made a reality for her. I would even wear the damn white dress if she wouldn't . . . I can't think the word.

My emotions are everywhere; now the thought sets in again in a much more melancholic manner: Gabriel will never meet my mother, and she will never meet him. The chances of it happening anyway were probably unlikely, but now they are inconceivable.

He looks into my eyes, offering a small, weak smile, "Thair, your plane does not leave for one hour and a half. I will stay. You cannot tell me to go. I will not go."

When he says this, I finally allow the tears to empty freely from my eyes. It was what my heart really wanted to hear, so I rest my head on his shoulder and cry and cry and cry. And cry. There is no one else in the world at that moment, just me and Gabriel. I am suspended in hell with an angel at my side. Maybe people are looking; I do not care. Gabriel holds me while I tremble and sob, and when it is time to go, he takes his hand and places it under my chin and gives me a kiss, lightly licking my lips, drinking my tears. "Thair, this will be hard for you. But I will call you. You will see. I will help you with this. *Te quiero un monton.*"

He helps me to my feet as we embrace for a last time. The ground below me disappears and I am getting sucked into a wormhole, losing my stability, feeling a bit dizzy again—but only for a moment; then I rebalance, and Gabriel steadies me. I hold on tight, not wanting to let him go, but it's time.

"Gabriel, thank you for everything. I . . . I . . . I will miss you. Good-bye."

I have read about this feeling but never really believed it existed. As I walk through the gate, a piece of my heart is ripped out of my chest: the mighty hand of Zeus works his fingers through every muscle fiber, into the rib cage, finds the beating sack and squeezes it until I gasp. I have no breath left, but I am still alive. I also have no choice but to follow my legs that are moving forward.

I don't look back.

Rancho Fierno
Saturday, July 30th

I gained a day in flight but lost so much. Rick meets me at the airport, and as soon as I see him, there's some small sense of relief. He hugs me tightly and a new waterfall of tears emerges from my swollen eyes. From Athens all the way to New York, all I did was look out of a black window and sob. There were moments when my eyes dried up, but as I closed them, a new set of tears found their way out. The poor lady beside me didn't know what to do, what to make of this sorry case that was huddled in the corner. At one point, she called over the flight attendant and asked if there was something they could give me. The flight attendant spoke sweetly, and I tried to take control of myself, but I had no control. On the connecting flight, a young man to my left offered me a sleeping pill; he said it would help me relax. I declined, but the quiet tears would not stop. Finally, out of pure exhaustion, sleep must have come.

Rick takes me immediately to Rancho Fierno, and on the way, we barely talk. He tries to ask me a few questions, but I have no words in me. I am anxious, nervous, and so afraid. When we get to the house, it looks so dark and foreboding. Rick tells me he can come in with me, and I say, yes, that would be nice.

At the front door, after a couple of light raps, I pull out my set of keys. A figure is behind the dark glass, so before I can get my key in the lock, my Thea Lena has opened the door. She is wearing an olive-green dress that has spaghetti straps, and her hair looks disheveled. Her face is rosy, and she looks young, vibrant; it's just the sadness in her eyes that brings me back to reality.

"*Ti kanis, koukla?*" She asks me how I am while stretching out her arms. I hug her, and we kiss on both cheeks, all in one very loving moment.

"How is Mama?" I plead.

A slight pause then, "Not well. Do you want to see her?"

I nod.

"Please be prepared—" She takes my hand and leads me to my mama. A young, thick, redheaded woman sits in the corner of my mother's bedroom reading a magazine. She gently excuses herself when we walk in. I see something in the bed, but I don't recognize it. It looks like a strange doll, an emaciated porcelain figure that is not beautiful, not frightening, just not of this world.

"Mama?" I lean down. "Mama?"

"Thair, you can talk to her, but she hasn't responded since yesterday. Mary is here from Scripps Hospice. Your mama had been waking up . . . screaming . . . so Mary is giving her Demerol to lessen her pain."

My dear, fragile mother waking up screaming? Acid burns my insides, but before I can say anything Thea Lena continues: "They tell us . . . it can happen any day now."

Suddenly, I am infuriated. How could this happen so quickly! I have only been gone for just more than a month and she wasn't even sick when I left! I have no tears just uncontained anger. I grab my aunt's hand and storm out of the room. *Tell me what happened? When did she get sick again? How long have you been here? Where is the cancer? What medicine is she taking? Why are you saying that SHE IS DYING? She will be fine! We will do alternative therapy! We will take her to a specialized center! NO! NO! NO! Don't say that! My God! NO!*

Rick hears all the screaming and comes into the kitchen and tries to approach me, but I push him away. My aunt stands there and tries to explain, but her face looks pale and clammy now.

"*Koukla*, please sit down. This is hard on all of us. I love my sister very much—"

"How can you say you love her and not allow her daughter to be with her! Why didn't you call me earlier and what about those emails?"

"Thair, I wrote them, but you have to understand, even if I didn't agree with what your mother was doing, it was her choice."

"WHAT DO YOU MEAN, HER CHOICE? HER CHOICE TO DIE?"

"Yes, if you want to look at it that way. It was her choice to die. At least to die this way. With dignity. She called the place you were staying a few weeks ago when she had taken a turn for the worse and talked to a Kyria Akrivi because you were out. The woman said you seemed so peaceful, so happy, so she didn't tell the woman why she had called. Your mother was adamant that I should not tell you to return."

Rick comes over and puts his hand on my shoulder, and this time I don't push him away. A desperate voice comes out of me, one I don't recognize, as I plead for her to tell me everything.

After she does, I try to lie down, but I can't relax.

Sunday, 3 a.m.

Thair's mother went to the doctor shortly before her yearly check-up with abdominal pain and to check a strange protrusion that was visible from the outside of her stomach. The doctor did a biopsy and he confirmed his worst suspicion: she had cancer again. This time it was ovarian cancer, one of the most aggressive, and she was already at stage four. There was really no hope, just a death sentence—only months to live. She could do chemotherapy, but it would just prolong the inevitable, and Phaedra did not want to *inconvenience* her daughter anymore since the result would be the same. She wanted to live her life to the fullest for as long as she could, and she did not want anyone except for her sister to know.

Phaedra asked Lena if she could come and stay with her in the middle of June, almost as if she had predicted the date of her own demise. Thea Lena wanted to come right away, but Phaedra, as always, had made up her mind about everything. She would be busy getting paperwork in order—a will, bills, and bank accounts—and she did not want or need any company, but she believed that by June, once her affairs were in order, she could use the help, and by then, she could spend quality time with her sister. Thea Lena had asked repeatedly about Thair, begged her sister to tell her only child, but Phaedra could not be persuaded; she was a stubborn Greek to the core. No. This was Thair's time now. She had been planning this trip for a year, and Phaedra would not tell her daughter because she was certain Thair would not go if she knew. After the pain she had caused Thair, she told her sister, she wanted Thair to travel and enjoy her time in Greece worry-free because Thair deserved it. Phaedra was always protecting Thair, a martyr until the end. So Thea Lena took a leave of absence from the orchestra and arrived just after Thair had left for Greece. For the first two weeks, Phaedra was doing so well, but then her health declined rapidly.

Thea Lena told Thair that during those initial weeks they had spent wonderful days together, cooking with vegetables from Phaedra's garden, watching old Elvis movies, sitting by the swimming pool, Phaedra in the shade wearing a big hat with her feet up and laughing. God, what Thair would do to hear her mother laugh again. Thair was livid that she was left out of this dying plan, but Thea Lena told her that Phaedra was unyielding. She did not want her sickness to disrupt her daughter's plans. Thair was pissed! Disrupt plans? What a ridiculous notion! There was no place on earth where Thair would rather have been than with her mother. She had the right, damn it, to be with her mama and see her through this! Not to come back from a holiday and see a lifeless corpse in the bed! It was so god damn fucking unfair!

For three days, I have been sitting vigil by mama's bedside whispering to her. Singing to her, telling her stories, reading to her—and nothing. I tell her all about Gabriel. All about Kamena Vourla. All about Meteora. The breathtaking monasteries in the sky. About Metsovo. But she remains so still that I repeatedly lift the covers to see if she is still breathing. My heart stops as I do this, and when I see the small heave of her chest, I lay the blanket down gently and continue with my stories. I even read her the stories I have written. I start at the very beginning, Yiayia's story, her story, my story. But I do not read her Sunday's entry. Or the one about the day she met Jessica.

I look for reactions from her when I take away Dita's virginity with words, or when I create Phaedra as a desperate air-conditioning-loving immigrant, but nothing. Not even a quiver of an eyelid. No response, just a ghostly figure, in the bed, lying there. I have selfishly asked Mary to back off of the high dosages of Demerol because of my desire to see her one more time—for her to see *me*, to know that I have come back to be with her. I just fear that my instruction to take away some of the morphine-type painkiller will cause her to wake with agonizing pain. But even with lower dosages of medication, she does not wake.

Gabriel calls several times a day, every day, and though his voice eases me, I have a hard time talking. Sometimes we stay on the line quietly and he patiently hears me cry; sometimes he describes the places we visited, the food we shared. Mostly, I cut the conversations short because I don't want to lose a moment with my mother.

On the fourth night of my return, when I can no longer find words or songs, Thea Lena takes over and forces me to get some rest. I retreat to my old bedroom, my cotton candy hell. I fall heavily on top of my bed, too exhausted, too sad, too depleted to put on pajamas or take a shower. From a turbulent sleep, I hear Thea Lena screaming: "Thair, *ella*! *Ella*! Come quickly!"

My heart is racing, what is happening? *No, God, please, please don't let it be what I am thinking. Please, God . . .*

My God, is this it? Is this how a precious life is taken from us? As my feet move faster than my mind, I stumble into a piece of furniture and knock over a small plant, but don't look back. I reach the bedroom. Thea Lena is hunched over my mama, holding her hand; despite Mama's pallid countenance, they both seem to be smiling. My mama is slightly propped up on the bed, several pillows behind her gaunt frame, her eyes halfway open. Her lips are light purple, and it looks like she wants to talk.

I sit cautiously on the bed for fear of crushing her, take my fingers and delicately move them across her forehead, "Mama, I'm here." I place my cheek next to hers and hold onto that moment forever. I'm fighting back the tears as I kiss her gently.

Her lips tremble, but there is no sound.

"Mama, you don't need to talk. I am here." My voice cracks, but

I continue, "I *love* you, Mama." I see her lips begin to move again as they struggle to form words, each attempt heart-wrenching. "Mama, please, relax. You don't have to talk."

Her body shakes a bit, her eyes protrude; she clearly wants to get these words out, but the pain that she is experiencing is written all over her glass face; the energy needed to use trite language is excruciating for her and for me. My throat fills with tears, but I refuse to show weakness, not here, not now; I need to be strong for her.

"*Ag-ape mou*—" she pushes the words out, "I—am so—rry. Please for—give meeee." Then she gasps, "Be ha—ppy with Je—Je—ssi—ca. I know you—lo—love herrrr. Be ha—ppy. *Sa—ga—po*," with that her chest heaves one more time, and she flattens into the pillows more than is humanly possible. But she looks peaceful, her mouth no longer quivering.

Her eyes are still slightly open when she looks at me. *What do I say?* Despite what I told her before I left, my mother must have believed that Jessica and I broke up because of her. To explain it *now*, *here*, that I do not love Jessica anymore, but that I am in love with a man I just met seems ridiculous—even unimportant. So instead, I take my mother's hand, and say, "Thank you, Mama. I love you. Please just try to relax."

"Thai—r?" she has more to say.

"Yes, Mama?"

"Did you fe—ed my Puss—a—ki?"

I couldn't help but laugh. My resilient mother. The great escape artist. On her death bed and she brings up her cat.

"Yes, Mama," I say as drops of water fall on her blanket, "Yes, I fed the cat."

"G—ood. I am go—ing to clo—se my eye—s now, o—kay?"

"Okay, Mama, sleep with—the—angels." I gulp and finish, hoping she can still hear me, "Mama, I love you *so* much."

But she doesn't say anything.

She never says anything again.

Encinitas, Rancho Fierno, Nowhere, Everywhere
Early November, 2005

There were days when Thair was quiet. Other days when she was loud. Some days, she cried. Other days, she just stared at a wall. Some days, she yelled; others, she wailed. Some days, she stayed in. Other days, she went out. But she was always alone. Nothing seemed right in the universe anymore. How was one supposed to live in this world when the one who brought you here was gone?

Her father was great. He came to San Diego and stayed with her for a few weeks. He helped her go through all her mother's belongings; helped her choose what to save, throw away, or donate. Sometimes he rented a movie and watched it with her or took her out to dinner. He was at her side the entire time. Even her stepmother came for a week and was a gentle figure, taking her shopping and buying Thair fabulous shoes, thinking it would brighten her day. It didn't.

Nothing was good anymore. Nothing—well, almost nothing. Except the phone calls.

"Hola, Thair."

"Hi, Gabriel."

"*Cómo está mi* Thair?"

"I'm okay."

"How was today?"

"It was okay."

"Did you have to do anything *h*ard?"

That hard "h"—such an endearing sound—made her think about the first time they talked outside of that café while she was having lunch.

"Thair? Are you there?"

"Oh, yeah, my dad and I went through loads of paperwork. Again. I hate it."

"Ayyy, Thair. I am sorry I cannot be there to help you. Did you decide what to do with . . . your mama's house?"

"No, it's just so hard to sell it. It's funny, I spent my youth hating Rancho Fierno, and now I just can't seem to leave the place. I spend more nights there than I do at my own home."

"Thair, it makes me sad to think of you all alone. You know that—"

"So tell me. How was your day?" she interrupted.

He would then tell her all about his day at school; he detailed each of his co-workers and they had become characters in her mind. Vanessa, the principal's assistant was dating Jorge, the thin guy who worked in Human Resources; one of the board members ran away to Costa Rica with another board member's wife; the Ambassador of the US had been on campus that day, so there was full security. Then he would tell her stories about his family: how one of his sisters was now engaged; how the one who was living in the US had moved back to Peru; how his mother had undergone hernia surgery, but was doing well; how his father had won a major golf match and was still glowing days later. For more than an hour, every single day, they talked. The calls made through phone cards were often scratchy and it was hard to hear, so they had found this new thing called Skype— free calls through the computer—and it was working out well. With a mini webcam installed, she could see his handsome face and warm eyes. They talked so often and so long that, at times, he seemed so close she could touch him.

But even with Gabriel's phone calls, weekends were awful. Weekdays were easier. She taught her classes, prepared for the next day's lesson, watched some TV and, generally, escaped quite well. Sometimes though, when brushing her teeth or after she turned off the light, she felt a cold, hollow sensation in the pit of her stomach. She felt so alone. In the beginning, she thought she would be able to *feel* her mother's presence, but she felt nothing. Never. None of that bullshit people said: "I can feel my loved one here with me." It was simply dust to dust.

Thair had an urn of her mother's ashes sitting on top of her wine bar that the damn cat almost knocked over. Thair freaked out and nearly killed the little shit. It was an ugly cat, brown spots and skittish, but it was the only thing that was her mother's that was still alive. All the plants she had taken from Phaedra's house had died. Even a large cactus she brought home with her had withered, turned sickly yellow, and toppled over. An Asian student had once told her that the health of a cactus was reflective of the health of a home. Great, she thought, and she put on gloves, wrapped the dead thing in a big, black garbage bag and stuffed it down the chute.

Phaedra's wish was that Thair spread her ashes over the island of Imbros one day (she knew this was her mother's conniving way of getting her to go back to Greece), but Thair had no travel plans, so they would sit in the urn between the Pinot Noir and Cabernet until further notice. She would pass the urn every day and talk to it, as if somewhere (in heaven?) her mother's bell rang, "Call for Phaedra! Your daughter is speaking to your ashes." But the ashes never responded. There was no cosmic force that moved them a bit, no sudden wind that opened the lid and let a few ashes fly, nothing to let Thair know that Phaedra's spirit was, in fact, somewhere in this universe.

"Thair, I know you don't want to talk about this . . . but your Thanksgiving break is coming soon. Do you think you want to visit me?"

"Oh, Gabriel."

"Thair, what you thinking?"

"I don't know. I do want to see you. Really, so very much. But I just can't imagine a vacation right now. It just doesn't seem right."

"Thair, it is not a vacation. It's for you to get away and meet family . . . uh, my family."

She couldn't help but feel lighter when he said these highly romantic things, but just like in Metsovo, sometimes it was too much—it just did not seem realistic. Go to Peru? See Gabriel? Then what?

Encinitas
Mid December, 2005

On Friday night I come home and put on my pajamas, make my tea, and wait for Gabriel to call. But he doesn't. I watch show after show. I don't even know what I am watching. I look up at the urn several times and want to cry, but crying would mean feeling, and today I am just numb. And it has little to do with Gabriel not calling. For the last few weeks, I have been in a ditch. It's dark and deep and wet. There's a ladder to crawl out, but I ignore it.

This month the pain is different. It has set in. She's not coming back. I go about my life but am not a very happy person and simply no fun to be around, oh, and I could give a shit. Rick and Frank separated after almost fifteen years together, so much for soul mates. It's all bullshit. Rick comes over and we mope around a bit, but then he leaves. I don't like his company, and he doesn't like mine. We are both so negative and, together, insufferable. Gabriel still calls, but I am curt and careless, yes, no, yes, no, no, no; compassionate sentences are hard to form. The last thing I can think about is going to Peru to visit, so his frustration seeps through the computer line.

I've turned off the webcam, so I only hear his voice now, can't bear to look at him. After these frigid conversations, I don't hear from him for a while; I assume he's pouting because he's not used to *this* Thair. When he does call again, after a few days, he tells me that he has been spending time with his family or going out with his friends. Sometimes he calls slightly inebriated and tells me he is still waiting for me, but adds, he will not wait forever. I don't say anything. I don't feel anything. When he says these things, I think: I don't like being with me, so why would he?

Thanksgiving has come and gone. In two weeks, it will be Christmas. My first Christmas without my mother. She was only fifty-nine. My God. I just don't understand *why*? Why, God, *why*?

———

It's Sunday. I'm still in the same pajamas from Friday night. I haven't taken a shower, and I am turned off by my own stench. I haven't eaten anything but cereal for the last two days, and there are dirty bowls scattered around the house. The TV is on loud. I think I hear another sound, but it doesn't register. Is the doorbell ringing?

Riiiing. Riiiing.

I tell myself to get up. I need to move, but I can't. Who could it be? As the ringing continues, I go to the bathroom and put on my robe.

Riiiing. Riiiing. It hasn't stopped. Now there is a heavy pounding on the door.

I stand on the other side and look through the peephole. *What the hell is he doing here?*

He stands there with a Trader Joe's bag and some flowers. I glance at the mirror, see that I look like a wreck, but don't care. I open the door.

He puts down the groceries, hands me the flowers, and gives me a long hug. I relax, and tears fall from my eyes.

"Thair, dear Thair, I am *so* sorry. We just heard."

"Hi, Ravi, thanks, come in."

I see him look around at my place and his nose lifts.

"Thair, *how are you*?"

I let out a feigned laugh, "Not great. This has been the toughest month."

"My mother ran into a woman who knows . . . I mean . . . who knew your mom. Anyway, she told my mom that . . . Phaedra . . . passed away."

Passed away! Damn euphemisms. I want to scream: she didn't pass anywhere! *She fucking died!* But instead I say: "That's okay. Thanks for coming now."

"Gosh, Thair, we were both so shocked. We both really cared for your mom. If I knew, I would have come earlier." He looks around again, "Have you had any help?"

"Nope, not lately anyway."

"What about . . . *that woman*?"

He sounds like my mother. *That woman.* "You mean, *Jessica*? Well, she came to see me, but if you're asking if we are still together, *no*, we separated a while ago." It is just too easy to get pissed these days, so I try to change my tone. "Everybody's been really great. From the colleges, the students, other teachers. Friends have been really supportive, but you know what, Ravi?" Here I go again, but I can't stop myself.

"What?"

"Sympathy is short lived."

"What do you mean?"

"Well, everyone feels bad for you when your mother dies, when your child gets some rare disease, or your husband is killed in some horrible war. Yeah, everyone feels bad initially; there are gifts and cards and warm meals and groceries," I say this while looking at the bag. "But then life takes over. People have their own problems, other obligations, and they forget all about you. But for those who are suffering, they don't forget. They live with their pain every god damn day." I let out a wicked laugh. "They say 'time heals all.' I am still waiting for time to heal my empty heart. It's been almost six months and you know what?"

"What?" he asks again hesitantly.

"Whoever created that dumbass quote lied. Time heals shit. It just makes you remember more, miss more, hate fucking life because your loved one is no longer in it."

There's a part of me that again feels guilty for my negative attitude. This nice guy comes over to share his condolences, and instead I rip into him with verbal diarrhea, using expletives like salt and pepper. And to think I disliked it when people had trash mouths, but today my anger is at the surface; pain makes people think they are entitled to be a bitch or an asshole. Right now, I feel like a lot of both.

"Thair," he comes over to me, gives me another hug.

From intense frustration, his warm arms around me feel so strangely comforting. We stand like this for a while and don't talk. He's rubbing my back. Then he draws a little away from me, gazes into my eyes and, fuck, is he trying to kiss me? I jerk myself away.

"Sorry, Thair. I don't know what came over me," he says, genuinely contrite.

"I think it's time for you to go. Please tell your mom thank you for thinking about me, and thanks for coming over, but I *am fine*."

Defeat overpowers me. I shut the door behind him. I take the urn off the shelf and place it on the floor in front of me; sitting cross-legged, I bend my head, my forehead touching the cool metal lid, and weep.

Our Story

Island of Kythnos, Greece
Mid July, 1989

Thair had just gotten out of the shower and was about ready to walk onto the balcony when she heard the whispered voices of her mother and grandmother. They were speaking in Greek, but it went something like this:

"Mama, have I disappointed you?"

A long pause. Then Thair's yiayia answered, "No."

"Then why do you hesitate to answer?"

"Because I am not disappointed with your choices, I am just sorry how they turned out."

"Because Gordon and I got divorced?"

"Because you never fell deeply in love with Gordon."

"Mama, I did love him, not completely, but I loved him enough. I loved him the way I saw you love Babba—enough."

"I wish I showed your father more how much I loved him. He was a good man, a very good man, but I didn't realize that until he was gone."

"So you were in love with him?"

"Phaedra, I loved him." She was not going to say more.

They sat quietly for a moment, staring into the sunset, sipping their Greek afternoon coffee.

Then Phaedra spoke, "Mama, I worry about Thair."

"I don't. She's a strong young woman. She will make wise choices. She has choices that you and I never had. She will find happiness. You'll see."

"And what about us?" Thair's mother said as she sat closer to her own mama, putting her head on Dita's shoulder.

Thair saw her yiayia smile. "We are strong women, too. We will be fine."

33

Thair's Story

Encinitas, CA
May 15th, 2006

Thair was sitting in Pannikin. It was the fifth month of the new year, and the San Diego sun was beating heavy on her shoulders, heating her body, and making her sunglasses slip off her face. It was good being around people again. Last night Rick threw Thair a surprise thirty-seventh birthday dinner at The Brigantine. About ten friends, including Emily and her husband, Mark, all showed up with gifts and heartwarming cards. Frank arrived late with a dozen yellow roses for Thair and a single red one for Rick. Frank and Rick still lived separately and were tentative around each other, but Thair could see something good happening again. When Frank laughed, Rick seemed lighter than he had in months. At one point, Frank and Thair had a quiet moment talking about their mothers; they both got a bit choked up but were also able to smile after each shared a fond and funny memory about each of these women. The entire night made Thair feel appreciated and loved, and not so alone. Much different than how she had felt at the beginning of the year when she had invitations for lunches and dinners but had always declined. Almost all winter break, she had spent alone in her condo with her mom's cat, Pussaki.

She even liked the little critter now and looked forward to the meows that greeted her every day after work.

For Christmas dinner, she was invited over to Emily's, but with the new baby and several of Mark's friends coming over, she really wanted something a bit quieter, so she decided instead to spend it with her father and his wife at the La Costa Resort. It was a cold dinner, but the company was good enough, and the champagne was even better. There were actually a few laughs during dinner with the two boys, her stepbrothers, and a few tears, when her father brought up his first trip to Greece and how he had met Phaedra. Thair's stepmother visibly did not like hearing that story, but she listened quietly because it obviously meant a lot to Thair. And, anyway, Thair's mom was gone now, absolutely no threat to this over-tanned, leathery blonde woman with big brown eyes who wore too much mascara but seemed to have a gentle heart.

The way Gordon had made it sound, he had been very much in love with Phaedra. Maybe he was, but he couldn't keep his pants zipped up. Thair didn't know what to think, but it really wasn't important anymore. What was important was that she had a little family again. When her mother was alive, Thair had no desire to reach out to her father or her stepbrothers, but now she was enjoying their company and even planned to visit Florida next year and maybe go to the Bahamas with them. A family vacation; imagine that, Mama, she said in her head, as she tilted her chin upwards and toasted her mother.

One day in late January when Thair was returning from Costamar College, she stopped by the gym to pay her outstanding bill. She bumped into her yoga teacher; they talked for a while and she invited Thair to a class she was giving in her home the following week: a yoga and healing session. Thair went, and though it felt weird at times with all the chanting, it reintroduced her to something she loved, so for the last few months, she was practicing regularly again. She was also reading great books, spending weekends taking long walks along the coast, eating salads with lots of feta cheese, olive oil, and red cherry tomatoes.

That's also when things started changing with Gabriel—or, more accurately, when the relationship changed for Thair. Gabriel hadn't called for almost two weeks and Thair sensed the end had arrived. While sitting on the floor, legs open wide, the urn in front of her, she admitted out loud what she had been afraid to think.

"Hi, Mama." Silence.

"Do you remember Gabriel? The Peruvian man I met in Greece last year?" Thair didn't tell her mother about him when she was conscious those last few minutes, but daily conversations with the urn detailed many of her memories, her philosophies, her struggles.

"Mama, I have been thinking about him a lot lately. About my life."

"Meow," Pussaki responded. She rubbed the cat's head while it sat next to her, looking at Thair with head tilted sideways, as if her furry friend were a psychiatrist listening to her crazy client.

"Mama, I think I blew it. I think I really . . . love . . . him, but I finally pushed him away."

"Meow."

"Mama, I am starting to feel happiness again. I don't need Gabriel, but I want him. He feels *right*."

But before she could reach out to Gabriel, he did something. It was almost Valentine's Day, and he knew how Thair felt about this silly holiday, but when she got home Friday from work, a large box sat on her doorstep. She picked it up; it was light. When she moved it around, it made a slight thudding sound. Foreign stamps decorated the front, and PERU was written with a big black marker. She smiled and unlocked her door quickly.

Thair took the package into the living room, poured herself a glass of wine, and stared at the box. Then she cut it open and slowly began unwrapping what was inside. Before she reached the last layer of brown paper, she held the object on her lap, and with her eyes closed, touched it all around. It felt like a big ball. With eyes still wide shut, she peeled away the final layer and then opened her eyes. A white and black soccer ball. A small card was taped to the ball, *Feliz día, Thair. It is not so compli-cated, Amor . . . de mi vida.*

It was nothing more than a soccer ball, just white with black pentagons. Two colors, one ball—two rolled into one. She and Gabriel had many differences, various obstacles, and yet, he was unequivocally the person she most desired. And he was, essentially, sitting on her lap. Thair felt her brain-hand and heart-hand reach for one another. They held on to each other tightly.

The next few weeks were tumultuous. She dreamt of Zeus, of Chronos, of Artemis. Some nights, she swam in the Mediterranean, other nights she drowned in the Pacific. She pictured herself and Gabriel tied together; sometimes it was their legs and they were in a silly three-legged race; other days she would dream about a white dress and a church and her mother seated on one of the pews. Some nights, she dreamt of the dreaded hospital bed and could hear her mother wailing. Those were nights when she would wake up in sweats, pulse beating wildly. Jolted awake, her head would be spinning, and then she would lie awake for hours and just think. There were still bad days. Bad nights. But there were a lot of good ones in between.

And today was a good one. As she sat in Pannikin Café and typed away on her computer, she realized the light was back. The pearl inside her soul was translucent—the dark grain of sand that is the inception of every pearl had been again covered by layers of light. As she touched her stomach, she visualized this pearl tucked under her skin, right behind her belly-button. The nucleus of her pearl, that nagging grain of sand, had been devoured, had disappeared, had dissipated entirely—even if not scientifically possible. But it had. It was gone; because even with science, there are miracles. She knew there was no more core heaviness. Undoubtedly, sadness is part of life and would return time to time, but Thair's soul was finally shining, white, and light.

Thair thought about her mother, the bedtime story, and how that Greek god had persuaded her to search for her Other Half, and, yes, she had stumbled upon Gabriel, had leaned on him, but—ultimately—she had made it out of the tunnel *alone*. Like most people, there had been conditions in her life that had kept her from reaching her potential, and since no two roads are the same, she had to do exactly what she had done, and the way she had done it, to get to where she was. She was always whole; she just had to figure that out. Like Aristotle's concept of *entelecheia*, she had blossomed and become who she was meant to be. And the possibilities were limitless.

So, this was the end of Thair's story.
Or the beginning. It would be a happy ending, regardless.

The End

———

I look at my last line. It's done. My yiayia's, my mama's, and now my story. I feel relieved, elated, free. And at peace.

I sit here for a few moments and just take in the sun's rays. I finger the wooden heart keychain I had bought for my mother in Metsovo. I take my car keys off it, leave on my condo key, and place it on the far end of the table. "Know Thyself." Socrates, Solon, and other great sages knew the secret so long ago. Finally, finally, these words inscribed on the Temple of Apollo at Delphi are now inscribed in my heart. I know myself. I know what I want. And I know how to move forward.

As I open another document and read the words, a huge grin spreads across my face. My letter of resignation, *nice*, I think, no resentment, just words of gratitude—inspired by the faces of hundreds of wonderful students, not endless hours on the freeway for minimal pay and little security. After sending my résumé, credentials, and several successful phone interviews, I landed the job, an overseas position at a prestigious private school. In Peru.

I am so excited that it's hard to sit still these days. I will drop off the letter at the college, pick up Pussaki's traveling papers from the vet, and then head to meet Rick. He said he'll be by around 2:00 p.m., says he has a nice couple who are interested in renting my condo.

That night I dream of Meteora, the Acropolis, Machu Picchu, and a big bowl of red Greek tomatoes.

Acknowledgments

First and foremost, I want to thank Hugo de La Rocha Sarmiento. You are my beginning and my end.

I also want to thank two women who read draft after draft and were always honest, supportive, and enthusiastic. The first is Bettina Faltermeier, my dearest friend whose integrity, sensitivity, and sense of independence taught me that a person can, indeed, be happy alone. Thank you for holding my hand every step of the way with this novel. The second is Vanessa Gubbins whose insight and feedback always gave me something to think about and made this a stronger story.

To my first four readers, Jean King, Claudia Cevenini, Vicki Macris, and Daphne Mila, thank you for your passionate responses and reading my novel in less than a week, making me feel like it was indeed a project that I should see through until the end.

To my writer buddies whose emails, phone calls, and cheerleading skills were endless in my moments of angst, thank you, Jim Mastro and especially my writer soul sister, Alicia Bien.

To Mark Clements and especially John Barnier, my editors, your guidance was so appreciated. To Brooke Warner, my publisher, Samantha Strom, my editorial project manager, the Sisterhood, and everyone at She Writes Press and SparkPoint Studio, thank you for giving this story legs.

To my colleagues and students for the past twenty-seven years, ευχαριστώ, gracias, and thank you; you've all helped me grow into a more compassionate and better educator. Michelle Lee, thank you for your big-hearted friendship, and for good friend Michelle Coff Barnier and her mother, Georgine Coff, who both lost the fight to ovarian cancer, thank you for your inspiration and your courage.

To my own dear mother, Mama Angela, thank you for being unapologetically you. You are so smart, so fiercely independent, and my role model of what happiness and resilience look like. I am the μῆλο, and you and Yiayia are my tree; I'm beyond blessed to have you two as my roots.

And, to my brother Ray, you are an indelible mark in my heart. I have so much love and respect for you. Thank you to my Peruvian and American families, especially to Tess and Drew who are examples of the new Wonder Women. And Achilles, Opa, and Oia who fill my days with slobber, snoring, stinky farts, and so much unconditional love. I never knew I could love four-legged creatures so much.

Thank you to my Greek family who have opened their arms up to me year after year, especially Lucy, my first best friend, and my yiayia and papou, whose summer house by the sea left me with my fondest childhood memories.

And thank you to Greece. My love affair with this country can best be described through Homer's epic poem. Odysseus had Circe and Calypso, two beautiful enchantresses, but he still wanted to go "home" to his Ithaca and to his Penelope. Your home is not necessarily better than anyone else's, but it's yours. After twenty long years, he goes back; one day, πρώτα ο θεός, I will have the sweet soil of Greece on my feet again permanently.

Mostly, I'm grateful that Chance (or Fate?) led me to Hobson's Choice, and I met my husband, so I don't have to fight or journey without him by my side. Hugo, you are my home. Thank you for your endless love, laughter, support, and even though I don't believe in a Príncipe Azul, I believe in you. You are my peace, and I love you with the whole of my being.

Questions and Topics for Discussion

1. The Prologue of *The Greek Persuasion* opens with an intriguing story from Plato's *Symposium* about Zeus and the Other Half. This lays out one of the more important themes of the novel. How does this story of "other halves" and "soccer-ball people" affect the protagonist's life? Did Phaedra do a disservice to Thair by telling her this bedtime story? Or is it a good idea not to settle and to seek a partner who is one's perfect fit? Do you believe in the Other Half? A Soul Mate? Or should people—men and women—be whole and happy alone?

2. Take a moment to discuss the structure of the narrative. When Thair writes her "stories," she uses a third-person perspective and past tense; otherwise, the novel is written in first-person present tense. Why do you think the author chose to use this structure? Did one of the "stories" capture your attention more than the others? Did you have a part of the novel that was your favorite? Which part and why?

3. What is the significance of the three sections: Change, Growth, and Peace?

4. The novel captures many attitudes about women and motherhood. In Dita's story, we read, "She was a mere woman with no hopes for a future." Do you think Dita had more choices at that time? Could she have done anything differently? "Mr. Wright had

been so wrong," Phaedra says, and she tells her daughter that she couldn't have gone back to Greece as a disgraced divorcée, so she chose to stay married for almost twenty years. Do you think these attitudes are still common today? What choices did Phaedra have growing up in Athens, and does her life seem better or worse in San Diego? Later, Thair states, "I think women try to do too much, and sometimes something has to give, and it's usually the marriage." Do you think some women can "do it all"—career, children, marriage—and be happy?

5. Take a moment to discuss Thair and Phaedra's relationship. Is Phaedra a sympathetic character? Do you believe she was a good mother? Did her traditional attitudes remain until the end of the novel, or did she change? Was Thair a good daughter? Should Thair have done anything differently to please her mother?

6. Thair has various romantic relationships in the novel. Discuss her relationships with James, the sad-eyed woman on the beach, Ravi, and Jessica. Are any of these characters someone you could fall in love with?

7. Angela, Thair's ex-student, gives her a phrase that changes her life: "No society dictating what's right and what's wrong. . . . You didn't see color, race, religion. Or even gender. . . . If only others were more open, then they would see that there are a helluva lot of people out there to love." Do you think this is true? Or do parents, society, religion, and traditions, in fact, dictate who we love?

8. Thair has a transformation in the novel and discusses her sexuality and LGBTQIA+ issues extensively. The novel takes place between 1999 and 2006. Do you think these stereotypes still exist? Do you think "bisexuality" is marginalized? Do you think there is such a thing as "heterosexual privilege"? What do you think about labels? Has the US and our world changed? She states that Rick and Frank can't marry legally. What are the laws in your state?

In your country? Do you think people in the LGBTQIA+ community should have the right to marry? Have or adopt children? Serve in the military? Hold the highest office? Be happy?

9. Discuss Thair and Gabriel's relationship. Thair says that at times he seems too good to be true. "And it's too much, like the stuff of trashy novels. But I kind of like it." Do you think she has met her Other Half? Thair says, "My brain-hand and heart-hand are reaching for each other . . . are they connecting?" What does this symbolize for Thair? Why does her relationship with Gabriel work? Do you think she could be happy with Gabriel forever?

10. "Can we only feel complete in the arms of our soul mate or can we find this wholeness alone? Or is mere *contentment* with someone the solution for loneliness?" What do you think? At the end of the novel, Thair says, "She was always whole; she just had to figure that out." Do you think Thair has found this wholeness alone, and is she finally comfortable in her own skin?

11. Red Greek tomatoes are an important symbol in the novel. First they are mentioned as "deep-red, delicious tomatoes" from Thair's yiayia's garden. Later, in the US, Thair says, "The tomatoes in the salad aren't red, instead an awful pink color." When she is thinking of breaking up with Jessica, she finds one in her fridge that is "reddish-purple, mushy, and has white fungus growing on its side." When she shares a meal with Gabriel, Thair says, "the red in the tomatoes is deeper." And, finally, the last line of the novel reads, "That night I dream of . . . a big bowl of red Greek tomatoes." What role does this fruit play? How is it used in the various scenes, and to what effect?

12. Why do you think the novel is called *The Greek Persuasion?* Here are some references in the novel: Thair says to James, "Obviously, this myth has persuaded you, too." Later, we read, "Thair wanting this fairy tale, this myth that her mama had persuaded her young

mind into believing was a true story, led to Ravi's walking out the door." Phaedra later tells her daughter, "I think you persuaded yourself into believing that you could only be happy in Greece." Finally, we read, "Thair thought about her mother, the bedtime story, and how that Greek god had persuaded her to search for her Other Half." Who or what is "The Greek"? Is it a person, a mythological character, a country, and/or an ideology?

13. Which scene in the book moved you the most? Which characters did you think were the most notable? Was the ending satisfying? Did you get choked up at all while reading the book? Did you find yourself thinking about, or agreeing or disagreeing with, any of the concepts that Thair mentions? Do you have a desire to visit Greece after reading this book? Are you Greek? Have you had a chance to visit the incredible places mentioned in *The Greek Persuasion*?

14. Analyze the final words mentioned in the novel: Meteora, the Acropolis, Machu Picchu—what can you say about those places, and why are they important to the novel's conclusion?

15. Finally, what will you remember most about *The Greek Persuasion*?

About the Author

Kimberly K. Robeson is a Greek-American assistant professor at Los Angeles Valley College, where she teaches world literature, creative writing, and composition, and is the coadvisor for the college's LGBTQ+ Club. She grew up in Greece, Saudi Arabia, South Africa, and California. She holds a master's degree in comparative literature and has taught English in Greece, Peru, and the United States for the past twenty-seven years. Kimberly, like her yiayia, has always been a storyteller, and Greece is always in her heart. She currently resides in Los Angeles with her husband, Hugo, and their three bulldogs, Achilles, Oia, and Opa. *The Greek Persuasion* is her debut novel.

SELECTED TITLES FROM SHE WRITES PRESS

She Writes Press is an independent publishing company
founded to serve women writers everywhere.
Visit us at www.shewritespress.com.

A Drop In The Ocean: A Novel by Jenni Ogden. $16.95, 978-1-63152-026-6.
When middle-aged Anna Fergusson's research lab is abruptly closed,
she flees Boston to an island on Australia's Great Barrier Reef—where,
amongst the seabirds, nesting turtles, and eccentric islanders, she finds a
family and learns some bittersweet lessons about love.

Play for Me by Céline Keating. $16.95, 978-1-63152-972-6
Middle-aged Lily impulsively joins a touring folk-rock band, leaving her
job and marriage behind in an attempt to find a second chance at life,
passion, and art

The Geometry of Love by Jessica Levine. $16.95, 978-1-938314-62-9
Torn between her need for stability and her desire for independence, an
aspiring poet grapples with questions of artistic inspiration, erotic love,
and infidelity.

Shelter Us by Laura Diamond. $16.95, 978-1-63152-970-2
Lawyer-turned-stay-at-home-mom Sarah Shaw is still struggling to find
a steady happiness after the death of her infant daughter when she meets
a young homeless mother and toddler she can't get out of her mind—and
becomes determined to rescue them.

Magic Flute by Patricia Minger. $16.95, 978-1-63152-093-8
When a car accident puts an end to ambitious flutist Liz Morgan's dreams,
she returns to her childhood hometown in Wales in an effort to reinvent
her path.

Stella Rose by Tammy Flanders Hetrick. $16.95, 978-1-63152-921-4
When her dying best friend asks her to take care of her sixteen-year-old
daughter, Abby says yes—but as she grapples with raising a grieving teenager, she realizes she didn't know her best friend as well as she thought
she did.